DIRTY AIR SERIES

THROTTLED

Book One

LAUREN ASHER

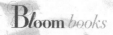

Published by Bloom Books, an imprint of Sourcebooks
P.O. Box 4410, Naperville, Illinois 60567-4410
(630) 961-3900
sourcebooks.com
PAH

Cataloging-in-Publication Data is on file with the Library of Congress.

Printed and bound in the United States of America.
10 9 8 7 6 5 4 3 2

Mom,
Thank you for everything,
including the holy water
you'll bathe me in after you read this book.

Playlist

God's Plan – Drake	3:19
High Horse – Kacey Musgraves	3:34
HUMBLE. – Kendrick Lamar	2:57
I Think He Knows – Taylor Swift	2:53
Antisocial – Ed Sheeran and Travis Scott	2:42
Mixed Emotions – Emily Weisband	2:40
Animals – Maroon 5	3:51
Bailando – Enrique Iglesias	4:04
Torn – Ava Max	3:18
Sorry (Latino Remix) – Justin Bieber ft. J. Balvin	3:40
Never Be the Same – Camila Cabello	3:47
Dusk Till Dawn – Zayn ft. Sia	3:59
Locked Out of Heaven – Bruno Mars	3:53
Proud – Marshmello	3:11
Anywhere – Rita Ora	3:36
Die a Happy Man – Thomas Rhett	3:47

PROLOGUE
Noah

TWO YEARS EARLIER

I inhale deeply, welcoming the smell of rubber and engine exhaust before I pull down the visor on my helmet. Gloved hands grip the steering wheel of my Bandini Formula 1 race car, my fingers trembling from the engine's vibrations while my race engineer talks into my earpiece. The Abu Dhabi Grand Prix crowd bursts with excitement as the crew pulls off my tire warmers. Yesterday's successful qualifier sets me up in a first-place grid spot, and as long as I don't fuck it up, the World Championship title will be mine for the taking.

Santiago Alatorre, a young driver who joined Formula 1 only a year ago, has been giving me a run for my money this race season. He and I have been battling it out all year long while we compete for the World Championship title.

Whenever I beat him and secure points for the

championship, he comes back with a vengeance, and he's successfully turned tonight's race into a tiebreaker.

No pressure.

I stare up at the moon for a few minutes before everyone scatters off the track. One by one, red lights illuminate above me, shining off the hood's glossy red paint.

Five. Four. Three. Two. One.

Fans silently wait, and I take a deep breath to calm my heart.

Lights shut off to signal the start of the Grand Prix. I press against the throttle, and my car rushes down the straight before I pull up to the first turn. Tires skid across the pavement, squeals sounding off behind me from other drivers. But I suffer from tunnel vision on the track. It's just me and the car.

"Noah, I want to let you know Liam Zander's behind you, followed by Jax Kingston and Santiago Alatorre. Keep up the pace, and mind your turns." The team principal's voice carries over the radio in my helmet.

I stay defensive of my position, making it difficult for anyone to overtake my car at the turns. The hum of the engine fills me with exhilaration as I speed down another straight at over two hundred miles per hour. Fans scream as I pass them. My foot presses on the brake seconds before I make another turn, soft tires screeching against the asphalt. Music to my ears.

The first few laps of the race go without a hitch. Adrenaline flows through my body as Liam's car comes up next to mine at one of the curves, the recognizable steel-gray paint glistening under the bright lights lighting the track. His engine roars.

I pull a risky move, pushing on the brake a few seconds later than recommended for a curb. Fiberglass trembles as the right tires lift off the ground before slamming back down. Liam pulls back, unable to pass me, as my car surges forward.

My race engineer talks into the radio. "That was a dangerous turn. Relax out there. You still have fifty-two more laps to go. No reason to drive cocky."

I chuckle at the advice. After a grueling season fighting off Liam, Santiago, and Jax, I have one last Grand Prix between me and the World Championship win.

Thankfully, my teammate and I already earned enough points as a team to secure the Constructors' Championship title for Bandini, although I won't be satisfied until I have both wins for the season.

"Santiago cut in front of Liam at the last turn. Don't underestimate him. He wants the win." More chatter echoes through the radio.

Speak of the devil. Santiago's royal-blue car shows up in my side mirror. I shake my head as my car hugs another turn. He acts like a young shit who tries to show off a little too much, attempting to make a name for himself with his team and the F1 circuit. His skills are decent for a new guy, but one too many close calls during this race season makes me hesitant to let him get close.

The fucker races right up to my rear wing, closing the gap between our cars—unwise for the narrow set of twists coming up. My heart pumps rapidly. Hands clench around the steering wheel as I take a few deep breaths. Inhale, exhale—yoga shit. I don't fold on my first-place spot, having no interest in letting

Santiago overtake my car. Gray pavement blurs past me. On the next straight, Santiago pulls up to my side, our wheels nearly touching. Just a few inches apart.

Both engines rev as the accelerators hit their maximum. I push into first place again at the next turn, my front wing creeping ahead of his.

Fuck me.

Instead of Santiago jerking back, he speeds up.

Motherfucking idiot.

The whole situation happens in slow motion, like a movie, playing frame by frame. Me, a useless bystander. Bandini's team principal yells in my ear about pulling back, but the sound of crunching metal tells me I'm too late.

Santiago's car grazes mine at about one hundred and ninety miles per hour, a catastrophic hit I won't recover from. I curse as the wheels of my car lift off the ground and I end up airborne, flying before making contact with the pavement.

My race car flips over twice and drags across the pavement, sparks flying around my head, concrete within touching distance. Thank fuck for the protective halo. The shrill sound of scraping steel hurts my ears until my car stops moving. Ragged breaths leave my lungs, pushing through my tight throat.

"Noah, are you okay? Any possible injuries? Help is on the way."

"Negative on any injuries. That piece of shit fucking hit me, knocked me out like a fucking bumper car." Anger courses through me at Santiago's carelessness. I plan on punching him the moment he enters the cooldown room after the race. Knock that pretty boy smile right off his face.

I can kiss my championship win goodbye. All thanks to Santiago and his stupidity, pulling a move he shouldn't have to get seconds ahead. Fucking reckless of him. My head clouds as adrenaline wears off and my body gives in to the pain.

"Fuck you, Santiago. Enjoy your title as Formula 1 World Champion because it'll be your last." I don't give a shit about everyone hearing my team radio. Let fans and him know I hate his guts. Santiago can act like hot shit now, but I'll come back for him. Asshole started a fight he won't win.

Black spots fog my vision. The combination of being upside down and being hit twice is too much for my body to handle. I'm helpless as the safety crew works to situate my car right side up, so I stew in my toxic mood and smack my hands against the steering wheel to the hammering of my heart.

I grunt at the medical team who check for any injuries. After an excruciating amount of time spent being poked and prodded at, my body gets an all clear with nothing to report except for a bruised ego and blood pressure through the roof.

Later, when I'm dropped off back at the Bandini suites, I surge past the pit crew to avoid pleasantries or fake claps on the back telling me how everything will be okay. I don't want to hear people say how I'll win the championship next year.

I take the steps up to my suite two at a time, ready for who waits behind the doors. My lungs burn from taking a deep breath. Fuck, more like ten breaths, in and out, the rhythm finally calming me.

I open the door to find two people I'd rather not see anytime soon. Preferably not within the next ten years, give or take. My dad paces the small suite, his broad shoulders commanding the space, chest heaving in and out to the tempo of his feet. His dark hair looks disheveled for once, and his deep blue eyes narrow at me. Mother dearest parks herself on a gray couch. Her icy eyes don't meet mine as she stares at her nails. Blond hair perfectly coifed, her body is posed against the cushions like the has-been model she is. Lucky for her, she sunk her claws into my dad and snagged the ultimate prize of a child with a famous F1 driver. She hit the DNA jackpot with a son who rivals the man she married.

Quite the family, right? A broken, mangled history of missed birthdays, uncelebrated holidays, and empty grandstands at most Formula 1 races. The only reason they both attended this Grand Prix was because Dad wanted to reminisce while Mom showed off to her friends how incredible life is for someone who birthed a racing all-star. Neither one came for me.

"What the fuck was that?" My dad's voice grates across my skin like a knife. His pointed eyes cut into mine, assessing for any signs of weakness. He suffers from resting dick face with wrinkles marring the sensitive skin near his eyes. Unfortunately for me, I look like him. Dark hair with a wave, blue eyes that challenge the Caribbean Sea, and a tall frame that stands toe-to-toe against him.

I place a palm against my race suit. "Well, shit. Someone told me I was driving for a top F1 team, but maybe I shouldn't have believed them."

"Someone told me you were supposed to be a world champion this year, but maybe I shouldn't have believed them," my dad's voice snaps back.

Ah, there's the viper we all know and hate. See, my dad may be a legend to everyone in the F1 community, but to me, he's a snake straight from the pits of hell. One sent from the devil himself. A venomous man who does nothing but scold me, funding my career with the lovely bonus of tearing me down whenever he has the chance. But in front of everyone else, he acts like a doting dad who supports my racing career, both financially and emotionally. He could win an Oscar for Best Supporting Jackass.

"Scared of me contesting your three-title standing? Thought you'd be happy with me staying in your shadow, forever trying to catch up to the *legendary* Nicholas Slade." Distaste colors my voice.

He closes the gap between us and grabs me like the good old days. His fists tighten around my race suit, eyes barely concealing the rage that bubbles within. I can tell he battles between hitting me and verbally sparring with me.

I roll my eyes, feigning indifference despite my heart rapidly beating in my chest. "Your predictability bores me. What are you going to do? Slap me around to remember how much of a dick you are?" My voice stays firm.

My dad and I have a tumultuous history at best. The first three years of my life were fun, but ever since I began karting, it was game over. Ironic how the best years of my life became the worst. Gone was the dad who took me to the park to ride my bike or throw a football around. Every year, he got worse when all I wanted to do was please him, pushing myself to become one of the best drivers in karts. Then it became Formula phases, forever seeking his love and approval at the expense of my childhood. Desperate for anything to stop his private rituals. Fans don't know the real me, the shit I dealt with to impress my dad, the weekly beatings I received if I placed anything below first. My ass never met a belt I liked.

Slaps became punches that upgraded into verbal lashings once I reached his height. My dad stripped away my childhood at the expense of my humanity. Because to survive the worst of them, you eventually become them.

I stare into my dad's eyes and look at the monster who made me. He got his wish. To please him and protect myself, I became everything he is, minus smacking people around. I'm an asshole with walls higher than the Grand fucking Canyon.

He leers at me, his words a snarl against his clenched teeth. "I lost thousands because of your shitty-ass display out there. Congratulations on being runner-up. Wonder how it feels to kiss a whole year of your life away. You can't live in my shadow when you don't deserve to breathe the same air as me."

His anger doesn't faze my mother, who sits there and watches us, eyes cold and dead, just like her personality. A useless waste of space who plays the role of a mother whenever convenient. She chooses to turn a blind eye every damn time he gets this way, indifference evident in her blank gaze. I'd honestly forget she talks except for when she calls me to ask for exclusive tickets and backstage passes.

"Then you should step away. Don't want to get near me because I hear being a loser is contagious." I grip his hands and push him the fuck off me. He doesn't back down, keeping eye to eye with me as he sneers.

"You're such a fuckup, ever since you were born. The only reason you got this far was because of me and my investments, since no other person would have sponsored your sorry ass. A pompous brat who acted out, pretending to be tough when you really cried into your pillow at night about a mommy who didn't love you and a daddy who beat your ass weekly."

I shrug, hoping to come off careless. Inside, my blood burns hot, edginess creeping up my spine in the hopes of a fight—an unlucky genetic inheritance from this man.

"Darn, Dad, sorry. Would you like to wipe your eyes with a couple of hundred-dollar bills? What a disappointment to raise someone who has three World Championship titles already."

"The disappointment wasn't raising you. It's seeing the pathetic excuse of a man you've become. Enjoy your second-place parade. I know it's been a while for me, but I heard the first-place view on the podium is best." He sends me an evil smile before stepping away.

Check-fucking-mate.

CHAPTER ONE
Maya

"Maya Alatorre, bachelor of arts in communications." The announcer states my degree in both English and Spanish. My parents and Santi beam at me from their seats off to the side of the stage, waving signs among other parents of graduates from the Universitat de Barcelona. I clutch the most expensive piece of paper in my hands, the rough texture pressing against my fingertips, reminding me of my efforts to graduate today.

I sit myself back in the sea of students cloaked in cheap polyester gowns. After a few speeches, we move our tassels to the side, signifying the end of our university days. Five grueling years and two major changes later, I can happily say I graduated. Turns out I wasn't cut out for a biology degree; I fainted during a dissection lab when my partner cut into a baby pig's stomach. And prelaw didn't exactly work out for me; I threw up in a nearby trash can during my first debate, forfeiting before the questions began. People would count these restarts as failures, but I think they built character. That and resilience for messing up.

It took me two internships to discover my interest in film and production. Finding jobs in film is a lot harder than I thought, so I get to add myself to the unemployed postgrad statistic.

My family meets me outside, the views of Barcelona greeting us while the cool December air brushes against my skin, which is poorly protected by the cheap grad outfit. We all pull in for a group hug before they take pictures of me. I get a boatload of congratulations and kisses, along with a slip of an envelope from my brother, Santiago.

"For the graduate. Took you long enough." He sends me a smile before smacking the top of my cap. We look similar yet different, thank God. Thick, dark hair matches our light brown eyes, long lashes, and olive skin. Our similarities end there. Santi inherited a tall gene from a distant relative while I stopped growing by eighth grade. He rocks week-old stubble and a goofy smile while I prefer a more mischievous grin that matches the glint in my eyes. He works out seven days a week while I count climbing up stairs to get to class as my daily cardio.

Santi's phone rings, and he steps away to answer it.

My mother poses me and takes more pictures. She and I look alike, all honey eyes, short stature, and hair with enough wave and volume to look good when I wake up.

"We're extremely proud of you. Both of our babies are out doing good things in the world," my mom says as she snaps a picture of me rolling my eyes. Her accent has a lull to it, a product of learning English from hotel guests at her job.

I groan when she smacks a big kiss on my cheek, leaving behind a smudge of her lipstick.

My dad mumbles about her needing to treat me like a grown woman. Look at me, now called a mature adult, all at the toss of a graduation cap. His smile reaches his brown eyes, wrinkles creasing at the corners as he looks down at me. He has thick hair that competes with Santi's, a short beard, and a lean frame. Santi looks like a younger, more muscular version of our dad.

"Who wants to grab dinner?" my dad says while rubbing his belly.

Santi steps back toward us, looking paler than usual. He comes up to my side and whispers into my ear, "Sorry about this. But they'll get pissed if they find out from someone who isn't me."

I look up at him, confused why he needs to say sorry.

Santi takes a deep breath before he breaks out a smile. "My agent just told me Bandini offered me a contract for next season."

Well, shit.

Santi doesn't need to steal my thunder when he robs the whole damn storm.

I place Santi's green smoothie on the table next to his workout bench. Four measly ounces of juice mock me, the goopy evidence supporting how I belong nowhere near a kitchen for the foreseeable future. Especially since green liquid still drips from the kitchen ceiling. What a mess. It's all fun and games until I forget to put the cap on the blender, making contents splatter everywhere, including my hair and clothes.

"I don't need you waiting on me hand and foot. You should be out having fun because we won't be back home for a while." He grunts as he lifts a weight above his chest.

"I want to make myself useful and not feel like I'm taking advantage of you for a free place to stay." I fidget with my hands while he counts his lifts, his deep exhales filling the silence.

Sleek equipment gleams under the overhead lights, a testament to his commitment to Formula 1. His new home is a far cry from the bedroom we shared while growing up. This new one has six bedrooms, a personal gym, a mini movie theater, and an Olympic-size pool. A whopping six thousand square feet.

He sighs. "Money isn't a worry anymore."

"I know, I know. But I want to make a name for myself because I can't live in your shadow forever." My hand itches to twirl a piece of my hair, but I resist the nervous tic.

I don't think I'll ever forget the ridiculous amount of zeros in his bank account. The first paycheck from F1 paid for my college in full. No questions asked.

Santi didn't blink when he signed the check like he expects to provide for our whole family now that he's made it big, which can't be further from the truth. We appreciate everything Santi does. His wanting to help in whatever way he can comes from a meaningful place rather than a sense of obligation.

When we were younger, our parents worked two jobs to

save up every penny for Santi's racing career. My dad repaired karts as a side gig while my mom cleaned houses on weekends. Unlike most wealthy "trust fund" kids in F1, my parents are middle-class on a good payday. Santi made a name for himself without the financial backing or a famous pedigree. He finally has sponsors who believe in him and his skills, making life easier and racing a hell of a lot more fun.

"I want you to come to my races this season. You can take the year to figure out what you want to do next. Plus, it'll be fun because this is our chance to finally travel together." He sends me a goofy smile from behind his barbell.

Santi gets to live out his fantasy of being a top F1 driver with Bandini—the best team in the sport. Driving for them is my brother's dream come true. I didn't hesitate to say yes when he originally asked me to join him a couple weeks ago, because my big brother is basically a superstar.

Sure, his bombshell of a revelation at my graduation stung, but I pushed past it because he had a valid reason for not wanting us to find out from an online article or the news.

Unlike other siblings, I don't mind sharing the limelight.

Most days.

"That's the plan. Your assistant sent me all the travel info and bookings."

It feels odd to say he has an assistant in the first place. She runs all his gigs, like checking in on his hotel accommodations, making sure he has weekly groceries, and booking sponsorships.

"Did you get the camera I picked out for you?"

I have no idea how to pay back his generosity, especially with such expensive gifts. He still buys me things even though he pays for everything. Lately, I struggle between feelings of guilt and gratitude.

"Yes, thanks again. I have it all set up, and I'm pumped to vlog. I already bought a handheld tripod to film F1 stuff." I smile down at him.

He doesn't miss a beat, lifting the weight over his chest as he continues to chat. "Can't wait to watch the videos once you start. And you have all your stuff packed up?"

"Yes, Dad, I got everything ready two days ago like you asked." I roll my eyes.

He chuckles as his almond-shaped eyes look into mine. "I hope I won't have to put up with this attitude all season long. I can't keep up with your teenage frame of mind."

"You're a year older than me, so relax with throwing the *teenager* word around. Any attitude issues are a thing of the past since I'm twenty-three, not fifteen."

His body shudders. *Good. That's what he gets for not thinking through his words.* He needs to watch what he says since film crews will follow him around all the time.

He gets up and wipes down his gym equipment because that's the kind of guy he is: put-together, organized, and responsible. Respectable people clean their workout equipment, making sure to put everything back where it belongs, while people like me never enter the gym to begin with.

Where Santi's dependable and secure, I tend to have good intentions with poor execution. I respect my brother's life decisions, but I'm in a transitional phase at the moment. So I get to travel the world, learn about myself, and grow up. Our family knows I have to pull it together eventually. And I most definitely will. But like a fine wine, I'm taking my time.

My *time* includes sipping drinks by the pool while Santi competes across the globe in twenty-one different races. No, I'm kidding. I love F1, which means I'll cheer him on every step of the way or every wheel rotation. But you get what I mean.

My brother and I did everything together while growing up. His kart races were what we all did as a family activity, and no one was shocked when he became an F1 driver—all at a world-record-breaking age of twenty-one years old. I can't imagine the gratification Santi experiences knowing that Bandini realizes his potential and wants to capitalize on it. His new contract reinforces his lifetime efforts in the racing community, representing a new chapter in his driving career.

Basically, my big bro has the talent and drive. Pun intended.

It's in Santi's weight room that I make a promise to him.

"I solemnly swear I'll be up to good."

His eyebrows draw together. "I'm not sure you know the meaning of the word."

I glare.

He snickers at me. "I'm kidding. Although you do know what they say about the youngest child."

My eyes roll. "I swear I got in trouble one time—"

"One?"

"Twice. Tops."

He softly shoves me, and I laugh.

Our parents show up an hour later for Sunday dinner. Mom's homecooked paella invades my nose while sangria coats my tongue. They beam when Santi and I tell them how I plan to join him for the race season, pride and happiness flowing off them.

"All your hard work has paid off, including those long days on the dirt tracks before you moved up to the big leagues with the Formula divisions. We appreciate all the sacrifices you made, including school." My dad tips his glass before taking a sip of his drink.

Our parents like to share their appreciation for everything Santi has done since he gained his massive contract with Bandini, including paying off the rest of their mortgage, setting up a savings account for them, and sending them on a vacation. More selfless acts from him.

An uncontrollable pang of jealousy runs through me at his ability to care for our family. The uncertainty of never living up to anything he does intimidates me. His success makes me happy—don't get me wrong—but I'm nervous about not accomplishing anything close to his greatness.

"We can't wait to visit Bandini when you compete in Barcelona for your home race." My mom claps her hands, a gesture I tend to copy. Her eyes shine under the chandelier in Santi's dining room while her brown hair flows around her.

Santi smiles at our parents. "I can't wait to be back and competing in Spain. Home races are the biggest races for drivers."

We all clink our glasses to Santi's words.

"It's great that you'll follow him around and keep him company. I'm sure it's lonely on the road. Plus, you'll have your vlog," Mom says between bites of her food.

I love her for including me in the conversation. She supports my whole process, sending me different articles and videos about marketing myself while building an audience.

I don't intend on following him around from country to country without purpose. While vlogs can't compare to driving around in the fastest and most expensive cars in the world, my ideas mean something to me.

"I can film everything since Santi bought me a camera. Hopefully I meet people along the way and make connections because I want to keep active while he's busy." I hold my chin up high, exuding confidence I don't entirely feel at the moment.

"We're happy you are going with him. Your mom and I worry about you and hope you find your way. Use that communications degree to its fullest potential." My dad runs a hand through his gray hair. He means well, and since my previous track history isn't the greatest, I can't judge him for it. Doubt seeps into my bones at his comment, but I push it away.

"Santi's lucky his life panned out like he wanted. He's an all-star at twenty-four years old. I'm only twenty-three, which means I have the world ahead of me." I shoot my parents a smile, ignoring the sense of panic running through me at disappointing them.

"I went over a few ground rules with Maya, you know, to keep her out of trouble. God forbid I find her drunk and crying on a bathroom floor to a sad love song."

I throw my cloth napkin at Santi. "That happened one time! It was my birthday, and they had just announced they were getting back together. I was super emotional, okay? Feelings hit me all at once, right there while I was washing my hands."

Everyone chuckles at the table.

"And I told her not to hand her camera over to random strangers because of the last incident." Santi's eyes shine with humor.

I withhold the urge to roll my eyes. "How was I supposed to expect that a random guy would run off with my phone when we asked for a picture? Who even does that? It goes against every code of ethics ever written." To be fair, some situations are a consequence of me being in the wrong place at the wrong time while trusting a shady person.

"People without morals, that's who. You should be careful with those types when you're gone. People need to go to church more." My mom makes the sign of the cross for good measure.

Leave it to my mom to think religion will solve everything.

I enjoy the rest of dinner with my family, grateful when the conversation sways away from me. No one gets how tough it is to live up to everything my brother does. Not that I want to, but still, Santi leaves behind colossal shoes my whole body can't fill. But I want to push negativity aside and enjoy the trips we have planned.

Because you know what's worse than complaining about your big brother?

Complaining about a big brother who is so damn perfect all the time.

CHAPTER TWO
Noah

I toss a pillow over my head to block out any light streaming through the window. Sheets rustle next to me, and a warm hand finds my dick under the covers.

"Okay, this is the time you grab your stuff and go." I point to the door while my other arm holds the pillow on my face. *Please don't be confrontational.*

"You're kicking me out of bed while my hand is on your cock? We had sex three hours ago." She fails to hide her disbelief.

She's smart and good with time.

"Yup, last night was fun and all, but I have to get up for practice. I enjoyed it. Thanks."

She snatches the pillow off my face, revealing a feisty woman with blond hair that's a ruffled mess and her makeup smeared. I smirk at a job well done.

Her eyes shoot daggers at me, matching the sneer on her

face. "You're as unbelievable as they say. Are you always such a dick to people?"

I blink a couple of times, not in the mood for her attitude. Talk about a complete one-eighty from last night. *Go figure.*

"I'm glad my reputation precedes me. You overstayed your welcome; be sure to be gone by the time I'm out of the shower." No use staying in bed. I get up with my dick hanging out and my ass on display. Her lips gape apart as I close the door on her face, ending our conversation. They always leave by the time I get out anyway.

I make it a long shower to avoid seeing the blond chick again. Amber-Aly-whatever her name is—shit if I know, since they eventually blur together, becoming one mindless fuck after another. Now with the season starting again, I won't be drinking like I did last night. I have to stay sharp and keep the sponsors happy. Getting drunk isn't a habit for me anyway, because I have to keep myself in top physical form.

I'm one of Formula 1's best, after all, which means I have an image to keep up.

See, to answer the chick's question, I'm a dick. But I don't exactly hide it. People like her don't sleep with people like me in hopes that I'll cuddle and say sweet nothings after a good screw. I find it hard to see where women like her come from, getting all flustered after a good lay, calling me all types of curse words. Can't help being the "fuck them and chuck them" type. But ladies know the score, lining up at nightclubs to salivate all over my Gucci loafers for a chance to go home with me. They use me as much as I use them. A quick, meaningless fuck to let off steam.

And I have a lot of steam to let out.

A couple weeks ago, Bandini signed Santiago Alatorre as a second driver. My rival is now my teammate. A scrappy little shit who likes to go balls to the wall, consequences be damned.

I can respect the fact that he drives well, but he has a lot to learn about the sport. A shit ton of lessons I'll happily teach. Like when to back the fuck off or how to apologize for a nearly fatal crash. Crap like that.

Unbelievable how Bandini welcomed him to the team despite our rocky history.

So I did what any reasonable person would do to pass time during winter break. I got shit-faced last night, where one drink turned into five, and here I am, being called a dick by another chick. Some consider me nice. I made sure she came multiple times before I did, because my nanny raised a gentleman after all, no thanks to my parents.

But I can't blame my terrible mood on a blond chick with a sour attitude. My anger is all due to Bandini's new contract with Santiago. Now I have to share my team with a guy I don't even like, our rivalry burning strong since he hit me during the Abu Dhabi Grand Prix. What a wreck, my car unrecognizable after that crash, retired and bent out of shape. My loss was Santiago's gain. He won a World Championship thanks to my collision. Doubt he loses sleep over it.

Santiago comes across as deceptively careless. Even in those tense situations, he calculatingly thinks about the moves he makes on the track, doing anything to end up on the podium. Ballsy motherfucker.

I have little respect for him since our collision, but I don't blame him like people say I do. At the time, I did. But after lots of thinking, I came to the conclusion that he didn't cost me the World Championship. That was all me. The real reason I can't stand him is because his rashness almost landed me in the hospital, a memory not easily forgotten.

I plan on playing civil with him since we have to act like teammates. We don't need to compare dick sizes to see who's the best when my driving does the talking. He gets to come onto my team and into my house and show his skills. Meaning I can sit back and relax while he proves himself worthy of the money they paid him this year. It will be intriguing to see where it goes and who performs better. No more excuses, because an even playing field means the better driver will win. And we all know who that is.

My phone rings on my dresser. *Father.*

I battle between picking up the phone and letting it go to voicemail. Deciding on the latter, I step away, but the phone rings again. Clever man knows I avoid any contact with him. Not wanting to prolong the inevitable, I take the call.

"Did you call me to wish me a Merry Christmas?" I shuffle the phone between my shoulder and ear while I grab my workout bag.

"I read the news. Bandini added that child to the team. What are they thinking? He's barely proven himself." His gruff voice reverberates through the small speaker, skipping over pleasantries.

"Nice to hear from you too." My words pack their usual bite because asshole genes run in the family.

"Cut the shit, Noah. This is serious, especially after he

screwed you over before. You've got to stay sharp this season and not let him get the upper hand."

"We can let the crash go since it was forever ago. I'm not worried about a driver who got lucky once." I double-check that the chick from earlier left, not wanting another encounter with her. *All clear.* I grab my keys and lock up my Monaco apartment.

"I didn't invest a ton of money into that company for them to mess around with your career. If they think a kid is going to get the best resources without showing his worth… What a sad mistake."

I rub my eyes. "We can see how he does before you pop off on some Bandini rep. I doubt he can beat me like that again since it was a fluke. A lucky hit where I lost control."

"Damn straight he won't. Don't fuck it up again; you don't want to crumble under pressure when you're at the height of your career."

Thanks for the love, Dad.

"Yup, sounds like me. Talk to you later. Bye." I don't wait for his reply before I hang up.

My dad can't help being an asshole, but the public likes him, so he saves all his pent-up issues for me. He gets his way no matter what. His solutions to problems include money, threats, and throwing his weight around. Me moving across the Atlantic Ocean hasn't put enough distance between us. Even with an insane time change between Europe and America, he finds a way to contact me.

Whatever races he graces with his presence end up being a shit show. Fans call me F1 royalty, an American prince because of my dad, the *amazing* Nicholas Slade, who is still called one of the greatest drivers in F1 history. Lucky me to have him breathing down my neck about everything I do wrong or where I can improve. Yes, he kick-started my career. I appreciate every investment he's made to help me along the way, but I race cars every weekend, proving to him and everyone else that I'll be a legend too. The driving world has changed a lot since he raced twenty years ago. Cars I drive today shit on whatever hunk of metal he drove, making the sport into what fans love today. A sport with drama, high speeds, and intense risks.

My phone pings from a new message.

DAD

Booked my flight to Barcelona.

Merry fucking Christmas to you too, Dad.

CHAPTER THREE
Maya

Three months have passed since Santiago signed his new deal with Bandini Racing. I am living with him while he gets ready for the new season, making sure to keep myself busy by starting my vlog. I want to share all my travels while I follow Santi around the world. My computer is jam-packed with research on different things to do in each city while he preps for races. Pride surges through me at my foresight to plan.

A mix of car exhaust and airport fuel wafts through the air as I inhale some fresh air after the long flight to Melbourne, Australia. Professionals call Santi's first Grand Prix of the season a "flyaway race" because it takes place outside of the sport's typical Europe circuits. It's the first one I've ever attended on a different *continent*, and I'm practically vibrating with excitement as our plane lands on the tarmac.

I say "G'day mate!" to one of the flight attendants as I exit the plane. A poorly executed slip of the tongue. She doesn't look amused in the slightest at my poor attempt to crack a joke, so I delete the saying off my phone once I step inside the airport.

I keep a translated list of popular phrases from each country we visit to prevent making myself look like a fool, at least not more than usual. *Note to self: double-check what phrases sound stupid.*

I stretch my sore legs after a twenty-hour flight from Madrid, my muscles thanking me for the special attention. Santi grabs my luggage off the carousel while I find the Bandini town car.

We get dropped off at the hotel where the team stays. I look around the elegant lobby, distracting myself with a funky art piece while Santi talks to the front desk. He texts his assistant to check each accommodation for two-room suites because he tends to be a needy man-child.

Our suite looks modern and fresh, with a minimalist color palette and a balcony overlooking the track. I throw myself on the living room couch. Comfortable cushions practically swallow me whole like a welcoming hug after a long day.

"I have to go to a couple sponsor meetings before working out kinks in the new car. You'll be good without me?" His brown eyes gaze down at me as he places a Bandini baseball cap over his head.

"Sure. I have plans for the day anyway. Don't worry about me." I shoot him a toothy grin.

"I'll always worry about you. You are a handful."

I send him a mock offended look. "No need to throw around charged words."

He waves at me over his shoulder before exiting the suite. I throw a pillow at the door as it closes, missing my opportunity by a few seconds.

I take in my surroundings. The suite can't compare to Santi's previous digs, our upgrade having a television the size of my bed back home, a dining table fit for eight people, and a large sectional that surrounds me.

After changing into my bathing suit and grabbing my camera, I check out the hotel. My stomach grumbles during my tour, encouraging me to grab a quick bite to eat before I head to the pool. I relax and doze off on a lounge chair, heat from the sun enveloping me like a warm blanket, tanning my skin. An afternoon nap tempts me, my body giving in to jet lag despite the regret I'll feel later about my decision.

"I have a press conference today, and I want you to come." Santi walks into my room and plops himself on my bed. His post-practice round makes him a sweaty, sticky mess, with dirty skin contrasting against the white comforter.

"Oh, please come lie on my bed in your sweaty clothes. Make yourself at home." My voice drips with sarcasm.

He ignores me as he grabs one of the pillows. I continue to put on my makeup, keeping it fresh and light, my go-to look. My skin glows in the mirror after my long tanning session turned nap yesterday.

He lets out a grunt. "Noah's an ass, and you keep me in check. I won't be an idiot if you're there. *Please* come."

His words distract me, and I stab myself in the eyeball

with my mascara wand. *Shit. Is there a greater pain than mascara on your eye?*

My heart accelerates at the thought of Noah Slade. He's hot, in a devilishly handsome kind of way. Messy hair so dark it looks black, sharp cheekbones that can shave ice, and lips every woman can envy. I see pictures of him everywhere—ads, commercials, gossip mags. You name it, he's been on it. Not to mention how my brother has stood at the podium with him multiple times. I may have watched one or twenty times on my TV at home. Hard to resist seeing Noah get showered with champagne on a podium while he beams down at the trophy in his hand.

I let out a sigh. Noah's the type of guy you don't bring home to mom; he's the one you screw around with before you find the guy you finally take home to mom, ensuring her you've moved on from your wild ways. His list of past partners happens to be longer than my grocery list and to-do list combined. Gross yet oddly fascinating how women like that.

"You do understand you're an adult, right? How on earth do I keep you in check?"

"Because I won't say anything too nasty for my sister's ears." Santi bats his long, dark lashes at me in a ridiculous gesture that softens my heart. Damn him and his goofiness. I fall for it every single time, a victim to his boyish ways.

"Your innocent ploy is nothing short of terrible. Is that how you get laid?"

He throws a pillow straight at my face, smudging my mascara even more.

"Ugh, you're messing up my makeup! Fine, I'll go. But get off my bed. *Now.*"

He hops off my bed triumphantly because I fell for his plan. Hook, line, and sinker.

"See you later. I'll send up someone to grab you when it's time." He taps away at his phone.

"The things I do for you. I'll try not to fall asleep on the side of the panel, but no promises."

He lets out a deep laugh. "F1 panels are juicy. You'll enjoy it. I know it." He leaves with a smile plastered on his face. I can't tell if he means to be serious when he rubs his hands together like an evil genius. Shady side-eye included.

I wrap up getting ready. An attendant shows me the way to the press conference area where my brother waves at me from the panel table. My grin mirrors his own. Warmth fills my heart at seeing him up there living his dream, wearing signature scarlet Bandini gear—everything he's wanted since he was a kid.

I snap a quick picture to post on my social media. Hate to break it to Santi's ever-growing fan club, but I've been his biggest one since we were kids, which makes joining him during the season that much more special.

After fiddling with my phone, I glance up at the panel, my eyes meeting Noah's blue ones—a strikingly beautiful color framed by dark lashes and brows. His plump lips turn down as he checks me out. My body heats at his appraisal, aware of the beautiful human in front of me because I can see. I find it impossible to calm my racing heart, thumping against my rib cage, as I take him in. *Fuck me.* I don't think I've ever thought a guy was so gorgeous until now.

He rakes a hand through his thick, unruly strands. His

hair looks like he continuously runs his fingers through the locks all day. Corded arms lay on the table, revealing tan skin and large hands, taking my mind to dirty places. Noah's lean kind of muscular is ideal for racing. Shit, the kind of muscular perfect for fucking against a door, in a shower, or on a counter. Vivid images fly through my head of Noah in compromising positions. My body hums with excitement at the sight of Noah smirking at me, my lower half clearly not understanding the difference between danger and lust. Turns out press conferences offer more eye candy than I thought.

I lick my lips at the sight of his arms. Nothing makes a girl swoon quite like a guy dedicated to his gym regimen, but this guy is more likely to commit to his gym than to another girl. He notices my reaction and winks at me. My cheeks flush at his attention, an embarrassing display that makes my attraction noticeable. *Can I be any more obvious?*

Frustration rushes through me, washing away thoughts of his lips against mine and his hands in my hair. How on earth will I survive a season around someone who looks like him?

God plays cruel jokes on me. Just when I promised to be good, he wants me to fall right into the arms of the devil. Men like Noah are only built for wickedness.

I force my eyes away and try to find something interesting in the room. *Oh look, a middle-aged man setting up his microphone. Riveting stuff.* The same man glares at me before he grumbles something about hot chicks not being allowed in the press room.

Noah's deep rumbling laugh sends a shiver up my spine. *Since when do laughs sound sexy?* My body finds it difficult to ignore him, my eyes wanting to pull back to him like a magnet. I refrain because I don't want to lead him on. But he makes my body stand to attention, my posture never looking better.

My interest in the reporter appears short-lived once questions come from all different directions. Each journalist reeks of desperation to add their tidbit, enthusiastically raising their hands every time a round of questions wraps up.

One question makes me pause my Instagram scrolling.

"What have you two been doing to prevent another Abu Dhabi situation?"

Ugh, this again? Aren't there juicier stories to bring up?

Noah seems to share my same sentiment, his low groan permeating through the crowd and gaining my attention.

"Are we seriously bringing up a race from two years ago? That's below you, Harold. Find fresher drama to bring up because your questions bore me."

Turns out Harold is the same reporter I was staring at earlier. My mouth drops open, shocked Noah Slade knows these reporters by name. He has no shame calling them out.

But Harold refuses to let Noah off easily, especially after a tongue-lashing.

"One would assume the competition is back in full force. How does it feel to be working closely with someone you publicly announced as a rival on the track?" Harold licks his lips at his own line of questioning. *Must be proud.*

Noah's jaw ticks, accentuating razor-sharp cheekbones. His icy gaze makes my blood run cold. "Seeing as we're teammates now, his performance is contingent on mine and vice versa.

I wish Santi the best of luck; this year will be competitive between everyone."

My brother opens his big mouth, piggybacking off Noah's last words. "We discussed team strategies and what situations can be prevented. I highly doubt Slade will make that mistake again."

Santi, so sharp in racing, so unaware of real life. Noah turns his head slowly toward my brother. I rub a palm across my face like it can rid the image of Noah's death glare and clenched jaw from my memory. *Abort, Santi.* Uncertain of who will say what next, the media room remains silent as reporters anxiously wait for a reply.

Noah faces the camera crews again. "We all learn from mistakes here. The sport is about growth and personal development on the track. Accidents happen. It's all about what you do after that matters."

One point for Noah Slade. He handles the situation like a pro who was well-trained by a publicist.

The rest of the press meeting remains mundane after the flair of drama, not as juicy as my brother promised. A blessing in disguise for him since he's already messed up.

Relief floods through me when an F1 member announces the end of the media conference. He reminds everyone about the gala being hosted tonight in honor of the Bandini drivers, plus information about a few other press sessions taking place after practice rounds and qualifiers. Excuses of how to get out of those pop up in my head. Thankfully for Santi, he can do most of them alone, minus Noah and myself.

Noah approaches us outside the press building. My skin

prickles at our closeness, his body hulking over my five-foot-two frame, making me feel smaller than usual.

"I don't know how your last team worked, but let me handle the big-boy questions. You should rewatch the tapes from Abu Dhabi if you think it was a mistake on my end, because it sure as fuck wasn't. That should be your first order of business around here. Well, that and staying the hell out of my way." His fists clench together, and his jaw ticks under pressure.

"I didn't mean for it to come out that way. I'm sorry. I wasn't thinking," my brother says in earnest.

"Clearly. You're new to the team, and we have a system here. One that doesn't include stupid answers. You should ask around if you're not sure how things work."

"There's no need to be rude to him. He said sorry," I snap, my eyes meeting Noah's cold glare. I can only take so much of his attitude when my brother's already said sorry. Santi acts tough, but issues affect him more than most, his emotions swirling inside him like a slow-moving tornado.

Noah's sapphire eyes trail down my body. He licks his bottom lip, drawing my attention toward them, noticing how the bottom is fuller than the top. They look soft and plump. Perfectly kissable.

Skin heats wherever his eyes roam. I feel betrayed by the way my body acts around him, like I can't control the draw I have toward him.

He opens his mouth. "Side pieces don't come to these types of things either, so she can stay away. Maybe you'll be less of a dumbass."

My head snaps up, waves of attraction replaced by anger.

All at the flip of a switch. He did not insinuate what I thought he did.

Before Santi or I can get a word out, he continues. His blue eyes gaze into mine, dancing with delight. "If you ever get bored of being with him, I'm always free. With age comes more experience." He shoots me a ridiculously smug smile, and I can't wait to knock it off his face.

I start toward him, wanting to get uncomfortably close, because death stares look better from inches away. Santi grabs my hand, halting my attempt to get up in Noah's space, but he can't stop my mouth. *Oh no.* My mouth has a mind of its own, and words flow without a second thought.

"He's my older brother, asshole. Can't you see the family resemblance? Or is the cloud of superiority around you so thick that you didn't notice?"

I imagine the wheels turning in Noah's head as he makes the connection. His eyes dart between Santi and me, looking at our dark hair, olive skin, and same honey-brown eyes. My head tilts to the side, and I shoot him a smirk.

His jaw drops open, and his cheeks tinge a light pink color. I gloat at his embarrassment, mentally dancing around at my sassiness. Everyone knows what they say about people who assume.

"I'm sorry. I clearly shouldn't have spoken to either of you like that." His voice has a hint of regret.

I shrug, ignoring the tug on my heart at his remorse, because I get petty when mad. Assholes don't do it for me, no matter how pretty their faces are.

My brother offers a handshake because he acts like a real

man. I try my best to disregard how good Noah's ass looks as he walks away, but I take a peek because a woman can only have so much restraint. He gives me one last look over his shoulder before he disappears around the corner of the building.

I sigh softly, my heart slowing down for the first time in an hour. Santi gives me a quizzical glance before we take off in the opposite direction. Looks like tonight's gala just got a lot more interesting.

CHAPTER FOUR
Noah

I mull over the conversation with Santiago and his sister while I eat lunch in the Bandini area. Santi has a sibling I had no clue existed. *Where was she throughout his racing debut?* I feel like I would've recognized her. Instead, I made myself look like an asshole on the first day. An image of her brown eyes boring into mine like she wants to skin me alive has singed itself into my brain. She's a stunning woman even when mad with flared nostrils, flushed cheeks, and waving hands.

I need to come up with a plan for the Bandini gala. It was never my intention to get off on the wrong foot with Santiago already, or his sister for that matter. Looking like a dick before the season begins doesn't make me happy. Santiago and I will spend countless hours together doing press tours and going to sponsor meetings, which means his sister will be around just as much.

I snapped when he blamed me for something that wasn't

my fault. Let this be a lesson for him not to open his mouth without thinking, a prime example of what can go wrong in the public eye, shitty consequences included. But it's not right how I took my anger out on his sister.

During our earlier walk-through of the track, I apologized to him again because I was ashamed of what I'd said. I'm not above cornering people to get what I want. He begrudgingly accepted my apology, his jaw tight as his fist squeezed my extended hand.

I spend the rest of the day sitting through more press sessions, the less desirable side of F1.

I make it back to my hotel room with enough time to get dressed for the event. Santiago and his sister plan on attending the gala, my thoughts confirmed when I discreetly asked around. No need to draw attention to myself.

The poorly lit lobby bar welcomes me as I order a scotch from the bartender. Out of the corner of my eye, I see a woman sitting in a booth, twirling a straw in her drink. She looks vaguely like Santiago's sister. I head on over to her, confirming she is, in fact, the Alatorre I need to speak to. *Perfect timing.* Getting an apology out now sounds like the best idea because I don't dance around problems to avoid confrontation.

Some people scurry at trouble. Me on the other hand? I drive my car straight into problems at two hundred miles per hour. Fuck the consequences.

"Do you mind if I sit here?"

Her body tenses at the sound of my voice. I'm not off to a great start by the looks of her grimace, rigid body posture, and stilled hand holding her straw. But I can work with it. I shoot her a dazzling smile that makes women drop to their knees. *Tested and verified.*

I remain motionless as her almond eyes look up at me. My heart rate speeds up as I gaze at her, taking in her smoky eyes that cloud at my perusal, lush lips that purse, and high cheekbones I want to run my knuckles across. Her dark hair piles on top of her head, begging to be let down. A few soft curls escape and trail down her thin neck. Her dress dips low, accentuating tan skin and a fully displayed back. My fingers itch to stroke her skin and test how soft it is.

She pulls me out of my thoughts. "And if I do mind?"

Shit. Forgot I asked her a question. "I would probably sit here anyway then." I give her a wide smile, enjoying her quick tongue.

"Fine. Go ahead." She lets out a soft sigh and waves toward the empty booth in front of her.

Don't need to be told twice. I settle myself into the seat, adjusting my pants because my semi hard-on is pressing against the zipper. My throat welcomes the burn from a swig of scotch. A little bit of liquid courage to make it through this conversation without flirting with her.

"I wanted to apologize about earlier, because I shouldn't have insinuated something like that. I'm not proud of myself for what I said."

Brown eyes linger on my face as she gauges my sincerity. I take another look at her, because shock still courses through me at how she disarms me. Her bone structure adds to her allure, along with full red-painted lips, long lashes, and dark hair that perfectly frames her tan face. With arresting brown eyes and a pout that I'm tempted to kiss away, she is gorgeous.

My head takes off. I imagine her red lips wrapped around my cock as she sucks me off, her lipstick marking me while my hands tug on her hair. Can't help my sexual appetite when I fuck like I race—wild, risky, and often. Blame the adrenaline rush or feeling like a god behind the wheel.

"It's fine." Her flat voice tells me differently. *Fine* is a woman's equivalent to a land mine, because you have absolutely no idea when or where that shit will explode.

"It isn't, and I don't want to annoy you anymore. Honestly. I want to put it behind us and say I'm sorry for insinuating you slept with your brother." I withhold the urge to cringe at my own stupidity.

"Consider it dealt with. Apology accepted." She fiddles with the straw of her drink.

"What are you doing here with your brother?" I take another sip of scotch, the cold liquid sliding against my tongue.

"I'm actually following him around this whole year." She tilts her head at me.

Great. She'll be spending ten months with us, and I already fucked up.

"You'll be attending a lot of races then. Are you a fan?"

A small smile tugs at her lips. "My weekends growing up included following my brother everywhere. Kart races, real races, all the Formula phases. He has the talent." She looks down at her hands. "Of course, I'm excited to join him because I'm proud of how far he has come. New car, team, and everything." She glances at me, her eyes gleaming in the low light of the bar while her lips fight a smile.

I smirk at her. "He'll be in good hands with the equipment

and engineers. Bandini cars are the best. There's a reason they're the most sought-after team, so it'll give him an advantage. But he still has to deal with me."

The sound of her soft laugh stirs something up inside me.

"How do you keep your ego in check?"

"I don't." My grin expands.

She rolls her eyes, and fuck if it doesn't turn me on. Her delicate features entice me, tempting me to scoot in closer to check her out and catch a peek at her chest. But I stop myself because I have a cap of one sleazy move per day.

I still can't believe I insinuated she slept with her brother. I'm losing my touch.

"You need someone to rein you in." Her cheeks turn a pretty shade of pink before she shakes her head. "I mean, not me, but it's always good to be grounded." She puts a stray curl behind her ear.

"Being grounded is dull. I don't drive cars at two hundred miles an hour to stay boring."

Her lips purse and her brows pinch together. "Being grounded isn't boring. It's realizing that, when all this"—she waves her arms around us—"is over, you still have people there for you in the end. Good people who are humble, because no one wants to hang around an asshole."

I'm going to guess I'm the asshole here. I sit with her words and consider my situation. But I know good people. Who is she to judge me when she's young and naïve?

Her phone rings. "I better get going. My ride is here."

"I'll walk you out."

Her face flashes with surprise before she recovers. Mine

probably matches hers, because I can't remember the last time I walked a girl out of anywhere except a club.

I get up from the booth and offer my hand, acting the part of a gentleman. She looks at it for a moment before placing her palm in mine. My skin buzzes at the physical contact. She shivers when my thumb runs across her palm, her soft skin smooth under my calloused digit.

Hmm. Her body reacts to mine in the same way.

I remove my hand from hers and place it on her exposed back as I lead us toward the entrance of the hotel. Our physical connection is an exciting development, one worth exploring further at another time. She sucks in a breath when I stroke my hand down the ridges of her spine. I tend to be a cheeky bastard. Her skin feels warm and soft beneath my palm, her shallow breaths matching the rhythm of our feet.

Maybe I'll enjoy having Santiago around after all, because it seems like his sister hanging with us will stimulate me. I want to see what other responses she has to me. Or under me. Or on top of me.

I need to get myself under control.

We exit the hotel to find her brother leaning against a town car near the entrance.

"Maya, let's go! The driver's been waiting." Santiago's voice booms off the walls.

Maya. I like the name.

She jumps a foot away from me, breaking our contact. Her eyes glare at me before she says a rushed goodbye and walks away. I shake my head, trying to rid my naughty thoughts, a gesture worth chuckling at. Her perky ass stands out, the tight black material of her dress hugging her curves. *Damn. I definitely will like seeing her around.*

Her brother helps her into the car before he turns back toward me. His stare speaks a silent warning I choose to ignore, instead deciding to shoot him a cocky grin and a chin tip. He disregards me and enters the car.

CHAPTER FIVE
Maya

The air in the car is thick with tension, and not the good kind. Bright lights reflect off the car's window as we pass through the city. Santiago hired a driver to take us to the gala, reminding me how I'm in over my head. A poser surrounded by the rich and famous.

"Why were you walking out of the hotel with *him*?" Santi seethes.

"He actually came to apologize for what he said at the press event. We chatted, and then I came outside. It's not a big deal. No need to get annoyed."

Placating Santi has been my job for years. He tends to be a situational hothead, much like other F1 drivers. High-stress situations usually call for it.

"You should stay away from him. Hell, stay away from most of the F1 drivers. They're not here for happily-ever-afters, white picket fences, a dog, and two kids. They fuck around. *A lot*." His hands clench in front of him.

"You are aware I lost my virginity, like, four years ago, right? No need to protect me anymore when my virtue is no longer intact."

If looks could kill, Santi would have murdered me twice already in this car alone. Wrong joke at the wrong time. *Message received.*

"I don't want to be aware. No. Keep that shit to yourself. These guys are different from boys you dated in college. They're the ultimate fuckboys. Liquor, ladies, maybe even drugs. Who the hell knows. I haven't hung around them much since I like to keep to myself."

"I'll be careful. But Noah is part of your team now. We're all stuck around one another, and I don't want things to be awkward with us. At least not more than they have to be."

No use denying my physical attraction toward Noah, but I can sure do my best for Santi. I owe him that much.

I give him a sweet smile while I pat his hand, hoping to calm him. His lips tip down. He must be concerned because none of my usual tactics are working on him.

"You're my little sister, so it's my job to protect you. Be careful, okay? I can't keep an eye on you all the time. Especially with someone like Noah. His bedroom has a revolving door and a waiting list."

My body tenses. *Thanks for the reminder.* Nothing like a classic man-whore, one so stuck in his ways he can't see straight. Good thing those types of relationships aren't on my radar.

"You don't need to worry about me. I'm up to only good, remember?" I shoot him a goofy smile.

He grins at my cute stupidity and tugs me in for a hug, constricting my air supply.

"I love you. You know that, right?" His chest vibrates while he speaks.

I return his hug with a squeeze. "Of course. I love you too. Now let's go party!"

The swanky event, in fact, surpasses my original idea of a sponsor party. I pictured old men rubbing elbows and chatting about their stocks, but it's all so much more. We walk into a ballroom decorated to the nines with crystals and flowers hanging from the ceiling, waiters walking around with food, and dripping champagne towers on several tables. I grab a couple of fancy-looking appetizers while I walk around the room.

Lots of bigwigs visit to shake hands with the elite of racing, but the scene includes unlimited alcohol, a decent DJ, and silk dancers spiraling from the ceiling. It resembles more of an overdone wedding than a gala for race car drivers, and I'm immediately entranced by our surroundings.

Santiago reluctantly leaves me to my own devices after being called over by his agent. He gives me a warning look before walking away, but I brush off his worries with a flick of my hand. I follow his rule of not talking to the other drivers, but he can't fault me when others talk to me, because I can't control everyone else. Loopholes make life interesting.

I occupy a seat at the bar when Noah shows up and sits next to me. His intoxicating cologne short-circuits my brain cells.

Somehow his hair already looks like a disheveled mess, and his bow tie lies crooked against his pressed shirt. His unruliness brings a smile to my face. Sturdy hands that caressed my spine an hour ago hold another glass of scotch. I regret looking Noah straight in the eye, caught off guard by a penetrating gaze, his deep blue eyes framed by thick, long lashes.

A simple smile he sends my way tugs at my lower half. I can't control my body's response to him, especially when he looks at me like he wants to kiss me.

"What's a pretty girl like you doing all alone at an event like this?" Noah's voice has a rough sound to it like he spent the night partying and drinking—sensual and gravelly all at once.

"Aw, you think I'm pretty. How charming. Santi left me alone because he's busy kissing ass." I point a pink-nailed finger toward my brother, who is chatting with a group of sponsors.

"More than that." Noah's megawatt smile makes my heart clench. *Well, don't you have a way with words.* "Ah, a day in the life of a celebrity. A tough cross to bear."

I chuckle. "I doubt I'll ever get used to hearing that. Can't imagine my brother as a celebrity. So weird."

"It takes time. Wait until he's followed around by paparazzi to the point where he can't even eat or shit in peace. This place corrupts the best of us, surrounded by endless money, booze, women—you name it. A playground for the privileged."

I turn toward him and glance down at his outfit. He pulls off a tuxedo, looking roguishly handsome with smooth material clinging to his body. My fingers twitch at the temptation to run through the tousled hair that hints at his rowdiness.

But I don't because it'll ruin my efforts to be good.

"Did this place change you?" I try to keep my voice neutral, not giving away any feelings. He's the last person Santi would want me to hang around with.

His eyes harden. "I was born into it. Son of a legend and all." He flashes me an eye roll. "So technically, no, since it's all I've ever known. Can't be corrupted by something that made you."

I scrunch my nose. "We aren't like that. We were raised in a small home by modest parents. Santi didn't even go to college, so he could race to make money. Gave up a lot to pursue a dream. He paid my parents back everything they've ever invested in him because it means the world to him to provide for them."

"Humble beginnings make the best success stories. Your brother signed a twenty-million-dollar contract though, and that's a lot of money, so with it comes responsibility." His eyes stare intensely into mine.

I sigh, aware of Santi's most recent financial gain. He may surround himself with pompous people, but he isn't like most of these greedy and egotistical guys.

Noah takes a big sip of his drink. I copy him, chugging my champagne—a dose of liquid confidence to dull my nerves.

"What was it like being a kid around here?" I look across the room, imagining a young Noah hanging out with these people.

"While growing up, I thought it was the coolest thing ever. And I still do. But my dad isn't exactly father of the year. Nannies took care of me while my mom was off yachting around the world. But woe is me, the hard life of someone who has it all." The sadness in his voice betrays his attempted nonchalance.

"Do your parents come to see your races?"

"Every now and then. Dad's coming to the Barcelona one. My mom's another story, occasionally popping in when it's most convenient for her and her friends." He tips his glass and clinks it against mine before we both drink to that notion.

I sense parent issues with this one.

He looks at me with bright eyes. "What about you? What brings you to the hectic life of F1 racing?"

"Do I need a reason besides my brother competing?" I smile at him.

"Well, I assumed you were here for me, but now that you mention it, that sounds plausible." He hits me with a playful grin that sparks something inside me.

I shake my head at him. "I just graduated, and I wanted to travel the world." I hold back on mentioning my vlog because I don't want to be judged by someone like him—a man who thrives and succeeds.

"Well, you picked the right year to join. You get to see beautiful destinations with a bonus of me kicking your brother's ass. You can't Pinterest that shit."

I throw my head back and laugh. His cockiness has no bounds, but I like the way he teases, uncaring with a glint of mischief in his eye.

"How do you fit your head in your helmet? I'm worried it must expand the more people stroke your ego," I say with fake concern.

"I have one custom made to avoid that issue."

"Sounds costly."

He shrugs. "Being the best comes with a hefty price tag."

"What? Your soul?"

His eyes glitter under the lights. Before he has a chance to answer me, someone calls him away. He looks unenthusiastic at the interruption, his feet remaining planted to the ground.

"Duty calls." I tilt my empty glass to him.

He sends me a smirk and mock salute as a goodbye.

I explore Melbourne on Friday since Santi has a busy day with practice and press events. As interesting as his plan sounds, I decline his invitation to join him.

I spend the day taking photos and discovering the city. A local street-art tour gains my interest, and I enjoy the ability to fade into the group while surrounding myself with fellow tourists. When I hang with Santi, it feels like I'm on display. The attention he receives stifles me. People always take pictures, ask questions, or request autographs. And I hate feeling watched. He tells me everyone eventually gets used to it and I won't notice them after a while.

That type of complacency scares me.

The rest of the day goes by quickly. Newfound privacy comforts me so much that I eat lunch alone, at a table for two no less. My solo day seems short-lived when an old man sits in the chair across from me. He eventually gains the courage to strike up a conversation after fifteen minutes. I politely engage in the discussion of his arthritis, nodding along like I understand the struggles of chronic pain. He even shows me about one hundred photos of his grandkids.

What can I say? I'm a sucker for never saying no, because how can I look that poor older man in the face and decline seeing photos of his little tater tot? His words, not mine. I can't. So I end up spending an hour entertaining a man named Steve, even offering him a signed Bandini baseball cap as a parting gift along with a promise to text him a picture of the track on race day. I don't know the risk of giving a grandpa my cell phone number, but he seems sweet, so I give in.

My mom calls me while I'm walking down a side street.

"*Cómo estás?*" My mom follows my vlog religiously, commenting on all my posts with encouraging messages and quotes. She's cute like that. I even get texts with GIFs as a way for her to express her feelings.

"I've been having fun so far. Santi's pretty busy with the business side of things. I don't know how he finds the energy."

We stayed out late, and he got up at the crack of dawn to go drive on the track. Meanwhile, I hit the snooze button about five times before I finally got up.

"He lives for the sport, so he puts up with the social side of things. Keep an eye on him because he works too hard." There goes my mom, always the worrier.

"I'll try my best. I can't do what he does, schmoozing and boozing. People here are snooty and full of themselves."

"I've been reading gossip about those different drivers. Men like Liam Zander and Noah Slade pop up all the time, and you should see what women say about them. Don't get me started on Jax. That man has trouble following him like a bad smell." Her voice fails to hide her disdain. I don't ask for more information because gross details don't interest me.

"Be careful what you read. They can start spinning stories about Santi one day. Reporters are aggressive. And they love an interesting story, whether it's true or not."

"Have you met his teammate?" She can't conceal her curiosity about Noah, and I can't blame her.

"Yeah, he's not as terrible as stories claim. But he's still the ass who thought I was Santi's girlfriend."

"*Que bruto*. Someone should've raised him better, given him extra love and attention. That must've been embarrassing for him."

"I think that's his problem. It must be such a lonely life for him, screwing around with whomever and having no one to celebrate wins with. His own family barely comes to the races. Like his dad visits a few times a year, his mom even less. Makes me wonder if there is more to this show he puts on. I doubt he even realizes it though, especially when people like him always think they're happy until they aren't anymore. But who knows? I'm speculating, and it's not fair to judge." Unfiltered words rush out of my mouth.

"*Cuídate*. Behind the glitz and glam, people live with lies and unhappiness."

I change the topic, not wanting to talk about Noah anymore. It feels wrong to expose the small truth he shared with me last night about his parents. My mom and I catch up on plans for the weekend, and not soon after, I hang up the phone and go back to the hotel.

Australian
Grand Prix

CHAPTER SIX
Noah

Qualifying on Saturday relies on a successful lap time since a position for Sunday's race depends on the qualifier. Getting a sucky start on Saturday makes the race a hell of a lot more difficult to win, although not impossible.

Just *improbable*.

Pole positions are my and everyone else's favorite. I can bounce back from a second-or third-place starting point, not needing to pressure myself to overperform. Back of the grid tends to be the worst. Ever since I joined Bandini's team, I rarely place below P3 anymore unless I received a grid penalty.

Squeals of the tires hitting the track bounce off the pit walls as I walk toward Bandini's area. Each team has their own garage on the pit lane where the team preps before the race, including small rooms above the workstation where Santi and I get ready. I gear up in my suite for my two practice sessions.

I complete two successful practice rounds like I wanted.

My qualifier went even better, landing me the pole position for the Australian Grand Prix. Best spot on the grid. Santiago isn't far behind, qualifying third, right behind Liam Zander. Not bad for the new guy.

For the sake of the team, I want him to succeed, since we also compete together during individual races. I'm not totally selfish. He needs to do well for us to win a separate team-based championship, the Constructors', which happens at the same time as the World Championship and is determined by how many points he and I collect during each race. A total of twenty-one races and two coinciding championships with a guy I can't stand.

Sounds like the start of a great season.

Santiago can settle for winning the Constructors' with me because I want to be the world champion this year. My teammate can keep his shiny consolation prize.

Santiago, Liam, and I attend a press conference meant for the top three qualifiers. I sit between the two of them as reporters hit us with questions.

"Liam, can you tell us about your strategy with McCoy this year?"

"Besides fucking through the McCoy family?" I whisper under my breath, the microphone attached to my cheek not picking up on my voice.

Liam chuckles and shakes his head. We fuck around with one another, keeping the conferences interesting while breaking up our routine.

"Team strategies are the best-kept secret. Can't have Bandini here catching on to all my tricks, particularly the hothead over there." Liam points to Santiago over my shoulder. "But we have big plans for the upcoming races, including new specs on our cars. Going to give Bandini a run for their money."

"What he means to say is the view sure looks nice behind P1." My gruff voice makes reporters laugh.

"P2 allows me to screw Noah's car from behind, hitting him at the right angle. Oh, wait. That's Santiago's job. My bad."

I smack Liam's backward ballcap off his head.

Thankfully, Santiago refrains from any stupid comments this time around. He looks at Liam and me oddly. I let Liam's comments slide because he's actually one of my good friends and greatest opponent, at least before Santiago came around. Our verbal sparring makes its rounds on social media every time, gaining thousands of likes and comments within an hour.

Liam's a German guy who drives with McCoy, another top team. Blond-haired, blue-eyed man with a god complex. I like him a lot since we became friends during our young karting days. Raced together in the Formula phases and even competed on the same team when he started, both rising up together.

He acts like a total douche to women, and that says a lot coming from someone like me. I may be an ass, but Liam can be worse. His preppy looks deceive the best of them. A ton of pressure rests on him this year because his contract with McCoy will expire, and he slept around with the owner's niece.

Unlike my preference for one-and-done situations, Liam actually keeps girls around for longer than one time. I can't fault him when women willingly agree. But his F1 seasons include one or two girls on rotation who eventually get their hearts broken, spilling their stories to the gossip rags. A yearly cycle. But now he needs to keep himself locked up like a good boy after pissing off Peter McCoy.

I occasionally watch the trashy gossip videos of us on YouTube, shameful to admit they entertain me. McCoy can't be happy with Liam. Recent videos have focused on Liam's lack of foresight, calling him out for fucking around during an important year. Sleeping with your boss's niece tends to stir up lots of emotions.

Maya hangs out in the corner of the press room, trying to blend into the wall. Fat chance that's possible. She looks beautiful in ripped jeans and a T-shirt that clings to her chest. Her wavy hair is up in a ponytail that bobs while she leisurely scrolls through her phone.

It annoys me how she only tunes in to Santi's answers, staring up from her phone every now and then to watch him. It's like Liam and I don't exist. If she doesn't care, then she shouldn't come. Plenty of reporters would kill for a spot in here. *Why does she find her brother fascinating?* It blows my mind how she looks at him like he hangs the moon for her, her eyes all proud and shit when he talks.

Is this usual sibling stuff? I glance over at Santi while he speaks, curious to see what gains her interest.

"Santiago, how do you feel about your new contract with your rival's team? Any stress that comes with driving against one of the greats?"

I school my features like a well-trained PR puppet. Inside, my irritation grows, an eye roll barely contained. When will these guys let go of the contract deal? They lack original questions, the same type asked each conference, forgoing the hype of the first race of the season.

"Uh, it's not about contracts but rather how well we drive. I don't think about dollar signs or Noah when I'm out there. I think about the next turn and the finish line, with a possible podium ending."

Okay, not bad. The team publicist must be helping him after yesterday's disaster.

"Noah, who do you consider to be your biggest threat this season?"

A cocky smile breaks out across my face. *Showtime.*

"I like to consider myself as my biggest threat. When I race, it's me versus my instincts. Everything around me disappears. I test myself, seeing how long I can wait before pressing the brake or how to overtake another person. I don't think about the other drivers out there more than I have to. That's where others screw up."

Camera bulbs flash in front of me and capture my confident smile. Maya shakes her head, apparently not a fan of my response. The idea displeases me. My eyebrows pinch together, and my lips turn down into a frown. Appearances represent everything in this line of work because fans buy into this shit and love it. They even make videos about our bizarre press conferences every race, like bromance videos and rival compilations. You name it, there's a video on it.

A reporter moves on to Liam, asking another pointed question. "Liam, what game plan do you have to clear your name in the media?"

"Why don't you ask me in a few months? I want to keep my plan to myself in case it goes wrong." Liam shrugs.

I nudge him with an elbow. "That tends to happen with him."

Liam turns toward me and brushes his eyebrow with his middle finger. My head drops back, and I laugh. I lift my head, catching Liam shooting Maya a grin that she returns, no longer inattentive. My fists tighten under the table as I stare straight ahead.

Liam can be considered a good-looking guy. A six-foot-tall German jock who needs a short beard to hide his baby face. Basically, a glorified tool. Women dig his positive vibes and carefree attitude, along with his preference for multiple repeats. Everything about him screams good parents who gave him sugar, spice, and everything nice. Unlike me, who reeks of broodiness and bad memories, driving away from my demons week after week.

We finish up answering questions, and I leave the stage. I don't want to be there for another minute more. I'm mentally done with today.

Nothing tops the buzz of a race day. Everyone deals with their pressure differently, tensions escalating as we approach the start time. Anticipation of events keeps everyone up and running. Sundays are my favorite day of the week because who needs a church when I have a front-row seat to heaven?

Every driver does quick rounds to appease fans and sponsors, including meet and greets, parades, and interviews—the usual crowd pleasing and ass-kissing. Following that, I do my typical engine checks and attend a prerace stage event with an end goal of alone time in my Bandini suite.

This sport exhausts the best of us. I love it, but it wears a person down through the years.

The small Bandini suites can't compare to the motorhomes the team builds during the European leg of the season. The plain room gets us by, with enough essentials to appease the drivers, including a couch and a mini fridge stocked with water.

Music is my preferred method of easing nerves before races. I have a playlist and everything for each day of racing, since I tend to be a creature of habit who prefers solitude. Unlike other drivers, I leave the celebrating for after a race when I actually win. No one likes a guy who parties prematurely and doesn't even end up on the podium. We leave that for the sucky teams.

Maya's laugh seeps through the thin walls. Santiago acts differently from other Bandini guys, not minding Maya hanging around with him while he preps for the race. Small quarters don't allow for much privacy around here. I try my best not to listen, but I find the task difficult with our shared wall, telling myself whatever I overhear isn't my fault.

Maya's voice carries into my room. "Remember when you had your first kart race? You almost threw up inside your helmet, your nerves shot after that kid nearly crashed into you."

I like the sound of Maya's soft laugh.

"It was intense. Never underestimate an adrenaline rush because they're no joke. I think it took an hour for my heart to slow down and the nausea to go away. How do you even remember that? You were, like, six at most."

"Mom showed me a video of that race. They were reminiscing the day you signed the Bandini contract, including showing me tons of videos of you in your kart. They're so proud of you." Maya's voice sounds sentimental.

My parents never filmed my races, let alone watched them with a wave of nostalgia.

"You know they're proud of you too, right? With starting up your own vlog and supporting me."

Maya sighs. "Yeah, but you're the success story, and they sacrificed everything for you. The vlog is starting out, and things like that take time. Let's see what happens because I don't want to disappoint myself or anyone else. It's hard to get a decent following."

"I'll share something you post to help you gain followers. Plus, you're around a bunch of famous people—word will get out eventually. Just watch."

Curiosity pushes me to see what she vlogs about. I pick up my phone and google her, quickly finding and bookmarking her channel for later when I have time to check it out.

I also go ahead and request to follow her on Instagram since she set her account to private. *Fuck it, why not. I'm curious, nothing more.*

Their voices drop too low for me to catch the rest of their conversation. I find it difficult to imagine a childhood like Maya's since I'm an only child with no competition for my parents' limited attention. Hit the parent jackpot. They never married, avoiding a financial train wreck, messy divorce, and custody agreement neither of them wanted.

I put my headphones on and tune out the rest of their conversation. Eavesdropping distracted me enough, pulling me away from my usual mental clearing before races.

Not soon after, Santiago and I prepare for our cars. We zip up our matching race suits and grab our helmets. His was custom-made by some Spanish artist, who created a design with the Spanish flag colors, the Bandini's logo, and the number seven while mine is painted red and covered in sponsor logos. Even the chrome visor has a sponsorship decal, making me feel like a walking advertisement whenever I put it on.

I touch the scarlet-red paint, my hand running across the signature glossy coat of Bandini cars, the warm engine running beneath my fingertips. Even after all these years with the team, I still do this same prerace ritual and trace over the front wing and the white number twenty-eight. I've had the opportunity to change it, but I've stuck with my number since I started, and I don't plan on ever switching it, even if I win another championship.

Fans call me superstitious, and they're right because switching to the number one seems like a sure way to ruin my shot at winning a championship again.

I lie down in my seat and strap myself into the cockpit, the clicking of the belt further securing me. One of the techs hands me my gloves and steering wheel as I take a few deep breaths to ease my nerves.

The crew and I roll up to the front of the group, situating me in the P1 spot while testing my radio connection. I grin to myself beneath my helmet. Pole position will always be the most ideal spot in the whole race, and pride fills me that I claimed it. Have to start the year with a boom.

My heart pounds in my chest, the rhythm similar to the shaking of the engine. The team slips off my tire warmers before they rush off the pavement. The drivers complete a formation lap, and I stop my car on the painted spot designated for P1.

The lights above begin to illuminate one by one.

Five. Four. Three. Two. One.

All five red lights shut off. My foot pushes on the accelerator, and my car speeds down the runway, hitting a neck-breaking pace as tires rub against the pavement. Commotion buzzes through my earpiece. Team members speak to me, telling me how Liam stays behind me, with Jax overtaking Santiago at the front.

Fuck, I love this feeling. Nerves fire off in my body as adrenaline seeps into my blood, the sound of tires screeching across the pavement competing with the whooshing in my ears. Bodily sensations breathe new life into me. The engine hums as I push the car to its max capacity, testing the limits of the new race car model. My lungs tighten in my chest as I approach the first turn. I tap into my reflexes, becoming one with the car.

The beautifully executed turn happens in a blink. I tune out most of the radio chatter that sounds off through my helmet, concentrating on breathing in and out to relax my heart rate.

I continue to hold down my position as the race leader while we twist and turn down the track. If the team didn't keep me updated, I'd lose count of the laps. My car rips through the track like nothing. Liam, who is in P2, tries to overtake me at one of the turns but fails, his car falling back behind mine, sucking up the dirty air. The team principal shares who else may threaten my lead.

The race is touch and go between Liam and me for a while. A similar season start—both of us vying for the top-place spot. We have a competitive relationship on the track, knowing each other's moves since we were kids in karts. Both of our teams strategize with us for ways to beat each other.

Santiago isn't even a blip on my radar, seeing as the team hasn't spoken a single word about him.

I take a quick pit stop halfway through the race to get new tires. My car stops in the pit lane, allowing the mechanics to take over with their drills and machines. Process takes one-point-eight seconds. I thank the team via radio for their quick turnover time. A speedy pit crew are the unsung heroes of F1, the ones who make the magic happen once I box in the garage area.

I talk back and forth with a race engineer during my drive, communicating competitors' positions and specs. He wants to check in on how the car feels for the first race. The team shares strategies, and I follow along for the most part, although I'm not afraid to voice my disagreement with some calls because they don't pay me millions to blindly follow every command. They trust me behind the wheel.

I continue to hold the front-runner position for most of the first fifty-seven laps. Liam overtakes me a couple times, but I beat him back into second place with a few beautifully executed overtakes and a well-timed pitstop. During one turn, our front wings get awfully close to grazing each other, but he pulls back at the last moment. With one lap left, Liam will come out in second place, and Santiago will end up in fourth.

The sweet sound of engines roaring fills my ears. My hands grip the steering wheel tightly as I make the last turn toward the finish line. I push down on the pedal a few seconds early, allowing me to surge past the waving checkered flag before Liam. Fans scream as they announce I won the race.

"Fuck yes, guys, what a big win! Thank you, everyone.

Amazing first race. Let's fucking go!" My foot lifts off the throttle as I rush down the straight.

The radio buzzes with cheers.

I throw my fist in the air, proud of a race well done. *Suck it, Santiago.*

Bahrain
Grand Prix

CHAPTER SEVEN
Maya

My heart speeds up as Noah passes the finish line. Santi follows soon after, his car a red blur as he flies past the checkered flag. His performance on the track will frustrate him despite driving well. He still gets points for the Constructors' Championship, but in the end, against these other guys, it's not good enough. That's the life of high stakes and large salaries. Plus, the pressure of a big racing team and a pricey contract are on my brother's mind.

I meet Santi near the pit area. He smiles at the team when he gets out of the car, shaking hands and thanking the pit crew—an image of good sportsmanship. His jaw twitches while he signs fans' gear at a crowd barrier. Not wanting to get in the way, I decide to meet him in his suite instead of waiting outside. Better for him to relax first.

By the time he's made his way back to his room, he looks calm. I get up from the small couch and give him a hug. His sweaty body plasters to mine as my lungs get a deep inhale of oil, sweat, and rubber. Kind of gross. I pretend to gag as I wrap my arms around him, my head barely reaching his shoulders.

"You tried hard. Fourth place is good, and you'll be on the podium next time."

He returns my hug. "I'm disappointed I didn't try to cut around more. I played it too safe because I was scared of messing up the car."

"You can't race with a fearful mindset. You never have before, and you shouldn't start now, not when you're racing against the best. Think of it as another car with plenty of parts to fix anything."

Despite today's cautious performance, Santi has a rep of being ruthless on the track.

"You're right. I'll bring my best next time. Screw it." He pulls away from me.

Santi beats himself up whenever he doesn't place on the podium. I believe he can succeed next time out on the track, especially with plenty of races for him to improve his standing for the World Championship.

"I'm going to have to show up at the after-party to congratulate Noah. It's what sponsors would want, and I don't want to look like a sore loser." He sticks his tongue out at me. "Top five isn't that bad for the first one. I'll bounce back." A telling smile crosses his face. Santi cares about losing, but he won't let it get in the way of his professionalism. What an adult.

Yay for team spirit.

"Then we better get going. Let's go wish Noah a job well done." I give him a mischievous grin.

Noah may put on a whole arrogant show, but he backs it up with his racing. His performance makes it obvious why fans love him.

I sense the excitement from the rowdy crowd once Santi and I walk up to the podium event. Groups of them gather around, bouncing along to the music streaming from the speakers on the stage, waving around face poster cutouts of Liam and Noah. I can't imagine being so famous that people actually pay for big blown-up pictures of your face. Watching my own face staring back at me would make me die of embarrassment, right there on the stage floor.

Santi and I hang out in a VIP area off to the side, enjoying the show from a less sweaty and chaotic distance. My preferable choice. We have a full visual of the winners' podium, including the perfect view of Noah spraying his champagne on Liam. I sigh at the display. Santi looks over at me and raises his brow. I cover up my laugh with a cough, embarrassment tingeing my cheeks.

In F1, champagne is the messier equivalent of confetti launchers at other sporting events. Drivers shake bottles and splatter the contents everywhere. The crowd roars as champagne splashes on them, opening their mouths to capture droplets. Who needs Girls Gone Wild when you have F1 podiums?

Santi drops his disappointed mood, replacing his frown with a smile as all of them celebrate onstage. He even cheers when they announce all the winners.

We find Noah, Liam, and the other winner outside the press building after a postrace conference to say congratulations to them. I choose to give a thumbs-up while saying hi, barely suppressing a groan at how awkward I look. *Smooth, Maya. Killing it.*

Noah lets out a gruff snicker at my attempt, along with Liam barking out a laugh, adding to my embarrassment. Can't fault myself when I have no idea how to greet them.

I stand around awkwardly. Santi offers Noah and Liam a typical guy handshake and slap on the back. Noah's eyes heat up at the sight of me, swirling with deeper shades of blue than usual as they trail down my body. He flatters me. Either he sucks at subtlety, or he doesn't care if I notice.

My breath hitches when I check him out in his red race suit. Tight material presses up against firm muscles, highlighting a strict workout schedule. His hair looks sweaty and unruly, with a few pieces sticking up in different directions, and his wicked smile shines. He makes wild look sexy. I glance away before he catches me staring at him like a weirdo.

Being around all these hot guys throws me off. I need to stop having these intrusive thoughts about Noah, especially since he's my brother's teammate. How do other women keep up with these men? My brain bombards itself with images of puppies and grandmas to avoid checking him out again.

Liam's eyes gaze up and down my body. These guys boost my self-esteem by the second because they don't give a damn about hiding their attraction. He gives me a lazy grin when he notices my lifted brow and crossed arms. But I feel disappointed when my body doesn't have the same reaction to Liam that it does with Noah, my insides not heating up from a glance. Not even a flare of attraction. No racing heartbeat or warmth pooling inside me at his perusal, only a basic acknowledgment of his good looks.

"I'm Liam. We haven't had a chance to meet yet, but I saw you in the press conference and had no clue you're Santi's sister. You were a sight for sore eyes in a sea of old male reporters." He takes my hand and gives it a kiss like a prince from the olden days. *Oh, this one is full of pickup lines.* Hanging around him will be a good time.

I chuckle, snapping back into the conversation. "I'm making it my mission to attend as few of those events as I can. It's surprising how they let you get away with taking shots at one another and at the reporters too."

Nothing short of a comedy roast each week with Liam and Noah teasing each other, their candidness pleasing reporters and fans.

Liam beams at me. "You haven't seen anything yet. Wait for the dirty race moves, crashes, and losing streaks. That's when it all gets exciting." Liam cups a hand to his face, like he shares a secret, except his voice keeps the same volume level. "Noah here is a sassy one when he gets mad."

Noah looks at Liam with a glare that gives me chills, a feeling running from the base of my neck to the bottom of my spine. His narrowed eyes are ones I'd hate to be on the receiving end of. *No thank you.* He can be intimidating as hell, but Liam seems unfazed as he laughs and nudges Noah in the arm.

"Told you." Liam winks at me. His blue eyes twinkle as he beams at me. He has this lightness about him that automatically brings a smile to my face.

Santi shifts his weight from foot to foot, a signal that he wants to get going, since we need to pack and get ready to travel to the next stop in the circuit. Blame the busy schedule and long flights.

"We'll see you in Bahrain. Maya and I head out tomorrow morning on an early flight. We better get going because we need to pack and everything." Santi runs a fidgety hand through his hair. He loves to pack three days before his flight ever leaves, so it must eat him alive to have put it off this long.

"Man, you'll have to come on my private jet next time. Maybe we can shift around a few flights so you both can join." Liam's eyes sparkle as he pulls the slick move. He has this devil-disguised-as-an-angel kind of look, with blond hair, baby blues, and gleaming white teeth. Although his exterior screams innocent, his eyes say everything but.

I give him a small smile in return, highly doubting that his invitation to fly in his jet has much to do with my brother. Probably has a lot more to do with me. Santi doesn't notice Liam's flirting, shocking since he bothered me all weekend about how these guys are after two things only: trophies and ladies. And preferably in that order.

"That'll be cool. We'll definitely take you up on the offer," my brother says.

Noah gives Liam a side glance and crosses his arms. *Did he just roll his eyes?*

I don't have a chance to analyze the situation further because Santi pulls me away.

My vlog picks up more followers after Santi put it on blast for a week while we were in Sakhir for the Bahrain Grand Prix—

growing from a few hundred followers to a solid thousand. The idea hits me of posting YouTube videos of vlogs from each stop on our list. Last week, I filmed during our time in Bahrain, including a video from the practice sessions and interviews with the fans around the racetrack.

I edit and share a video of Santi placing fourth again in the Bahrain Grand Prix. Another loss for him, which makes for an unhappy brother. He says he's worked out the kinks of his new car. We move along, ready to hit the next race, time passing quickly with all the traveling from city to city.

Followers comment on how they love seeing behind-the-scenes footage of F1 racing. Turns out a lot of subscribers enjoy that part of my vlog, asking for more webisodes. After all the positive feedback, I dedicate a portion of videos to F1 racing and related activities. Not exactly my original plan, but hey, give the fans what they want. The change helps my numbers increase within a short amount of time. Thousands tune in weekly for the new videos.

New follower requests flood my Instagram, including Noah, Liam, and a few other drivers. I accept them and decide to keep my profile private from fans because I want to separate my vlog from my personal life.

Liam and Noah give my channel a shout-out on their own social media platforms when I tag them in racing clips. My numbers skyrocket, blowing my mind. Amazing what two pretty boys can do. By the time we fly to the third race of the season, I already have over ten thousand followers. *Ten points for Maya growing up! Look, Ma, I made it!*

We land in Shanghai for the Chinese Grand Prix. Santi

takes off soon after we get set up in our hotel room, since he scheduled tons of meetings. I hang around the suite and relax after a long flight because my body aches from sitting upright for hours. Another race, another basic hotel suite. White sheets and understated color palettes have become a staple of my life.

I eventually head over to the Bandini motorhome, located right next to the Shanghai racetrack. Easy access allows the crew to take breaks during busy days. It runs like a mini headquarters, with suites for the drivers to hang around along with meeting rooms for pre- and postrace consultations.

While grabbing a snack to eat, I run into someone. My eyes meet a pair of green ones that belong to a woman about my same height. She looks about my age with her blond hair wrapped up in a top knot, golden pieces escaping the haphazard hairdo. Dressed casually, she rocks a white slogan T-shirt, jeans with more holes than fabric, and white Adidas. She gives off a California beachy vibe from American television shows.

"Oh, sorry about that. I'm such a clumsy person." Her neck and chest turn a shade of pink that contrasts against her tan skin.

"It's no problem. I run into things all the time too. I haven't seen you around here before." *That sounded weirder out loud.*

"I'm Sophie. You probably haven't because I just got here." She offers her hand, and I take it.

"Maya. I haven't seen anyone my age except my brother. Glad I ran into you—literally."

She laughs. "It's my first time joining the race. I wrapped up my classes early for the year to spend time with my dad while he tours. Can't say no to a free vacation."

"I graduated in December! And who's your dad? I guess he's with Bandini then?" I wave around the lobby of the motorhome that bustles with activity.

She fidgets with her gold star necklace. "My dad is the team principal. He's the one who runs the show around here."

"Oh wow. And you're going to be here for the rest of the season?" I try not to sound too excited because I don't want to scare her off yet. But the idea of a new friend sounds nice.

"I'm going to try to convince my dad to let me take my fall classes online so I can stick around for the whole schedule. It's my first time around since I was younger, so I have to take advantage." Her smile makes the dimples in her cheeks pop out.

"Nice, we can hang out, since I'm going to be here for the whole season. It'll be awesome to have someone my age keeping me young." I smile at her.

"What's the deal with everyone around here? Spill the deets." She abandons her previous nervousness.

Does she get tense when people bring up her dad and his job? He keeps Bandini up and running because team principals are bosses without owning the company.

We both pull out a chair at one of the nearby tables, ready to chat and eat.

"If you're not yet aware, my brother is Santiago Alatorre."

Her eyes bulge out of her head. "No way. I can totally see it now that you mention it though. He's got that young Spanish hottie vibe going for him."

I hold back a groan. Can't say I think of my brother in that way, nor will I ever.

"Yeah, we both have the typical dark hair, brown eyes thing going for us, even though I'm the better-looking sibling. But don't tell him that. These drivers and their egos, fragile little things." I give her a cheeky grin.

"He's the new guy around here. Must be a lot of pressure to keep up with some of the best. How's he getting along with Noah?"

"Uh, it's been all right so far. They haven't crashed in the past two races. Go team." I do a cheerleader arm pump.

Sophie lets out a snort. "My dad was stressed to sign your brother on. He worried about how Noah would take it since he's been with Bandini for years. An original Bandini boy. The team doesn't take on young drivers—it's like their standard—but your brother's a world champion now, which makes him a hot commodity in this industry." She lifts one brow on command.

I lift a shoulder. "Yeah, he's grateful to be a part of the best team. I still think it's crazy he's one of the youngest members to ever join Bandini. But Noah has handled the transition okay, seeing as he hasn't chewed out my brother yet. Well, besides after the first press conference."

She waves her hand at my words. "Those meetings are fifty percent serious and fifty percent drama. Fans love to watch, sitting on the edge of their couches." She looks at me pointedly before continuing. "Be careful with Noah though. I hear all kinds of stories from my dad and other people."

"Like what?" I lean in, not wanting to miss a word of Sophie's insider info.

"He's cocky, self-assured, and kind of a jerk. Plus, he sleeps with lots of groupies. Yuck, yuck, and yuck. He's the guy your dad threatens to bury in a cement block. Well, at least my dad would, said so himself before I joined the season." Her nose scrunches. Seems like her dad may be slightly overprotective. "But Noah has a right to be confident, being a three-time World Championship winner and all at such a young age. He can race for years to come if he wants."

"Lovely. Nothing like a good playboy story to start the year off strong." Sarcasm weighs my words down.

"My dad has dealt with one too many phone calls from sponsors who were concerned with his behavior. But what can my dad do? Noah remains a professional out on the track, and he has proven to be one of the best drivers out there. He could just chill with the confidence sometimes."

"You know, Sophie, I think you and I are going to get along fine."

She returns my smile. We clink our water bottles together, cheering to our new friendship.

CHAPTER EIGHT
Maya

Turns out Sophie and I mesh well together. We both love listening to similar music, eating the same Ben & Jerry's ice cream flavor, and spending all our money at local boutiques instead of designer stores. Fundamental pillars of friendship.

I like having a new partner to attend sponsor events, press meetings, and any other snore-worthy activities. Especially one as quick and witty as Sophie. She comes off sassier than I'm used to, but I like how she doesn't take shit from anyone.

I tell Santi that I'll meet him at the sponsored event since Sophie and I will take a car together. He fails to hide his curiosity when he asks to meet the new friend I made, claiming he wants to make sure I'm not out corrupting a poor soul. His overprotection has hit new levels ever since we joined the F1 season.

"Okay, break down the guys for me. I haven't been around

these people for, like, three years." Sophie doesn't miss a beat, wanting a rundown before we've seen any of them inside the ballroom. Not that I blame her. I wish I had been half as prepared because these men ooze confidence and sensuality.

"You know my brother and Noah, obviously. I met Liam at the other race, and he's a total flirt. No promises that he may or may not eye-fuck you. Just a warning."

Sophie's eyes narrow. "I haven't seen him since before my freshman year of college. But I've read stories of him in the tabloids. Lately he's been popping up everywhere after he slept with his boss's niece." Her lips tip down in a frown.

I cringe at the information about Liam because what a low blow for his standing with McCoy. Bad timing with his contract renewal.

"Yeah, I don't know how wrong the gossip columns are about these guys, so I barely pay attention to them. But that's all I can share because I haven't met any of the other drivers yet."

"This sponsor event is for the entire Grand Prix, so I'm sure you'll see them in all their hotness, at least from far away. Sometimes I question if it's a requirement for F1 drivers to be ridiculously attractive. Sex sure sells." She lifts one brow.

I shake my head at her comment. Her assumption can't be far off, at least from the press videos and interviews I've seen on YouTube over the years.

We enter the ballroom. There are ginormous chandeliers hanging from the ceiling, dimly illuminating the room as classical music fills the air, while waiters offer appetizers and small plates of food. I love attending these events to see what party planners come up with. The venue looks beautiful and extravagant, bright lights glistening off my sequined dress.

Sophie and I make our way toward the bar, linking our arms together to make it through the crowd, sliding past a series of suits. Alcohol is a must at these types of events. I quickly learned that lesson after one too many boring conversations about race cars and bank accounts.

Sophie pulls us into an empty spot at the bar. Liam conveniently occupies the area next to her, not holding back as his eyes roam over her.

"Sophie, I haven't seen you in years." His baby blues smolder.

I try not to feel offended that he shares an interest in her after flirting with me. But I guess I should expect it, since all these guys have overactive sex drives.

"Liam." She nods her head politely. Strange way to greet someone you haven't seen in a while.

"What can I get you two fine ladies?" He waggles his brows.

"Isn't it an open bar?" Sophie's wit shines through, and I love it. She may become my favorite person during this whole championship business.

"Doesn't mean I can't order it for you. Make a man feel useful." He places a hand on his chest and pouts his lip.

"Because you, of all people, need your ego stroked more than usual. Yeah right… But I'll take a Moscow mule." Sophie flashes a smirk, making a dimple pop out.

He grins at her before he looks at me expectantly.

"I'll have the same."

Liam politely covers the tip for the bartender, making himself needed after all.

"Why do you two want to spend your night hanging with stuffy men? They're such a bore." He clinks his beer bottle to our glasses along with a quick *cheers* before he takes a swig.

Sophie's eyes stay planted on Liam as his lips tug on the bottle. "I'm on the hunt for my future husband. Was thinking of someone between the ages of forty and fifty. Old enough to pay for everything I want, young enough to not have a wrinkly dick."

I choke on my drink. Sophie shrugs at me while Liam's eyes linger on her chest for a second too long.

Pull it together, man.

"Sixty and older means you'll only have to rinse your mouth with bleach for ten years instead of twenty." Liam weighs the invisible options in his hands, beer bottle bobbing along with him.

"Unlike Sophie, who wants to become a mail-order bride, I came because my brother drags me everywhere."

"How's your brother transitioning with our broody prince?" Liam turns toward me before his eyes drift back to his new interest. His eyes narrow at her lips wrapping around a straw, eye-fucking her as she sucks on her drink.

I shoot him a look that tells him he can't bang my new friend because I actually want her to join me at events. Hopefully, my eyes say, "hands off." Nights like these tend to be lonely and dull with Santi always being busy.

He catches it and subtly nods with understanding. *Good.*

"Sophie's dad handles them, giving them enough love and attention to not make them jealous."

"He's a hard chief, running his team in tip-top shape while expecting the most from them. I wonder what it's like growing up in his home. Care to share?" Liam looks eagerly at Sophie while flashing her a bright smile.

"Wouldn't you like to know. Can't reveal our secrets to the enemy." Sophie pretends to seal her lips.

"I drive for a different team. Not quite enemies. Don't be dramatic."

"Oh, that's rich coming from you. Drama seems to follow you wherever you go." Sophie says the words with a smile on her face.

Liam's smile becomes a full-blown grin. "Keeping tabs on me?"

Sophie's cheeks flush at Liam's raised brow before she takes a drawn-out suck from her straw.

I break it up. *"All right.* Oh look, it's Noah."

I grab on to Noah's arm and drag him into the conversation, no longer wishing to be the third wheel.

Noah looks down at my arm like it offends him. *This is going swell.*

"Noah, this is Sophie. Sophie, Noah." I speak without thinking.

"We know each other. I've been on her dad's team for five years." He gives me a puzzled look that is immediately replaced with one of hunger as his eyes take me in, raking down my red dress. *Thank you, Sophie, for the outfit idea.*

My stomach dips as I check out his tux, a new weakness of mine. *Resist the bow tie, Maya.* This weekly situation tortures me. *What have I done to deserve this type of punishment?*

No matter how many times I tell my brain Noah isn't worth the trouble, my body won't agree. Out of nowhere, his index finger drags across my knuckles, an electric connection sparking at his touch. My drink sloshes when I pull my hand away in a jerky motion. Cool liquid trickles down my skin.

Noah's thumb picks up the droplets before he brings the pad to his mouth, his eyes remaining on mine. *Oh my God.*

I inhale deeply, filling my lungs with air. He shoots me a telling wink.

I let out a breath of relief as Noah talks, placing his hand in his pocket.

He smiles at Sophie in a caring way. "Nice to see you though, Sophie. Your dad sure sounds happy to have you visiting us. He talked all about it at lunch the other day, not shutting up about you finishing your degree. Says you should manage my funds."

Sophie gives a shake of her head. "And he told me lots about his dream team and how smitten he is with all the new changes. Are you playing nice with this one's brother?" She points at me and smiles.

Thank you for bringing up his rival, Sophie. Is it too late to cancel our friendship?

Noah chuckles. "Don't insult me. I thought I was his dream driver. But yes. I share all my toys with Santiago, making sure to play nice together at recess."

I roll my eyes at his smug smile, questioning why I thought bringing Noah here was a good idea. Just when I think he can be normal, he turns into an arrogant jerk.

Our exchange is saved yet again by a random guy. Based on his looks alone, I peg him as an F1 driver.

His British accent breaks up the current conversation. "Hey guys. What an event, am I right?"

Sophie and I both swoon at the Englishman in front of us, his accent packing a punch. The Brit greets us with hazel eyes, bronzed skin, and tight curly hair trimmed close to his scalp on the sides of his head. His unbuttoned black shirt displays neck tattoos trailing down the small reveal of his chest. He nails the quintessential bad boy look. A tattooed hand grips a glass tumbler, showing off inked knuckles and fingers.

Liam and Noah greet the stranger and introduce him as Jax, Liam's teammate.

"Who are these lush young ladies? You two have been holding out on me, I see." He gives Liam and Noah a wild smile and tips his glass up to them.

Sophie blushes, not immune to his charm. F1 hires the lookers of the group. Honestly, I doubt I'm any better off at the moment, with my cheeks matching the color of my dress.

"I'm Maya Alatorre, and this is Sophie Mitchell." *Go me for getting the words out.*

"Quite a duo you two have here." He shakes his head at Liam and Noah.

"We wanted to keep them away from your ugly face. Don't want to scare the girls away before they get to spend more time with us." Liam tips his beer in Jax's direction before taking a swig.

Noah suppresses a groan, barely audible over my laugh.

"Who knows? Maybe we can have them root for McCoy over Bandini one day. Women tend to be suckers for our accents." Jax lays the British accent on real thick this time.

"I'd rather *die* than cheer for your team." Sophie looks mock disgusted with a wrinkled nose and wide eyes.

"Don't go saying things you don't mean. One day in my pit garage and you'll be wishing you never have to leave." Liam smiles suggestively at Sophie. She smacks him on the arm before messing around with her drink again.

"Catch you all later." Jax tips his glass toward us before he steps away from the conversation.

Sophie practically drools on her dress, unprepared for the hotness that seeps out of F1 drivers. I tried to warn her earlier.

"Nice chatting with you both. We're going to be on our way now. Thanks for the drinks, Liam." I shoot him a grin while grabbing Sophie's hand and tugging her away.

"The drinks are free. Seriously, Liam, you're strapped for cash? McCoy not paying you enough?" Noah's voice carries over the music.

Liam lets out a deep laugh while I run away from Noah, because bow ties are my kryptonite.

Not Noah. Nope.

CHAPTER NINE
Maya

The crowd stirs with enthusiasm as pit mechanics prepare for the Chinese Grand Prix. Team members huddle around the cars, conducting engine checks and ensuring everything looks good to go. It's chaotic yet organized all at once. Hundreds of people help run the operation, from feeding drivers to running electrical tests on Bandini cars.

Noah goes through his solitary prerace ritual. I don't blame him for his preference, with the immense amount of pressure during every race, plus how draining fans and crowds can be. Santi and I hang out while he signs hats and gear for fans. He likes how I keep him company, telling me it eases his prerace jitters. Whatever works for him.

I enter the suite area, silence welcoming me since most of the crew work in the garage, making sure the cars are in top condition for the race.

On my way to the bathroom, I slam into a firm body,

confirming how running into people is becoming my specialty. A hand grabs my arm and steadies me. My eyes land on Noah's face, his deep blue eyes piercing mine. His hand remains on my arm while goose bumps break out across my skin.

I sigh at the contact, not liking these uncontrollable physiological responses. "I'm so sorry. I should watch where I am going." First Sophie, now him.

He pulls down his headphones. "No problem. These halls are pretty tight." His voice rumbles.

Why can't he have a nasally voice that throws me off, something to take away part of his sex appeal? I doubt it's too much to ask.

My eyes have a mind of their own, taking a quick peek at his body because I lack self-control. His race suit fits snugly against him, emphasizing his muscular form, the vibrant red color flattering his tan skin. My eyes close in a useless effort to try to rid the image of him. I wish Santi had an unattractive teammate, because I'd describe this experience as the worst kind of punishment.

"Have to get used to how busy it is around here on race days. What are you up to in there? You always seem quiet." I point my head in the direction of his door.

He taps his headphones. "I listen to music and get in the mental state for racing. Give myself a pep talk and work out."

"*You* need a pep talk? I can't believe it. I thought the fantastic Noah Slade could do no wrong, with no feat too scary." I look up at the ceiling wistfully as I place a hand on my heart.

His smirk falls, but he recovers quickly. "Even the best

need to get motivated. We drive cars at super speeds, so it can still be intimidating as fuck."

His arm grabs mine again and pulls me toward the wall. An attendant runs by, hands full of car parts and bags.

"Gotta be careful around here. You're small enough to be run over by a cart or something."

I look up into Noah's eyes and immediately regret it. His shade of blue easily becomes my favorite, reminding me of Barcelona's coastal waters.

"Good to know. I'll leave you to it then." My hand taps on his headphones before I turn toward Santi's room. I need distance from him, anything to break his arm away from mine.

"Wait." A calloused hand strokes my arm again, heating my skin where his touch lingers. Noah's lack of personal space frustrates me. His touchiness overwhelms me and overrides my brain, making me crave him. My body refuses to follow my brain's memo about Noah being bad news.

"Uh…" I can't form logical sentences while his hand lingers on my arm.

Not sure where this is going, a feeling of uneasiness flows through me.

Noah speaks up. "Why do you spend time with your brother before races? It's distracting."

I blink once, twice. And one more time for good measure. *Okay then, who died and made you king?*

His fingers trace patterns on my skin like he didn't say something rude. I doubt he grasps how his words come across to others. Why would he when he always gets what he wants anyway and is never told the words *no* or *please*? Entitled prick.

Dislike rolls through me at the response my body has toward him, the way my heartbeat picks up at his touch and how it ignites something inside me. I stare at his hands and will them away. He has strong hands that look large enough to dominate. Ones I want to feel on me, touching and squeezing.

My physical restraint around him is commendable. I deserve my own trophy and champagne shower, especially when his intoxicating clean scent confuses me. He makes it challenging to think about anything but him.

"It's not disturbing to my brother, and that's who matters to me. No offense." My breathy voice doesn't pack the punch I intend. I blame Noah's stupid hands for disrupting my brain cells, making me unable to form coherent sentences.

"I can hear you through the walls sometimes, your laughs included. Must be fun in there."

My body tenses at his admission. He sounds sincere. Maybe even wistful? I can't tell if I am imagining things, guessing emotions that could be wrong.

"I'll be sure to keep my voice down and not laugh too much. Don't want to disturb the champ and all." Sarcasm packs a blow this time around. *High five to myself.*

I confidently gaze into Noah's eyes again as he lets out a deep sigh. "I'm sorry. I didn't mean to offend you."

A little too late for that.

My gaze remains on his face, silently encouraging him to continue. I can wait for apologies.

"I'm not used to you or Santi being here. It's usually quiet on race days. My old teammate was like me; he typically listened to music and worked out. He took naps too. I don't mean to make you feel bad about it, so please don't take it the wrong way." He shifts his weight from one foot to the other.

He comes across genuine at least. His hand runs through his hair, making the dark strands stick up everywhere. A typical look for him. I smile at his state of disarray, aware I've found Noah's nervous tic. Who would have guessed the hotshot had one?

"It's okay. I don't want to be distracting for anyone either. I'll keep it down." I offer a sincere smile.

"All right, thanks." He turns toward his door.

"Noah." His name rolls off my tongue, prompting him to look over his shoulder. "Good luck today."

"Thank you."

Part of my heart melts at the sight of him winking before he closes the door.

I lean against a wall and wait for my heart to stop racing. Once I finally relax, I enter Santi's room again.

Liam leads the group today with pole position. Finally, a change of pace from Noah's usual P1 spot, with my brother as runner-up and Noah in P3. A third-place qualifier for Mr. Slade. What a tragedy. Bandini and McCoy outperform other drivers every time, which seems unfair since money makes all the difference in a sport like this. Top teams hire the best engineers and crew. A couple others follow close behind, working toward upper grid positions and better cars.

Drivers take off down the track once the lights fade from above the grid. The smell of fuel fills the air, strangely calming me. My hands clap as cars drive by. I love standing near the track's safety fence, feeling the vibrations of the engines as the cars rip past the lane, metal rings trembling underneath my fingers as I clutch the barrier.

On TV, cars may look like they hit normal speeds, but in person, F1 race cars rush past in a blur of colors and a burst of air, the roar of engines rivaling the crowd's cheers. My dark waves blow in the wind as Bandini's red cars fly by. The fast pace makes it difficult to tell which car Noah drives versus Santi, making me tune in to the speakers for race standings. Sparks fly as cars brush up against the pavement. Others cruise by, a mix of colors ranging from gray to pink. Race car models vary from sleek to clunky. I film the event from the sidelines today, wanting to stand at a popular turn overlooking the finish line.

No significant hiccups occur within the first twenty minutes. During the twelfth lap, a driver runs into a barrier, his car hitting protective blockades. Water splashes against the track from exploding plastic jugs. The driver unbuckles himself and yells expletives before throwing his helmet. He ends up kneeling next to his wrecked car, his body tense and shaking. Fans underestimate how emotional drivers get when they crash. A failure to complete a race. After all the hard work and sacrifices from the team, they retire with no points for the championship.

I turn my camera back toward the racetrack, getting fantastic shots of McCoy and Bandini cars rushing by, metal frames nearly touching as they try to pass each other. The howl of the engines brings a smile to my lips.

Liam and Noah fight it out for first and second place throughout the first forty laps. Excitement has yet to wear off after the first hour of watching them compete against each other, the crowd still yelling chants and cheers. My legs cramp at standing for an hour and a half. In hindsight, I should have packed a chair and snacks.

By lap fifty, my brother tails Noah's race car. Santi's defensiveness keeps me on edge. I grip the fence as they careen down the track, Noah holding his lead. Santi's car hangs uncomfortably close to Noah's. *Too freaking close.* During a straight stretch, my brother speeds up before he swerves while trying to get around Noah.

I gasp as the front wing of my brother's car hits the back of Noah's race car. Santi spirals out behind him, both cars trembling as they drag across the pavement. My brother has crashed into Noah at about one hundred and eighty miles per hour. The Bandini cars spin around like two red yo-yos across the track, the drivers unable to do anything about the loss of control. My stomach lurches. The crowd quiets and listens to the grating sound of metal, a path of sparks and smoke trailing behind the Bandini cars. Their cars finally stop near a side barrier. Smoke plumes from both engines and billows up into the blue sky.

Shit. Noah and Santi climb out of their cars. The safety team ensures that the drivers remain uninjured while a tractor picks up the messed-up Bandini cars with a crane. Noah flails his arms around at my brother. He tosses his helmet off to the side while he grabs my brother by the race suit and pushes him. My brother catches his footing before he falls over.

I take in a deep breath, relief rushing through me that they are both safe. The risk of crashing always hangs over the heads of drivers in this sport. Some have died during crashes like today. But most drivers get out of their cars unharmed because of all the safety precautions, like fireproof race suits, helmets, and the bar above the car that protects the driver from barrel rolls. This crash proves why F1 has safety protocols in the first place.

The broadcaster announces that Noah and Santi will retire for the rest of the race, the worst news for the Bandini team. A major loss since neither teammate will receive points for the Constructors' Championship. Plus, it's a strike against my brother's confidence.

I wait for them in the pit suites, in the same hallway where I ran into Noah earlier. Noah and Santi make their presence known the moment they enter.

"What the fuck were you thinking? What type of reckless, amateur shit are you trying to pull here? That crappy move cost us everything today."

My body stiffens at the way Noah talks to my brother. I peek around the hall's corner, wanting to get a look at the scene. Noah's back faces me while my brother looks furious, a rare happening for him. He has flushed cheeks, narrowed eyes, and pinched brows.

My brother's eyes flare. "I already said I'm sorry twice, Slade. Do you want to kiss and make up?"

Last-name dropping and the sarcasm dripping from Santi's voice are never a good sign.

"If you want to prove your worth, try to do it without

crashing a million-dollar car. It'll serve you better in the long run. But if you wanted to ride my cock, all you had to do was ask nicely." Noah's hard voice carries through the halls.

"Fuck you. You act like your God's gift to earth. News flash, I'll beat you one day, and so will everyone else. Get over yourself."

My eyes strain, and I press a hand against my mouth. Noah doesn't respond. He turns toward my hiding place in the hallway and practically runs me over on his way to his room. His hands grab on to me, stabilizing my body before I topple over.

Dull eyes and rosy cheeks greet me.

"Sorry," he mumbles before shutting the door to his room.

My heart squeezes at how unhappy he looks. I don't want to feel bad for him, because he acts like a dick to my brother, but I can't help pitying him. It sucks how my brother made a stupid move that has severe repercussions for the team. Points aside, morale between these two can't be lower.

I enter Santi's suite to sit on the couch when Noah's phone rings next door. He rarely gets phone calls, so I can't fight my curiosity. I try my best not to listen in on what happens in his suite. And by trying my best, I mean I currently have a cup held up against the wall to try to amplify the noise. All I get are muffled words. A pretty unsuccessful spy mission if I do say so myself, my ears only catching a few words like *father* and *crash*.

Santi comes into the room while I google how people use glasses to eavesdrop. He eyes the empty cup in my hand curiously but doesn't mention anything about it, choosing to ignore my playful smile.

Santi plops himself on the couch next to me and lets out a sigh, the defeated look on his face pulling at my heartstrings. His fingers fumble with unzipping his race suit while his feet toe off his sneakers. He puts his head in his hands. The room fills with the sound of his deep breaths in and out.

I give him a few moments before I probe. "How did the talk with the chief engineer and Noah go?"

I learn from my mistakes, making sure to keep my voice low enough for Noah not to overhear us.

"Noah's pissed to say the least. And I get it because I fucked up bad. But I apologized to him the moment we got out of the cars and when we got back here. I hadn't even seen the footage yet, but I knew it was my fault."

"He shouldn't have yelled at you like that in front of everyone, making a scene. It's wrong and embarrassing for both of you. And not mature when you already said sorry."

Okay, the volume of my voice has increased a bit. Noah may or may not be listening in on our conversation at this moment, no thanks to me.

"I screwed him out of a good number of points. It's going to take time to recover from that loss. I would be angry too if it were me." Santi's hands pull at his hair while his face stares at the floor.

"You are both teammates trying to figure each other out. The two of you have different styles of racing, and you need to find your groove and work together." I root for both of them. For the sake of Bandini and the Constructors', they need to put aside this rivalry between them.

"F1 Corporate will make us do a postrace conference

together to represent Bandini." He looks up at me finally. His red-rimmed eyes lack their usual shine, and his sadness makes my heart hurt for him.

I take a deep breath, knowing what I have to do. "I'll join you. What's the worst that could happen? It's not like you can crash again."

Famous last words.

The press meeting is not the same as watching Santi and Noah crash in real life. On the racetrack, you can't see or feel the tension between the drivers. Except for the team radio, but not many people listen in unless the videos end up on YouTube.

See, in a press meeting, all the emotions hang around like unwanted groupies. Reporters salivate at the idea of these two guys sitting on a duo panel. Tension fills the room like a dense cloud, my brother shifting in his seat while Noah's gaze focuses on the bright lights in front of him. I cringe at the awkwardness between them. The guys have many cameras on them, making it hard to hide anything.

I take back my previous comments about press conferences being yawn-worthy. I'd take snooze fests over train wrecks any day of the week.

Noah's jaw ticks when the reporter asks Santi a question.

"It shouldn't have happened today. Our team lost a lot of points because of it."

The reporter doesn't let Santi off easily because good answers don't sell magazine covers.

"Is it true that the team engineer told you to brake the car and pull off Noah's tail, but you didn't listen?"

My brother moves around in his seat. "I don't want to discuss it. The team already lost today. It's bad for us. Do we need to harp on the logistics of how I messed up?"

Noah subtly shakes his head before his sharp eyes look straight ahead. He replaced his tight race suit with a sponsor polo shirt, his hair pressing smoothly against his scalp with not a single dark strand out of place yet. I prefer his charming wickedness over this sad state any day of the week. His arms cross against his chest, bringing my attention to the ridges of muscle etched into them, tan skin gleaming under bright lights.

I check out reporters around the room, searching for any distractions, but my eyes drift back to the press table and roam over Noah again. *Ugh. Why does he have to be my brother's racing rival?*

I shift on my feet, my sneakers scuffing against the slick tile. My attention snaps back to my brother, choosing to ignore my attraction toward Noah because I don't want to accept those feelings. Instead, I list off all the reasons Noah's bad news in my head.

It's way too soon.

I barely know him.

He's my brother's teammate. Rival even.

He's a man-whore with more hookups than the whole Formula 1 grid combined.

He looks like he'll screw with my head as well as he'll screw me in bed.

Working out all the reasons why Noah Slade is a bad idea is

a useful distraction, keeping me away from the drama ensuing in front of me.

I tune in again when the reporters decide to move their attention to Noah.

"Noah, tell us your thoughts on the situation."

These reporters decide today is the day for such open-ended inquiries.

"It's a shitty situation that should have never happened. Santi's apologized, and we are sorry. Our racing team has to fix our mistake, and we're appreciative of their efforts to get our cars up and running for the next race. We love this sport, bad accidents aside. We're not in it to retire early from the race and go home empty-handed. This is the worst-case example of teamwork, but we'll work on it."

He handles questions like a professional. *Not bad.*

My brother visibly relaxes in his seat, relief evident in his eyes.

My expectations for today didn't include Noah acting like such a pro. He pushes aside his earlier bad mood in front of the cameras, presenting himself as the ultimate teammate. I can see why Bandini keeps him around besides his talent behind the wheel. His appearance makes it obvious why women gravitate toward him, with him being such a smooth talker, willing to put on a show.

The rest of the conference is dull. I sneak glances at Noah because what is a girl to do during the rest of a boring meeting? He catches me staring at him, making my cheeks flush.

And that wicked smile he sends me when the cameras stop rolling? The one promising more? Yup. I see it.

Oh man, I'm in trouble.

Miami
Grand Pix

CHAPTER TEN
Noah

Maya totally tries to hide how she checks me out. I no longer think its mild curiosity, chalking up her initial reactions as her way of sizing up her brother's new teammate. But we've danced around each other for a month, ever since the season started, glancing at each other and avoiding physical contact. She fills me with a different excitement—because of her and the reactions she thinks go unnoticed.

My new relationship with Santi is already off to a bad start. No need to fuck it up more with a quick hookup, no matter how hot his sister is. And I mean she is a drop-dead gorgeous woman. Thoughts plague me about ways I would defile her, like wrapping her ponytail around my arm while her lush lips wrap around my cock, pump after pump until I finish. I'm a dirty bastard, but I can't do that to my teammate—no matter how much I want to. So I lock up my fantasies for another time with another girl.

I don't shit where I sleep. Period. End of story.

My dick retaliates against my brain though, because I steal glances at her across the Bandini garage. I could lie to myself and say its sheer curiosity. Based on the way my cock hardens around her, it's more than that, and frustration runs through me at denying myself.

I'm ashamed to admit I jerk off in the bathroom sometimes after seeing Maya. No use denying my terrible habit. It happens mainly after races, with all the pent-up adrenaline begging for release. But she always hangs around, so lately I've been taking a lot of cold showers, trying to rid the images of her from my head. She wears these tight shorts that show off her tan legs, plus she looks fucking fantastic in Bandini shirts. It brings out a possessive side of me, happy to see her in my team's colors, bobbing around the pit garage with her camera.

Can I ask the chief to ban attire like hers altogether from Bandini's motorhome? May solve half of my problems.

She bends over the cockpit of Santi's car, checking out the inside with one of the engine mechanics.

The mechanic darts his eyes everywhere except on Maya's jean-clad ass hanging in the air. Thank God she didn't wear her scrappy shorts that look shredded and two washes away from breaking apart. I can only take so much. She doesn't even notice how the pit barely buzzes with noise as she busies herself with filming the inside of Santi's car for her vlog.

I shift my jeans because my aching cock is pulsing uncomfortably against my zipper. My eyes glance around the rest of the room, catching how the pit crew steals glances at her perky ass. And I don't like it one bit. Where the fuck is Santiago when you need him?

Santiago, please come collect your sister. She fucks up everyone's work schedule.

Thank God Maya finally pops her head out. Her hair lacks her usual ponytail with wavy brown strands flowing down her back and framing her face. I'd consider her angelic-looking, except her body is meant for sin—to fuck hard and long. My type of damnation. I suppress a laugh at the comical display of many heads snapping back to their jobs. A hum of drills and the beeps of computers start back up again, heads no longer facing in Maya's direction.

Her smile beams at me once I catch her attention, filling my chest with a kind of warmth I don't recognize often. I return her smile with one of my own because I'm not a total asshole. My eyes snap toward the small black camera and tripod she grips in her tiny hand, the lens taunting me as she inches toward me.

Ah, explains the warm smile. I shake my head at her cleverness, a smirk replacing my grin.

"And here we have Bandini's finest, but not to me, because I still think my brother is the best. It's Noah Slade. Say hi to everyone." She points the thing directly up at me, not asking for approval. I like how she's the type to ask for forgiveness instead of permission. Reminds me of myself.

I don't like interviews that aren't mandatory. But fuck it, if it helps her get new followers, I can go along with it.

A megawatt smile breaks out across my face. I lie and

tell myself I do it for the fans, but my dick and I both know what's up.

"A real vlogger shouldn't be biased," I grumble.

Her soft and breathy laugh makes the tripod shake, and damn if it isn't the best sound I'll hear all day. What other noises can I get her to make between the two of us?

Get your head out of the pit lane, Noah.

"More on that later, everyone. So, Noah."

My stiff cock stands to attention at the way my name rolls off her tongue, sultry and lulling on the vowels. I shift my feet subtly to ease the ache.

I would love to hear her repeat my name under different circumstances. Behind closed doors, where no one can hear us, preferably without clothes on.

What a sick joke on me where I crave attention from the one girl I want but can't have. And even worse, she remains oblivious. I want to spend more time around her and suck up her happiness like the goddamn black hole I am.

Maya resumes, unaware of my inner conflict. "Would you want to give the fans a tour of your own car?" She bats her eyelashes, laying the charm on real thick. Her brown eyes gleam up at me. Damn, who the fuck could resist looks like that?

"Sure, fuck it. Why not."

Nice, Noah. Cursing on camera.

Her head bobs with excitement at my agreement. Knowing her, she's resisting clapping her hands because of the camera.

We walk over to my car. Engineers take the cover off to

give me easy cockpit access. My hand drags across the front of the car, giving the hood extra attention. Maya's eyes darken as she focuses on my hands. Further evidence that she is affected by me too, proving our attraction is not one-sided. My brain logs this information for another time.

If she wasn't Santi's sister, I would invite her back to my hotel room and show her a good time, help her give in to temptation. But since she is, I have to be respectful. Not typically my status quo.

I do it for the good of the team of course.

"Care to share with viewers what it's like behind the wheel?" Her lips tip upward.

I nudge a pit crew attendant. "Hey, can you grab my steering wheel? Please."

He hurries away at my request.

"While we wait, I'll give fans a tour. New watchers of the sport don't know how we F1 drivers are practically lying down inside the car. Sometimes it's even hard to see over our steering wheels. Makes turns more difficult if you can imagine." I casually lean against the car.

Maya's bright smile encourages me to keep going.

"Depending on the type of damage we sustain during the race, the pit crew may have the spare part needed to fix it. Here's the wheel now."

Maya steps into me, angling the camera to get a good shot. I inhale the fresh floral scent of her perfume, a recognizably addicting smell.

I explain the mechanism and buttons on the wheel. Bandini likes to keep tight-lipped about our technology, so

I withhold spilling any trade secrets. Maya nods along while paying attention to everything I say. Her head bobs, and small smiles make my heart clench—a new sensation that spreads through my chest, unlike any feeling from winning a race.

I wrap up my explanations. She flips the camera screen up and turns the tripod toward the two of us. Her body presses against my side as she tries to get us both in the frame, distracting me with the contact of her skin.

I shake my head at her attempt to film us together with her short arms. The camera cuts off part of my head, prompting me to grab the tripod and fix the angle to fit us in the frame. Her intoxicating scent washes over me again. The smell of her turns me on, like fucked-up pheromones drawing me in, showing how screwed I am.

"And that's what it's like behind a driver's steering wheel. For my next video, I'll be meeting up with the pit crew as they tackle the Miami Grand Prix."

I smile down at her. Her enthusiasm about her vlogging rubs off on me, uncharacteristically agreeing to this segment despite my usual distaste for these kinds of things. Not to mention how I check out her Instagram daily since she approved my request. My dirty little secret.

I lie to myself about how I don't want to miss out on her vlogs when I appear in them. But I have a hard time convincing myself when I check out her travel videos too, curious about what she does during her free time away from the racetrack.

"Any last words you want to share with Bandini fans?" She nudges me with her elbow.

"Tune in next week to see me kick Santiago's ass." I smile at the camera.

She laughs and elbows me harder this time, the tiny bone barely making a dent.

"Spoken like the conceited athlete we all know. See you next time." She waves goodbye to the camera and shuts it off.

I take in one last breath of her addicting smell before she pulls away, the heat of her body gone.

Yup. I'm a sick motherfucker.

"Thanks for doing that. I wasn't sure if you would, to be honest." She tucks a loose lock of hair behind her ear.

Her nervousness comes back in full force, guilt tugging at the few heartstrings I have left. I can't help being an asshole.

"No problem. Can't have you only showing Santiago's side of things. It's good PR for the company anyway." *Right.* I have trouble believing my own lie despite how easily it flows off my tongue.

"Yeah sure…" Her voice tells me she doesn't buy my brand of bullshit. "Maybe you can join another time. I better get going since I have to edit all this before tomorrow. See you around!" She sends me one last smile over her shoulder.

"Bye," I grumble, hating how her departure makes me feel…

Lonely.

Spanish
Grand Pix

CHAPTER ELEVEN
Maya

upload the video I filmed in the garage where Noah made his cameo appearance. The comments section floods with positivity and excitement. People share how they're happy to see Noah in a more relaxed setting, away from the press circuit and racetrack. Hard to miss the barrage of horny women asking to be Noah's baby mama.

With every day I spend around Noah, I learn more about who he is once the cameras stop rolling. Before qualifiers, he likes to drink two espresso shots, which can result in him bouncing off the walls for a solid hour. Turns out he loves to chat while espresso runs through his veins. He also enjoys a session of yoga early in the morning before race days, a tradition he invited me to join during the last Grand Prix. Safe to say yoga is not my workout of choice. *Namaste in bed, thank you very much.*

Noah even tugs on my ponytail now whenever he passes by

me. At some point, lines blurred as we accepted a new level of comfortability with one another.

I learn details about him that chip away at my resolve, making it hard to resist him. He is no longer just a conceited guy who makes my eyes roll into the back of my head. Don't get me wrong. He still acts smug as hell—that has not changed. But I like it. The more time I spend around him, the more he draws me in.

Imagine my surprise when my usual mantras won't work anymore.

Not even I'm only up to good.

Because I want to be really bad.

Hooking up with Noah is the same as picking up two BOGO pints of Ben & Jerry's. It sounds and tastes like a great idea at first, but you overestimate your self-control, and next thing you know, the whole thing is gone and you have a stomachache.

Basically, Noah is a heartache disguised in pretty packaging. He has the same allure as a pint of chocolate fudge brownie ice cream.

And no sex on earth is worth his kind of trouble.

See, Mom, I told you I would try to be more responsible! Look at me go.

The current standings of the F1 World Championship include Noah in first place, Liam in second, and Santi in third. My brother bounces back up the ranks after his second-place performance in Miami.

Noah is a force to be reckoned with. His confidence is well-deserved because the guy is a badass behind the wheel with spot-on instincts and fast reflexes. My brother could learn a lot from him if they put aside their dislike for each other. Things have been tense since the Shanghai fender bender, their dynamic not entirely back to normal despite how two weeks have passed.

The best thing about this next Grand Prix is that we get to go back home to Spain. My mouth waters at the idea of eating tapas, and my chest warms whenever I think of being reunited with my parents again. They will visit us and watch Santi race. We look forward to returning to our home country after being gone for two months, because time flies by while on the road.

That's why my resolve slips around Noah. We've played around each other for months, with me putting in extra effort to resist his sex appeal. Hard stuff when he wears his race suit.

Our driver drops us off at the F1 paddock area. My eyes widen with surprise as I take in all the different buildings made out of motorhomes, a distinct setup compared to previous races.

No words pass my lips as we walk down the row of uniquely colored buildings. Each team has their own motorhome with dining halls, meeting rooms, and larger suites. The building allows for a place of relaxation during the hustle and bustle of the busy race week. We still have our hotel rooms to sleep in, but this is where Santi and Noah spend a lot of their downtime.

We stop next to Bandini's motorhome. Red paint gleams under the sun, looking sleek and modern while still carrying the classic feel of the brand.

The motorhome has a luxurious feel when compared to pit suites from the flyaway races. People hang by the bar and restaurant on the bottom floor. Santi shows me the upper levels, including private suites and an outdoor patio where I see myself setting up my laptop to edit videos and content.

Bandini's motorhome shows how much funding the brand has from sponsors, including Noah's dad, who invests heavily in the team. Supposedly it looks good to have a previous race legend backing a brand.

I get tugged to the side before I can enter the suite.

"I need your help," Sophie whispers despite us standing in an empty hall. Her wide green eyes and heavy breathing make me hesitant.

"With what? And why are you whispering?"

"I was invited on a date." She chews on her cheek.

"That's great! Do you need help picking out an outfit?" Her glare makes me stop clapping my hands together. "Or not?"

"Not. This is the worst thing. Liam bet if he placed on the podium in Miami, we would have to go on a date. I stupidly agreed because I was buzzed at a sponsor event. Plus, his previous track history was awful so I didn't think he would actually make it."

My eyes widen. "Oh, you didn't." Bets never ever end well.

"Tragic, I know. So I'm going to go because I don't rescind bets. But…he never specified the type of date." Her smug grin sets off a few alarms.

"Am I missing out on different types?" Not exactly connecting the dots here.

"I'm going on a double date. And you're coming with me." Her small hands grip my arms.

"What! No way," I sputter.

She's crazy. The last thing I want to do is go on a double

date with them. Talk about awkward. Sophie and Liam have enough sexual tension between the two of them to make me sweat. And I highly doubt Liam wants a double date to start with, seeing as he salivates when Sophie gets close.

"It'll be us, Liam, and Jax. You remember him, right? British, hot, looks like he wants you to call him daddy in bed. It's a win-win for us." She gives me a sickly sweet smile.

I burst out laughing. "Where do you even come up with this stuff?"

"I'm full of ideas. Will you do it for me? Your only friend here?" Sophie clasps her hands together and rocks back and forth on her feet. She plays the innocent card well. I grimace at how it works on me, a sucker for helping others no matter how bad the idea sounds.

"I'm game. But I'm only doing this for you. When is it?"

"Tonight! Before they get busy with the prerace stuff." Sophie rubs her necklace. She throws this on me on the same day. How thoughtful.

Lovely. I'm bursting with excitement here.

"My brother is going to kill me," I mutter.

"Oh, nonsense. He hooks up with a few ladies on the side anyway. He gets it."

Who the hell says things like that? She should count herself lucky that I like her and she's one of my only friends here.

"Ugh, come on. Get a filter. Gross." I stick my tongue out at her. That's absolutely the last thing I want to hear about, like ever. Right up there with hearing how my parents still have sex together.

"We better go pick out our outfits. We should look our

best." She grips my hand in hers, demonstrating a shocking amount of strength for a tiny person.

The whole thing may be a terrible idea, but at least I can look good while doing it.

We end up going shopping together around the streets of Barcelona. I don't mind because I love feeling surrounded by my type of people for the first time in months. Hearing others speak Spanish and smelling fresh food from different restaurants makes me feel at home.

Sophie and I grab lunch together at one of the local spots. We chat while stuffing our faces with tapas, draining the contents of our sangria glasses. *Home sweet home.*

Sophie's cheeks flush, alcohol getting to her head, as she admits a fascinating tidbit of information to me.

"One of the reasons I'm stuck going on this date isn't only because of the bet." She lets out a deep breath.

My eyebrows draw up. I keep quiet, not wanting to interrupt and make her lose her nerve. Call me curious to get more information about her and Liam.

Sophie rattles on. "I created a fuck-it list for my time traveling with Bandini. Basically, it's a mix of different things I googled, from normal bucket list stuff to sexy items."

I choke on my drink. "Did sweet Sophie come up with a naughty bucket list? How bold of you." I waggle my brows at her.

She snorts, not holding back. "I was tired of living the perfect life my dad wanted. So I decided to create a list before I came here." She pulls out a small, laminated square from her purse, unfolding the page so it becomes the size of a standard piece of paper. I have no clue how she did that.

I check out the different items, my eyebrows rising at a few of them.

"Then what's the connection to Liam?"

"Well…remember the time we sang karaoke in Shanghai?"

I nod my head.

She swallows a gulp of sangria before continuing. "The list fell out of my bag, and Liam grabbed it. He knows about it and added, 'Go on a date with a bad boy.' See?"

Black scrawl mars the bottom of the page, messing up her perfectly color-coded list of items. Dots connect in my head.

"Oh my God, he offered to help with these?"

A red flush crawls from Sophie's neck to her cheeks.

"I only agreed to this one date. That's it, no others because I don't want his help. No matter how hard he tries. But I wanted to tell you because we're friends and all, which means we share everything together." Her honesty fills me with happiness, knowing our friendship has reached a new level of trust.

My brother did, in fact, disagree with the date. Not a shocker.

He paces the floor of my room while I finish getting ready, his feet dragging across the carpet while he mumbles to himself. I snicker as he runs a hand down his face for the fourth time today.

"You're going to give yourself wrinkles by thirty if you keep that up." I point to his face with my mascara wand.

He crosses his arms against his chest and scowls at me.

"Why Jax and Liam? Seriously, it couldn't be anyone besides them?"

I give him a pointed look. *Yeah, right. Imagine if I had said Noah asked me on a date.*

"What about the nice guy you talked to at the press conference last week? Nerdy, has a comb-over, but can ask a decent question?"

If the comb-over isn't enough to warn me away, the suspenders are a hard no.

I shake my head at him and exhale. "It's a favor for Sophie. She begged me to join her because she didn't want to go alone with Liam. So here I am. No need to freak out about it."

He should congratulate me for sacrificing myself for the greater good and my friendship.

"Do you need to wear *that*?"

I look down at my short red dress and shrug. "Eh, it's cute. I don't want to be underdressed since we're going to a nice restaurant."

A growl of frustration leaves his lips. His overprotection may be sweet, but the charm wears off pretty quickly when I deal with it weekly.

"Don't worry, big bro. I'm not even interested in Jax. I would rather be in the hotel room in my pajamas than going out right now." I find minimal appeal in attending a fancy dinner, unlike my brother who lives for this life, with crowds of people feeding his energy. He loves the glam and glitz of the F1 community. But me? I prefer a cozy life of snuggling up with a good book or a new TV show.

I shudder at the thought of him hooking up with girls. *Damn, Sophie, why did you have to tell me about that?*

"Fine, but try to be back here before midnight. I won't be

able to fall asleep thinking you're out there with them." He doesn't have to tell me twice because I like midnight bedtimes.

The last thing my brother hears is my laugh as I exit the hotel room, the door thudding behind my back. My eyes meet Noah's as he exits his room.

Seriously, he stays on our same floor?

These run-ins are becoming way too common with us. It concerns me since I feel like he's wearing me down, little by little.

His gaze explores my body before he closes his eyes, his lips moving like he's saying a silent prayer. His reaction tells me I get a gold star for the red dress choice.

I giggle at the sight of him being rattled, which is so unlike his usual calm and collected self.

"Going somewhere?" His blue eyes reflect two dark pools. My breaths shallow as his eyes rake down my body again. He follows me to the hotel's elevator bank, meeting my strides, step for step.

I take a deep breath before I respond to him. But I realize a little too late how much of a terrible idea it is as his smell engulfs me and makes my brain foggy.

Clean, fresh, bone-jumping worthy.

Another deep inhale before I speak. "Yeah, I'm going to dinner since we have a free night and all."

Wednesdays are relaxation days for crew and people like me who don't have to do too much.

He presses the elevator button and turns toward me. "Few and far between with such a busy race schedule. Who are you going to dinner with?"

All right, back to asking about the date.

"Sophie and, uh, Liam...and Jax." My execution is anything but smooth.

He remains silent as he checks out my outfit again, lingering on my legs before his eyes meet mine. I send a prayer for someone to get me out of here ASAP. The elevator takes forever, the lit-up button taunting me as I will it to come quicker.

"Hmm, I didn't get an invite." He pulls his phone out of his pocket and scrolls through it, searching for an invite that never happened.

I use the opportunity to check him out. Powerful forearms taunt me, on full display because of the rolled-up sleeves of his button-down shirt, along with jeans that hug his tight ass and muscular legs. His dark hair is slicked back, not yet disturbed by his fingers. My teeth bite down on my bottom lip to suppress a groan.

His lips turn down as he locks his phone, making me feel both satisfied and sad for him. *Is it possible to have such a mix?* Noah screws up everything inside me, including my common sense.

I shrug at his response, playing it off even though my heart races in my chest. "Maybe they thought you were busy. We'll be sure to invite you next time."

We won't, because there can't be a next time.

The doors open. *Thank the Lord.* We both enter at the same time, brushing against each other. My body responds to the physical contact, desperately wanting more, but my brain makes a wise decision to situate myself in the opposite corner of the elevator.

"Yeah, maybe. Where are you having dinner then?" He runs a hand through his hair, now messing it up like I knew he would. I smirk at his signature style.

"I think it's called Bouquet. An expensive place I assume based on the outfits Sophie picked out." I bring his attention back to me. *Crap.*

He coughs. "Hmm." One word that has a heavy weight to it, stifling us in this stuffy box.

He remains silent for the rest of the descent. Air charges as movie scenes of couples hooking up in elevators flash through my mind. My body presses up against the side of the cart, my hands gripping onto the cool hand rail as I rid the dirty thoughts from my head. Our closeness and the delicious fumes of his cologne wreak havoc on my body.

He glances over at me one more time before the doors open up to the lobby and I dart out. I peek over my shoulder and give him a quick wave, my spine tingling at his devilish smile, feeling his eyes on me as I power walk to the group. The glint in his eye and the smile on his face promise more.

That's a problem for future me.

Damn, I coined my new mantra.

We're two drinks into the night, and dare I say, the date is turning out to be a fun time.

Liam whispers a few sweet nothings into Sophie's ear. Every time he says something to her, she takes a chug of wine like a messed-up drinking game between the two of them.

Jax comes across as a nice guy. A bit withdrawn but funny

and edgy. Sophie's daddy comment pops up in my head, because I mean, come on. The guy is sexy. But honestly, does she think he does that? She wouldn't say something that ridiculous if there wasn't a little bit of truth in it.

Jax has curly hair he inherited from a combination of his "mum" and his dad, who is one of the best Black boxers from the United Kingdom. He gets his hazel eyes, sharp cheekbones, and pouty lips from his Swedish side. A total knockout with muscles and brains to match. I ask him about his family, but he closes himself off, switching the subject back to me.

Jax can check off most people's hot-guy boxes, but I can't figure out what doesn't work for me. *Maybe I don't like tattoos?* He tells me they cover his body, black ink peeking out from the collar of his button-down shirt. Intricate designs cover his knuckles and right hand. I ask about a couple of them, but there are too many to get into.

When he grabs my hand across the table, my body doesn't respond to it; it's the equivalent of holding a stranger's hand. I frown at the lack of flutters in my stomach or racing heartbeat. By the time we order our entrées, I've come to the conclusion that I don't feel a sexual connection, which is fine because it puts less pressure on me. Friendship sounds like a good idea.

"Oh, hi, guys. I heard you were out here tonight. I think my invite got lost in the mail."

My stomach flips at the sound of Noah's voice. I suppress the temptation to rub my eyes as though he'd disappear from my vision.

Heat rushes up my chest and neck. Liam and Jax look confused, and a surge of guilt rushes through me. Sophie kicks me under the table, and I kick her back. I have no words to explain what is happening now, despite the questionable look she sends me.

Liam and Jax greet him reluctantly. Sophie and I get up from the table to give him quick hugs, except Noah holds on to me a second longer than necessary, a clear fuck-you to Jax. I choose to ignore him as I struggle to process everything.

What the hell? Why is he even here?

"So what gives? It's unlike both of you not to invite me somewhere."

My mouth falls open at Noah's boldness. I fight the urge to bolt from the table and make a run for it, deciding to deal with the consequences of my big mouth. How responsible of me.

Noah's hand rests on my chair, distracting me from the table, instead choosing to concentrate on how warmth radiates from his body. He pretends I didn't tell him about this double date. I feel like this is an episode of *The Twilight Zone*, the strange occurrences just part of the show.

"We're on a double date." Liam blushes while rubbing the back of his neck.

"Oh, a double date? Mind if I crash it for a second?" Noah doesn't mean to ask for permission, seeing as he commandeers the situation. He pulls up an empty seat next to Jax and me. I have a feeling he wants to stay for longer than a moment when he grabs my menu from my hands. My throat bobs as his fingers brush against mine.

I pull away from his touch and rub my temple with my hand, attempting to prevent a tension headache. Could be a good excuse to get out of this situation.

"Seeing as you are already sitting, does it even matter?" Liam fails to hide his annoyance.

My head snaps up and catches his stormy blue eyes. Sophie covers up her laugh with her hand, the muffled sound carrying past her fingers. At least one of us finds this amusing.

"Is Team McCoy trying to snag information from our Bandini ladies?" Noah rests his elbows on the table and places his chin on top of his knuckles. He doesn't pull off the innocent look well with his wicked gleam and smirk.

I speak up. "Because everything goes back to racing for you. It's not because they're interested in hanging out with us outside a track, right? God forbid that were to happen." My statement silences the table as everyone stares at me.

Noah's lips gape before he clears his throat. "I didn't mean that. I was only joking around..." And there goes another hand through his hair. I gloat at his embarrassment because he deserves it after crashing our date and making dumb assumptions.

"I thought you would be busy since you usually are on Wednesdays. Jax was free and agreed to join. It's nothing personal." Liam returns to his usual pacifist self.

Everyone in the racing world is well aware of Noah's Wednesday ritual. Those days usually include models, fine dining, and an exclusive tour of his bedroom. Every tabloid knows it, and hell, I know it, no matter how much I want to ignore it.

"I would've canceled any plans to come. They're not that important anyway."

Wow. Way to make any of the girls you sleep with feel

special. His wicked Wednesday ritual leaves a bad taste in my mouth.

Noah cocks his head to the side when he catches me scrunching my nose.

Jax and Liam offer him blank looks. They don't hide how much they want him to leave, but Noah steamrolls along, his presence authoritative.

"Maya, you're from Spain, right? Are you from Barcelona?" He acts like we are the only ones at the table, going as far as to turn his back on Jax.

"No, I was born in Asturias. It's up north." I respond to the whole group, my eyes pleading with Sophie's, looking for an out. I'd wave my white napkin in surrender if it meant escaping this situation.

"But you went to university here?" He asks.

My brows pinch together. "Yes."

How did he know that?

"Does that mean you know where all the good bars are?" Sophie finally chimes in. *That's my girl.*

I bark out a laugh.

"I like your laugh. It's cute," Noah says.

My cheeks warm at his comment. *Cute?* Since when has that word ever left Noah Slade's lips before? Sophie's wide eyes meet mine.

Jax and Liam stare at Noah. Even Noah looks surprised at what came out of his mouth while another hand runs through his hair. Someone should tell him about his noticeable tic because it gives him away.

We continue the conversation like Noah didn't act

extremely out of character. I choose to overlook what he said, preferring my usual ignoring techniques with anything related to Noah. If it makes my heart race and my thighs clench, I pretend it never happened. Works like a charm. At least so far during our time at different Grand Prix stops, except we never find ourselves this close together.

A muscular thigh brushes against mine under the table, his existence made known as a hum of energy courses up my leg. His proximity muddles my brain. I push my thighs together, half to avoid him, half to ease any aches that happen whenever he gets near me.

Every day, I convince myself that I don't need someone like him in my life—a guy who breaks hearts as a side gig. I prefer to keep things simple and avoid problems. Label it a sixth sense...or an in-depth Google search. I still regret that one because nothing good ever comes from checking out famous people online.

We carry on with our dinner. Noah orders something to eat when our appetizers come out. Jax and Liam give up on the double-date idea at this point, filling me with relief.

Liam covers the check at the end of the night. I can only imagine how expensive this place is, even though I ordered something cheap on the menu. Hanging around guys who make more money in a year than I expect to make in a lifetime makes me uncomfortable.

Noah unexpectedly wraps his arm around my waist while we wait for the driver to pick us up at the valet area. My body jolts at the contact of our bodies pressing together. What has gotten into him today? The moment I think I have him all figured out, he does something like this, switching up the game on me.

"Maya and I can ride back together since we're staying at the same hotel." His hand possessively splays across my stomach, holding me hostage.

I like it as much as I hate it. My body tries to wiggle away from him, but I stop once my ass rubs against his front.

I choose to ignore the bulge I feel pressing against me.

Nope. Not today, Satan. Stop tempting me.

"What a great idea. Can I tag along? I'm staying there too." Sophie shimmies on over to us, her green eyes humorously gazing at me.

Noah's arms squeeze me before he lets go. Sophie winks at me, and I'd give her a hug if it didn't draw attention to us.

Liam chuckles. "Trying to run away from me? This doesn't count as a date, thanks to Noah and his love for messing shit up. A bet's a bet. Unless…you want to back out? What did we say was the price for whoever quits? I can't remember. Maybe we can check your list."

Uh-oh. Liam doesn't seem like he will let Sophie off easily. Jax and Noah look confused at the mention of a list, but Sophie's nostrils flare as she glosses over the information.

"Mm-hmm, I don't need money to keep me honest. I'm no quitter." She says a quick goodbye before walking toward the street.

"Thanks for dinner. We will have to do this another time." I give Liam and Jax quick hugs.

"Un-fucking-likely." Noah says the word low enough for only me to hear.

I shake my head and walk away to join Sophie in the car.

This night did not go exactly how I thought it would.

CHAPTER TWELVE
Noah

I spend time relaxing on Bandini's deck after a successful qualifier. Barcelona's afternoon sun warms my skin as I lounge on a couch overlooking the ocean, blue waves rolling against the sandy coast while birds fly above.

It's purely coincidental when the Alatorre family shows up on the deck. I take the opportunity to watch Maya and Santiago hang out with their parents, curious to see what their dynamic is like with the people who raised them. Something heavy presses against my lungs at the idea of not having a family supporting me at a race. Must be nice to share the weekend with people you love.

I never had that. My dad usually shows up for the Sunday race and ditches after I place on the podium. He doesn't care to join me at different events, forgoing a postrace dinner unless he wants something. Manipulative motherfucker. My mother equally disappoints, recently contacting me to hook her up with tickets for her and her friends to see a race. The usual shit from them both.

Maya's mom looks like an older version of her daughter, making it easy to see where Maya gets her good looks from. Her dad rocks Bandini's gear and a permanent smile while his gray hair peeks out from underneath a scarlet cap. Their parents seem to be loving the F1 experience.

I find it difficult to ignore the pang of jealousy swirling around in my chest, mixing in with sadness and wistfulness— an unwelcome feeling I want to push away. Maya's family seems simple yet extremely happy, making it hard to overlook how I grew up with a crappy dad and an absentee mom. And it annoys me because I never wanted for anything except attention, something fundamental yet robbed from me. The Alatorres' ordinariness and my shitty thoughts put me in a negative mental space.

My scowl lifts to a smile at the sight of Maya coming up to me. Her brown hair bobs in the usual ponytail I love to pull, held up with a scrunchie, along with ripped overalls and a white top. I don't miss the hint of cleavage. The outfit would look ridiculous on anyone, except Maya's sensual enough to pull it off. A fucked-up nineties girl grinning at me.

"Hey, want to come and meet my parents? They've asked about you a few times, wanting to know who Santi has to compete against every week." She focuses on her feet, absentmindedly pushing around invisible dirt with her sneaker.

If it puts a smile on your face…sure, why not.

I get up and introduce myself. Her mother pulls me in for a surprise hug, showing me how touchy-feely her family is.

"Maya shares such nice things about you. It was kind of you to help her with her videos."

Not what I expected to come out of her mouth. *Maya says good things?* I look over at the girl I can't get out of my head lately. Her face turns red as she stares at her sneakers again, making my small smile break out into a full-blown grin.

"It's no problem. I had fun helping her out."

"She's lucky to have you around. Especially since she's all alone when Santi is busy. We tell him he works too hard."

I doubt her mother would have the same opinions about me if she knew half the thoughts I have about her daughter.

Her dad glares at me like he wants to assess me from the inside out. He acts like he can read the expression on my face, his scrutiny and deep brown eyes making me shift uncomfortably.

"Take care of my little girl." Hidden meaning fills his statement.

I don't try to get into his daughter's pants; I just think about it a lot. But I've been respectful compared to the way I act with girls I want to fuck. He should be grateful.

Call me an entitled prick. Fuck if I care.

"Santi's not the one who needs help because he was always our good kid. Maya, on the other hand—" Her mother brushes a stray lock of hair out of Maya's face. "Trouble. But the good kind with such a big heart. She's a little rebellious like her dad." Maya's mom smiles up at her husband with love and affection.

I chuckle. "What is the good kind of trouble? I'm curious how I can sell that one to my PR team when I mess up again."

"She always has good intentions, but they sometimes miss their mark. Overall, she's the best daughter anyone could ask for." Maya's mom gazes at me with the warmth only a mother can have.

"Mom," Maya groans. "Stop talking like I'm not right here." Her honey-brown eyes look at me for the first time in a while. "Ignore her. She loves telling ridiculous stories."

"Do you know she used to steal Santi's kart and ride it around the neighborhood? She was only five years old. Santi exploded when she put a couple of unicorn stickers on the steering wheel."

I barely contain a laugh as Maya rubs her face, hiding behind small hands.

"Ugh, not a good moment. Santi was mad at me for weeks." Maya's lips turn down.

"You liked karting?" I pull on her ponytail to get her attention.

Santi's eyes narrow in on my hand while her dad scowls at me. *Message received.*

"I did it a few times on the side, but it was more Santi's thing. I liked to do whatever he did, including beating boys his age." She smiles up at me.

Damn, my chest tightens at her smile, proof of how much of a sucker I am for them lately.

"How about the time she tried to forge her middle-school report card?" Santi fails to control his amusement.

Maya's cheeks turn into two bright red blobs.

"Maya Alatorre, did you live a life hardened by crime?" I scoff.

"Oh, I remember this one since her mother made me punish her after. Always got stuck disciplining. She actually took her report card out of the mailbox and tried to white-out her bad conduct grade. She sealed the envelope with a steamer before putting it back. If we hadn't been so angry, we would have been impressed. She cried when I took away her cell phone for a week." Her dad joins in on the fun.

Maya looks everywhere but at me.

"You guys are literally the worst. Santi, if you keep it up, I'll tell Mom and Dad about the time you drove their car at fourteen because you wanted to go do doughnuts outside."

Oh shit. The looks on her parents' faces tell me they don't know about this story. Maya's statement shuts up Santiago quicker than I ever could.

He puts his hands up in a mock surrender.

"Truce. No need to fight so dirty."

The idea of Maya fighting dirty entices me.

Fuck.

I banish those thoughts, choosing to focus on having a normal conversation with my teammate's parents. We all end up having a good time together until my dad shows up on the deck, sneaky like a snake with enough venom to match. I am surprised he showed up earlier than race day, a rarity that makes me regret skillfully avoiding his phone calls for two days.

The time we spend apart never seems long enough. Cold eyes land on me, two blue orbs as inviting as skinny-dipping in the Arctic Ocean. He keeps his dark hair slicked back and his suit perfectly pressed with not a wrinkle in sight. To others, he comes off as welcoming, but his deceptiveness covers up all the darkness simmering beneath his skin.

Maya eyes him curiously. My dad ignores her family,

passing by them without a glance. He comes to greet me, giving me a pat on the back, acting happy to see me. Nicholas Slade couldn't give less of a shit if he tried. But since he cares about a show and his image, my life acts as a side project to keep him busy from decaying during retirement.

He watches Maya's family suspiciously, paying attention to them for the first time by assessing each of them. Competitors getting along is his worst nightmare. And for a moment, I forgot Santiago and I are just that, talking with his family like we don't have a rivalry.

It felt nice. To be the three of us hanging out with their parents, the race on the back burner while they got to know me. Parents who actually seemed curious to ask me questions and learn about the man outside a Bandini car.

"Son, a second of your time?" The tic in my dad's jaw tells me everything words won't.

"I'll see you all later at the event." I throw the statement over my shoulder as I follow my dad toward the suites.

"You ignored my calls. I fly all the way out here for you, and this is how you treat me? I expect better from my son."

Right, we both know why he comes out to these events.

I bite back a snarky comment. "I've been busy qualifying and getting ready for tomorrow. It's good that you found me between events." *Lies.* But I've learned from the biggest fraud of them all.

"Yeah. We need to come up with a plan for tomorrow."

We enter my private room. My dad settles into one of the couches, a dark cloud against the white walls of the room as he sucks the energy from me. He grabs one of the red pillows and props himself up against it.

"How are you going to go about winning the race?" He jumps into it.

I haven't seen him in almost a year, and he doesn't even ask how I am, unsurprising but still grating on my nerves.

"By giving it my all?" I meet with strategists and engineers for hours each week to prepare for every single race. Don't need his shitty two cents.

"It's Santiago's home race. That means it's a big one for him. You should have seen his parade today. Thousands showed up."

"That's awesome for him. A home race is usually the best for those drivers, and I'm lucky to have two this year. After attending the Miami Grand Prix, I can't wait to head back to the States for the Austin one." My mouth waters at the idea of barbecue food.

"Well, you obviously need to wipe the floor with him tomorrow. There's nothing worse than losing in your hometown," my dad sneers.

I struggle to hide my irritation. Racing fuels a passion of mine while easing the edginess inside me. Yeah, it's a job, but it's much more because I enjoy it and compete against the best. My dad sucks the fun and excitement out of anything, making everything a rivalry. No wonder he had no friends back in his day.

"Sure, Dad. I'll try my best."

"You better. I'm here, and the press will eat that shit up. They love a good father-son moment." He treats me like a shiny accessory.

"I need to get going. It's a busy night before the race tomorrow." I throw him a wave before taking off.

Race day in Barcelona. The crowds bounce around in the stands, charged up with excitement. Machines buzz, drills hum, and computers beep in the pit. Sophie's dad tests out the team radio in my ear to ensure we have an open line of communication.

I zip up my racing suit and put on my flame-retardant headgear. I look down at my helmet, savoring the moment of representing Bandini's brand and appeasing my fans. This life is all I know, and it brings me comfort to put on my helmet. *Honey, I'm home.*

Crew members push my car toward my grid location. Liam has pole position, while I'm second, and Santiago's third.

Before a race, I spend hours studying the track, making sure I've memorized all the turns. A total of sixty-six laps made up of sixteen turns stand between me and the Spanish Grand Prix's podium.

The race kicks off with a bang. An American team driver crashes his car into the barrier on the first turn, taking down two other drivers with him. What a shit show as metal flies around and cars run into one another.

Liam holds first place for the first few laps. We play a game between the two of us, me trying to pull up to his side and him being aggressive on the turns. Sweat trickles down my neck as my skin warms from the heat of the engine. I take a couple sips of my drink to stay hydrated, because nothing is worse than getting woozy as I drive around at top speeds.

I narrowly avoid clipping Liam's tire at one of the sharper turns. He pulls away from the curve, flashing me a glove-clad middle finger. His rattled state makes me chuckle. The car continues hauling ass down the racetrack as I hit a main straight. An opportunity for overtaking presents itself when Liam lets down his defenses for a split second. I pass him at one of the turns. My foot presses on the accelerator, allowing my car to pick up speed and race down the straights, leaving Liam in my rearview mirror. *Too bad, so sad.*

Fans wave their Spanish flags and big face cutouts of Santiago in the air. They blur past me as I continue down the track.

Negative thoughts fill my head about the crap my dad said yesterday. I don't want to be a teammate who steps on others, trying to one-up them every time, acting like my father. No one likes a piece of shit. The type who takes everything, not caring how it affects the other person. Santi's had a rough go starting out this season. His rashness fucks me up, but he wants to win as much as anyone else.

Losing in Austin would suck. How disappointing—all those fans showing up, hoping you represent them well but falling short.

Fuck me, I hate thinking while racing.

After a pit stop, I make my way back up the race ranks from fourth to first again. I hold on to my first-place spot for another twenty-six laps.

"Noah, Santiago's gaining speed behind you. He's in second now. For the love of God, don't crash into each other at a turn." My radio relays the team principal's message.

"Copy. What happened to Liam?" I growl at his words because I'm not crashing into anyone today.

"Don't worry about that now. Santiago is behind you by about five seconds. Be careful not to let him overtake you."

"Got it, thanks."

My defensive position at the head of the pack takes minimal effort to keep. Blurring crowds welcome me as I pass the starting point again, a wave of red and gold colors flying by me, matching the Spanish flag the Alatorres had earlier. Their cheers get louder as Santiago passes them while he closes the gap behind me. A few seconds away from me now. If I were Santiago, I would do anything to win this race.

He tails me the whole time, waiting for me to slip up.

The image of Maya and her family coming all this way to see him succeed flies through my mind. *Shit.* I try to push away the thoughts, but the invasive images don't let up, accompanied by sounds of Maya's laughs and cheers. My hands grip the steering wheel as I think about the sacrifices his parents made for his career. Sacrifices Maya made living in his shadow. Never being one to steal the spotlight, preferring to dance around in the dark while her brother gets all the attention. Unfortunately for her, people like me thrive in the shadows.

Fuck. I never think this much during a race, like ever, because thinking makes me stupid. Thinking leads me to come up with my rash, selfless plan in the first place.

A fucking anomaly.

On the sixtieth lap, I let down my defenses more. I do it slowly, making sloppier turns, allowing more space for anyone to overtake me, while I still stay in control of my car. Messing up too quickly would draw negative attention to myself.

"Noah, is everything all right? Santiago's gaining speed. He wants to overtake you. Make your turns tighter."

"Copy. I think something's off with the car, but I can't figure it out. Do you see anything on the screens?" I sure as shit know there is nothing wrong, but I have to milk it to the point where I believe my own words. Fans can tune into my team radio via live television.

"Nothing over here. Can you describe what's happening? We can figure it out for you." My engineer sounds hopeful.

"Not really. I think there's something wrong with the steering wheel. It feels loose." The lie leaves my lips easily as I make another bad turn.

"Got it. Just keep going, and we'll figure it out later." They all buy it, my authentic display working on the team. I still want to land on the podium anyway.

By lap sixty-four, I make worse turns that leave me open for an overtaking. To no one's surprise, Santiago passes me at one of the corners, rattling my car as he zooms by.

My lips lift at the corners.

The crowd goes wild, releasing deafening roars when Santiago crosses the finish line first, red smoke billowing up into the air from canisters. I solidify my second place on the podium when I get the next checkered flag.

Better luck next time.

Santiago's family celebrates behind the barrier next to the podiums as they watch us on the stage. His parents light up the entire stage with their smiles alone. Maya has decked herself out in Bandini gear, with a Spanish flag wrapped around her as she dances around to the music streaming from the stage speakers. Watching her happy makes my heart clench like a chick.

Usually, when I meet a woman, the first thing that attracts me is a set of perky tits, a tight ass, and seductive lips. But for the first time in my life, I'm interested in someone for a different reason. With Maya, the most beautiful thing about her is how her eyes light up with happiness when she grins, an infectious smile that makes my lips turn up every time. Her beam is hands down one of my favorite things. A bubble of positive energy, dancing in circles without a care in the world.

Does she have a great body? Sure.

But at this moment, her smile draws me to her. I want to keep them all to myself and bottle them up for the bad days. Don't get me started on her laughs. I feel them all the way down to my cock, every single time.

Champagne sprays all around me, but I barely pay attention, too enamored by her.

And fuck, it scares me.

I smirk one last time at the sight of her before turning back to the rest of the crowd. They chant my name, and although it feels great to hear them, nothing beats the smile on Maya's face as she watches us.

My dad paces the motorhome's lobby after the winners' ceremony. He follows me to the private suite area, his agitation evident in his jerky steps. The sounds of our shoes against the smooth floor distract me. I pull him away from others because we don't need an audience for his explosion. He enters the suite first, and before I have a chance to close the door, he shoves me toward the center of the room. His dirty move catches me off guard. My feet trip on the slick tile, but I right myself before hitting a couch.

So this is how today is going to go.

"What the fuck, Noah? You call that racing?" His voice echoes off the walls. *Someone's cranky about my second-place win.*

"Last time I checked, we called it racing. But maybe the concepts have changed since you last drove. It's been a while."

My dad's chest heaves up and down as his eyes dart around, wild and uncontrolled. It's the same look he gave me every time I failed to land on a shitty kart podium or crashed my F2 car. A glare he saved for our alone time in his office before he smacked my ass into the next day. Lucky for us, bruises aren't visible when you wear race suits daily. Not a single scar was left on my skin except for the mangled remains of my heart, a mistrusting organ ruined by the man before me. A cliché of the worst kind.

"I don't sponsor this team to see a shitty performance like that from my own son. I don't buy your crap with the steering wheel. All the tests came back fine; nothing seemed loose." His voice gets louder as his agitation grows.

My face remains flat because I don't feed into his anger. The fallout from his rage is a lesson I don't wish to revisit anytime soon, at least not in this lifetime.

I look over his shoulder and catch the suite door ajar, a shocked Maya staring back at me through the crack with a hand covering her mouth. Acting like Spanish Nancy Drew, piecing together what I did.

Just a bad day in racing. Steering wheel problems happen all the time.

"There was something off. Hopefully they find out what happens before the next race. That way, I can get first place next time."

"Bullshit! Don't try to pull something over on me, acting all coy. You know I basically fund your career here. People would kill for your seat. I could replace you like that." He snaps his fingers.

"Go ahead. I'm sure McCoy would offer me a seat in a heartbeat. That team probably pays more than Bandini does anyway. Wouldn't you like that?"

A resounding crack fills the small room as my head snaps to the side. My dad fucking backhanded me. I try my hardest not to start something with him, my breaths becoming labored as my self-control teeters. Maya's gasp and the whooshing sound in my ears make it difficult to make out any other noises.

I wipe away blood trickling down my mouth. It feels like I'm ten years old again, getting third place in a kart race, my dad pissed and taking his anger out on me. *Looks like old tricks never die.*

"Oh, Father, I thought we were past this. You should put more meaning behind a hit like that. Maybe age is getting to you."

"I thought we were moving on from your shitty attitude, but I guess I was wrong. Fix yourself up. You look like a fucking mess."

Thank fuck Maya has the foresight to disappear, because my dad barrels through, ending our crappy conversation. I take a deep breath before looking into the hall, surprised yet relieved to find it empty, a nosy Maya long gone.

Spanish
Grand Pix

CHAPTER THIRTEEN
Maya

Holy shit.

Holy fucking shit.

I can't get the image out of my head of Noah's dad hitting him because how does someone hit their thirty-year-old child?

My brain runs a million miles an hour, unable to keep up with the surplus of information. The steering wheel problems, the race, his dad freaking hitting him across the face. The way Noah's eyes looked into mine, sad and so damn lost. It gutted me to see him like that. Stripped down to nothing more than a man with weaknesses and a fractured past. Nothing like the cocky man I see daily, unaffected and disinterested in the people around him.

My family shows up in Santi's suite five minutes after the Slades' fight. No one notices my silence or how my leg bounces up and down while I mull over what I saw: a family dynamic no one knows about. I took an Intro to Psych course, and I know the stats about parents hitting their kids. This is not a one-time thing, a fluke because of a messed-up steering wheel or a lost race.

Noah's dad is an awful father who lives through his son.

I spend time with my family before excusing myself. Santi looks at me weirdly before returning his attention to my parents, their wide smiles bright after his success today.

I go to the kitchen and grab an ice pack, the cold plastic numbing my hand as I walk up to Noah's suite. My stomach rolls from nerves because I don't want to overstep after his bad day. Another deep breath expands my lungs. I wait for a moment, unsure if I should knock on his door.

I dig deep and lightly rap my knuckles.

The door opens a crack. A moody Noah looks down at me, blue eyes shadowed by a Bandini hat situated low on his face, a poor attempt at hiding his reddened skin.

"Hey, I come bearing gifts." I jiggle the ice pack. No point in hiding what I saw earlier.

Noah pushes his door open wide, and I pass through. His suite has the same layout as Santi's with plain white walls and red accents with Bandini's logo covering one wall. He takes a seat on one of the white couches, grabbing the extended ice pack while I take up a spot on the opposite side.

"Come to admit you suck at eavesdropping?"

My cheeks flush at his tactlessness. "Well, sorry." Might as well apologize even though they left the door open.

"And sorry you saw that. I should have closed the door, but he surprised me for the first time in a while."

Noah's words tug at me. His statement is a lot to unpack, and I don't understand why he apologizes. My head pounds as I wrap my mind around Noah's toxic history with his dad.

"You don't need to be sorry. He's a total ass. You warned me a while ago, but I guess I didn't think it was that bad."

Noah winces as he presses the ice pack against his face. "No one knows." He lets out a deep and shaky sigh.

My stomach dips with unease at his lowered defenses, a rare sighting for someone as confident and self-assured as him.

"I'm going to go out on a limb here and assume this isn't the first time he's hit you."

Noah's blank gaze reveals enough.

"How long has he been doing this? That's not right. It's not how parents should be, especially at your age. You could kick his ass into next week."

"A while, but I'd rather no one finds out, so let's keep it between us."

My heart cracks at his admission. I can't imagine growing up with someone rude, condescending, and disgustingly competitive. Hard to picture what Noah's life was like. He puts on an image for others, but is this what he deals with once the lights shut off?

Santi and I don't share Noah's problems because our parents have always treated us with respect and love. Growing up without wealth could be a better option. I live a happy life, and no one holds money over my head. Not Santi, who pays for a lot of things. Even though I make money from YouTube ads and sponsorships, the funds don't have the same weight as an F1 contract.

"I won't tell anyone. But I don't understand why you cover up for him." A wave of nausea hits me as I consider how people act around his dad, idolizing him as a racing legend. Fans call Noah the American prince. One stuck wearing a crown heavy from deceit and expectations. No matter how much Noah dislikes his dad, he lives in his legacy.

"Who would believe me? He's a racing icon and a big sponsor for this team. People see what they want to see anyway." His head faces up to the ceiling. Liquid from the ice pack drips onto his race suit, running down the red fabric like tears. *How symbolic.*

"I don't know. Anyone. There's always someone filming something. Cameras catch everything nowadays."

I recognize how I saw Noah how I wanted, believing the show he puts on for everyone. Smug, overconfident, rebellious. My chest tightens at my quick judgment.

"Please leave it alone." His voice has a sense of finality to it.

I drop that part of the conversation because I don't want to push him too far when he opens up to me.

I choose to address the second issue because I can't help myself. "Is it true what he said? About your steering wheel?"

He lets out another deep sigh. "Don't trust everything you hear. My dad gets pissy when I don't place first. My steering wheel was loose, no matter what people say." The words leave through gritted teeth.

"But you were in the lead for, like, forty laps. Defensiveness is your thing."

"Maya."

His gravelly voice captures my attention, and I look up into his intense blue eyes. My name rolls off his tongue, hitting me in the heart and below the belt at once.

"Drop it. Forget what he said. Your brother won the Spanish Grand Prix fair and square. You should be happy for him instead of thinking up conspiracy theories."

His eyes dart to the side as he avoids my gaze for a second too long.

Holy shit. Noah totally threw the race. Why would he lose?

We sit together in silence. I attempt to work through these new revelations, getting lost in my own world, not noticing how he gets up and sits next to me.

He clasps my hand in his, ice pack long forgotten. My pulse quickens at the contact. I tell myself it must be because his hand is freezing from the ice, the cool touch jolting my body. It has nothing to do with our connection. *Right?*

I try to pull my hand away, but he holds on, his calloused fingers brushing against mine. My skin tingles where his thumb lazily rubs against my hand.

"Listen. Let's forget what my dad said. No need to give attention to a piece of shit who gets mad when I don't place first. He's irrelevant and barely shows up anymore, that is unless it's convenient for him and his bank account."

"Uh, yeah. Sure." I barely pay attention to what he says. My eyes stay pinned on his tan hand engulfing my small one, his thick thumb brushing against my bony knuckle in a mindless pattern.

The room warms as tension thickens, choking me as it wraps around my head and my heart. His silent confession about the race feels like too much between us. I don't want to share secrets together, opening myself up even more to him, a point we can't turn back from.

But he doesn't need to admit anything to me. He threw his chance at winning today, from a quick gaze and a bob of his Adam's apple. Label it a sixth sense for bullshit.

Relief fills me when his hand stops caressing mine. I finally breathe easier, gaining the mental clarity to tug my hand away.

"I better get going. I'm going to dinner with my family before the after-party. Maybe we will see you there."

I lean over him and give him a kiss on the cheek that isn't red. His breath catches at the touch while my lips tingle at the contact, lingering a second too long.

I bounce out of my seat and reach for the door handle before he can react.

He remains sitting on the couch, unfazed, except for a tiny lift at the corner of his mouth. If I didn't know him, then I would have missed it. But we've spent two months together, and I've been learning his tics, the tells he gives when no one watches him.

"See you later. Thanks...for coming over. And the ice pack." He repeats the same jiggle I did earlier.

I laugh at his ridiculousness, blue eyes lighting up when they land on me.

"No problem." I don't bother looking over my shoulder as I softly shut the door.

Noah doesn't show up to the main after-party. I hate to admit it feels off without him there, missing how he entertains me while Santi and Sophie are busy.

During the party, it hits me how much trouble I'm in. A cardinal sin has been broken.

I think I *like* Noah Slade.

Monaco
Grand Pix

CHAPTER FOURTEEN
Maya

Monaco. The ultimate race to attend. Bandini's week is packed with events before the world-famous Grand Prix de Monaco, known as one of the oldest races in F1 history, fueled by wealth and luxury. Celebrities from all over the world come to attend. Yachts litter the sea, glittering under the bright sun as I observe from our hotel room.

The Bandini team schedules a week packed with boat trips, interviews, galas—you name it, they have it. Which means I get to go too. My supportive sister role has no bounds, and although I usually try to avoid these types of events, I don't complain about this race week.

Because not even I can resist a party with a bunch of celebrities.

Monte Carlo is the coolest place ever. Pictures don't do it justice; they're unable to capture the picturesque shoreline and old-world feel. I can't believe Santi wants to buy an apartment here. We picked one out earlier in the week before he got busy, a modern two-bedroom overlooking the Mediterranean Sea.

I can tell the stress is getting to him. He seems edgier than usual, getting heated at smaller things, like when I left my makeup all over the bathroom counter. Monaco's race is a big deal, and he feels pressure from Bandini to perform well. It doesn't help that this circuit happens to be one of Noah's best, a place where his racing skills shine.

What exactly am I doing on a Tuesday in Monaco?

I'm on a boat.

Bragging isn't something I usually do, but come on. This is Monaco… By boat, I mean one that is at least a hundred feet long, the white fiberglass gleaming under the hot summer day.

My body lies on a lounge chair on the front deck of the McFloating Mansion. I already toured the four different floors, drank a cocktail on the back deck, and did a vlog interview with my brother while breathing in the crisp ocean breeze. Talk about living my best life this week.

I grab a sunscreen bottle out of my bag because my skin is warming under the intense sun. Noah, a man with impeccable timing, decides to plant himself in a lounge chair next to me.

"Avoiding the sun?" He taps at the pink bottle in my hand.

Dark sunglasses make it difficult to see and read the emotions swirling within his blue irises. To be honest, his whole look unsettles me. His preppy bathing suit looks shorter than regular swim trunks, accentuating muscular thighs and calves. Plus, he's lost his shirt somewhere between the cocktail hour and now. My eyes flick across his tan, sculpted body before focusing on the deck.

"No tan is worth aging when I'm already naturally golden." My heart quickens when he leans in closer.

His hand brushes against mine, causing an intense buzz of energy, one that never goes away no matter how many times his skin touches mine. He grabs the sunscreen bottle right out of my hand.

"Uh. I can handle that!" I sound breathy. *Can he tell?*

His cocky grin tells me that yes, he can. I grab my sunglasses from the top of my head and pull them down onto my face, creating a barrier because two can play this game. An immature move I have no problem with.

"Turn around. I'll help you."

Is it possible to die of a heart attack at twenty-three? What are the stats?

I pull out my cell phone, desperate to check.

"What on earth are you so interested in now? Every time I'm around you, you're always doing something fidgety."

I want to disappear in the lounge cushions or melt away into the sea. He's onto me.

He plucks my phone straight out of my hands.

"Excuse me! Hand it back. Now." I use my best mom voice, but it lacks the desired effect, making Noah chuckle instead. *Going to suck at punishing my kids one day.*

He ignores me, choosing to swat away my grabby hands.

"*What are the chances of dying of a heart attack at twenty-three?* Seriously, you're googling this? I didn't know I had such an effect on you. You flatter me."

I shoot him my best scowl, but he just laughs. A full throw-your-head-back laugh, and if I weren't peeved, I'd find it extremely attractive. *Who am I kidding?* I do. Annoyed or not, this man is fine. Handsome and absolutely fuckable.

I take advantage of his moment of weakness and snatch my phone back.

He rotates his finger in a motion to get things moving here, his previous task no longer put off. I reluctantly turn and lie down stomach first on the reclined lounge chair. Noah sits by my side, the cushion dipping under his weight as his thigh presses against my body.

He toys with my red bikini strap before squirting the sunscreen bottle. "You look good in red."

Does his voice sound huskier? Is it just me? I can't see his face since I'm looking out at the Mediterranean Sea.

My body jerks when the cold liquid hits my back. I lie to myself, chalking up my goose bumps to the cold sunscreen. Not because of Noah rubbing sunscreen all over my back. *Nope.*

I tell myself so many lies about Noah that I convince myself to go to the local confessional. A priest will have a field day with this type of stuff, offering sage advice before sending me off with at least five Hail Marys. I can't blame myself. Noah has the sex appeal of about one hundred men combined, making this whole process hard.

My arms grow heavy as he continues to rub lotion into my back; I'm enjoying the feeling of being cared for while Noah's hands caress me. His strokes leave a path of warmth behind them. I let out an embarrassing moan that I try to cover up with a cough.

His laugh—all throaty and deep—makes my body sing. He acts like this is natural, just the two of us hanging out on our private yacht, enjoying a casual day on the water. We might as well be, because not one person passes by to save me.

He can't see my face, thankfully, because my cheeks sear at his unrelenting touch.

And that's not the only thing heating up.

My core pulses at the attention from him. How long has it been since I've slept with a guy? Maybe my junior year of college? My brain draws up a blank, which I don't find to be a good sign. I decide this must be my issue with him. Not because he knocks off every attractive thing on my checklist.

Sure.

His hands move to the dip in my lower back, and I groan as they knead my skin.

I'm so very fucked.

My body hums with excitement at Noah's touch, not understanding why this is all so very, very wrong.

He pulls me out of my thoughts.

"Did I tell you that you look beautiful today?"

Nope, you didn't. But I'll take it now, with my head pressed against the comfy lounge chair as his hands rub my back. I don't think he has a drop of sunscreen left on his fingers.

"Hmm. Not sure."

Okay, good job. That didn't sound half as desperate as your moan.

"You look stunning today." He ramps up his charm.

He shocks me by doing the unthinkable. I suck in a breath as his lips press against the curve of my neck. *Swoon.* It takes everything in me not to bolt from the chair. My fingernails claw into the seat fabric to hold still, leaving indentations to match the ones Noah burns into my brain.

My body feels on fire, and my most intimate places are worse off. How is it possible to get turned on by sunscreen application? There should be a warning label on the back of the bottle for this. Screw damaging rays, this shit with Noah burns me up worse than any SPF below fifty.

He lets out another chuckle that prompts me to turn around and face him.

He looks unaffected, and it ticks me off. I check for signs. His eyes remain hidden, and his face looks neutral. My eyes skip past his golden chest and abs because I have absolutely no time or restraint for that.

I smirk at the bulge in his bathing suit. His cheeky grin makes me want to kiss it off his face, replacing the humor in his eyes with lust.

Our attraction threatens our semblance of normalcy with each other. Not sure what to make of this. I need time to process, concoct an avoidance plan, set up defenses against the ultimate playboy. This will take effort. I may even need Sophie's help with reinforcements because plans are her thing; she's been successfully avoiding her attraction to Liam like a plague.

Thou shall not bang your brother's teammate rings in my ears, a new mantra for me by now. Yes, my mantra list continues to grow, but you haven't met Noah Slade. You don't understand how sensuality seeps from his pores. Never underestimate the power of pheromones and wicked smiles.

He even makes sunscreen application into some kind of foreplay.

Guilt rushes through me because I don't want to be

attracted to Noah. Although he does nice things for me, he stills acts like a dick to Santi. I'm a walking contradiction at the moment, battling the pros and cons, weighing catastrophic situations if Noah and I got together.

Noah gets up from my chair, placing the offensive sunscreen bottle next to me. A wave of uncertainty passes through me. Part of me wants to make him stay while the other part of me wants him to go. My brain needs to digest this information. His boner distracts me enough, drawing my attention to it, the bulge looking much larger as he stands. I need it removed from my vicinity ASAP.

He tugs on my ponytail. I smile up at him because somehow, it's become our thing.

How can he be so hot yet so cute at the same time? Troubling.

"Don't think too hard. You'll be stuck battling the 'what if you dos' and the 'what if you don'ts' instead of living in the moment. Call me if you need my help again. I'll be around." He gives me one last cocky smile before disappearing below the deck.

I let out a deep sigh.

I'm so royally screwed, by the F1's American prince no less.

I can lie and pretend I'm a mature woman. I can say I've kept it cool in front of Noah and my brother. But I haven't. Why bother lying when I suck at it anyway?

My butt plants itself on the bench inside a local priest's confessional. My mother loves how I've found time to go to church while in Monaco. The priest wishes me lots of luck with my life and tells me to go to Mass more. It feels good to let it all out, even to a man of the cloth, like my own therapist on the road. I'd describe the experience as cathartic. No shame as I spill my guts to him, letting it all out in a confessional booth.

Surprisingly, he sends me off with three Hail Marys, two Our Fathers, and a bottle of holy water to cleanse myself whenever I have impure thoughts. *Confessions come with goody bags. Who knew?*

I start a new avoiding Noah campaign. It goes strong for two days, thanks to Sophie's obsession with lists and plans. Two long days. If anyone understood the amount of effort it takes to avoid him, they would be impressed. He and my brother have to do everything together in Monaco, since a united team looks great to the public.

I spend a lot of my time in our Monaco hotel avoiding parties and cocktail hours. To pass the time, I book myself a massage. It doesn't yield the same physical reaction as Noah's back rub, but I attribute it to having a female massage therapist. She doesn't physically do it for me. Santi covers the cost, but unbeknownst to him, he basically rewards me for my good efforts at avoiding Noah. I take one for the team here.

I would count my evading techniques as successful, at least until my brother asks if I can attend a fashion show that apparently is a big deal. An A-list event I should be grateful to have an invite to.

Santi makes me watch him practice his runway walk to make sure he looks good. He loves the limelight, but not this kind—with the expectation to model. And I do not blame him at all. If I did a show like this, I would definitely fall flat on my face before rolling into the pool.

"Do you really need me there?" *Please say no.* I can only execute so much control around Noah. And once you add a tux element into the mix, it's a recipe for disaster.

I feel like my brother sets me up for failure here.

"I never thought I'd have to convince you to go to this. Everyone wants a ticket." He pouts at me, a bit extra for his standards. It impresses me yet flusters me all the same because he uses my own strategies to get me to agree.

I can't get out of this when his words sound absolute. So I engage in the next step of a desperate woman's plan.

I bargain.

"Can Sophie come—if she doesn't have an invite already— because I don't want to be alone during it." *I don't trust myself,* I mentally add before putting my two hands together in a silent plea.

He texts away on his phone, searching for the answer to my question, unable to resist my charm.

"All right, I got her a ticket too. But you both have to behave because I won't be out there protecting you from the old men."

"But I've always wanted a sugar daddy!" I whine while throwing my hands up in the air.

He throws a pillow at my face. Santi may have won this battle, but I'll win the war.

CHAPTER FIFTEEN
Maya

can't believe you scored us tickets for the fashion show. It's one of the biggest events of the year." Sophie bounces up and down in a chair. We went on a shopping spree earlier to buy dresses for the event after she claimed what we had wasn't enough.

"Oh, believe it. We better finish getting ready. The car's coming in twenty." I don't feel guilty about using Sophie as a cockblocker because her enjoyment rubs off on me.

Two birds, please meet my one stone.

I run a hand down the silky material of my blue dress. Looking at it now, I realize the blue matches the color of Noah's eyes.

Fuck me. A fashion equivalent of a Freudian slip.

I grab my heels and book it out of the hotel room, wanting to get this night over with.

Sophie can't stop chattering the whole car ride to the

oceanfront destination. "Did you know all the guys will be modeling tonight?"

Can't say I did.

"Are you excited for anyone in particular?" I want to pull any information about her thing with Liam. Sophie hides her attraction well, but I catch the briefest glances she gives him. She tells me they're "just friends" ever since she pulled that card on him after our fail of a double date.

"Mm, no. Such an odd question. Are you?" She stares at me. *Point taken.*

We arrive at the fashion show location soon after. A cross-shaped stage floats in the center of a pool, lit from within and emitting a purplish glow. We make out different yachts anchored out in the ocean. The event bustles with enjoyment from the attendees while waiters walk around with food and drinks. Music streams from speakers around us.

"Let's get a drink. Time to get this party started." Sophie pulls me toward the bar area. She handles ordering. "Can we have four shots of your finest tequila?"

My eyebrows rise. *Two shots already?* "I don't want to end up a blubbering, drunk mess tonight. Tequila makes me embarrassing." Hard to forget how I cried in a bathroom. I blame my favorite boy band getting back together and tequila.

"Relax." She pats my arm for good measure. "We can get buzzed now so we can enjoy the show. We won't have more until the alcohol wears off."

She slides the two glasses toward me, and we knock back the shots.

Sophie was right. This fashion show is way better with a buzz. Guys strut their stuff down the stage, each looking handsome in their different evening wear. I even whistle when Noah comes out. Not my fault he looks beyond fuckable in his tux, which calls out to me.

Whoops. This is the alcohol talking. A slip of the tongue. I do not want to fuck Noah Slade. I nudge Sophie when Liam comes out, his body pressed against the tailor-made suit and his blond hair slicked back in his usual style. He even points her out of the crowd and sends her a wink. That one is a flirt, and honestly, I have no idea how Sophie resists him because her eyes light up whenever she sees him.

Once the show finishes, Sophie and I get the party started. Sophie bribes the DJ to let us behind his setup. She spins the turntables while I pick out songs from a playlist. We get a few people to bounce up and down, creating a small mosh pit at the center of the dance floor. I don't think I've laughed any harder than I have with her.

A Bandini rep eventually pulls us away from the DJ area after we play our third reggaeton song. Apparently, it's not well-suited for the elite crowd.

Two older guys ask us to dance, and we agree. Not exactly my type but the haze of alcohol says yes for me as they pull us toward the dance floor. Sophie and I aren't drunk. Only a little on the tipsy side, still managing to stay put together.

A crowd of dancing couples engulfs us. I dance around with a middle-aged man who has gelled-back hair and smells strongly of alcohol. My eyes search for Sophie between songs, but I can't find her. The man's hand creeps its way toward my ass at the same moment as I conveniently step on his toes. Hard. He lets out a yelp while I fake an apology.

Music shifts to a classic salsa song DJs play at our clubs back home. A shadow looms over my dance partner. By now, I can recognize the reason for the tingle in my spine anywhere. Two months of resisting him does that. Strobe lights basking him in an ominous glow, my naughty knight in a shining tux sizes up my pervy dance partner.

"Mind if I cut in?" Noah's irritated voice carries over the music. *Or am I hearing things?* Alcohol confuses my brain.

The man sputters out a reply as he lets me go. Noah grabs my hand while placing another at the dip in my back right above my ass. It feels way less invasive than my previous dance partner, like his hand should be there. Plus, Noah doesn't smell like whiskey and old money. He needs to bottle up his scent and sell it on the mass market. I would buy a few bottles and spray it on my pillows at night, not creepily of course.

I smile at the idea. *Real mature, Maya.*

He shakes his head like he can't believe the sorry state I'm in at the moment. He and I both.

I place a hand on his shoulder. His tux feels smooth under my fingertips, the strained material pressing against his muscles.

"I thought you were avoiding me because I haven't seen you at any of the events this week."

I think out my reply carefully. Well, as carefully as alcohol allows me to.

"Where did you learn to dance salsa?" *Suave change of subject if I do say so myself.*

His deep laugh makes me feel all warm inside.

"I lived in Europe long enough to pick up on it." He sways us to the music.

A kernel of jealousy blossoms at the idea of Noah dancing with other girls.

"Hmm. Cool." I feign indifference, but I can't tell if I succeeded.

Noah turns me, pulling my back to his front. My ass presses against his crotch as his hand runs down my arm.

"Uh, we learned two different types of salsa. They didn't teach me this in class."

The rumble of his chest is the only response I get.

I look around, curious if anyone else sees this. My body molds into his. A crowd of people dances to the music, oblivious to Noah's advances as his stiff cock presses against my ass cheeks. I press into him, unintentionally of course.

Sign me up for the next confession slot.

Turns out Noah seems into this back-and-forth, or lack thereof. He moves us along to the music. One of his hands presses on my hip, holding me flush against him while his other hand pushes my hair away from my neck.

"Did you wear that color dress for me?" His husky voice makes my head swim. *How can he tell what color my dress is when it's dark outside?*

"It's navy. What do you mean?" Okay, it isn't. But boys suck at knowing anything beyond basic colors.

"Hmm, weird. It looks like the same color as my eyes. But maybe I'm wrong, just seeing things."

"That's often a sign of narcissism. You should get yourself checked out when you have a chance. I don't do everything to appease you." Unfiltered words flow from my mouth.

He shuts me up by pushing his rigid length into me. I groan at the feeling, my body heating up at his boldness.

"Tell me you're not affected by this connection between us." His husky whisper sends a shiver down my spine. He trails a finger down the length of my throat to my collarbone, stopping right above my cleavage.

No way I will admit anything to him.

"Not sure what you're talking about. Do you try this with other women?" Alcohol makes me stupid. So, so stupid.

"I think you know." His hands grip me possessively as our hips move to the music.

I withhold a moan as my head rolls back into his chest, his dick pressing into my ass, a hint at the size of him.

He blows hot air into the shell of my ear, causing my core to pulse with need. My body burns wherever he touches, his fingers skimming down the smooth material of my dress. A delicate layer protecting my body from his touch.

"You drive me crazy. I keep thinking about fucking you, wondering how you sound when you explode in ecstasy. The moans you'll make while you greedily take my cock. Is it breathy? Loud?"

My stomach flutters at the sensation of his teeth grazing

my earlobe. I tilt my head to the side, giving him better access to my neck, his lips trailing kisses down the curve of it. His touch makes me pant. My resolve slips, begging me to give in to him.

Take me home, I want to say. But I don't, letting my body say the words my mouth can't get out.

It's a problem for future me.

What's one night with him? We're adults who can keep a secret.

Noah senses my submission. His lips press against the hollow of my throat, his tongue darting out to taste me, making my body shudder as he sucks on the sensitive skin.

Someone grabs my hand and tugs me away, cold air hitting my skin in Noah's absence. He growls at the intrusion.

"Maya, just the girl I've been looking for. Your brother is searching for you. You remember him, right? Noah's *teammate*." Sophie emphasizes her words. How did she even find us in this crowd, a cluster of bodies dancing together?

I shake away the lust-induced cloud. Music thumping in the background washes over me, reminding me of where we are. Dance lights illuminate my shoes. If I click them together, can I go home?

"I better get going. Sister duties and all. Thanks for the dance," my voice rasps.

Whatever we did is nothing like any dance I've experienced in my life. My eyes meet Noah's intense ones, a swirl of lust and frustration evident even in the dark.

"This isn't over." His husky voice hints at a promise.

"It is for now, Romeo. Let's go, Juliet." Sophie pulls me away, proving herself to be the best cockblocker.

She keeps her cool until we find an empty corner.

"Uh, where's my brother?"

"Who the heck knows? I needed an excuse to get you out of there before you and Noah screwed each other on the dance floor. What happened to you staying away from him? I was practically fanning myself while watching the two of you." She demonstrates with her hands.

My lips tip up in a smile. "I didn't peg you for a voyeur."

"You're not using your shitty evasion techniques on me. I see through them a mile away; don't insult my talents. Are you trying to get with him or avoid him? You need to decide." She taps her sneaker on the ground and crosses her arms, a ridiculous look only Sophie can pull off, her fluffy dress and white sneakers shining in the dark.

"I don't really know." I shrug because I genuinely don't know what to make of this thing between Noah and me. An out-of-control magnetism I can't describe.

"You two were all over each other, so I'm not buying it. What are you going to do about this thing between you both?"

"Uh, 'thing' is a bit of a stretch. That's the closest we've ever gotten to each other. Attraction, yes. Thing, no." I shake my head from side to side.

Her elevated eyebrow fails to reassure me. "You're into your brother's teammate. And rival I might add."

"N-no," I stutter. My weight shifts from foot to foot. "I'm

sexually attracted to him. Not, like, into him as a person, because I barely know him."

"*Right*." She draws the word out. "We'll have to keep you away from him."

"We?" My turn to be confused.

"Liam and I. Duh. That's what friends do."

Never have I been so thankful for a friend. Sophie and I stumble out of the party hand in hand, leaving behind sucky decisions and bad boys.

CHAPTER SIXTEEN
Noah

I'm into Maya. Like *really* into her. She scrolls through her phone, unaware of her surroundings or of me checking her out.

I want to hash it out, test the physical connection to its maximum. See how explosive the sex is. Fuck her against every hard surface in my apartment and show her a good time. The idea of exclusive fuck buddies for the rest of the championship can be on the table if our sex proves to be as good as I imagine. Never had a permanent fuck buddy before, but I think we can be that great together.

Liam jerks me out of my daydream. He nudges my side and looks toward the cameras and reporters in front of us.

"I wasn't paying attention to the question. Can you repeat it?" I offer a sly grin.

The group of reporters snickers at my honesty. Maya glances at me with lit-up eyes as her chest shakes from withheld laughter.

"What strategies have you taken to defend your undefeated Monaco Grand Prix title?" The reporter stammers out his question again.

"Uh, well, I usually get in the car and practice. Try to go my fastest. You know, the basics." I play the jokester today. Stifled laughs carry through the crowd while a couple cameras click, taking photos and videos.

Everyone knows I hate questions like these. This reporter is probably new and unaware of my preference. Viewers eat this up, loving the way I act and how I present myself. They're fans of mine for a reason.

Reporters drone on. Not wanting to make myself look like a total idiot before a race, I make sure to pay attention to them this time. Sponsors may assume I partied too hard in Monaco. I even listen when they ask Santi how he feels about his second-place qualifier.

"Pretty good. It's nice when my hard work pays off. Last year, I retired early from Monaco after an engine failure, so I'm excited to get back out there and compete against people I've looked up to for years."

I nod, impressed with his answer. It seems like he's been working on his PR skills.

Once the press conference ends, I stroll off the stage and head straight to Maya. "Funny, I never saw you again after the fashion show. Where did you disappear to?" Both my dick and I are curious where she and Sophie ran off to.

She keeps scrolling through her phone. I push one finger down on it, revealing the screen. *She's ignoring me for social media?*

I press the lock button on the side of her phone. The dark screen taunts her to look up at me, and she plays right into my hand.

I don't like how her brown eyes intensely stare into mine, guarded and unexpressive.

"I spent time with my brother and Sophie before calling it an early night." Her eyes dart to the side while answering.

"Funny thing, because I ran into your brother five minutes after you left. He was surprised when I asked if he was able to get in contact with you. He tried to call you, but you didn't pick up. We ended up spending the rest of the night talking with sponsors." I shrug, trying to come off unfazed. In reality, it ticks me off how Sophie dragged Maya away. How messed up. Sadly, I had to whack off in the bathroom after Maya left to relieve the raging hard-on I had. Embarrassing as fuck. Sophie's the worst cockblocker ever, taking Maya away right when she gave in to me.

The pink shade of her cheeks deepens, revealing enough to me.

"Would you look at the two of you, all cozy and shit. What secrets are you discussing? How to beat me tomorrow?"

I roll my eyes at Liam's interruption before I run a hand down my face. Can Maya and I not get a second alone?

"I'm spying for my brother. My loyalty is always to him." Maya taps her Bandini hat. The brim shows an embroidered seven on it. What would it be like if she wore my number twenty-eight? I envision her in a shirt with my name on it instead of Santiago's.

She screws me all up inside, making me want ridiculous things.

"I better get going anyway because Santi and I have a lunch to go to. Good luck tomorrow, Liam. See you later, Noah." She scurries away.

"Bro, you don't want to tap that. She's your teammate's sister. Not worth it."

Liam telling me to not hook up with someone is unheard of, the equivalent of him telling me to throw a race. It just isn't done.

"Seeing as you tap anything with two legs and fake boobs, why are you giving me advice right now?" I struggle to cover up my annoyance. That came out rough, even for my standards.

Liam puts both palms in the air. "Whoa, no need to take it out on me. Or make it personal for that matter. If you need to fuck someone, pick a girl up at one of the events. They're easy ass."

Therein lies the problem. I have no interest in hooking up with a random chick, and I haven't for a while. When was the last time I slept with someone casually like that?

Liam mistakes my silence for acceptance. "Listen, bro. A word of advice—even though you're being a dick right now. People like Maya don't casually hook up with people like us. She's the type to get feelings and end up wanting more." Liam shudders dramatically.

"What's wrong with feelings?"

He looks at me like I've grown two heads. Granted, I guess I usually don't care for women's feelings.

"They develop into more. Then it becomes proposals, sacrifices, babies crying. The works. One day, you wake up and wonder where time went. You'll be forty years old, your wife will barely fuck you anymore, and next thing you know, you're masturbating to porn every day to get by."

I still jack off now. Not exactly a trade-off.

Liam comes off uncharacteristically bitter, which I find weird because his parents have a perfect marriage. I mean, I'm already thirty. Not like I want to be alone for the rest of my life, only while I compete in racing and live on the road.

"Not sure how hooking up with Maya turned into a ten-year life plan. But thanks for your concern." I pat him on the shoulder while rolling my eyes.

"I want to warn you. She's one of those girls who'll bring you to your knees. I'm telling you. You'll be wondering where you went wrong, swapping out new girls for the same chick. Same pussy for the rest of your life."

His vision of marriage is kind of dark, unlike his usually optimistic self. Don't know what crawled up his ass today. I leave him behind, my mood tainted by his words.

The day of the Monaco race, I search around for Maya because I don't see or hear from her. I end up in the Bandini bar area in a last-ditch effort to find her. Sophie sips espresso at one of the tables, casually flipping through a magazine, not a care in the world.

"Have you seen Maya?" I keep my voice low as I plant my butt in the chair across from her.

She sips her drink. "Like recently?"

Why is she playing dumb? "Yes. Within the last few hours?" It takes effort to keep my teeth from grinding. My dentist won't be happy with me next time he sees me.

She finds my reaction funny, her eyes betraying her amusement. "Why do you want to know?"

"Answer the damn question. Not that hard," I blurt out.

Her eyes roll at my rough tone. I've visited her house during the holidays, so we've known each other casually for years. She reminds me of an annoying third cousin because we're not close enough to be considered siblings.

"No need to get your race suit in a twist. She decided to watch like a normal bystander today, wanting to film the experience for her vlog."

Doesn't Maya know that's not a good idea? People will recognize her; drunks will try to grope her. I don't like the thought of her being out there by herself.

"Why aren't you out there with her?" *In other words, why are you sitting here drinking coffee while your friend is out by herself in a chaotic crowd?*

"I was going to hang out in the pit with my dad. This is one of the biggest races of the year, so I'm sure it'll be crazy down there."

I pull out my phone before she finishes her sentence. She watches as I tap around on the screen.

I break the silence after a few minutes. "What's your number?"

"Seriously, you try to hit on me after you ask where my friend is? You were dry humping her the other day."

My jaw clenches. "No. You're skipping out on the pit today. Your dad sent me a ticket, beyond enthused that you want to see the race like a true fan."

I smirk at her wide eyes while she tells me her number. She

doesn't speak another word, thank God. Maya can avoid me all she wants, but it doesn't mean she has to do it alone. I'll get my way eventually. These types of games don't faze me because I have enough stamina to outdo her.

My lips twitch as I think up a plan to get her alone after the race. She can evade me all she wants, but it doesn't mean I need to. *Two can play this game.*

CHAPTER SEVENTEEN
Maya

I hear Sophie before I see her. She yells at a guy to stop accosting her in the stands. Her vocab choices are something else, a testament to reading one too many classic novels.

She makes her way toward the seat next to mine and settles down. We look the same, twinning in Bandini polos and ear protection gear.

"What are you doing here? I thought you wanted to spend time in the pit."

Nearby fans give us weird looks. I tug my hat lower on my face and pull down my sound-reducing earmuffs to hear her better.

She shrugs, picking up that trick from me. I nudge her in the ribs.

"Ouch. Fine. No need to get physical. Noah cornered me earlier, asking where you were." She rubs her rib.

Did I hear her right? "And you ended up here how?"

"Noah forced me to, I guess so you're not alone."

It shocks me that he even cares.

"Did he say anything else?" I fiddle with the settings on my camera.

"He said, and I quote"—her voice drops lower to imitate Noah's—"I didn't know she was a fan of hiding. Let her know when I find her, she won't like it. I was the champ at hide-and-seek growing up."

"*What*? Seriously?" My voice screeches.

"No! That's a terrible pickup line. He's better than that. I'm messing with you." Her laugh fills the silence. She's giving me a severe case of emotional whiplash today. "But there was some observable tension. I may conclude that he likes when you hang out on race days?"

"I didn't think he cared if I was around on Sundays."

Her eyes shine. "Hmm. I don't know about that. Noah seemed agitated that you weren't around earlier. At least enough to ask me about it."

Announcers cut off our conversation, letting the crowd know the race will begin momentarily.

The crowd quiets down as red lights flash above the grid. Everyone holds their breath for the start of the race, electric energy charging the stands as race car engines rev. My heart beats along with the flashing signals above the grid. The moment the lights change, cars take off down the track toward the first turn.

The Monaco Grand Prix circuit can be unforgiving, especially if a driver makes an error, like under- or overestimating speed during a curve.

Noah keeps his lead around the first bend, with my brother not far behind. Santiago's car zooms down one of the straightaways before turning another tight corner. Liam and Jax compete against each other for the third position.

Monaco's track seems unlike any other in the Grand Prix schedule. Constricted roads keep cars compacted, not allowing much room for mistakes. Jax and Liam avoid a disastrous collision with each other at one of the turns. Pieces of metal fly as the cars graze each other, the sound of clanging metal against the ground ringing across the track. The crowd gasps as Jax's car careens toward the side. He uses his momentum to get back on the track, narrowly avoiding a catastrophic crash.

Hums of the cars zipping across the pavement fill me with excitement as Noah and Santi pass us, completing their first lap. The crowd feels alive and energetic, chanting out the names of their favorite drivers while waving flags and signs in the air. My own body pulses with exhilaration as Sophie and I get up to cheer. Fans hang out on nearby balconies, overlooking the race from hotel rooms.

The smell of burning rubber fills my nose, a scent I've come to love during my time here.

Noah continues to fight for the lead with my brother. He remains defensive of his position, which makes it hard for Santi and others to get ahead of him. My brother tries to overtake him multiple times but can't since the Monaco track makes it tough to rise up the ranks. Often, the position a driver starts with is the one they end with so long as the team nails their pit stop strategy. Race strategy and not crashing the car matters, but the entire podium can change within a few seconds.

At one of the sharper turns, my brother tries to overtake Noah again. He does it sloppily, brushing Noah's front wing, causing Noah's car to fall behind. My brother secures the first-place position. Noah must be pissed because he detests when cars have contact with each other. The whole race turns out to be a messy one with shrapnel flying and cars colliding.

The crowd grows silent as Liam crashes into one of the barriers. His front tire flies off, and the severe damage makes him retire from the race early. He splays his hands against his helmet as the cameras pan over him. Sophie's eyes cloud and her teeth chew on her bottom lip.

During one of the final laps, my brother lets down his defensive position enough for Noah to sneak up next to him. Their front wings drive side by side, almost touching, as they race down a straight together. They approach a narrow corner. I hold my breath, unable to look away as Noah accelerates while turning. His side tires lift from the ground, losing important contact and traction to turn, a dangerous move that pays off as his car surges past Santi's, securing first place again. The crowd goes wild at the move Noah pulled, and I'm finding it hard to hide my bounce of excitement.

Noah ends up passing the finish line first. A checkered flag waves in the air, rustling against the wind. The fans eagerly cheer when they announce Noah as the winner of the Grand Prix de Monaco. Sophie and I bounce up and down when my brother zooms past the finish line as the runner-up.

Bandini had a great racing day. They prove time and time again to be one of the strongest teams with Noah and Santi at the wheel, another race closer to winning the Constructors' Championship.

Sophie and I wait with the masses while the drivers complete their victory lap. We end up leaving the stadium area once the guys start their usual press circuit.

We meet up with the Bandini team at the winners' podium. Noah stands in the middle, with Santi and Jax at his sides. It fills me with happiness to see both of the Bandini boys getting along with each other, laughing at something going on between the three drivers.

Santi and Jax pour champagne all over Noah. The crowd screams as champagne sprays all over them, the sticky alcohol making the air smell like a classy frat party. The podium area is a mosh pit of alcohol and cheering fans.

Noah notices me from my spot behind the blockades, shooting me a panty-melting grin. He tips his big champagne bottle to me before he chugs. I smile back at him and give him a thumbs-up, incredibly proud of him. The sight of his lips wrapped around the bottle brings naughty thoughts to the forefront of my mind.

Sophie joins her dad in the celebrations with the pit team while I head back toward the suites to chill while Santi does his other interviews.

I wait in the suite, surprised when the door opens earlier than I thought.

"Hey, you're back earlier—" I stop midsentence when Noah smiles at me.

He recently took a shower. His hair is slicked back, no evidence of his hands raking through the strands yet. A new Bandini shirt presses against the tight muscles of his chest. I lick my lips as my eyes roam over the rest of him, taking in expensive-looking jeans that cling to his legs.

"What are you doing here? Your suite is next door." I don't like the mischievous grin plastered on his face at the moment. Not one bit.

He closes the distance, shushing me by pressing his finger up against my lips.

"I came to collect my postrace winnings." He drags a calloused finger from my lips to my throat.

"Uh, I'm pretty sure they already gave you the trophy," I whisper huskily.

Noah's grin widens as his blue eyes pierce mine. The air in the small room feels heavy, like all the oxygen was sucked out of it. He's a hurricane catching me in the eye of the storm, giving me a false sense of security before the winds pick up again. A catastrophic and relentless disaster in the making.

He steps away from me. The click of the lock sounds loud, sending a shiver up my back.

"This isn't funny, Noah. Go to your own suite." I take a step back while he takes a few steps forward, eliminating the gap.

"I'm not trying to be funny. You've been avoiding me."

Uh, yes, I have. After the fashion show, I've made myself scarce around here. I don't trust my urges around him, but I don't say anything because his ego gets fed enough.

"Not sure what you're talking about. I've been busy." I'd probably sound ten times more convincing if my voice wasn't rasping. My body betrays me, unable to keep up with Noah's persistence.

"I follow you, and I've seen your recent posts."

Oh. This is the second time he's mentioned watching them.

I didn't even think he had the time to see them, but he must have checked out my movie and spa day posts.

"Sometimes you need a day off."

"You took two." The back of his hand strokes my face. *When did he get so close? And why does that feel amazing?*

I shut my eyes at the incredible contact.

The same hand wraps around the back of my head and pulls me forward. My eyes snap open. His clean scent surrounds me and muddles my thoughts. He doesn't give me another second to think before his mouth is on mine, soft lips pressing against my own.

At first, the kiss is soft and sweet—innocent and unexpected from a man like him. He plays, leaving behind gentle pecks.

His teeth graze my bottom lip, rough with a bite of pain. I gasp at the sensation. His tongue takes the opportunity to invade my mouth and stroke against mine, a relentless exploration demanding everything from me. He tastes like mint and champagne, a shockingly wonderful combination. Kissing him is a mind-numbing experience. His hands roam over my body, pulling me into him as his mouth stifles my moan. An impressive erection pushes against my jeans. One of his hands runs through my hair while the other grips my face, making it impossible for me to get away. Not like I want to. Oh no, when I commit to being bad, I'm all in.

My heart hammers in my chest. I wrap my arms around Noah's neck, pulling him in closer, giving in to our attraction. His hair feels soft and smooth beneath my fingers as I run them through his strands. My knees threaten to buckle. I try to make sense of all the sensations happening inside me, experiencing the best kiss of my life—both intoxicating and exhilarating. My body feels like putty in his hands, begging to be touched.

"Why is my door locked? Hello, Maya, are you in there? Open up."

My brother's voice hits me like an ice-cold shower. Pounding fists against the door beat alongside my heart.

I break apart from Noah's mouth and take a few steps back, nearly stumbling over the couch. A disheveled mess of hair makes me smile. His eyes stare at me, wild-looking and hazy, and his pants have a prominent swell. I can't deny the pride that surges through me about doing that to him.

Go me.

He holds up a finger to his mouth. One side of his mouth tips up, and his eyes shine, swirling shades of blue I've come to like. How is he always so unaffected? It seems unfair. I look back down at his pants to double-check.

Nope, he's affected.

The doorknob rattles, guilt replacing the pride I felt seconds ago. Santi would kill me if he found me in here with Noah.

"*Carajo*. How is my room locked? Who has the key?" My brother's voice fades away with the sound of his footsteps.

"You need to go *now*. I'll make sure he left." I push past Noah.

He grabs my elbow and pulls me back toward him. A quick peck silences me. My brain hasn't caught up to my body yet, leaning back into him like we can continue what happened.

"Relax. He doesn't have to know." His wicked eyes graze over me one more time before he exits the room.

I plop myself down on the couch, running a hand down my face. *What the hell did I do? I can't do this to Santi. Can I?*

Why did one kiss feel like it opened me up for anything?

Two weeks have passed since the kiss. I needed to take a temporary leave of absence from the race schedule, which meant I skipped out on the Canadian Grand Prix. Santi begged me to come, but I made up an excuse about wanting to go home. Lying to him made me feel worse, my stomach in endless knots as I packed my bags and purchased a ticket to Spain. I told him the traveling exhausts me. Which isn't far from the truth; I can't help how the man we travel with tires me emotionally and physically. Life's all about semantics.

Sophie pled with me too, but my mind was made up. I needed to clear my head.

Jax took home the trophy for the race with Liam being runner-up, and my brother placing third. For the first time this season, Noah didn't make it to the podium.

Sophie must have given Noah my number because he sent me multiple texts last week. I made an incognito contact name for him, just in case Santi gets a hold of my phone.

Media outlets call Noah the American prince, but I've found a more suitable nickname for him.

AMERICAN DEVIL

Are you flying in late? Santiago is here but you aren't.

AMERICAN DEVIL

Found out from your brother that you're not coming. Isn't he superstitious? You've been to every race so far.

AMERICAN DEVIL

Didn't place on the podium. Maybe I'm the superstitious one.

My stomach dipped at the last one. I didn't want Noah to do poorly, since he is my brother's teammate, but he didn't lose because I wasn't there.

I pulled up a video interview of Noah after the race, telling myself I did it to ease my curiosity.

Noah looked good in his red race suit with his sweaty hair plastered to his head. He rocked the messy look.

The reporter jammed the foam microphone in Noah's face.

"What happened today out there on the track?"

"Just an off day. It happens. I'm happy for my teammate and my friends who did place." His tight smile begged to differ.

"Have anything different planned for the next race?"

Noah glanced at the camera. His deep blue eyes looked hazy, blocking off any readable emotions.

"I think I need to change up my prerace ritual. A couple things might not be working for me anymore. But more on that later. Don't want to reveal my secrets." He ended the interview with a lazy smile.

After watching his interview yesterday, I ignored his texts for a whole day. I lasted twenty-four hours before giving in to answering him, the image of him frowning into the camera plaguing my thoughts. Three thousand miles do nothing to ease the pull he has on me.

> **ME**
> I'm sure you'll place next time. You're one of the best.

> **AMERICAN DEVIL**
> Are you coming to that one? Did you get my earlier messages? I didn't get a response.

I would never peg someone like him to question if I got his messages. Has he ever sent that to a woman before? The notion makes me take pity on him and answer quicker than usual.

> **ME**
> I'll be there. Needed a vacation from all the traveling.

I choose to ignore his second message because he crosses lines I'm not ready for yet.

> **AMERICAN DEVIL**
> Good. See you then.

That went easier than I thought. I need to face him, but I need a game plan first, particularly a Sophie-made plan.

Azerbaijan
Grand Pix

CHAPTER EIGHTEEN
Noah

s this what it feels like to be ghosted? I've done it to girls in the past, but I've never been on the receiving end. And to be honest, it totally sucks. *Karma really is a bitch after all.*

I haven't seen Maya since Monaco. She barely answers any of my messages, which makes me second-guess if I kissed her too soon. *Me, second-guessing. What a joke.* Sometimes she seems in to me, but stuff she does makes me uncertain. A foreign sensation to say the least.

I land in Baku two days earlier to get acclimated to the city. That and I want to be around when Santi and his sister arrive because I want to catch Maya when he leaves.

Wednesday goes by without a sign of her during our sponsor meetings and ass-kissing specials. But Maya doesn't come to any of them. I worry she wants to back out of coming to another race because of me.

I give in to my curiosity and ask Santi about her while

we walk back to the hospitality suites after our press conference.

"Where's your sister been?"

He turns his head slowly toward me, revealing squinted eyes and a tight jaw. I don't get intimidated by him. His scary face comes off like a puppy dog, not threatening like his dad's.

"Busy. She visited our parents back in Spain. Why?" He glares at me.

"Was curious why she didn't come to the last race. Wondered how it would affect your racing." My cocky grin seems to placate him. Back to our usually scheduled programming with each other—me being the cocky asshole and him taking it.

He scoffs. "I did fine. I raced without my sister by my side for years while she was in college. You're the one who struggled this time."

Santi has a fight in him. *Good to know.*

"Yup. You win some, you lose some." I shrug. "Is she coming to this race?" I can't tell if my voice sounds disinterested enough.

"Yeah. She's already here."

I follow Santi to the hospitality suite, disappointed when Maya isn't there.

"Is Maya hanging out in there?"

He stares at me, his head tilting to the side as his lips press together in a tight line. "Nah, she went to hang out with Sophie. Said something about exploring the city for her vlog."

My eyes nearly bug out of my head. They're out alone in a random city they've never visited before where the people speak a different language. What if someone recognizes them?

"They should be more careful. Why do you let them go out by themselves? That's irresponsible."

Santi's gaze hardens. "I can take care of my sister. It's a safe city."

"I think you forget you're worth over twenty million dollars now. Why do you think people are kidnapped for ransom? Hint, it's not always for pretty looks."

His ignorance grates on me.

Santi's jaw ticks. He takes a couple of deep breaths while I stare him down. I piss him off, but he can be a real idiot sometimes.

"Thanks for the advice." He enters his suite and slams the door.

I text Maya to check if she still has a pulse.

MAYA

Thanks for asking. We're all good. Going to dinner and then bed. Good luck at practice tomorrow.

I need to come up with something to do together that doesn't include me shoving my tongue down her throat. Which I still want to do, but we have to do fun stuff too. A plan comes to mind, so I enlist my friends to help me. She needs to see what she can have if she gives us a chance.

"Grab the girls and meet me at the Baku kart area."

Liam stares at me like I'm talking to him in another language. Yeah, he speaks German, but he understands English fine.

"Why are we doing this again?" His voice matches the incredulous look on his face.

"Because I want us all to have fun before the race. What's so hard to believe?" I control the urge to roll my eyes.

"Uh yeah. Your usual prerace fun involves being balls deep inside a model."

I punch him in the arm. "Fuck you. Don't tell Maya I planned this because then she won't come." My teeth grind together—my new bad habit lately, kind of like stalking Maya's social media accounts. I've become *that* guy. The one checking her profile to the point of addiction, sneaking quick glances at what she does to fill the void of her absence.

Jax and Liam can take credit while I pretend to join because I don't want her to find out I put in this much effort. Her avoiding me for weeks forced me to plan something drastic for her attention.

"All right, no need to hit so hard. I'll meet you there." He rubs his arm and pouts.

Liam pulls up to the kart track an hour later. Jax, Maya, and Sophie hop out of the rental car. I didn't invite Santi because I'm not a total dumbass, mainly because he's been paying extra attention to me recently, sneaking random glances whenever his sister gets close.

Maya's mouth gapes open when she sees me standing there.

"We're going karting?" Sophie claps her hands and bounces around, her blond braids swaying around her while Liam checks her out. He gives me a hard time with Maya when he makes heart eyes at Sophie.

"I haven't done this since I was a kid." Maya looks at the

helmet in my hand. She blushes when I pass it to her, our hands grazing against each other.

"You only had an opportunity to ride karts when you stole your brother's. So here's your chance to drive them for real. Don't put any unicorn stickers on them." That totally makes it sound like I planned this. There goes my idea of her not knowing about it. *Real subtle, Noah.*

"Oh no. But you guys are professionals. How is that even remotely fair?" Sophie crosses her arms over her chest.

Maya rubs her hands together while she shoots Sophie a grin full of mischief.

"Sophie, they're used to fast cars. We've got this."

That gleam in her eye? Definitely should be worried; no doubt she wants to kick our asses.

Turns out Maya does precisely that on the first run. I had no clue she was talented with a kart, and fuck, it turns me on. I could blame the fact that I haven't kart raced in a while, but she's a natural at it. Absolutely wiped the track with us.

My dick twitches at Maya sitting there, gloating in her kart, arms up in the air in triumph. She looks sexy as fuck with her helmet and borrowed race suit. I didn't peg myself for having a racing fetish, but looking at her now makes me rethink the idea, especially when she whips off her helmet to reveal messy hair.

An unknown sensation surges through me from the top of my head to the tips of my toes at planning something she likes. She smiles at Sophie from the mini podium they have, meant for kids. I wish she would smile at me like she does with others, beautiful with a hint of trouble. Liam and I grab the champagne bottles I kept hidden in a bag and spray them all over the girls.

"Hello, aren't we the ones who should be spraying champagne?" Maya gets the words out between laughs.

Liam and I pass them new bottles that are the same ones we use on the stage. Went for the full F1 effect today. I pop the cork before letting go, the bottle nearly dropping before Maya grips it with two hands.

Maya proceeds to pour it all over me. The cool liquid runs down my shirt, wet material plastering to my torso. Her eyes heat up at the sight of my abs before they roam over my body. I give her a wicked smile. She hops off the stage, lunging to the side, but my reflexes make me quicker.

I haul her over my shoulder like a fireman's carry. She squirms about, making it difficult for me to hold on to her. My hand smacks her ass playfully to get her to stop.

"Ay! Watch it. That's the no-go zone." She shakes from laughter.

No clue what the no-go zone is, but I'm all for exploring it. She should know by now that I don't follow the rules, preferring to bend them into submission.

"Precious cargo. Everyone, please move out of the way."

Kids and parents part at my request. Maya's giggles turn into a snort, which makes her laugh more, her body vibrating against mine.

"The blood's rushing to my head. I can't think straight."

"Join the club." I refer to a different head than she is. She gets the joke a second too late, and her body shakes from more laughter.

"Oh my God, you can't say stuff like that. Like ever."

More laughs as I smack her ass again. I love the feel of it beneath my palm, my dick stirring while a smile breaks out on my face.

I carry her to the waiting town car. We all drive back to the hotel, soaking wet from champagne. Maya gives me the biggest grin that reaches her eyes, and damn if my lungs don't burn at my sudden intake of breath.

"Hi, everyone. Maya here with the amazing Noah Slade. He agreed to do an exclusive interview for me."

She looks gorgeous with her hair down. Today, she wears shorts that show off her golden legs, ones I want wrapped around my waist while I pound into her. I'm so curious to hear the different noises she makes during sex. Is she a screamer? A moaner? I'll volunteer to figure it out.

She smiles at the camera she situated on a rolling cart in the pit garage. We position ourselves next to my race car, the vibrant red calling my name as Maya's ass leans against it. Low beeps from the pit computers sound off in the background.

"You think I'm amazing?" I forget the camera for a second. Like the sad sap I am lately around her, I love hearing anything she has to share, any revelation about her feelings. A fucking breadcrumb would be nice. She taunts me daily despite the way she guards herself, keeping her lips sealed, both literally and figuratively. There are few opportunities for us to be alone. Sophie magically finds us every time we get a moment by ourselves, which makes me want to take drastic measures to spend time with her, including this exclusive interview.

And everyone knows I hate interviews.

She rolls her eyes with minimal effort. "Hush. I wonder if you consume extra calories to feed your ego. Anyway, fans want a backstage exclusive. They're curious to learn more about you. So I copied a famous game called Web's Most Searched Answers."

She passes me a cardboard poster with my name in a Google search bar, along with a bunch of tape-covered questions. I recognize it so I guess I'm famous enough to play it.

"Our first question is…" She expectantly looks at me, making me smile. Her parted lips tempt me to take a risk and kiss her.

I cough to cover up a groan, and then I tear off the tape for the first piece of paper.

"*What is Noah Slade's height?* Well, I'm six foot. Which is considered on the taller end for F1. They make the cars to fit around our bodies specifically. My feet are near the tip of the front wing up against the pedals."

Her hands motion for me to continue. *All right, I get it.*

"*Who is Noah Slade and Santiago Alatorre?*" I pause. "I'm Noah. No surprise there. And Santiago is my partner and Maya's brother." I point at her like an idiot, because obviously they know that. "He's a Spanish dude who's loud and rarely beats me at racing. Still needs to work on his overtaking skills and not crashing into me from behind."

Maya sticks her tongue out at me, making me think about her tongue on other places of my body. Not a convenient time for a boner with cameras rolling. I shift against the hood of the car, discreetly adjusting my pants.

"Ha. Ha. Everyone can tune in for your comedy career once you're done with racing."

Fat chance that happens. I chuckle as I rip off the tape to reveal another question.

"*What is Noah Slade's net worth?* I'm not one to brag because that's not polite and I was raised better. But I think last time I checked, about three hundred million. Give or take. Received good advice from my financial advisor about always investing your money. Don't let it sit in the bank gathering dust. So that's what I do to multiply the amount I do have. Not to mention real estate investments."

Maya lets out a low whistle. "I'm impressed. We're talking to a world champion here who gives free monetary advice."

"You know what they say...the bigger the bank account..." I waggle my brows.

Maya ignores the camera and throws her head back. I love the sound of her laugh; pride surges through me at amusing her. Her exposed neck entices my inconvenient one-track mind.

"*Who is Noah Slade's wife?*"

Wow, she picked hard-hitting questions here.

I continue. "I'm currently on the market. I've never married someone, so that's a negative. Is the statement no wife, happy life?" I wink at the camera.

"I think you mean happy wife, happy life." Maya blushes and shakes her head.

I chuckle before I keep going. "*Where does Noah Slade live?* I'm not going to give away my addresses here because I can't have paparazzi and fans at my doors all the time. My limited privacy is the best part of the offseason. But I own an apartment in Monaco, a house in Italy, and a loft in London. Favorite place to live is off the Amalfi Coast during F1's winter breaks. Hands down the best food and views."

"Who can resist gelato? I've never been to Italy, but the food is my favorite. I can't wait until the stop in Monza. All right, two more left." She clasps her hands together and looks at me. She crosses her legs again, drawing my attention toward them once more. I lick my bottom lip before continuing.

"When is Noah Slade retiring?" I blink at the board. I never think about retiring, choosing instead to focus on the next year. I'm still young enough to not worry about it. But the question makes me think about what I'll do once I hit my late thirties.

"I bet you anything that Liam and Jax google this yearly. They're probably waiting for my announcement since they're younger. I don't doubt it." Blood rushes to my dick at the sound of her giggle. I need to get out of here before I do something stupid on camera. "Uh, I haven't considered retiring anytime soon. But I imagine if I meet someone special and have kids, I may consider what's best for my family. But for now, I plan on kicking everyone's asses."

Maya looks surprised at my answer. Hell, I am too. When the fuck have I thought about having kids or a wife? But the answer falls from my lips with ease, like I think about the notion occasionally.

"You never know what could happen in the future. But I'm sure you have plenty of time to figure it out. F1 drivers don't retire until, like, forty years old. Basically, you'll be ancient once you leave here. Okay, last one."

Is that even what I want? To keep racing at the risk of not having a life to go back to once it's all done? I don't want to be like my dad, who parties with twentysomethings on private yachts, cruising around by myself. The thought creeps me out.

"Best Noah Slade team radio?" My team radio videos on YouTube are hilarious. "If you look me up on the internet, you can find lots of videos of me cursing at the team and myself. A team radio is how Bandini and I communicate about race stats, car info, and problems. My personal favorite video is the British Grand Prix from 2014. Watch it if you haven't seen it. You'll be entertained. The pit crew forgot to connect my water pump, and I was basically a cranky baby without a bottle for an hour."

I glance at Maya. Her eyes look up at me and fill my chest with a warm feeling.

"Thank you so much for joining us, Noah. Those were the most googled questions people wanted answered about Noah, so I decided to go straight to the source. This week, I'll have exclusive footage from the McCoy team, including interviews with Liam and Jax. Stay tuned. Subscribe if you haven't already. See you next time!" She waves to her camera before shutting it off.

She looks like a natural, both gorgeous and confident. It's cool she's found something she can be passionate about. Especially if it keeps her entertained and coming back to all the races because I don't mind these one-on-one interviews at all.

"You forgot one more question." I don't think as the words leave my mouth. It seems like the perfect chance to have her alone without any interruptions of the blond-haired, green-eyed variety.

Maya stares up at me, confusion lining her face.

"Will Noah Slade ask Maya Alatorre on a date?" I flinch at my pathetic pickup line. *Not exactly my best work.* I blame it on being out of practice, not the way my heart races in my chest at the fear of her rejecting me.

"A date? You don't date." She messes around with her camera tripod.

My hand engulfs hers to stop her fidgeting. Her body tenses as I rub my thumb across her knuckles, something I noticed she liked during the few times I've done it.

"I want to try. What's one date?"

"Uh, for someone who doesn't ever date…everything." She tugs on her hand, trying to free it, but I don't let it go. Not until I get what I want.

"It's one date. Don't be dramatic. I'm not asking for a forever… Are you scared?" I goad her. "We don't need to put labels on anything. Let's have fun."

"Of course I'm not scared. You just want to have *fun*?" Her brows raise, and her lips form a tight line.

Maybe she won't be happy with no labels, even though most chicks I get with don't mind. Or maybe *fun* was the wrong word to say because now she looks at me in a way I can't read.

"Then go on a date with me. Tomorrow?" I can't tell if she wants to shut me down.

"My brother can't know. He would lock me up before killing you," she sputters.

All right, she didn't say no. I can work with it.

"What he doesn't know won't kill him. We're only having a good time together." I want to tell her to stop making a big deal of this. *Hasn't she tried no strings attached?* But she agrees, making it a win for me. If there is something I live by, it's how there's no time like the present.

I stride away, throwing a victorious grin over my shoulder.

Azerbaijan
Grand Prix

CHAPTER NINETEEN
Maya

No way. I'm not getting on that thing." I cross my two index fingers in front of me in an X. If only my mom could see me making responsible decisions. She'd be proud.

"Live a little." Noah's eyes gleam while mine narrow, not sharing his amused look. He looks eerie with a flickering light above our heads, foreshadowing this bad idea.

A shiny motorbike brings a frown to my face, the steel-gray paint polished and sleek, like an alien spaceship. It should come with a warning label.

Hell, Noah should have a walking, talking warning sign.

We wage a battle of wills in the parking garage of the hotel we're both staying at with Bandini. The garage makes the perfect place to meet up for our date since we can avoid the paparazzi and my brother. Just Noah, me, and a dimly lit lot. I don't have my usual chaperones keeping me in check. Much to

Sophie's dismay earlier, I declined her invitation to third wheel our date. Appreciate her loyalty though.

"Come on. It's not scary. I promise."

I roll my eyes. Anyone will say that to get me on the back of a contraption.

He steps toward me, wearing down my defenses. He talks low and slow to me like I'm a scared dog in an alleyway.

I push my lower lip out and cross my arms, not above pouting to get my way. If it works on my parents, then it could work on Noah.

But he doesn't take the bait. I need to work on my delivery because it sucks.

"Don't make me carry you onto it. I've driven motorcycles since I was thirteen. I'm still alive." He waves down his body, bringing my attention to his leather jacket and dark jeans. His outfit screams bad boy in every good kind of way. Instead of making me feel better, he distracts me with his tight-fitting shirt, which accentuates his firm muscles.

How does he make casual look so good?

"Is that supposed to make me feel better? That's illegal! Who in their right mind would let a child on a motorbike?" Did anyone ever watch over him as a kid?

He chuckles, not bothering to address my comment. Instead, he grabs a black helmet from the seat and puts it on my head, adjusting the straps to fit my chin. I'd consider it a lovely gesture if my heart wasn't in my throat at the moment.

I wasn't exactly expecting this when he told me to wear jeans and a comfortable top earlier.

"You're one hard date to please," he grumbles.

I'd rather not have my body splayed across a street like roadkill.

"Have you even been on a real date? Usually normal people go to a restaurant, have dinner, and end it all with a kiss. Stay within the comfort zone." I paint a picture for him since he seems like a visual kind of guy.

His chest rumbles with laughter. "I've dated before, but I'm far from normal. Why wine and dine you? I'm going to get what I want anyway." He waggles his brows.

Well, excuse me. I can't ignore the pang of jealousy when he mentions other dates. For once, his arrogant attitude wears on me.

Who does he think he is? Sex with me is not a given.

"That's one of the worst things a first date has ever told me."

Another hand tugs through his hair as he sighs. He may be sharp on the racetrack, but his people skills suck. I withhold the temptation to stick my tongue out at him because it'll encourage him more.

"It gets cold with the wind. Take my jacket." He slides the leather jacket off his back and passes it to me. The moment I put it on, a smell that's distinctly his with a hint of leather surrounds me. It calms me down a teensy bit.

"Please do this for me? It'll be fun, I promise. If you hate it, I'll park the bike and order us an Uber."

His sincerity does me in. I accept my fate and walk up to the spaceship.

It's one date.

I sigh. "All right. Because you asked nicely."

He gives me a wicked grin.

I'm so screwed.

Five minutes later, we speed down one of Baku's seaside streets. The smell of the water relaxes me as the city lights blur past us. Lucky for him, I don't suffer from motion sickness because this bike hits maximum speeds. I grip on to Noah's waist for dear life as tires tear across the pavement. My hands accidentally brush up against his abs, and I casually run a finger across them, interested in counting the ridges. He laughs at my failed attempt to be subtle. The rumbling sensation of the motorbike beneath my ass and touching his abs is turning me on.

Did he plan this on purpose? My body presses up against him, and my arms wrap around him, leaving no space. Even my legs plaster tightly against his to make sure I don't fall off. If it wasn't risky, I'd wrap them around him as an extra safety precaution. The whole situation comes across as intimate despite my bubbling anxiety.

Everything feels different with only Noah and me. No press, no friends, no distractions. We strip away all the extra stuff getting in the way of us spending alone time together.

He streams music through a pair of speakers, making the whole experience much more enjoyable than I thought. Sea mist hits my face as we get closer to the beach, and I love every second of it. I won't admit it to his face though because he gets to gloat enough as it is.

Noah eventually pulls the bike into a secluded area by the shore. I hop off, anxious to break our physical connection. My chest tightens at the scene in front of us.

A couple of lanterns outline a picnic area, looking unexpectedly romantic.

"Just fun?" I mumble under my breath, the date not screaming casual to me.

"Relax. Don't make a big deal out of it." He grabs my hand and pulls me toward the colorful blanket.

I settle into one of the cushions on the sand. A picnic basket is open off to the side, along with a bucket with chilled wine. The sound of waves crashing against the shore makes the perfect soundtrack.

A wave of uneasiness threatens to take away my happiness. Noah's lips say casual, but his actions speak differently. People propose in less cute ways. I take a deep breath of the salty sea air to calm me down, hoping a few inhales can cure my insecurity about Noah's intentions.

"How did you plan all this?"

"I had a little help." He shoots me a rare shy smile.

"Right. Busy life of an F1 driver." It impresses me how he made an effort to make sure something nice was planned.

"We can pretend for a night that none of that exists. No talk of your brother, and no bringing up Baku. You're a girl and I'm a guy on a normal date." He flashes me his usual mischievous smile.

Did I say he looks like trouble already? *Still waiting on the warning label.*

I agree to his terms. We eat together, talking about anything and everything. He tells me about TV shows he loves, food he misses from back home, and his favorite places in America. I say how I've never been to them, and he insists that I need to see the Grand Canyon before I die. I tell him about my failed attempts at graduating on time, being held back a year after I figured out I wasn't meant to be a Spanish Elle Woods attending Harvard.

"Let's play a game." Noah hits me with a mischievous grin.

"Seriously?"

"Dead serious. Ever heard of two truths and a lie?"

I roll my eyes with minimal effort. "What are you, eighteen and attending your first college party?"

Noah lets out a rough laugh. "I never went to college. Entertain me?"

I nod because I'd do just about anything with him smiling at me the way he does.

"Whoever loses has to chug straight from the wine bottle for five seconds." His smile reaches his blue eyes as the candlelight flickers across his skin.

"Okay, since this is your bright idea to get me tipsy, you can go first."

He chuckles to himself. "I'm an only child. I spend thirty minutes a day watching the news. And I lost my virginity in the back of a pickup truck."

I cough at his last statement, aware of how this game will go after one round.

"Pickup truck is a lie. You look like a thousand-thread-count kind of guy."

His eyes light up. "Nope. You got it wrong. I hate the news, so I stay away from that shit."

Well, damn. Guess Noah is an American boy after all, getting down and dirty in the bed of a truck. I grab the wine bottle and take a chug, holding up a finger for each second that ticks by.

"Your turn." He winks at me.

"My brother announced his Bandini contract on the same day as my graduation. I've gotten into five fender benders. I crashed my brother's first date."

"Five fender benders? That's excessive for someone young."

I shake my head and point to the bottle sitting next to us. "Nope. I never crashed my brother's first date, even though my parents wanted me to. Santi paid me fifty euros to watch a different movie. He got his hookup while I got a new pair of shoes."

"One, how do you still have a license? And two, your brother told everyone about his Bandini deal on your special day? How fucked up," Noah says before taking a chug from the bottle I drank from, his lips wrapped around the same spot mine touched.

I shrug. "I can still drive because the officer felt bad when I cried, begging me to stop. And Santi couldn't help the bad timing."

"Sometimes he can be a real dumbass. He could have waited a day at least."

Guilt runs through me at us talking about Santi this way because I love my brother. Noah doesn't care much for him. Stupid to hope they could get along—for the sake of the team or for me.

"He has the best heart. Truly. I can't get mad at him for more than a day at most. Not even when he stole all my Barbies and shaved their hair off."

"That should have been the first sign of his instability."

A loud laugh escapes my mouth. We play a few more rounds with me losing a couple times while Noah guesses my lies with ease, surprising me with how he sees through my bullshit. Wine calms my nerves and takes away my awkwardness. I learn a few things about Noah, like how he skipped senior prom because of a race and how he spent seven different Christmases by himself since his parents were both traveling. A truth I guessed as a lie because who spends the holidays alone?

We move on from our game. I share the success of my social media platforms and how, for the first time, I feel like I found my place. How I don't worry as much anymore about being successful or comparing myself to Santi's career.

"What's your favorite part of creating content?" He gives me his full attention, his blue eyes wandering over my face.

"Mm, that's a tough question. It originally started out as a travel vlog, but now everyone loves how I work with F1 and Bandini. Fans seem to be super into it. And they're constantly sending me new ideas of things to do or people to interview."

"I wonder if I'm the best part." His cheeky grin makes me show one of my own.

"I doubt it because people beg for Liam and Jax. Must be their accents."

He scoffs. "It's tough to compete with Jax's British accent. Liam on the other hand... German tends to lack sexiness."

I shake my head from side to side because Liam sounds fine. "There's a reason people like Prince Harry. Or any attractive British guy."

"You find Jax attractive?" His tight smile tells me I didn't say the right thing.

"I mean, people find him attractive. But I went on a double

date with him and realized he's not my type." I trip over my own words, wanting to put them out there.

"It wasn't a double date because I was there. That makes it automatically friends hanging out." His eyes glint in the soft lighting.

"Liam's been asking Sophie for a redo, but she keeps saying no."

"We don't want that to happen," his voice rumbles.

When did he get close to me? Our hands are practically touching.

"And why not?" Another breathy sentence from me.

"Because I already called dibs on you." His intense gaze makes me shudder.

"You can't call dibs on people. You sound like a B-list rom-com."

"But I fuck like an A-list porno."

Okay then. Who says romance is dead? My throat tightens as his eyes lower, taking me in. He closes the space between us.

A hand tugs my head toward him. Our lips meet. But unlike our first kiss, this one demands. Noah takes everything from me all at once, his lips brushing against mine, intense and irresistible. This somehow beats our first kiss. We have no one around to stop us, no interruptions to pull us away from each other this time.

One of his hands grips my hair and tugs. The quick bite of pain makes me gasp, giving his tongue access to my mouth. It strokes mine possessively, branding me, not giving me a second to overthink anything. My tongue meets his and strokes back. I want to taste him and make him crave me just as much.

"Why not? We can call it quits when the season's over. No harm done."

I seriously doubt that because I can tell from a couple of kisses that's not the case. It hurts to hear him be cavalier about it, but it's not unexpected from someone like him.

His reaction gives me more strength about my decision.

"Uh. I don't think that's true. At least for me. I don't want to catch feelings for someone who isn't looking for a relationship. I'm not *that* type of girl, a no-strings-attached person." I clasp my hands on my lap, preventing any fidgeting. I've only had a handful of exclusive boyfriends in my life.

"Feelings?" His voice gives away his aversion to the idea.

Note to self: he's not a fan of that F word.

"Yes, feelings. People like you leave a trail of broken hearts behind. I don't want to be one of them, another notch in your damaged bedpost."

"I'm not looking for a girlfriend. I have a crazy schedule, and racing is my life, so I can't promise you anything but something sexual. And that we'll have the best sex you've ever had in your life. I can tell by our connection."

My exact worry. Looking at him weakens my resolve, but I need to stay strong.

"I'm the type who needs more than a physical relationship with someone. I'm not the booze-and-banging type you usually hang around with. I can't change who I am to be what you want."

"You're really going to deny yourself this?" His reaction shows me how no one denies him. Evidence of his messed-up childhood, the ultimate only-child syndrome shining through.

He trails a finger down my neck toward my chest. I gasp at the scorching sensation his finger leaves behind, unhappy how my body becomes aware of his touch instantaneously. It's a shame to deny what my body craves.

"Yes." My panting voice doesn't exude the firmness I need it to. I swat his hands away, ending his spell. "We can stay friends. Not the benefits kind though, but I'll avoid you less." I nod, convincing myself that this is the right decision. My honesty about avoiding him feels like progress.

"Right."

His blank expression fills me with dread. *Am I making the right decision?*

Our dinner went well. Comfortable and easy, something that feels like it can be much more than a casual fling. But people like him don't fall in love. I don't need to open myself up to potential misery with someone from Bandini.

Noah gets up and reaches out for my hand. My skin warms at his touch. *Yup.* I absolutely made the right choice because this is a one-way ticket to heartache. We walk through the sand toward his motorbike. I look back at the picnic area, my heart tightening at the abandoned sight of it. Despite the less than ideal ending, this was one of the best dates I've ever been on, and I'll always remember it.

I put on the helmet and his jacket without a fight, a chill running through me at this ending. The smell of him is intoxicating and unfair, like it's wrong to breathe in.

Noah stays quiet as he gets on the bike, his mind drifting off to somewhere else, erecting a wall between us. I don't give him a hard time getting on. He starts up the engine, and we take off back toward the hotel. The ride feels shorter, as if Noah's desperate to get us back. I don't take it personally.

He drops me off in the parking garage shortly after, pulling the motorbike up to the elevator like a gentleman.

"If it were another life, I'd probably do right by you. I'd take you on dates and try harder. But that's not who I am or how I was raised. I don't know how to be the kind of emotional guy you desire."

My eyes water, clouding my vision. Everything feels final. We've circled one another for three months, and now it's over, gone in the blink of an eye. I respect him for sharing and being honest about who he is.

"Thank you for a great date. It'll be a hard one to top, even with everything." I sneakily inhale one last breath of his jacket before passing it back to him.

"Likewise." His cocky grin doesn't exactly reach his eyes.

"I better get going. Santi will be wondering where I went for so long."

He presses the button. "Yeah, sure." His arms pull me in for a hug while his lips brush softly against mine, giving me a goodbye kiss that should be reserved for lovers—intimate, kind, and packed with unspoken words. My heart perks up before he pulls away.

Elevator doors open, the empty car a welcoming sight. I walk in and turn around.

"Bye, Noah. See you tomorrow."

His intense gaze is the last thing I see before the doors close.

CHAPTER TWENTY
Noah

The first thing I feel when I wake up is the pulsing of my head.

The second thing I feel is a hand crawling up my chest.

The third thing I feel is intense regret.

Fuck. Please tell me it's Maya's hand.

I look down at long, red nails. Maya's don't look like these talons scratching at my chest, preferring natural nail colors. These hands are a symbol of my past. Nausea crawls up my throat as I lay my head back down on a pillow.

I comb through the memories of last night, of how I took Maya out on the date I planned. Never thought I could have such a good time with someone while doing absolutely nothing except eating, drinking, and kissing.

The date was my favorite, at least out of my short list.

And the erotic way Maya kisses. *Fuck me.* Kissing her feels like I did it wrong with all the women before her.

But what the fuck happened after? I struggle to remember what I did once she pulled the stops on me. Images flash of her rejecting me with sadness in her eyes, knowing I can't give her what she needs. The ultimate blow still feels fresh based on the way my chest constricts at the thought.

Memories hit me all at once, flooding my brain with unwanted recollections. Lots of shots. Liam and Jax at a club, groups of women coming on to us at our VIP table. It feels like I went back to a time before I met Maya.

Shit. My crappy decisions proved Maya's point of not being the type of guy she wants to date. Not in the slightest. I sure as fuck wouldn't want to date someone like me.

My back lifts off the mattress, and a blond girl topples off me.

"You need to go. Now," my voice rasps. Another reminder of my bad decisions, along with my dry mouth and aversion to sunlight.

I don't want to spend another moment with this woman, the look and feel of her all wrong. Her rose scent, mixed in with the smell of sex and booze, chokes me, incomparable to Maya's fresh one. My stomach revolts at the thought of how badly I fucked up.

I head to the bathroom, choosing to brush my teeth first, wanting to cleanse my mouth from the taste of that woman and alcohol. My battered face makes me wince. Disgust rolls through me at my sunken eyes and pale, sickly skin.

I take a shower, eager to rid myself of the woman's smell and everything else associated with her and a bad ending to my night. By the time I get out, there's no sign of her, except for the underwear she left on a pillow. My body shudders as I dump her souvenir in the trash.

I pull my phone from the plug, glad I remembered to charge my battery. At least I made one responsible decision because overall, I'm a fucking idiot.

Are you shitting me? I didn't set my alarm, missing my practice sessions.

Shit. Shit. Shit!

I bolt out of my hotel room, desperate to make it to my qualifier on time.

I've never been so damn irresponsible in my life.

It doesn't shock me when my day goes from bad to the fucking worst. My qualifier starts out as a shit show. I rush to get my race suit on and chug a gallon of water to make sure I don't pass out behind the wheel under the hot conditions. Sophie's dad looks pissed as fuck about my tardiness, glaring at me as I swallow down a granola bar.

He fails to hide his distaste. "You look like shit. You're not a young kid anymore, staying up late to party. I expect this from anyone but you." His sneer tells me everything. James Mitchell isn't one to fuck around with because he has balls bigger than King Kong. His green eyes stare down at me while he runs an agitated hand across his face. His gray hair remains in place, unlike mine standing up in different directions, the waves untamed from my hands.

"I'm extremely sorry. This will never happen again." No apologies can erase my terrible decisions.

I trip over my feet while rushing to my car. I'm a hot, crappy mess, and fuck if it isn't humbling. Embarrassed doesn't begin to describe how I feel. Bandini mechanics look down at me, unsure how to help, as I clamber into my car. Sweat clings to my chest before the engine starts up, a shitty omen for my fuck-tastic day.

The beginning of my qualifier goes okay as my car takes down the first straightaway. That is until I make it past my first turn. Bile creeps up my throat during most of the turns after, the curves of the track not faring well with the alcohol seeping from my pores. I spend all my mental energy on not blowing chunks inside my helmet.

My nasty hangover doesn't pair nicely with my car going two hundred miles an hour round and round the track. The qualifier performance is sloppy and unprofessional. The usual hum of the engine fills me with dread, guilt eating away at me as I think about Maya and how she might feel if she heard about my night.

Sweat trickles down my back, soaking the material of my fireproof gear as I careen across the track. Fans watch the worst display of my entire racing career.

I rush out of my car once the qualifier finishes. My body revolts against me as I throw up twice near a patch of grass close to the pit area, the acidic taste making me nauseous all over again. All this happens while a local camera crew films me. Somehow, I find enough self-control to not flip them off, instead choosing to give a thumbs-up to the camera while I hunch over.

My car places fourteenth for the race. Fucking fourteenth

out of twenty drivers. I haven't had such an embarrassing placement since I started out in F1, and I don't know if I'll live this one down.

The only small blessing from today is how I don't have to attend the press conference meant exclusively for the top three drivers. I guess sucking comes with benefits.

Since Santi has the pole position, he'll be distracted. I need to find Maya and apologize for everything. Like for taking her out on a date and fucking another girl in the same day. Even if she's disinterested in hooking up with me, it's wrong.

I spot Sophie and Maya talking with Liam and Jax on the main road near all the hospitality suites. A cold feeling creeps its way up my spine at the sight of Jax pulling her in for a hug. It shouldn't upset me, but shit, it stings to see her wrapping her arms around him and laughing, unaware of how he got a blow job at the table last night from a random chick.

I don't have a right to feel jealous, since I can't give her what she wants. But I can't control it; my fists clench at the sight of them, envy whirling inside me like toxic air.

Maya's eyes catch mine. The smile she had before slips from her face, and it pisses me off how I've turned her mood sour in two seconds flat.

I stroll up to the guys, keeping it casual even though I barely have it together inside.

"Shit luck today, bro." Liam doesn't look the least bit fazed from last night. *Was I the only one who got seriously fucked up?* Come to think of it, he was sober as hell. I don't even think he blinked at any other girls who came on to us. *Shit.*

"Never going out the night before a qualifier again. That

was a terrible idea, man." Jax pats my shoulder as he throws me under the bus.

Fuck you very much, Jax.

"You guys look like you had quite the night. Ballsy move before a qualifier." Sophie's narrowed eyes glare into mine.

"Mm, that's why my brother is the best. He puts the team first." Maya's polite smile doesn't reach her flat eyes.

"Yeah, yeah, we get it already. You adore Santiago. At least pretend you want us to do well too." Liam knocks Maya's hat off her head and offers her a shrug. She laughs at him.

I want to record the sound for the bad days, like today, because I'm the biggest idiot.

"We better get going. Girls' day and all." Sophie links her arm in Maya's. They head off after saying their goodbyes with Maya ignoring me. It fucking sucks.

"Bro, you got smashed last night. You wouldn't shut up about her." Liam nods his head in the direction Maya left in.

Jax shakes his head. "It was a sad sight until you took that girl home. You even called her Maya once, but she shrugged it off. What was her name? Beatrice?"

Thank you, Jax, for bringing up the last thing I want to think about. I flip him off.

"She was hot. You always get the good ladies." Liam's arms cross against his chest.

"I'm surprised she even went home with him. He kept talking about Maya rejecting him, how she doesn't want a playboy like him." Jax chuckles to himself.

"Okay, guys, I get it. It was a pathetic night. Can we not

bring it up anymore? Like ever." My clipped voice matches my declining patience.

"All right. No need to get pissy at us." Liam's last words end that conversation.

I take off in the direction of the Bandini motorhome because I have another round of apologies to get out to Sophie's dad and the pit crew.

Unlike the last time Maya avoided me, we both keep our distance this time. Me because of shame. Her probably because I gross her out, not that I blame her at all.

The rest of Saturday is uneventful, which fills me with relief. I recover from my awful hangover, trying to overhydrate because race-day conditions are hot, and alcohol dehydrates like no other. No doubt I'll sweat out three pounds of body weight at least.

On race day, I eavesdrop on Santiago and Maya's conversation, desperate to feel close to her. She keeps her voice low and inaudible. To avoid punching a wall out of frustration, I exit my suite to go to the pit area.

I run through some engine checks and attend a prerace briefing. Busying myself keeps me from doing something stupid, like finding Maya and giving in to her demands while begging for forgiveness. After wrapping up with the top engineers, I head back toward the garage.

I silently curse at Maya sitting next to the computer bay. She wears one of the engineer's headsets so she can listen in on Santi's team radio. A churning feeling of jealousy swirls in the pit of my stomach. Being jealous of her brother...a new low.

A lot of contradictory feelings mix inside my head. Maya rejects me because she wants more than I can give her, but I don't even know how to try to give her what she wants.

Her vlog camera swings around in full force, filming the busy race-day activities.

I find it difficult to ignore her voice while I discuss the logistics of the car and any last-minute tune-ups. She tours the place and introduces members of the team, a sweet gesture to show off the men and women who are essential to Bandini. Her voice raves about how the crew keeps everything up and running, even introducing them by name, proof of her connection to the team. She has this way of charming people. Unlike me, who has a way of fucking up with people.

I try to hide my shock when she walks up to my car.

"Here we have Slade's team."

I see we are back to last names now.

She does a spin to get everyone in the camera shot. "They're busy doing last-minute checks on his car. He has a big task of catching up to Santiago, Liam, and Jax, since he starts in P14 today. It's his worst start since he began racing in F1. Better luck next time."

Thanks, Maya. I take it because I deserve it and more.

I wave at the camera as she pans over my car. Her fruity shampoo hits my senses, instantly bringing me back to a few days ago. Her lips on mine, the sounds she made when I touched her, when I grinded into her. My dick twitches in my race suit. *Great.*

She moves on to interview one of the head engineers. He subtly checks out Maya's chest in between questions, and it takes everything in me not to push him away.

Concentrate on your car. You're about to go race, and you don't have time to worry about her.

I decide to ignore Maya for the rest of the prep. No need for any more distractions, least of all from her, since she decided she doesn't want anything casual. She rejected me. Her loss.

I lose the race big time. But I worked my ass off to get out of fourteenth position, and considering where I started, I'm happy with placing eighth. Santi and I even get points for the Constructors'.

I head to my suite, not wanting to check out the podium celebrations today despite being glad for Jax and Liam. Santiago too, I guess. But it was a good day for McCoy, which means a bad one for Bandini.

Maya sits out on the empty balcony of the hospitality area, lying across a couch, cell phone in hand. I like to head up here when I have a bad day, but it looks like she beat me to it.

"Was she worth it?" She baits me, not glancing up from her phone screen. My irritability grows with every second she refuses to look at me.

"Who?" I play stupid because I don't want to deal with this shit anymore. We aren't boyfriend and girlfriend.

"The woman from last night."

My lips twitch up at her word choice. "Oh, her." That gets her to look up at me. I don't like her stormy gaze, the way she comes off indifferent to a situation that bothers the fuck out of her. I'd rather have her mad at me than feel nothing at all.

I meant it when I said I'm a selfish bastard.

"Yup." Her lips pop on the last letter.

"She was a decent lay." I shrug, coming off uncaring, even though my throat feels like I swallowed glass. It feels wrong to lie like this, my words hurting her because I take my anger on myself out on her.

"Mm. Wonder how much alcohol you had to drink to wipe the taste of me from your mouth. Doubt the girl minded though. Desperation always trumps common sense."

Fuck. She has me there. I'm stunned stupid, unable to get any words out.

"They'll never be as good as what we could have. But this is why people like you never have happily-ever-afters. You're so jaded, you can't see the best things until it's too late."

She gets up, not bothering to give me one last look as she leaves the balcony.

My stomach drops at not being worth a backward glance.

Belgian
Grand Pix

CHAPTER TWENTY-ONE
Maya

I avoid everything Noah-related for weeks. Anytime I find him in the Bandini suites, I walk the other way. Things sit heavy between us. And not in the "hot and heavy" kind of way. Much more like the "my heart hurts whenever I see him" kind of way.

How I feel about him is messy. It doesn't fit nicely into checked boxes or a pros and cons list. I struggle to understand my conflicting emotions, which ends up pissing me off more. Part of me wishes he could commit to trying a real relationship, while another part of me thinks he's not even worth the trouble.

He should have waited at least a day before hooking up with someone else. It's basically common courtesy.

How do you fuck another woman right after you go on a date with someone else? It's cold and disgusting. I honestly didn't expect that from him.

Every time I run into Noah, I feign indifference, choosing

to ignore the way my heart beats faster around him, how my body heats when his eyes roam over me, or the hint of sadness that crosses his face when I ignore him.

I thrust myself into taking my content to the next level. Seven hundred thousand people follow me across different platforms, and the ads on my videos turn a nice profit. Sponsors reach out to partner with me, something I never thought was possible. My platforms have surpassed everything I'd ever dreamed of. Sophie and I visit different places in every city we travel to, making the most of my time with Bandini while the explorations conveniently keep me away from Noah.

The month-long summer break between the first and second half of the season couldn't have come at a better time. I try to lie to myself and say I don't miss Noah over the vacation. But I do. I check out his social media accounts daily, except he keeps quiet, not posting anything but a couple pictures of the Italian coast. Even gossip accounts have nothing to report on him. He's taken a break from everything. And maybe it's a good thing, seeing as his previous indiscretions finally cycled out of the media.

I spend the vacation with my family, including Santi. Besides the temporary bouts of missing Noah, I have a good time.

Sophie comes to Spain to visit us during the last week of the break. My parents welcome her like a second daughter, sharing how grateful they are for me to have someone to spend time with besides Santi.

Sophie and I come up with the best plan. A talent of hers.

"Repeat the plan back to me. I want to make sure you're

convinced." Sophie paints her nails in my bedroom. Tomorrow, we both fly together to the next race because she wants to prep me before seeing Noah at the Belgian Grand Prix.

I jokingly roll my eyes even though I appreciate her friendship and dedication to making sure I keep out of trouble.

"All right. Since I'm now a mature woman who knows better, I'm going to be civil and nice. I don't need to play games with him. We are two adults who can get along for the sake of the team."

Sophie smiles up at the quote she makes me repeat every time I bring up Noah. "And…" She waves her hand expectantly.

"I will not give in."

"In to what exactly? I need to hear you say it."

Ugh, she actually wants me to repeat it.

"I will not fall for his rough yet sweet personality, rock-hard abs, kissable lips, or fuckable body." My new go-to chant.

Her green eyes sparkle. "Attagirl. I'm so proud. Look how quickly you grew in a month. Vacation glow looks good on you." She pinches my cheeks.

"Why does this feel like it's going to be a disaster?"

"Stop your catastrophizing. You're going to give yourself a migraine. What's the goal for the second half of the season? Maybe we need to run through it one more time."

She's so full of it. But I give in because she flashes me two dimples.

"Grow my vlog, find a nice man to go on a couple of dates with, and spend time with my best friend."

Sophie claps her hands like I'm a child saying my first words. The display comes off dramatic and silly, but it fits her.

"Yes, girl. Cheers to that!" We clink our glasses and sip our wine.

The cold liquid soothes my throat. "Where does one find nice men in F1 anyway? I'm curious."

"Leave that up to me. I'm your fairy godmother, but instead of waving a magic wand, I use a magic dildo. Works like a charm. It's guaranteed to land you the best dick you've ever had."

Wine nearly streams out of my nose.

Not sure what I volunteered myself for, but I can't help feeling worried.

CHAPTER TWENTY-TWO
Noah

I regret how I went about everything in Baku, including how my anger got the best of me after the race, making stupid statements to Maya. I messed up big time with her. But I want to fix it and make things right.

I spend a good portion of the break working out kinks in my car and strategizing with the team for the second half of the championship season.

But I also spend time going to therapy.

Yup. Let that sink in for a second. Me in therapy.

I sit in my psychologist's office, attending one of my two weekly sessions. One session per week wouldn't cut it because I need to work through a ton of shit about my parents, relationships, and my issues with commitment. And I don't have a lot of time before the next race.

The whole process has been a lot to take in. Some days, I leave sessions pissed off, while other times, I leave sad because of how fucked up my parents are and the damage they've caused. Therapy is an emotional struggle that drains me worse than driving one hundred laps around a Grand Prix track.

"What holds you back from wanting a relationship?" My therapist's brown eyes gaze at me from across the room as he sits casually in his beige chair. I sit on a leather couch, switching between staring up at the ceiling and meeting his gaze.

"I'm not sure. It's kind of a mixture of different things. I've never even tried to have a real girlfriend before."

"Walk me through the combination of reasons." His hands clasp together across his knee. He looks put together with his gray hair combed over and his pressed suit.

"I don't even know what a good relationship looks like. My parents didn't love each other. I was a credit line at Barney's for my mom, an endless tie to my dad's bank account. So I'm not sure what real love even looks or feels like. That's a scary thought in itself." How can I recognize something I have no clue about?

"If you could describe love to me, what would you say?" His questions never let me off easy. No, I consider them shit-stirring instead of open-ended.

"Hmm." I rub the back of my neck. "I think love is about happiness and sacrifice. Compromising instead of arguing. Having someone who is always there for you even when you don't deserve it. Loving someone means you want to spend the rest of your life with them, on the good days and the bad days and everything in between."

He looks proud of what I said, nodding along with me and hanging on each word. A small ounce of pride rushes through me at my thoughtful answer.

"Those are all great ideas of love. And what would be the reasons holding you back from trying with someone? Let's use Maya as an example since you bring her up during our sessions."

I sit and think about his question for a full minute. He doesn't push me when I stay quiet, instead preferring to wait it out, putting less pressure on me to fill the silence.

"I think I'm afraid." The words leave my lips in a whisper. I don't like admitting fear about anything when I drive cars faster than any other man in the world, for fuck's sake.

"Fear is not always a weakness. It's what you do with the fear that shows your true strength. What exactly are you afraid of?" This man and his board of inspirational quotes.

"Not giving it my best and failing. Disappointing her and not being able to be there when she needs me. Breaking her heart and mine in the process. The thought of giving someone power over me…" I look down at my hands. Rough fingertips press together in a fidgeting motion that reminds me of Maya. Ever since Baku, thinking about her makes my chest constrict weirdly like it recognizes how much of a dumbass I am.

"Those are all reasons anyone would be afraid and worried about trying. You're not alone in thinking that. A lot of people share similar reservations when they start a relationship because loving someone makes you vulnerable."

I didn't know that.

"How would you feel if Maya dated another person who is willing to love her like you described earlier?"

I clench my hands. The thought of her dating, kissing, or fucking another guy makes me sick. I don't deserve her, but screw anyone else who tries.

"I wouldn't like it one fucking bit."

"And why is that?" He doesn't flinch at my cursing, further evidence of why I like this man.

"Because I would be wishing it was me who could do those things with her."

My admission sits with us like a third person. Minutes pass by as I devise a plan, the sound of the clock ticking to the rhythm of my bouncing leg.

"I think I have an idea for what I need to do. But I want to run it by you."

My therapist smiles at me. He helps me build confidence, listening to my ideas while offering insight and opposing viewpoints. I'm fucking done sitting on the sidelines thinking about my mistakes, because I'm the type to be on the front of the grid with a pole-position start.

Time to get my trophy.

CHAPTER TWENTY-THREE
Maya

"L isten, the last date was bad, but this one will be better. I pinky promise. We can ditch together if it goes terrible." Sophie holds my hand before linking our pinkies together, forcing a promise on me before I agree.

I groan. Another date sounds like a terrible idea. "The last one included a guy bringing out photos of his family and ex-wife. He even told me how they got married and divorced, tearing up as the waiter brought out our dessert. I'll never look at tiramisu the same way again."

"Okay, I get it. That wasn't my best work. I'm still fixing the kinks in my magic wand dildo thing. But I picked two good ones this time." Her green eyes fill with hope.

"That sounds so wrong. Who are the new guys?"

Since we can both suffer together, I give in to the plan. I don't want to risk it with another disastrous date because a woman can only take so many photo albums.

"They're two top engineers for McCoy. I met one of them at a press conference my dad was talking in. They're sweet, I swear. Cross my heart." She drags her index finger in an X motion.

I nod along, agreeing to the plan because of Sophie's good intentions.

"Yay. You won't regret it! They even got us reservations at the nicest restaurant in Milan. Because nothing says a good date like pasta!" She claps her hands and drags us to my hotel room to pick our outfits. For someone who loves sneakers and T-shirts, she sure enjoys getting dressed up.

Here we are on a date the night before a qualifier round, sitting across from two good-looking guys. Sophie shoots me a grin when they look at their menus.

I agreed to this date for her because she's seemed to struggle with Liam ever since they went to Canada. Not that she opens up about it.

The man Sophie set me up with has a head of blond hair that curls at the ends. He looks kind of cute in a sweet way, and he even has a hint of an accent I can't place. Candlelight dances off his brown eyes as he stares into mine.

"What's it like to be a vlogger for Bandini? At McCoy, we always watch them, hoping you'll drop trade secrets." My date, Daniel, smiles wide.

I shake my head. "I'm careful to make sure that doesn't happen. I think they would flag my videos and not allow me to film anymore." I make a zipping motion with my fingers and throw the invisible key over my shoulder.

"Which videos have you seen?" Sophie jumps in, her blond space buns bobbing.

"We watch a lot of them, and they look pretty well done. Do you edit them yourself?" Her date, John, asks.

"I've learned how to edit better as I continue to make more videos. I'm sure I could upgrade my equipment once it takes off because nice cameras are worth thousands of dollars."

"By taking off, she means more than a million followers. She's close to eight hundred thousand already." Sophie beams like a proud mom.

"How much did you pay Noah to do those videos? Especially the question ones because he never does stuff like that. He even declined Sports Daily when they asked for a similar one."

My eyes burn at the memory. Nothing like bringing up Noah to dampen my mood, except my date has no idea about Noah and me, let alone how the industry works.

"I paid him nothing since he volunteered, and I didn't exactly strong-arm him into it. Plus, we don't really pay for things like that in this kind of work. Famous people usually do it if they want to. If not, they say no." I scrunch my nose at Daniel's misunderstanding.

"Doubt anyone could say no to you, not even the great Noah Slade."

Daniel's smile doesn't fill me with warmth like Noah's did. I give a weak smile back, not exactly enjoying how he brings up Noah and Bandini.

Sophie gives my knee a squeeze under the table, finding the perfectly painful pressure point. I force the idea of him out of my head. Her new project includes conditioning me into not thinking about Noah anymore, going as far as watching videos on Pavlov's dog.

"Excuse me. I'll be right back. I need to use the restroom." I push my chair out with more force than I'd intended. It knocks into the back of another person's seat, causing the occupant to glare at me. "I'm so sorry." I speed walk out of there and dart into the dark hallway near the bathrooms.

I pull out my phone to distract myself while keeping track of time. Scrolling through my social media feed comforts me.

A finger hovers over the power button right before the screen shuts off.

I breathe in a smell that's distinctly Noah.

Oh God, why does my luck suck so bad lately?

"Date going that terrible?" His hoarse voice grabs my attention, and my heart rate picks up. Calloused fingers lift my chin, making my body respond to him instantaneously like we haven't spent a month apart. Poor lighting in the hall doesn't give me much to look at. I breathe in the smell of him because I'm a glutton for punishment. His textured thumb drags across my lips.

"What are you doing here?" *Did my voice sound husky?* I can't hear it over the blood rushing through my ears.

"I'm out at dinner with friends. It's a popular restaurant."

Okay, so at least he doesn't follow me around. That would be a bit concerning.

Noah's dark silhouette blocks any light, making it difficult to distinguish his features in the dim hall. His lips brush against mine. My lips tingle from the barest touch, a mere caress I feel guilty enjoying. I tilt my neck to the side to evade his lips.

He chuckles. His lips trail down my neck instead, leaving light kisses behind.

"I've missed you." The three words he says feel like everything I want to hear. They make my heart ache because he can't give me what I want, no matter how much I crave it.

"You can't miss what you've never had." If I wasn't currently occupied, I'd clap myself on the back for that one.

"What if I told you I've changed, that the break did me good?" He gets the words out before his lips suck on my neck, what I deem to be my weak spot. Our chemistry has not wavered. It feels as charged as ever; as his lips drag across my skin, my body unconsciously arches into him.

The betrayal.

"Not sure if I believe you. Actions speak louder than words."

Trashy tabloids have kept quiet since the blond woman in Baku. He may speak the truth, but I don't want to chance it, putting myself out there to get hurt.

"Let me show you. Just give me a real chance."

His lips find mine again. But this time, his kiss dominates the situation, just like him, crashing against me and tearing down my walls. His tongue strokes the seam of my lips, seeking entrance.

I keep them sealed off, preventing him from taking the kiss further. He nips at my bottom lip in a silent demand for me to open up to him. His teeth graze and pull, causing me to groan at the feeling.

"Uh. Oh man, I'll come back later."

My head snaps up at the stranger's voice. I bury my face

in Noah's button-down shirt, which is a bad idea because the addicting smell of him makes me lightheaded.

I don't move until the stranger's footsteps disappear.

"Hear me out. Let me expla—" his voice croaks.

Nope. Need to get out of this situation ASAP.

"Um. Uh…I have to go." I take off in the direction of my table, leaving a grumbling Noah behind me, not bothering to steal a second glance at him. My brain tells me to run away from Noah while my body tells me to run toward him.

Sophie's eyes narrow at me when I settle back in my seat, making me feel even worse about what happened.

I ignore her side glances throughout the night because we can have story time later.

My stomach twists in knots as Sophie stares at me from across the room, her sneaker tapping against the carpet. She reads my body language while she sits on the sectional couch in Santi's suite. My eyes gaze around at the plain hotel room in a struggle to find anything interesting to look at. Basically, anything but her face would do.

"What did we say about him?" She won't let me off easy, her voice laced with disappointment.

"Well, I didn't *exactly* fall for his rough yet sweet personality, kissable lips, fuckable body, or rock-hard abs. Honestly, he cornered me in the hallway. I didn't even know he was there. It's not like I chose the restaurant." I may or may not have practiced that line in the bathroom earlier.

"And what, he tripped and his lips fell on yours?" She

waves her hands around. *Yup. Definitely ticked off.* My silence doesn't bode well with her because she paces the room, agitated and grumbling about how all her plans fail. "Don't you dare try to play it off in your pretty head. That's a ridiculous idea. You came back to the table a mess, and your lips looked like you sucked his dick in the bathroom. *Did you*? Or did he suck on them like a Hoover vacuum?"

I have no clue how she says the most ridiculous things as seriously as she does, not even cracking a smile.

My chest and face feel fifty shades of pink. I dramatically throw myself face-first onto the couch in front of us, grabbing a pillow to drown her out. She means well and all, but it doesn't make it easier.

"I'm sorry. I won't do it again. I learned my lesson." Cushions muffle my voice.

"I sure hope so. Daniel is a nice guy who's hesitant about giving you another chance." She plucks the pillow from my face and stares at me, green eyes glittering under the dim lighting.

"You talked to him about it?" I cringe at my whininess.

She shakes her head. "Not exactly. But I can read these things. Call it intuition."

"Next one will go better. Maybe we shouldn't go somewhere public." I get her hopes up, pretending to agree to another date I have no intention of following through on. No need to lead a poor guy on when my mind is on someone else.

"I don't think it'll happen because we are engaging in stage two of the plan."

Sophie's second phase fills me with uncertainty.

I glance up from my pity corner on the couch. She taps away at her phone, ignoring me.

"I'm bringing in reinforcements." *Tap. Tap. Tap.* Her fingers moving against her phone fills the quiet.

"Should I be worried?"

She shoots me a mischievous smile.

Well, that answers my question.

Singapore
Grand Prix

CHAPTER TWENTY-FOUR
Noah

I try to pinpoint the exact moment my friends started ditching me. Was it after Germany? Or France?

I can't exactly place it, but ever since the summer break, I barely hang with Liam and Jax. Every week, they come up with excuses about being busy. By the time we show up in Singapore for the Grand Prix, they're nowhere to be found. Yet again.

The only time I see them is during a press conference after Saturday's qualifier. I ended up driving well and have pole position for tomorrow, securing the best spot at one of the few night races we have. At least things with racing look promising.

Do they not want to hang out with me because I win a lot? The championship gets competitive after all. Maybe they keep their distance for the brand's sake, since teams don't encourage us to hang out and play nice. But when I think back on times in the past, they never got this way, which means it has to be something else.

I hang out all alone in my hotel room, overlooking the city, checking out the view of the famous trees and Marina Bay Sands buildings. Singapore bustles with activity before the race. People flood the sidewalks, looking like ants from my suite's balcony.

Despite all the action, for the first time, I feel lonely.

I'm putting it out there. My therapist would be proud.

I sit on the couch for a few minutes, processing what it feels like to have no one around. My friends rarely respond to my messages. We haven't planned a night out, a strange occurrence for them in the biggest party city on the Grand Prix schedule.

Even Maya avoids me ever since I kissed her in the Milan restaurant two weeks ago. She sticks to Santi's side like a stage-five clinger, playing it smart because I'd never do anything in front of him. But she won't give me a chance to explain myself either. I want to tell her I'm ready to try with her, the whole deal, no more fucking around.

I can't stand how she evades me. So I do what usually calms me and drowns out the thoughts in my head. I pull up Maya's vlog on my laptop and click yesterday's upload. My heart drops at her stunning smile, her brown eyes staring into the camera with happiness as she holds a lens to her face.

"Hi, everyone, welcome back. This week, we are in Singapore, and it's honestly one of the coolest cities we've visited so far during the championship. I'm here with Sophie, Jax, and Liam."

Now I have my answer about my friends' whereabouts. My

teeth clench at the sight of them all smiling into Maya's camera like they didn't ignore my two texts to hang out.

"We're here at the Gardens by the Bay. Viewers asked for a Web's Most Asked Questions with Jax, Britain's favorite playboy. Liam decided to tag along because he has a serious case of FOMO."

You're not the only one, buddy.

"We decided to do a combination deal here. It's the best of both worlds. I asked viewers what their most pressing questions were about these two clowns. I wrote down the top ones because my social media was flooded with options. Ready?"

Sophie grabs the camera and films Liam, Jax, and Maya sitting on a bench with the supertrees in the background. *Fan-fucking-tastic.* A few people walk behind them and wave at the camera.

A burning sensation settles in my gut.

"Some are embarrassing, and others are outright silly, but I can't be biased. I picked whichever ones were asked the most." Maya smiles as she pulls out a paper with a list of questions.

I remember the time I told her she can't be biased. Guess she keeps me in mind someway, making me smile.

My laptop bounces to the rhythm of my knee, nervousness and curiosity coursing through me about where this will go. Most of the questions she asks Liam and Jax are about F1 and the guys' racing careers. Seven minutes pass before Maya asks about personal issues. Can't help feeling like a stalker watching them like this, but she does post it publicly. Screw it.

"Jax or Liam. Or both. The lady subscribers wonder about your relationship status."

They high-five each other behind Maya like they're five years old.

"I can answer for myself. I'm single and ready to mingle. Meet me at the Singapore party after the Grand Prix if you're interested in hanging out and getting to know me." Jax rubs a tattooed finger across his chin.

Liam grins, not answering the question, that sly little shit.

Maya pretends to gag. "You heard it here first, everyone. I am *not* dating either one of these guys. We're all friends." She nods enthusiastically.

Liam stays silent, winking at the camera and tapping his fingers on his thigh.

Do they hang out this much? How did I miss this?

I pull up Liam's social media page. His most recent images are of him and Jax or the four of them out touring whatever city we are in. Plus, a few hard-to-miss posts of him and Sophie.

When did he clean up his act?

Jax's profile looks similar. He has a picture of him and Maya in a photo booth from a gala event. I recognize the background because I was there too, yet I don't remember seeing Maya there.

Where did they even find the time for all this shit? But more importantly, could I make time for something besides racing?

I land myself on the Singapore podium. Second place. *Woo-fucking-hoo.*

This time, the champagne showers don't feel as fun. The

crowd roars but I ignore them, my eyes landing on Maya standing behind a barrier as she cheers Santi on. My eyes stay glued to her for minutes. Her grin falters when she catches me looking at her, but she regains her composure. Jax and I end up spraying champagne on Santi since he impressively won the whole thing. This race is a challenge. Humidity is disgustingly high, making it hard for us to race with our heads fully in it. I think I lost at least five pounds after racing today. Not joking. Sweat still drips down my back, clinging to my race suit.

Attendants escort us to the press conference after we all have a weight check, an ice bucket bath, and a quick shower. The idea of answering more questions fills me with dread because I'm not in the mood for reporters.

It stuns me to find Maya in her usual corner of the press conference. She gives me a tight smile before Sophie whispers something in her ear, her throat dipping back as she lets out a laugh. Carefree and so damn beautiful. I lick my lips at the sight of her, the hollow part of her neck easily becoming one of my favorite places—to kiss, to touch, to nip.

I'm thankful for the table in front of me because I don't need *that* problem on camera today.

Since press conferences can be boring as fuck, I run through my plan for tonight. I can't skip out on the Singapore after-party Maya mentioned. She glances at me, making my lips tip up into a naughty smile, the first one I've given her in a while.

Her eyes widen.

If only she knew what was coming. I'm done playing games; I'm getting my checkered flag.

I pull out the big guns for this. And by big guns, I mean Sophie because she's the equivalent of a grenade launcher and semiautomatic rifle combined. Without her on my side, the plan is hopeless.

I text her after the press conference to please meet me in my hotel room. She grumbles about it until I text her with praying hands and a promise for chocolate-chip cookies. Girl hasn't changed in all the years I've known her.

"What do you want, Slade?" Her icy glare could make a normal man cry, but instead, I grin. How formal of her to use my last name.

I make myself comfortable on the couch, since Sophie refuses to sit. She stands in a power pose, ready to take me on, hands on her hips. An intimidation stance that barely reaches past my head.

"I'm coming to you for help because I really need it. And trust me, I do."

Sophie blows a bubble with her gum before popping it, the sound breaking the tension in the room. She looks like a Barbie version of a mob boss.

"How can I help you? I don't even know what you want." She likes to play dumb, batting her eyelashes at me.

"I think you do." *Let's cut the bullshit.*

"I want to hear you say it. The first step in fixing a problem is admitting you have one in the first place."

Yup. This is why Liam can't help being around her. She gives him a run for his money, all sassy and shit.

I suppress a groan and tug at my hair. "I like Maya."

Her blank gaze gives nothing away. She blinks a couple of times, waiting for me to continue.

"And I messed up. I thought I knew what I wanted. But in reality, I didn't."

"Tell me more." She sits down, her pose looking like my therapist.

"I took her out on a date. I'm sure you're aware of that."

She nods.

"And it didn't exactly end well. I told her I could only offer physical stuff. No attachments or frills, and she wanted more."

"No duh. And what do you want now?" Her gaze reminds me of her dad, staring into me like she can sense my sincerity.

I look away from her intense scrutiny. "I think I want more."

"I don't think you should do anything unless you *know* you want more. Maya's the sweetest. She doesn't need someone who isn't willing to go all the way. Like make sacrifices for her."

My fists tighten in front of me. "I can try. I never even wanted this before. But seeing her all the time, from far away, I feel terrible. I struggle not to go up and talk to her or even kiss her. I want a chance. But I need your help." I glance at Sophie.

She looks at me with a genuine smile and warm eyes, the opposite of how she was when the conversation began. "Share with me what you have planned. I'll see what I can do on my end."

I'm nervous because I don't know if Sophie will hold up her end of the deal. Hell, she concocted half of the plan after she deemed my original one unfit. Once I told her I seriously wanted to date Maya, Sophie became a lot more willing to help, coming up with a few ideas she thinks Maya would like. She nixed my original plan to show up at the after-party, telling me Maya doesn't function well past 12 a.m. Lucky for me, Singapore Grand Prix weekend includes events until the following Monday because they love to party over here.

I sit at an empty table at an exclusive restaurant. Sophie secured a private room that will force Maya to give me her undivided attention for at least an hour, but I hope for more if I buy a good bottle of wine. Because who can resist that? My fingers tap against the table, a nervous tic I picked up from the fidgeter herself.

Finally, after what feels like forever, someone knocks on the door.

"Okay, you guys. This is the strangest dinner plan ever—" Her voice cuts off when her eyes land on me sitting alone.

Her eyes widen while her mouth drops open. She's dressed up in a sexy black cocktail dress with her dark hair flowing around her face in waves, adding to her gorgeousness. I take a deep breath to settle my own nerves.

I stand and walk up to her slowly to prevent her from fleeing.

"What's going on?" Her eyes dart around the room, taking in the two seats before they land on me.

"Let me explain over dinner." My hand clutches hers as I walk her toward the chair across from mine, hoping she decides to stay. I pull out her seat and usher her into it. A compliant Maya may be my favorite version of her.

"I'm confused. I'm guessing Sophie is in on this plan?" She lets out an adorable soft curse under her breath.

"Correct. Let's order a drink first because we can both use one."

We get situated and order our food right away at Maya's insistence. I take her biting on her lip as a guilty sign that she wants to leave as soon as possible.

I sigh before speaking. "I had two months to get you out of my system. And trust me, I tried."

She flinches at my words.

Fuck, come on. I suck at expressing myself. "Not like that. I mean, I had to sit with my own decisions."

She relaxes in her chair. I take another deep breath, calming my nerves. *Think before you speak.*

"I thought it would get easier with time. But you avoided me, which sucked. I went from seeing you every day and talking to you and spending time together to nothing."

"I wasn't trying to ignore you." Her eyes flick across the room.

I give her a pointed look.

"Okay, fine. I was trying to a teensy bit. I told you what I wanted, and you rejected me. I can't expect you to change any more than I expect myself to. It's not fair to either one of us."

"Well, I have changed, and I want to try to give you what you want. Spending all that time alone, I realized I want what you want. To spend time with you before and after races, like going on dates, hanging out at events, being lazy in bed together after mind-blowing sex. Give me all the strings attached." The thought of rejection makes my stomach drop.

Her eyebrows dart up. "How do I know you won't back out the moment you get scared?"

I don't blame her for being skeptical when I haven't exactly proven myself yet. "You don't. And I don't either. But it's what I can give you for now. The real question is, are you willing to take it?"

She can back out at any moment. I can tell she thinks hard about it by the way she works her bottom lip between her teeth.

She looks down at her hands. "I guess we can give it a try. What changed your mind?"

Something warm spreads through my chest, eating away at the uncertainty and nervousness from before. Her agreement is all I need.

I lift her chin up, craving eye contact. "I mean it when I say I spent a lot of time alone. I reflected on what was stopping me from trying this out with you. Our chemistry is"—her lips capture my attention—"explosive. But I also know there's more. I like being around you, especially when you give me all your attention. I like when you film me without asking because you're afraid of me saying no, even though you can get me to agree to anything. I love the way you laugh almost as much as the way you find your shoes interesting when you get nervous. I really like the special noises you save just for me when I kiss you and the smiles you give me when no one is looking. I'm serious about trying it all with you. No holding back. I even met with someone to talk about my own issues and reservations, because when I do something, I go all in." *Clearly came down with a severe case of word vomit.*

She looks as surprised as I feel about revealing my secret.

And fuck, vulnerability scares me, but I can trust Maya. I *need* to trust her. For once in my life, I don't view leaning on someone else as a negative.

"I'm proud of you. That's a huge step." She grabs my hand and gives it a squeeze. A buzz similar to sticking my finger in an electrical socket courses up my arm.

I nod, not wanting to break the moment by hashing out my parental issues. "I've missed being around you."

"I have too. It's not the easiest thing—avoiding you when all my fans are dying to hear and see more of you." She shoots me a wink. "I had to fill the time with other interviews."

My breath hitches at the easygoing smile on her face, finally getting the grin I've waited weeks for. She fills me with hope. It's a new feeling, wanting someone to believe in me while desiring to prove myself worthy of her.

"We should give the subscribers what they want. I watch your videos." My cheeks heat up at my admission. I chug wine before I continue, needing extra help tonight. "I may be partial, but I think I'm better clickbait than Jax or Liam."

Her giggle fills the room. It's the best thing I've heard all week, even better than winning second place.

And it hits me.

Shit.

CHAPTER TWENTY-FIVE
Maya

We are doing this. Noah and me.

I never imagined he would come around. Days turned into weeks since the Baku disaster, and he didn't make a move, except for the time in Italy.

Noah hires a car to take us to a party, the lights of the city passing us by. He grips my hand on his lap, occasionally giving it a squeeze, checking that I'm still here.

"I don't want my brother to know. At least not yet." I look at him head-on, no shoes stealing my attention this time.

The temperature in the car drops a couple degrees. It may sound dramatic, but I swear it happens.

"Why?" His edgy voice makes me frown.

My eyes plead with his. "It's new. I don't want to distract him from the championship since you're both teammates and he won't like it. He tends to be overprotective of me."

Noah doesn't talk for a full minute. I shift in my seat,

waiting for him to say anything. His frown makes me wish I could take back my words.

"I'm not happy about it because I don't want to treat you like a dirty secret. I'm happy to be with you…but if that's what you want, I'll respect it." He shrugs.

"If it works out, I'll tell him after the championship, once everything is finalized for him."

His blue eyes stay pinned to mine. "It's going to work out, so we'll tell him when you're ready." His clipped voice has a finality to it.

"Thank you." I move close to him and wrap my arms around his waist, a new gesture that feels right. He gives the top of my head a quick kiss before he returns my hug.

"Now, time for kissing and making up. I hear that's the best part." He mumbles the words into my hair.

My laugh makes his chest rumble.

I can now confidently say kissing and making up might be my favorite part too.

I've watched extravagant weddings on television, even a few crazy sweet sixteen parties where a kid cries over getting the wrong colored convertible. All those parties one-up each other with new levels of craziness. If I combined every single overdone party known to man, that would sum up what Noah and I walk into for the Singapore celebration. Do all local events look like this—filled with indulgence, celebrities, and glam bordering on obscene? It's a party Gatsby would envy. But I love every second of it, soaking up the activities, including a side stage where people perform.

People say this is one of the best parties of the entire championship. None of the galas so far hold a candle to it. We stand on the rooftop of the most famous building in the city, overlooking the whole island, the supertrees glowing while buildings around us light up.

"Amazing, isn't it? Plus, now I have a date, which makes it ten times better." Noah's hand grips my waist.

His sexy smirk makes my heart pick up and my thighs clench. I sigh at the grin he saves especially for me. He wears a navy-blue tux today with black lapels and a crisp white shirt. I love the look on him, especially when my eyes gaze at the bow tie. He looks dreamy.

He gives me a peck on the lips. My body stills as I search around nervously for my brother.

"I'll keep an eye out for him. Don't worry." Noah's gruff voice vibrates against my chest.

Lying to my brother makes me sick with worry, making it difficult to fully enjoy attending the event with Noah.

Darkness cloaks us, giving us the ability to disappear into large crowds of people, becoming one of the many partygoers. We grab drinks at the bar before we search for our friends.

We find them soon after, Noah's fingers tensing before he removes them from my waist. The loss of contact makes me frown. But it's a necessary precaution at the moment, at least for the next two months until the World Championship is over.

We pull up to the table Jax and Liam reserved, bottles of alcohol set up in the center. Sophie sits next to them. I take up a spot next to her while Noah sits on the opposite side with the boys.

"Did it work out between you two?" She yells over the music into my ear.

I nod my head up and down in confirmation. "I'm surprised you helped pull that plan off. What happened to saying no to fuckable bodies?"

She winks at me. I laugh because it looks way more like a twitch.

"This time, it was worth it. I have faith it'll all work out. The magic dildo told me so." Both of her dimples show.

"Hey, I finally found you. Didn't see you earlier." My brother pulls me up for a hug. His words tug at my thin resolve, my lies building a wall around myself.

I play off my discomfort. "You've been busy being a champion and all. Must be such a hard life. Hopefully your hand hasn't cramped from carrying the trophy around all day."

"If I have to do another interview, I'll scream. How do you guys ever get used to this?" He glances at the guys, who send him a hello.

"You don't. Eventually press conferences become a running joke. Check some of ours out on YouTube." Liam hands a shot glass to my brother before tipping his own back. He pours alcohol for the rest of us.

Sophie and I knock ours back at the same time, my nose scrunching as the alcohol burns my throat.

I try to pace myself throughout the night. *A for effort. F for execution.*

I'm drunk by 12 a.m. Liam and Sophie dance around together. Both look smashed, Sophie stepping all over his toes with her sneakers, but he takes it like a man, chuckling at her drunken display. Pretty much everyone has let go and is having a good time except Noah. My brother left, so I get the all clear to scoot over to his side of the couch.

"Why are you sober?" I try to pout my numb lips.

"I think I'm going to cool it on the alcohol for a while."

Right. He and alcohol have a rough history.

My heart thumps in my chest as he smiles down at me. "You have such a good smile. It's not fair. I want to look that good." My fingers touch his face, grazing the rough stubble beneath them, imagining how it would feel in other places.

His chest shakes from laughing. "You look even better." He brushes my hair out of my eyes like a gentleman. His lips brush up against my temple, pressing sweetly before leaving again.

"Your kisses are the best. Like nothing I've ever had," I whisper-shout.

"Oh, tell me more." He lures me in, wanting to hear my drunk confessions.

I glance around to confirm Santi's gone. *All clear.*

"They turn me on. Like a lot." *Killing the sexy game, I think.* But he snickers at me instead of answering.

"What's so funny? Why are you laughing at me? I'm busy flirting. Hello." I push at his shoulder to make him stop.

He shoots me a breathtaking smile. My arms cross over my

chest, his eyes narrowing as he stares down at my cleavage. I return the favor by checking him out. His messy hair does it for me, along with the bow tie he already undid an hour ago. *Sigh*.

I grin. "Let's blow this popsicle stand."

He throws his head back and lets out a roar of laughter. I like being funny.

"Should I take that as a yes?" I clap my hands together.

"Sure, Maya. Let's go. Meet me outside in five minutes." Noah gets up from the table and says his goodbyes to the group. He acts like an expert at this incognito stuff to the point that someone could think we'd planned it all before.

I scroll through my phone, a hard job when all I want to do is get up and leave with Noah.

I wait for a total of four minutes before making my grand exit. My brother mopes at my departure after I find him schmoozing with sponsors. His sulking looks vaguely like mine, and I don't like how much I corrupt him.

I check the town car's license plate like Noah told me to. Numbers blur but it looks about right. My body falls into the bench seat dramatically, my dress swooshing around me as material flies everywhere.

The ride back to the hotel is quick with our driver adjusting his rearview mirror in hopes of sneaking a peek at our heavy petting and toe-curling kisses in the back seat. Noah barks at him to cut it out and to keep his eyes on the road. The older man sputters out an apology, the sound of his mirror returning back to normal making me laugh. At least until Noah shuts me up with more kisses.

I struggle to keep my eyes open by the time we pull into

the hotel. Alcohol hits me all at once, my body giving up the battle to stay awake. We both get out of the car at the same time since the hotel looks empty.

Noah practically carries me to the elevators. My feet are finding it difficult to keep up with his pace; they're dragging behind me as he holds me up.

I'm a giggling mess, but he joins me like a good sport.

It's all fun and games until he rejects my advances in his room.

"What do you mean, no?" My vision clouds as I take in a blurry Noah, his tux jacket abandoned and his bow tie lost somewhere in the car ride. He snickers when I stomp my foot for good measure.

"You're drunk. I don't want to risk you not remembering the first time I fuck you. I'm a gentleman, meaning I want to fuck you sober."

"I'll remember. I promise." I lift up two fingers like a scout's honor. He props up one more to show me how it's really done.

"What do I know? I wasn't a Girl Scout."

Noah laughs as he pulls me toward the bed. It's one of my favorite sounds, gruff and short. He shows me exactly what he can do even if I'm drunk.

CHAPTER TWENTY-SIX
Maya

I wake up the next morning not being able to breathe. Something heavy lies on my chest, making it difficult for my lungs to expand, not to mention the warmth against my side.

I bolt up and try to piece together what happened. My body relaxes when I find Noah's golden arm wrapped around my stomach. He rolls onto his other side at my jolt, replacing me with a pillow, looking innocent as he hugs it. I smile down at him and enjoy a younger-looking Noah.

My memories come back of how we stayed in his room last night, making out like teenagers.

My phone buzzes on the nightstand with a text from Santi.

SANTI

Where are you? You didn't sleep in your bed.

A wave of shame hits me as I type out another lie. My thumb hovers over the Send button, unsure about how far my deception will go. But Santi wouldn't understand. At least not during this season, with tensions through the roof between him and Noah. I seal my fate by pressing Send.

ME

Stayed with Sophie. Did you just get to the room?

SANTI

Uh, yeah. I'll text you after I take a nap.

A nap at 9 a.m.? He's always preferred to be private about his love life ever since he and his high-school girlfriend broke up after he chose F1 over her. Now my brother keeps his heart locked up like a maximum-security prison.

I squeal when Noah's arms tug me back to bed, ending my conversation with Santi. Warm sheets wrap around my body as Noah pulls me into his chest.

"What are you doing up this early?"

I dig how his voice sounds extra gravelly in the morning.

I lay my head on his chest. "Santi texted me to check in. Told him I'm staying with Sophie."

"Mm. When does your flight take off?" His fingers drag through my hair, untangling knotted strands.

"Later today on a red-eye. We're flying straight to the next race."

He pauses his hand movements. "You know what that means?"

Can't say I do. My brain doesn't function in the morning without coffee.

My voice strains. "No. But tell me."

More running of fingers through my hair. "Now that you're sober enough to consent, I have a few things in mind."

Noah's lips find mine, kissing me senseless. I break away after a few minutes.

"I want to shower first. I feel gross after the club last night." My nose scrunches at the thought of not washing off my makeup. I may or may not look like a raccoon, but I need a mirror to confirm.

"What a great idea. Let me help you." Noah hauls me out of bed and toward the bathroom. He places me on my feet before he sets up the shower, turning knobs and checking the temperature.

"It's a tough task. Are you sure you're up for the job?" I bat my lashes.

I don't even know if I'm up for the job. *Are we doing this? Going all the way?*

Noah answers the question for me when he pulls off the big T-shirt I wore to sleep. I don't even question how I ended up in said T-shirt, but I'm going with the flow, not wanting to kill the moment.

"You're so beautiful." He runs a hand through his already messy hair. His eyes roam over my body, taking me in. The way he looks at me makes me feel sexy, invigorated, and brazen.

I find it tough to distinguish steam from tension in the bathroom. It's hot, he's hot, the whole situation is fucking hot. My body feels feverish as he slowly appraises me again. His fingers drag across the slopes of my breasts, my skin pebbling at his touch, while excitement bubbles within me. His hand finds the clasp of my bra, and he snaps it off, leaving only my lace panties. The last barrier between us.

My boobs bounce as I move closer to him. I decide he looks entirely overdressed and his boxer briefs need to go. My hand dips below his waistband, brushing against his cock, swiping at the bead of precum on his tip. His body tenses and he groans.

"Let me help you out of these." I pull at the waistband and drag them down his muscular legs. He kicks them off, exposing me to his naked glory.

My oh my, is it a sight indeed. People rave about American football or hockey players or any other type of sport. Ladies don't understand how sexy F1 drivers are. I pant at the image of Noah standing before me, all his golden skin visible, muscles tensing at my assessment. *I was right*. He does have rock-hard abs, a fuckable body, and kissable lips. He even has a defined V-cut that I want to run my tongue across. His cock is huge, begging to be touched, licked, and fucked. I'm game for all of the above.

"God. How many hours do you work out in a day?" The question slips past my lips without a filter.

He chuckles to himself, making me glad I got my stupid question out of the way. His body isn't even remotely fair. I shut my eyes and open them back up to make sure I see everything right.

I bite my lip at the sight of him. He pulls me toward him, ending our eye-fucking session.

"How about I show you how much stamina I build up from

my workouts? That's the most impressive part." He runs his hand down my spine.

I'm sold.

Our shower remains temporarily forgotten. His lips find mine, his tempo desperate, persistent, and careless. Teeth gnash, bite, and suck. Sensations overwhelm me, making me question if this is too much. I can combust here with a few touches to my center. His tongue strokes mine, invading my mouth and taking me prisoner. *Sign me up for this life sentence.* My heart hammers in my chest, unable to settle down at Noah's relentless kisses. Hands grope his body, testing, touching, wanting, and assessing the ridges of his muscles as I memorize every part of him.

His hands find my underwear. Fingers trail the outside until they dip into my core. I groan as his fingers rub against me, making my body pulse with need.

A snapping sound rings over our labored breaths before loose lace falls at my feet.

"You tore my underwear? I've never had that happen before. I thought that was a thing in movies."

His husky laugh turns me on even more.

"I'm not like any of the guys you've been with before. I may not be your first fuck, but I might as well be." His domineering words ignite every nerve ending in my body.

Noah seals his possessiveness with a kiss. He demands everything from me, leaving no room for objections as he shatters any last bits of insecurity about us.

He lifts me in one easy swoop, my legs instinctively wrapping around his waist as he carries me to the shower. Our lips break contact when he situates us under the waterfall of hot water.

He pushes me against the shower tiles while his mouth finds mine again. Our kisses become lazier, less hurried, as we enjoy the time together. It's the sweetest he's ever kissed me before.

He puts me down and grabs the soap bar. His heavy gaze follows the contours of my body as he runs the soap across my skin, starting with my neck. Suds start to pour down my breasts. He spends extra time there as he brings my nipples to two sharp points. His hand creeps slowly down my stomach, making sure to soap up every part of me. My knees wobble at his caresses. But he takes his job seriously, being extremely thorough, learning every curve and dip of my body.

My breaths come out labored as his hands dip between my legs. His fingers find my center, but he remains focused on his task. I moan as he washes me in my most intimate place and cleans every part of me. He continues to lather me, all the way down to my feet.

A comfortable silence cloaks us; the only sounds in the shower include running water and our heavy breathing. Neither of us want to break the moment with words. I copy his same movements, running my hands across his chest, spreading soapy bubbles. I relish the feel of him, his muscles straining under my touch. He closes his eyes, enjoying my touch, a moan slipping past his lips. Damn, I feel powerful making him feel just as good.

I commit to my cause, soaping him up wherever my hands go, roaming down his body and the ridges of his stomach. He groans as my small hands wrap around his cock. I pump once, twice, until he places his hand over mine.

"Your hand feels so fucking good, but you don't have to do it if you don't want to. We can wait."

My lips smirk at him. I love how he'd hold off for me, but I'm more than ready to go, not needing his chivalry.

I move along, kneeling to wash his legs. My hands return to his cock after I ditch the soap. My hand wraps around it before I take him in my mouth, the taste of him both salty and clean. His head tilts back against the shower tiles, and he lets out a moan as my tongue traces along his shaft. Vibrations from my laugh prompt him to fist my wet hair in his hands and tug. I pull away to look up at him, interested in getting a read on the situation, seeing a disarmed Noah at my mercy.

"Don't stop now. Finish what you started," he growls before tugging on my hair.

All righty then. Don't have to tell me twice.

I suck him off like it's an Olympic sport. I lick, stroke, and graze my teeth to add a different sensation. He groans, pulling on my hair. His reactions make me feel powerful, seductive, and turned on. My other hand massages his balls, giving them extra attention. Our eyes connect, blue eyes piercing mine as he brands my heart along with my body.

"Where the fuck did you learn to suck cock so good? Shit." He moans as I suck him even deeper than before. His cock grazes the back of my mouth, testing my gag reflex. "Actually, wait. Don't answer me, Maya. Shit, feels fucking amazing."

I'd laugh if I wasn't occupied.

His hands tug at my hair again, the sting turning me on more.

A tingling sensation creeps up my spine. My hand that was massaging his balls moves toward my center. I touch myself, feeling how needy I am. He takes control of my head and allows my other hand to play with my breasts. His hands push my head up and down his thick shaft while I stroke myself in desperation. I insert two fingers, slowly pumping to the rhythm of me sucking his cock.

He looks down at me pleasuring myself. His lazy smile excites me, igniting me from my heart to my clit.

"Holy shit, you're so sexy. Look at you, sucking my cock while getting yourself off. Oh my God. You better be ready because I'm going to come. Now's your chance to back out."

I'm right there with him, my strokes becoming more frantic. No way in hell I'm not tasting him. His release hits the back of my throat, and I swallow everything he offers. He pulls out after finishing, giving me a moment to find relief. I moan as I explode on my own hand. Stars dance behind my eyelids as I come down from my haze, water falling on me while I sit in an unholy prayer pose. No Hail Mary can save me from him. I glance up at him, offering a playful grin in return.

"You're going to be the death of me. I just fucking know it." Noah lifts me off the floor and shuts off the water. He grabs us two fluffy towels, paying special attention to me as he wipes me dry.

I wrap the fluffy towel around me like a dress while he wraps my wet hair in another towel. The gesture makes my heart squeeze, aware of how I've never had someone take care of me like this before.

We end up back on the bed, but this time, the experience

feels different. Noah's movements show no rush to get this show on the road. I sit up as he removes the towel from my head and tosses it over the side of the bed, landing with a thud on the carpet. My eyes bulge at the brush in his hand. I let out a soft moan as he gets behind me and brushes my hair, starting at the bottom, removing knots meticulously.

"This is single-handedly one of the best things a guy has ever done for me." My eyes close, enjoying the feeling of the brush running through my wet hair. I have no shame. Noah brushing my hair turns me on, the sensory experience making my heart swirl with emotions I can't place.

He laughs. "You're setting the bar too low for me."

Noah enjoys the task, giving it his all. Once all the knots are gone, he returns the brush to the bathroom. I turn toward his standing form next to the bed.

"You're gorgeous. A natural beauty." His heated gaze travels down my towel-clad body, taking in my hotel fashion piece. Who knew I could make a towel look sexy?

One second, he stands beside the bed, and in the next moment, he kneels on the floor while his hands pull my legs toward the edge of the mattress.

I think I died and went to heaven.

Noah stares at me with intense eyes as he plucks the towel off me, exposing me again to him.

"I've thought about this for months. We're going to enjoy every second of it because I'm in no hurry."

I gasp when his fingers find my core. They part me, and his mouth replaces his fingers, making me lift off the bed at the feeling of his tongue brushing against me. One of his hands pushes me back down and holds me there. His mouth is a relentless torture of the best kind, the mind-numbing type. I'm not sure if I could tell you my own name. He knows what to do, making the guys from my past look like amateurs. Let this be the only time I thank all the women before me.

Noah really is a fucking champion. Someone give this man a trophy.

He licks me, marking me, clearly enjoying the sounds that fall past my lips. Shit, it feels good. His strokes change speed and pressure, lapping at my center, making the most of the whole experience. The rough texture of his tongue makes my core pulse. He adds two fingers that slide easily inside me, my body aching for his touch as his pumps match his licks. Pressure inside me builds.

"I'm so close. Oh my God, Noah."

His throat rumbles. The sensation of that combined with the unyielding pump of his fingers pushes me over the edge. I combust, my brain soaring away from me. His licks continue as I come down from my high—a lust-induced haze that beats any drug. My brain shuts down, a prickling sensation traveling down my spine all the way to my curled toes.

He gives me a sweet kiss right at my core, making me melt on the spot.

Here lies Maya Alatorre.

"Death by orgasm. Seems like a good way to go." My face heats at my mistake in saying that aloud.

He chuckles. "We're not done yet. Save your eulogy for after the finale." His wicked grin brings a smile to my face and a warmth to my center.

He keeps me in this position as he searches for what I assume is a condom in the nightstand. I frown when he pulls one out, questioning how he knew one would be there in the first place.

He looks down at me, his smile dropping until realization dawns across his face. He sifts through the nightstand, pulling out a box that still has the plastic wrapping. His knees hit the hotel carpet, making us eye level.

"Brand-new pack. I'm serious when I say I haven't been with anyone. Not since that day." His eyes flit to the side, shame marring his face about Baku.

"I believe you. You said you want to try, that you're all in?" I look into his blue eyes, giving him an out in case he wants to take it.

Noah doesn't blink. "Maya, I'm willing to try. You won't regret it. I swear."

I bring my lips to his, sealing his words with a kiss. He breaks the moment as he stands up, his eyes darkening as he gazes down my body again.

He fists his dick and pumps a few times, precum dripping from the tip, enticing me. I lick my lips at the sight.

"Next time." His thumb rubs the drop before he brings it to my mouth.

I suck on the pad of his thumb, tasting his saltiness. His eyes darken as I lick and nibble.

"You're a naughty little thing. I would have never guessed that you like to play dirty."

The quintessential sound of foil ripping fills me with excitement. "You haven't seen anything yet." Yup. Those words came out of my mouth. I blame him, because I'm not usually such a mouthy one, but he boosts my confidence.

He smiles while shaking his head. "I'm going to hold you to that."

Noah gives no warning, no sweet words before he grabs my legs and thrusts himself into me, the hotel bed perfectly situated for this position. My eyes water at the amazing feeling of him filling me. His dick is big, and I haven't exactly done this in a while. But he reads my body like he's been doing this to me forever. His fingers find my clit, rubbing it, making my body pulse with pleasure instead of pain. I forget the uncomfortable feeling of him stretching me to my limits.

"You'll get used to it. I promise." He kisses my lips softly. Another kind gesture, his words sinking into me and taking residence in my heart.

He moves inside me, his previous sweetness abandoned.

"Holy shit." Words breathlessly escape my lips.

"If I had known it would be this good, I don't think I would have held back for this long." His groans fill the room.

I grab the sheets above my head, desperate for something to ground me as he pounds into me slowly.

He stares into my eyes as he finds an amazing tempo. Our bodies move together in harmony, our chemistry nothing short of fantastic.

Noah drives it home. He grabs each of my legs and places them over his shoulder blades. The position makes his dick feel like I'm being fucked for the first time. A sweet torment. His pumps speed up as he slides easily in and out of me. Rough hands rove over my breasts, pinching my nipples. I arch my back, unable to regulate my body's responses, his movements becoming eager and uncontrolled.

"Oh. My. God." My voice comes off as nothing more than a hoarse whisper.

He changes his position slightly, making his dick rub against my G-spot. Noah controls the situation. My body quakes as he continues to thrust into me, strategically hitting my spot every time. I throw my head back as my spine curves up toward him.

"You feel fucking amazing. Tell me you're almost there."

He doesn't wait for a response. My body says everything my mouth can't with nothing but moans and groans passing my lips. One hand finds my clit while the other grips one of my ass cheeks. He pulls my ass up off the bed, taking advantage of the angle. His roughness adds to his appeal, showing me how eager he is, and fuck it feels good. His desperation is my gain.

"Yes!"

My body vibrates, my release closing in. I can tell by the strain in Noah's face he follows right behind me.

"Noah…" I don't recognize my own voice, the neediness foreign to my ears.

"Fuck yeah, babe, I'm there with you."

Simple words push me over the edge. I explode around him, my moan echoing off the hotel walls. He fucks me like a man possessed, his body straining as he holds me in the position he needs while I lose myself in my climax.

Noah's stunning smile is the last thing I see before my eyes close. His orgasm hits him, his cock twitching inside me as he rides out his release. Frantic pumps become slower, lazier before his body shudders. He stays inside me for a little while, not wanting to break our connection.

We groan together when he pulls out of me after a few minutes.

"You're so damn perfect, inside and out." Noah brushes loose hair out of my face, running a knuckle across my flushed cheeks.

I smile at him. "You're not too bad yourself."

He gives me a kiss before he takes care of the condom in the bathroom. When he comes back, he drags me to the head of the bed. We lie there together. I bask in the afterglow of the best sex of my life.

"Fuck, Maya. That was the best sex I've ever had."

I smile into his chest. *Likewise.*

Malaysian
Grand Pix

CHAPTER TWENTY-SEVEN
Maya

Someone knocks on the hotel door, pulling me away from my computer. I open the door to find Noah leaning against the frame. He glides past me and walks into the room, taking up a spot against the gray sectional before I sit.

"I want to ask you out on a date."

I check the time on my phone. "At ten in the morning?" Staying in the hotel room sounds like a fine idea, unless the date he plans involves brunch and mimosas. I can get behind that.

"Exactly why we better get going." He pulls me off the couch and toward the bedroom to get ready.

I smack his hands away when he tries to help me take off my pajamas. "Hands off or else we'll never make it."

He chuckles to himself.

"Does this date involve breakfast food?" *Please say yes.*

"Nope. But afterward, we can get something to eat."

He won't share information. *Suspicious.*

Noah's eyes gleam. I should be concerned because that look usually leads to hours in the bedroom. Take my word for it because we've bounced around each other's hotel rooms for the past week at all hours of the day.

But I go along with his plan because it's nice of him to set up a date. Noah claims he's changed. Who am I to rain on his parade?

I still can't deny my apprehension about the whole thing. Not the sex part. That part is banging. Okay, I know that pun is bad. I blame all the social media captions I have to come up with because being clever is basically a full-time job.

But everything else between Noah and me still remains questionable. It's brand-spanking-new with us being in the relationship honeymoon stage. Ask me again once the going gets tough. Like when my lies to my brother about my whereabouts blow up in my face.

Positive energy flows right out of me the moment Noah pulls up to the location of our first real date. An odd choice for a one-on-one.

I drag my body out of the car and take a step apart from him the moment we get within range of the video cameras in the Bandini pit. We still have to keep up appearances in front of my brother and everyone else who can spill our secret. Only Sophie can be trusted.

"Our date is at the racetrack?"

My eyes assess the crowd in front of us. Not sure why he wants to visit the location for the next race. Should I be worried about future dates if he thinks this is a good spot for our first official one as a new couple?

I'll have to take charge of the next one.

Noah rubs his hands together. "Think of this as a trust exercise. You know how people do trust falls?"

"Uh. Sure?" I nod along. Uncertainty creeps up my spine when he smiles down at me.

"So I don't want to worry about how you might not trust me yet. I want to make sure you do. Because that's the foundation of relationships." He sounds confident about all this.

What podcasts does he listen to? I don't know whether I should be concerned or impressed.

"Your smile makes me a little nervous," I blurt out. Nothing good comes from his shit-eating grin, the same look I give my parents when I'm hiding something.

He walks toward Bandini's pit area, a silent command to follow him. I wish I had stayed in the car. Distant sounds of tires squealing across pavement alert my senses.

A group of people rallies around the pit area. Camera crews film people getting inside neon-colored Bandini cars, perfectly lined, making up the entire rainbow.

I make the mistake of reading the banner above our heads. *Bandini Race Day Experience. Drive like an F1 driver.*

Oh no.

His hand gives mine a reassuring squeeze before he drops it.

"Please tell me we're doing a press appearance." My voice sounds stronger than I feel.

Hope surges through me at the idea of coming to watch and cheer fans on. Noah can take them for a spin while I stand behind the barriers, a few fist pumps in the air to sell my enthusiasm while he careens down the track.

"We are." He reveals nothing more.

My heart rate slows down, confident the date is what I expect. Safety barrier, here I come.

He speaks again. "But we're filming from inside that car."

Oh shit. Please tell me he means I'm going to look inside the car for two seconds. Slap the hands of the nerds who design the cars, take a quick photo, throw a thumbs-up. A girl can dream.

My eyes follow his pointing finger. They land directly on a neon-green Bandini car with open scissor doors. It looks like a car from the future, estimated at about $500,000.

"I am not setting a foot behind a steering wheel." *Over my dead body. Hard no.*

"You don't have to worry about that." He fills me with faith before ripping it away. "I'm going to be behind the wheel."

I need to put in a Bandini work order for this man to get a warning sign.

Noah all but drags me to the neon-green beauty with black leather seats and vibrant piping, stitching, and accent lighting.

A Bandini employee passes me a helmet. I don't put up much of a verbal fight with Noah because people watch us, and I can't be too embarrassing. A press crew follows us, eating up my reluctant display like I drag my feet for the fun of it. My stomach protests, my face most likely matching the green shade of our car.

I take deep breaths, trying to relax.

"Here we have Noah Slade taking Maya Alatorre onto the track. Maya, how do you feel about being driven around by one of the best race car drivers out there?" A reporter jams a foam microphone in my face.

"Nauseous?" my voice rasps.

The reporter laughs at me like I mean it as a joke. I shoot Noah a glare, questioning if it's too late to back out. My eyes dart between the car and the pit lane, estimating how quickly I can run before Noah catches up to me.

"It's interesting Maya chose to come out with you instead of her brother today. Any thoughts on this, Noah?"

My palm drags down my face. *Deep breaths.*

"I can't help that she wants to try out the track with me when she's watched her brother drive for years. But there's nothing like taking someone's racetrack virginity."

Pretty sure his response turned me on, and I'm halfway convinced I'm dating the devil in disguise.

He shoots me a wink. "We're going to get going. See you later, guys." He waves at the reporters like the natural he is.

Following his lead, I hop into the passenger's side.

Noah's eyes gleam. "You packed your camera, right?"

I pull the camera out of my purse. He takes it from my hands and sets it up on a conveniently placed camera mount.

"My heart may explode out of my chest. I might not make it through the whole thing."

He chuckles. "You'll be okay. We're only going to go about one hundred and thirty to one hundred and fifty miles per hour. That's not too bad. It's our trust test, remember?"

I no longer feel bad for disgruntled coworkers who have to do trust falls during employee retreats. That has nothing on this cruel version.

I never did find out the recovery rate for having a heart attack at twenty-three. *Regrets.*

"Jesus, take the wheel." I make the sign of the cross before putting on my helmet.

"You may have called me God last night, but I'm the only one behind the wheel today." The smug man fucking winks.

His hand finds the stick shift, and we propel down the grid area. He laughs as we make it past the first turn, tires screeching against the pavement while he speeds up again.

"Damn, I didn't hear you scream like that last night. Do I need to change my technique?"

"You perv! This is terrifying. *Oh my God*. How do you do this all the time? How is this even legal?" I'd slap his arm if I wasn't plastered to the side of the car.

"I love it. Just relax and enjoy." His voice does nothing to calm me.

"Never tell a woman to relax!" I scream again as we drift on another turn. It's touch and go with my heart, stopping every time Noah turns the car before picking back up again as he races down the track.

Another scream erupts from my mouth. I don't have the chance to feel embarrassed, the loud shrieks pouring out of me with no control.

The engine purrs as Noah's lead foot hits the accelerator. His hand does a bunch of shift changes, which are honestly kind of hot because his muscles strain and tense. I distract myself by staring at him in his element, a smile plastered on his face, beaming at my reactions. My screams stop long enough for me to check out how happy he looks.

He hits me with a megawatt grin. If my body wasn't already in fight-or-flight mode, my heart rate would have sped up.

"Eyes on the track! Hello!" I snap my fingers and point at the pavement in front of us.

He chuckles while he turns into another straight section, the car vrooming as he presses on the throttle.

"I could do this track in my sleep. It's an easy one."

"That's great and all, but I'd rather live to see tomorrow." I take another deep breath.

He laughs as he checks me out. "Do you trust me yet?"

"I trust that you're secretly a psycho. What kind of first date is this? Haven't you ever seen an episode of *The Last Rose?* This date is far from swoon-worthy!" I grip onto the side of the car for dear life. Those top handlebar things every car has? Yeah, I learn their true purpose, my knuckles whitening as I hold on with all my might.

Can he quit laughing at me?

"That's not the answer I wanted to hear. I'll have to step it up."

That, friends, is exactly the type of thing no one asks for. It's meme-worthy.

His hands turn knobs on the center console.

"Uh, what are you doing?" My stomach churns as my body bounces up and down, the car revolting against the high speeds Noah pushes it to. The death contraption continues to zoom past empty grandstands. Speakers sound off for the first time the entire trip, the robotic voice sending a chill down my spine.

Traction control disabled.

My head whips to face Noah, my helmet bouncing off the window. The movement jars me. Even I know the importance of traction control…it prevents the one thing Noah wants to do.

He shrugs, sealing our fate.

His hands turn the wheel, our car drifting across the pavement before spinning in doughnuts. Tires squeal against the track. A cloud of smoke swirls around us from rubber burning, floating up into the sky along with my sanity.

"I trust you! I'll never not trust you ever again. You're the best driver ever. You'll always keep me safe. Are you satisfied now?" I half laugh, half scream the words, sounding like someone who belongs in a psychotic thriller movie. There may even be a tear or two leaking from my eyes, but if Noah asks me, I'll deny it.

He stops the doughnuts, and we both end up breaking out in a fit of laughter. His hand grabs mine and brings it up to his lips for a kiss, my previous fear forgotten.

"To answer your question from before, yes I've seen *The Last Rose*. I took notes. This is the first of many for us, so I had to make it unforgettable."

He hits me with a devilish grin before I flash him one of my own.

CHAPTER TWENTY-EIGHT
Noah

There are only two things that can suck the happiness straight out of me.

One is any type of news of someone dying.

And two is my dad.

The second reason sends me a deceitful grin that makes my stomach shrivel up. He stands next to my car in the pit area, his negative energy pulsing around him. Not exactly what I need before a practice session.

Over the years, I've become a pro at avoiding my dad, an easier task since I've never liked being around him when he gets angry. Now that I've outgrown him, he moves on from hitting me to verbal lashings. The time Maya saw him smack me…that was unlike him. He usually keeps calm nowadays, at least physically, choosing to flip out when I perform less than perfectly on the track.

"Dad, what are you doing here?" What I really want to say

is *Dad, get the fuck out of here. I can't stand you.* But I don't say what I wish to because I prefer professionalism. Unfortunately, my dad funded a lot of my career at the start, his name carrying weight at Bandini. It was his racing team after all.

"After your poor display at the last couple of races, I wanted to check in."

Sure you did.

But this is my life. Anything below first place might as well be last. The only thing keeping me calm is the sound of race cars zooming by while I breathe in the smell of fresh car wax.

"Right. Hopefully this one will go better." I can win the Japanese Grand Prix since I've done it in the past.

"And here we are getting ready for the next practice session. Santiago, do you have anything to say to your fans?"

For fuck's sake, Maya has the worst timing.

My dad ogles her as she spins around in the garage. *Gross.* She keeps going, asking Santiago questions.

My dad focuses back on me. "She's a news reporter now? What's she doing in the pit area? It's no place for a woman." He still lives in an era where women get married and live the rest of their sad lives in the four walls of their home. *Times have changed, Pops.*

"Nope. Santiago's sister vlogs." *My girlfriend,* I wish to say.

Maya and I haven't talked about titles yet. We only hashed things out two weeks ago in Singapore. But everything about us feels title-worthy because we spend lots of time together whenever Santiago isn't around. In my bed, in hers, in one of the private suites, and secret dates in the cities we visit. My sex drive with Maya rivals that of an eighteen-year-old.

I don't like how my dad looks at her, pissing me off even more.

"Hmm. She shouldn't be filming." His growl of a voice does nothing to intimidate me.

"They already gave her the go-ahead for it. It's been good publicity and nice for branding since she has a lot of followers." *Shit. Did my voice sound like I am proud of her?*

My dad assesses me, giving me the fucking chills. His perceptiveness makes him cruel because he didn't get where he is today by being stupid.

"I guess it's fine," he says.

Everything about his face screams how it isn't. His eyebrows raise, he rubs his chin, and his eyes have an evil spark. A montage of every villain from every movie.

"I better get ready for another practice round. I'll see you later?" I don't want to leave him alone here with Maya, but I have to.

I sneak up next to her before hopping into my car.

"Stay away from my dad. He's a sneaky piece of shit."

Her eyes widen. "Good luck out there!" She gets my message, her retreating form comforting me as I get in the cockpit of my car.

Maya's hand strokes my chest. Instead of attending a sponsor event tonight, we both made up an excuse about wanting to stay in. Together, we watch a new season of Area 52—a show we both love about a secret military facility that was created after Area 51 was targeted by conspiracy theorists and alien enthusiasts.

"I don't think it's going to end well. I always thought he was a bad guy...but he's not. And now they killed him."

Her tears dampen my shirt as she cries over a fictional man who doesn't exist.

Wow, she really gets into shows.

"Do you always cry during sad scenes?" I pull her into a hug. It's cute, endearing even. But I don't want her to cry over something not real.

"I have a lot of feelings. Okay?" Her eyes glisten as she looks up at me.

I give her a soft kiss on her forehead, her sigh making me smirk.

And the action continues on the TV. Maya snaps her head back, eagerly watching the next part.

I have learned my lesson. Next time, I plan on picking the most boring show, solely so I can steal Maya's attention away. Over the last few hours, anytime I try, she swats my hand away whenever I put a move on her.

"You need to stop sighing every time that guy is on the screen. This crush has gotten out of hand."

My heart surges at the sound of her laugh. A weird feeling I've grown accustomed to whenever I hang around Maya, similar to how my dick gets rock-hard whenever she gets near me.

"I can't help it. That hair, his babysitting skills. Even his personality. Sigh."

How the mighty have fallen, becoming jealous over a TV character. "I can babysit. And my hair is definitely better. Personality? I sure as fuck hope mine's nicer seeing as I'm a real person. And I am older, wiser. I can fucking kick ass with a baseball bat." I flex my arms around her for emphasis.

"What does older and wiser have to do with the appeal?" Her chest shakes against mine.

She's totally teasing me. So I do what any logical man would do in my position. I shut off the TV and show her exactly how more experience comes with age. She stops complaining about the show the moment my lips find her clit.

I creep around, listening in on Santi and Maya's conversation. It's not my fault they're so loud and we share the same walls. Right?

I'm jealous of Santi. There. I put it out there.

Maya spends the whole morning before the race with him, hanging out while I spend the day by myself. She hides who we are from him because she doesn't want to upset him or inconvenience him before the final race.

Unfortunately for the Alatorre siblings, I'm not above eavesdropping.

"What are you going to do once the season's over?" Santi's voice carries through the thin walls.

"Mm, I don't know. I've started to fall into my own thing with my F1 content. I have over nine hundred thousand followers across all my social media platforms. That's, like, amazing growth for a career that started only eight months ago. The travel vlogging is nice, but behind-the-scenes F1 videos are what make me trendy and different."

Pride in her voice brings a smile to my face. I watch her

videos when I miss her or boredom strikes or Santi steals her away because Maya feels too guilty to say no.

We've already traveled with F1 for eight months, with Maya and I dating exclusively for the last four weeks.

"But is that really a job? Following me around?"

What an idiot.

"Uh. I don't follow you around." Maya's voice hesitates, unsure how to handle Santi's obliviousness.

"I don't mean to put you down. But don't you want a nice, stable job? One closer to home with less traveling? I can't have you here forever."

You can't. But I can.

Or at least until Maya doesn't want to be around anymore, *if* she doesn't. We still need to find our footing together.

I think up opinions like I'm part of the conversation.

She lets out a deep sigh loud enough for me to hear. Never a good sign.

"I'm living in the moment. I'm young. I have time to figure my life out. You don't know much about social media, but it's growing. Vlogging and short-form content are huge industries with good pay by views. And sponsorships."

"That's always your problem though. You may live in the moment, but you gotta grow up sometime. Are videos a career?"

"Wow...*okay.* I don't know what made you so pissed off today, but you're being a crappy brother right now. I'm going to take a walk."

An idea hits me. I open the door to my suite the moment Maya walks past it, pulling her inside.

"What are you—"

My hand covers her mouth before she can get out another word. I bring my index finger up to my lips. Her eyes change from dull to gleaming because I can now change her mood for the positive. *Fan-fucking-tastic.*

I remove my hand from her mouth and lock the door behind her.

I check the time on the clock. We have thirty minutes before I need to check in at the pit.

"Think you can keep quiet?" I whisper. Her brother is a few feet away, and the walls are thinner than a fucking condom.

She bobs her head up and down, eyes lit with excitement.

"Always enthusiastic." I trail a finger from her neck to her chest. My hands find the hem of her Bandini polo and pull it over her head, revealing a white lace bra that makes my dick pulse.

She toys with the zipper of my race suit.

"You look so hot in this. I almost don't want to unzip it." Her words bring a smile to my face.

I shut her up with a kiss so Santiago doesn't hear us. My tongue explores her mouth, enjoying her exclusive taste, one I find addicting as hell. A magnetic energy flows around us, always pulling me back toward her. Not that I want to stay away. Our tongues dance and tease each other. Our kiss stifles her moan as my hands explore her body, my rough fingers brushing against her smooth skin.

My hands palm her perfect tits. I pull down the soft cups of her bra, revealing her perky breasts and tight, pink nipples. The best fucking sight. I trail wet kisses down her neck, sucking to the point of marking her. Fuck would I like to. But I move along because I don't have enough time.

My dick throbs, rock-hard in my suit and craving her attention.

Her hands get caught up in my hair, tugging me along for encouragement. I'm a man on a mission with a time limit.

"Shh." I rub the rough pad of my thumb against her lips. Her heavy breathing might give us away.

She nods, staring down at me while I pull one of her taut nipples into my mouth. Her back arches as she pushes herself closer to me. I suck one nipple to a solid point before moving on to the other, my tongue trailing along the divot in her chest.

My other hand finds the button of her jeans. I dip my hand below, finding her slick and ready for me. Talk about the best fucking feeling, to turn her on with minimal effort required.

Her wild eyes and messy hair drive me crazy. Nothing compares to satiating the hunger between us, being able to please her to the point of oblivion.

Maya's hand touches the outline of my dick through the race suit. She palms me, doing soft movements up and down.

"Time to take this off," she says in a husky murmur.

Good girl.

The thrilling sound of the zipper rings through the room. Maybe Maya corrupts me just as much because I never do anything like this before a race.

I pull my arms out of the top part of the suit and finish unzipping to my waistline. The clock tells me we have fifteen minutes left. While I wish I had more time with her, a quickie will do. She tugs my dick out from the tight layers of flame-retardant material.

She gets down on her knees. The sight alone makes my

dick pulse, precum leaking from the tip before she grabs on to it. Her tongue darts out to lick the white bead.

My head drops back.

Shit, her mouth feels good.

She traces lazy lines with her tongue across the shaft. It's perfect. She's perfect. All so motherfucking perfect.

She takes me in her mouth, a warm, wet heaven welcoming my cock. Her tongue drags along the underside of my shaft as she pulls her mouth back and forth. She sucks, pumps, and licks me. Sensations make my brain short-circuit.

She pumps me into her mouth with one hand while another grips my ass. I regain enough mental clarity to pull her up, her lips popping as my dick bobs.

"Nope. That's not how this is going to go today."

Her honey-brown eyes narrow. I trail my thumb across her plump lips, loving how she looks after sucking me off. A brief kiss wipes the frown off her face.

I tug down her jeans and thong. She's right there with me, fumbling with taking off her sneakers. The best kind of teamwork.

Red numbers on the clock mock me.

"Now you have to be quiet," I whisper before licking the shell of her ear, her body breaking out in goose bumps.

She likes the quiet game we play, wondering who will mess up first.

I place her hands on the side of the gray couch. The suite is small, not meant for sex. But fuck it, I can make the layout work with a little extra effort.

"Keep your hands there." I grab a condom from my wallet.

Thank God for planning ahead.

I turn back toward Maya. The sight of her perky ass in the air, leaning against the arm of the couch, ready for me. Her tits hang out and her back arches. It's a lot to take in. She bites down on her lip, hitting me with the hungry look in her eyes as she checks out my dick.

I slip the condom on.

"Too bad your suit isn't sex-friendly," her voice rasps.

"My my, do you have a thing for race suits? Should I be concerned? I can lock you away from the other drivers and keep you here for myself."

My hands palm her ass, eliciting a light moan from her. One finger slides down the crease of her ass until I reach her slick folds. I plunge a finger inside, and then another, her wetness surrounding me.

I lean in close to her ear. "Always ready for me. Tell me, do you get this way while watching me race? Does it turn you on?"

She nods her head, the silent admission exciting me.

"It's a dangerous sport. High speeds. Collisions." I leave a path of kisses down her spine.

She turns her head to look at me over her shoulder.

"I'll let you in on a secret though... Fucking you is the equivalent of winning a World Championship. I could never win again and be perfectly fine so long as you're by my side. In my bed. Me inside you. I like you *a lot*."

She doesn't have a second to register my words. I have the foresight to cover her mouth with my hand before I thrust into her wet pussy. My teeth grit together as I hold back a groan, her body accepting my cock and gripping me like no other. Our connected bodies moving in unison mesmerizes me.

And fuck if that doesn't do something to me, a wave of possessiveness rushing through me as I drag my slick dick out, soaked to the hilt.

She feels tighter in this position, my pants concealed because I don't want Santi to hear me. I let my hand go from her mouth once the shock factor is done.

Maya claws at the fabric on the couch, a gorgeous image of her rattled by me. I ram into her again and savor the feel of her squeezing my dick.

She's heaven. Perfect for me.

My hand grips her ponytail, wrapping it around my arm, thick strands brushing against my skin. I tug, fulfilling a fantasy I've thought about since meeting her.

Her body pulses at the mix of pain and pleasure. Her skin warms beneath the touch of my other hand. I squeeze her tit, loving the feel of her pebbled nipple beneath my palm.

I want her to know I'm the only one who can fuck her like this, make her feel like this. I want to ruin her for any man who dares to try to come after me.

I fuck her like she's the last woman on earth. Because to me, she might as well be.

She does a good job keeping quiet, only letting out a few whimpers here and there. I pull on her hair again in a silent demand to look at me. She blows me away with a view of her brown eyes, hazy from lust, matching flushed cheeks and lips plump from my ravaging. I could come right there at the sight of her.

But I don't.

Because good guys finish last.

My grip becomes more possessive on her hip as I pump unrelentingly into her. I angle myself to hit her G-spot. Her whole body convulses around me, her reaction pulling a smirk from me.

I stroke her special spot and give it all my attention. My dick slides back and forth like never before, her arousal encouraging me as my thrusts become sloppier, less controlled. It feels like magic when she shatters around my cock. Her heavy breathing fills the silent room, her chest heaving up and down as she stares at me with a lazy smile.

Her orgasm gives me the final push. I thrust into her without holding back, balls slapping against her ass as she takes it all. I groan as I find my release. My toes curl at the feeling of her squeezing me, practically pleading for more. The whole thing seems fucking poetic.

My lips kiss her neck as I pull out of her. I dump the condom in the trash and situate my suit, wishing we had more time.

Maya keeps to the same spot, lying over the side of the couch with her eyes closed. Her back moves to the steady rhythm of her breathing. I grab her clothes from the floor, wanting to help her in whatever way, when she finally speaks.

"I think you've ruined me." Her whispered voice rings through the quiet.

Shit. That's the best thing I've heard all day.

CHAPTER TWENTY-NINE
Maya

walk into the pit area to wish Santi good luck. Noah fucked my bad mood right out of me, curing me from Santi's negative words.

"Where did you go?" He looks at me with soft eyes and a weak smile.

"I took a walk. I needed a break from our conversation."

Can he tell Noah just fucked me? Post-sex afterglow tends to be a thing.

"You look like you've been crying. I'm sorry if I upset you. I just want to make sure you'll be okay and find what you love to do."

My cheeks heat. Not exactly the crying he's thinking about. His apology makes my heart squeeze, guilt eating up any leftover lust.

"Mm, yeah. I appreciate it. But I am happy, and everything will be fine. I like following everyone, and I've made good friends. You don't need to worry about me anymore."

He pulls me in for a hug, our previous conversation abandoned. "You know I love you, right?"

My eyes roll with the least amount of effort because his corny phrase always gets me. I can't hold an argument against him for more than an hour anyway. "You tell me all the time. I love you too. Now go kick some ass. Preferably Slade's."

"Hey! I heard that. You both act like I'm not here." Noah's voice booms over the buzz of the pit crew and machines.

My body warms in recognition. I'm so screwed with him, both literally and figuratively.

"You've won three World Championships already. Save some for the little guys." Santi's voice carries over the other noises.

"I'm glad you're not ashamed of being little. That's mature of you. You know what they say—it's not the size but what you do with it that matters." Noah smirks at my brother.

Santi groans while I bark out a laugh.

"You're a piece of shit, Slade." Santi's words don't have the same kick. "Speaking of dicks, what the hell was going on in your room? Changing up your prerace routine? It's usually silent, but your couch kept hitting the wall, in a rhythm, I might add." Santi's knowing smile says it all.

My throat closes tight, my brain jumping to the worst kind of conclusions. I let out a breath when I find Santi not looking at me.

Noah returns a wicked smile and shrugs. "Sorry about that. I'll be more quiet next time."

If the world could swallow me up whole, now would be the perfect time.

But it doesn't.

"Maybe I need to follow the same ritual. I wonder if that's how you win so much." My brother, the idiot, smiles at Noah.

If I had a drink, this would be the moment I'd spit the contents out all over my brother. *Oh my God. You definitely don't want to, Santi. Can you shut up already?*

My eyes dart around the garage, avoiding eye contact at all costs with both of them. Santi gives me a quick peck on the head before hopping into his car.

Noah and Santi wish each other good luck before they take off for the grid. I stay behind in the pit area for this race, watching overhead on the TV monitors while Sophie hangs out with her dad. A pit crew member hands me a headset so I can hear what Santi says while he races.

Noah takes off in first place, no surprise there. Cameras switch between overhead shots and driver first-person cameos. Over the past few races, I've caught myself cheering for him as much as I do for Santi.

Noah drives swiftly as he cruises along the pavement. My brother keeps close behind, battling it out for second place with Liam. Noah holds a good distance ahead and avoids any major collisions with other drivers. My brother sets a great pace, with Liam behind his rear wing. The aerodynamics of the car make it difficult for Liam to overtake my brother. Air becomes a vortex inside the track, compromising the speed of any driver who tries to pass the leader.

Santi catches up to Noah, but he's no match for Noah's defensiveness on this track. Noah's turns stay tight, falling right in the middle, making it so no driver can surpass him. My heart races as Noah creates a comfortable distance between himself and my brother.

Commentators go crazy as drivers fight for second- and third-place spots. Jax flies by Liam, pulling in close behind my brother. A pit stop will decide who gets out on top between them. Jax overtakes Santi at a narrow turn, causing my brother to spin out before he regains control.

Cars go around and around, lap after lap, rankings switching among drivers. Jax gains speed on Noah, not compromising a potential first-place win for McCoy. I like Jax's style compared to the boys at Bandini. He makes deliberate moves rivaling Noah's, willing to do anything to get leverage on the first-place driver.

Noah's dad interrupts me, his voice pulling me away from the TV. I withhold my sneer. Noah opened up to me about his dad's anger management issues, telling me all about the unknown side of Nicholas Slade.

He takes up a spot next to me, staring up at the TV like he shares my same emotional investment. A comical display because his intentions become clear once he opens his mouth.

"You both think you're clever, hiding what you're doing."

My body stills, but my eyes remain on the TV. Noah and Jax compete for first place. Mechanics buzz as Noah pulls in for his pit stop, distracting me from his dad as the team puts on his new tires. The process finishes in under two seconds. I forget about his dad standing beside me until he fake coughs.

"What do you think Santiago and I are doing exactly?" I withhold an urge to run away.

His laugh makes my skin crawl.

Is it possible to hate someone without knowing much about him? Because what I know is enough. Who the hell hits their child for losing kart races? A man with a small dick and a fragile ego.

"You're fucking my son. It's so obvious from watching you two in the pit area earlier."

My neck heats up, prickling at the dangerous man next to me. My fingers twirl a piece of hair to stop my fidgeting. I avert his gaze, staring up at the TV.

"That's quite a theory. Are you so bored with attending races that you need to come up with stories?" I come off way more confident than I feel.

"You're a smart girl. If you mess around with Noah, and his performance isn't what I expect…"

I keep silent. He wants a fight that I don't need to entertain.

"I'll make sure your brother doesn't have another contract renewal. Not to mention you'll never walk into a Bandini suite again. I don't mess around. I play to win."

I turn my head, taking in his cold stare before returning it with one of my own. His threats don't scare me. No need to give him any semblance of control over me.

"Not sure what you think is happening. I'm sorry you're worried about Noah's performance. But what he does out there is all on him." My voice sounds sickly sweet to my own ears.

He leaves with a smirk on his face, proving to be the asshole Noah described.

"We need to talk." Santi lays himself against the headboard of my bed, occupying the space next to me. Yesterday was a rough day for him after placing fourth in the race. He made his rounds to appease fans, but the loss ate away at him, and he closed himself off in the hotel suite for the rest of the night.

Only room service could push him to leave the four walls of his bedroom.

"About?" my voice croaks. Paranoia riddles my brain, playing tricks on me as I worry if Noah's dad told Santi about my secret relationship. I wouldn't put anything past that vile man.

"We didn't have a chance to talk in private about yesterday. I came off like an asshole, and I'm sorry. A lot has been on my mind with Bandini, and I worry about you on top of everything else." His brown eyes pierce mine.

"There isn't anything else to discuss. I get how you want what's best for me." I squirm against the bedspread, unable to find a comfortable position.

"You've been kind of distant, and I don't know what's going on. I thought you might want to go back home, but I overstepped."

My chest tightens at his sincerity. "No. That's not it."

"You'd be honest if something was bothering you, right? This world is hard, but I appreciate having you here. It's made the season much better."

Please, stab me one more time in the heart.

"Of course. You're my best friend." A lump in my throat makes swallowing difficult.

"Now that our feelings shit is out of the way, I've been dying to watch a new season of Area 52. Let's see it while I have free time."

I end up watching the same season twice because guilt has a funny way of making me do just about anything for my brother.

CHAPTER THIRTY
Noah

I ended up placing second in yesterday's race. Jax put up one hell of a fight for the first-place spot, deserving his win. The hard track and my placement keep me pleased with my performance.

My dad, on the other hand, is not.

Regrettably, he invited me to dinner, a rare occasion, since he never stays after a race, choosing to leave as soon as he can. The whole idea of dinner puts me on high alert. I can count on one hand the total number of outings we've had together since I joined F1.

To put it short, my father deserves to be fucked right up the ass with a tub of extra strength Icy Hot for lube.

He comes off condescending to me and the waiters. My hands curl every time he speaks to someone with a chip the size of a twenty-pound kettlebell on his shoulder. It takes everything in me to not jump over the table and pull him by the shirt, spit in his face, and rip him a new asshole to match his personality.

My chest tightens at the thought of acting similarly to him. I want to forget the countless girls, the cockiness, and my attitude. To protect myself, I gave up bits and pieces until I was devoid of feeling. Deception plays cruel jokes on people. Turns out while I busied myself with putting on a show, I was the person I lied to most. Eventually I believed all the deceits, the excuses I made for my shitty attitude and moodiness, becoming the asshole I was escaping.

My dad's piss-poor attitude drives home all the points I've learned along the way this year. And the worst part? I actually feel bad for my dad. I pity him.

Nicholas Slade has no one, using money and power to get his way, never loving someone else. How can he when the man he adores happens to be his own reflection? To be honest, he doesn't love me. Fuck, he doesn't even *like* me, let alone share any semblance of the four-letter L word. He's a selfish bastard who lives vicariously through me.

But to move forward in life, I have to face these issues from my past. My therapist will be pleased with how I sit silently, taking deep breaths, putting up with his shit.

I put out a lifeline for him. A test of sorts.

"Maya mentioned you chatted at the race together." My voice stays relaxed despite a tingling sensation growing inside me.

"Mm, yeah. She's a pretty piece of ass. When are you going to drop the bomb on Santiago? It's a smart plan, fucking with his head before the final race of the season." His grin leaves a bitter taste in my mouth. How does he sleep at night? Restless, with a soul as black as the darkness that surrounds him.

"She's my girlfriend."

Not officially. But he doesn't need to know.

He tilts his head at me, offering a sinister smile. "If that's what you call your fuck buddies now, all the power to you."

My skin wants to crawl off my body and take up shop somewhere else. I attempt to give him a chance, waging an internal war.

"I'm probably going to marry her one day. I think she's the one." I say the words with confidence.

The idea is a little premature, sure. But I have a good feeling about her. Maya breathes new life into me, not wanting to piece me together but accepting all my jagged parts. Waking up next to her makes my mornings, not because of her phenomenal blow jobs but for the special smile she gives me when I hit her snooze button five times. I love the way she lies in bed reading books in the middle of the day, unbothered and shooing me away when she hits a good part. She brushes off my gruff attitude with a smile and a kiss because I can be a moody asshole when I don't place first—conditioned because of the shitty man sitting in front of me. Most of all, I like how she makes me want to be a better person. For her, for me, for the whole goddamn world.

My dad gives me a tight smile. "Better hire a lawyer for a prenup then. Women like her are only after one thing, and it's not your shining personality and good looks."

My facade drops. I run out of fucks to give him because he is too far gone to help. I made sure to prepare for this exact moment because I had anticipated the stunt he pulled with Maya. After all, I've watched him for years. I didn't expect him to threaten Santi's contract because I thought he would come after mine.

I let out a long exhale. He looks up at me, his dark eyes glaring at me.

"After spending time with people who care about me, I realized some things. People who love you spend time with you both on and off the track. They go to events and stay until the end to be around you because they want to. It's not about whether you win or lose. I'm a world champion, and you treat me like a piece of shit on your shoe. Inconvenient and unwanted."

He tries to say something, but I throw up my hand to shut him up. The upscale restaurant he chose allows us the privacy we need for this heart-to-black-fucking-heart.

"And you threaten my girlfriend? You actually fucking told her that her brother may lose a contract with Bandini? Like, how sad and shitty is your life that you'd do that? I'm done trying with you. You've been a crappy dad my whole life, only caring when it benefits you. In the end, being in my life is more about your image than about being there for me."

I only pay attention to his rapid blinking and lowering my heart rate.

"You can't cut me out when I sponsor your team. I was serious about Santiago's contract renewal. Try me." He hisses like the fucking snake he is.

"Oh, Father. The thing is I have it all handled. Bandini no longer needs your generous donations. I attended almost every sponsor event, meeting, and gala held this year, slowly securing enough sponsorships to outbid yours. You're done with *my* team. Feel free to back another group if you want. Not sure if they need a donor with a crappier attitude than the sewer you crawled out of, but hell, you are a legend after all."

"This isn't over. I'm still a sponsor this year, so I'll do whatever the hell I want."

I throw my cloth napkin on the table. "I don't give a fuck. Do whatever you feel like, but stay the hell out of my way."

No need to sit around and spend another minute with this man, my stomach threatening to rid itself of shame and a sixty-dollar steak.

He doesn't bother with an apology.

I leave my past behind at the table of some fancy-ass restaurant. Fuck him to the farthest galaxy and back because the moon is just too damn close for comfort.

CHAPTER THIRTY-ONE

Maya

"Today we're here with Santiago, since he gets jealous of all the attention I give other drivers."

My brother and I sit at a sleek bar top in the Bandini motorhome. I line up two shot glasses next to a bottle of tequila while Santi smiles at the camera situated on an adjacent table.

"Santi admitted he's down about not making it on the podium the other day. So we are going to do an exclusive episode of Tequila Talks because we still haven't learned tequila doesn't fix our problems. I hope this episode goes better than the last one. I'll ask him a series of questions where he has to take a shot whenever he refuses to answer. I end the show after four because he weighs a lot, and I can't pick his butt up off the floor. Blame their strict workout regimen and muscle mass."

My brother flexes his bicep at the camera.

"Warning: I didn't come up with these questions. I want to clarify since fans want answers to things I *do not* need to know about my brother." My lips purse at the horny bunch of fans out there—way more than I expect, all tapping away in my inbox about these guys.

I exaggerate a shudder at his mischievous grin and stick my tongue out at him.

"Favorite thing about your sister?" I bat my lashes at him.

"Hmm, who came up with that question?" His brow lifts.

I shrug and fail to answer.

"I love her passion, fearlessness, and carefree personality."

Aw, how sweet.

"Who knew you had such kind thoughts about me? Okay, next question. The worst part about F1?"

"Hands down the fact that I don't sleep in my bed for months at a time. I miss coming home."

Ah, the not so glam side of traveling the world.

"What you really miss is your gym and bubble baths." I smile at my brother.

"Bath bombs don't feel the same in a hotel bathtub." He pouts.

I suppress a laugh. "Best part of having a teammate?"

"The shared points you get together. Plus, personal tips and recommendations." Santi genuinely smiles at the camera.

"Ugh. I hate this one. Your favorite sex position?"

He winks at the camera and knocks back a shot. *Good answer.*

"Glad that's past us. Next, any special girl in your life?"

He flips his empty shot glass. "Not since high school."

"See, girls, boys are sensitive just like us. They get their heart broken once, and it's game over."

He chuckles to himself. "See, guys, girls are annoying as ever, no matter the age."

Oh, burn. "Moving on—"

"What's going on here?" Noah's voice makes my stomach flip.

"Tequila Talks. Want to join?" My brother has loose lips after one shot.

Sure enough, Noah grabs the extra glass and fills it up. He sits in the seat next to me, ready for questions.

My eyes dart between Noah and Santi. "Wait, he can't join. I don't have questions for him."

"Ask him the same ones." Santi offers me a quizzical look.

"Lovely." My jaw hurts from my teeth grinding.

Noah dares to look smug. *All right, he asked for it.*

"If you could go on a date with any celebrity, who would it be?" I give the camera a warm smile before turning toward the guys.

Noah coughs. I did try to stop him.

"Definitely the woman from the World Cup commercial that everyone was talking about. That girl is fine," my brother blurts out.

My hands fidget in front of me, anticipating whatever response Noah comes up with.

He mutters a curse before speaking. "Hmm. Juliana Santos-Carvalho?"

A supermodel? Really?

If glares could kill, this man would be dead on the spot.

"Sorry, ladies. It seems like unless you're a supermodel, you're out of luck with these two."

My brother chuckles while Noah keeps quiet, pleasing me. "Favorite F1 team besides Bandini?"

My brother strokes his chin as Noah takes it away.

"McCoy for me. I like the guys and their work ethic. They're great competition, always pushing us to do our best."

"My old team, Albrecht. That's a given from our previous history. There's no bad blood since I left. And the guys hustle."

I move on. "Name five things you look for in your dream girl."

"Attractive, smart, into F1..." Santi pauses. "Oh, family-oriented, and nice."

Noah takes a few seconds to come up with an answer, his intense gaze warming me up inside. I become fascinated with picking at the label of the tequila bottle.

"Beautiful, both inside and out. Funny enough to get my asshole sense of humor. Someone who wants to have a family and likes me for me rather than for fame. And a girl who will travel around the world with me because this job is constantly on the go."

I think my ovaries explode but it's hard to tell. *Moving on.*

"Best sex story?" *Did the camera catch my cringing?* I'll have to rewatch later while I edit.

My brother takes a breath before talking. "Well, there was this one time—"

My elbow hits him in the ribs. *Hell. No.*

Noah winks at me before knocking back his shot like the champ he is. *Oh, what a simple wink can do to me.* My lips tip up in a telling smile.

The game keeps going with questions taking a turn away from sex and love interests.

For the first time since Santi started at Bandini, he and Noah get along. It gives me hope that they can be friends after Noah and I come out about our relationship.

But you know what they say about the best-laid plans…

CHAPTER THIRTY-TWO
Noah

Maya tells her brother she wants to sleep over at Sophie's suite tonight. But in reality, we planned an all-nighter together after her Tequila Talks vlog, lying naked in the hotel bed.

"You know I don't want to get with Juliana Santos-Carvalho, right? I needed to say a name."

She sighs. Not exactly the reaction I want.

"Yeah. But you've been with models like her. That's a lot to compete with when I'm nothing like those girls."

My bad decisions rear their ugly heads again. Except this time, I want to banish them forever, no longer proud of my shitty past. Pack them away in a cardboard box along with my bad memories.

"Have you googled me?" I roll on top of her. My hand softly grips her chin, stroking her soft skin.

"*Maybe.* I was curious." Her eyes look up toward the ceiling.

"Google will be the death of me. Don't look at that shit. It's not worth your time or energy when people spin stories to make money." My lips softly peck at her cheeks between words. "You're. The. Most. Lovely. Woman. To. Me."

She giggles at all the kisses I plant on her face. My lips find hers, my tongue caressing her closed lips, wanting access. I fucking hate when she closes herself off. I slide my hands down her body, wanting her to respond to me. My hands stroke the entrance of her pussy and tease her into giving me what I want.

She moans when I dip a finger inside her, my dick stirring at her arousal. I deepen the kiss, wanting to show her how I crave and want her. Desire and desperation swirl inside me. My knee pushes her legs apart, and I roll my hard cock against her center. Her groan makes my cock pulse against her smooth skin, her arousal coating my dick as I grind into her. Lust makes my head cloudy, but I need to prove my point.

"I really like you, Maya. I want to spend every day with you, both in here and out there once you let me. Will you be my girlfriend? Officially?"

The way she smiles at me makes my heart skip and my dick ache. She pulls me down for another kiss that speaks volumes because who the hell needs words when their body does the talking?

I struggle to stay awake at the sponsor event, another gala where lots of old men open their big wallets. A dime a dozen around here. With age comes less willingness to attend these events, wanting to ditch the moment I arrive because I have no interest in kissing ass. Not to mention how I can't even have my girlfriend by my side since she hangs out with Santi.

So I do what any horny male would do. I text Maya to meet me in the empty ballroom next door.

She shows up ten minutes later, the darkness of the ballroom cloaking her as she stands near the double-door entrance. Low lighting makes her shape undistinguishable.

"Do you have a public fetish I should be worried about? This is becoming a common occurrence for us." Her voice sounds low and husky.

"Why don't you come over and find out?"

She strolls toward me, moving around piles of stacked chairs and empty tables spread throughout the room. My lungs welcome the scent of her shampoo mixed with a light floral perfume. I could get high off the smell of her alone.

She tugs on my bow tie, loosening it.

"I love seeing you in a tux. It's one of my favorite things."

I can wear a tux every day if it makes her happy. "I love seeing you naked. But this will have to do for now." I hiss when I tug up the hem of her lace dress. "You're not wearing underwear? This whole time?"

She replies with a breathy laugh.

I bite down on my lip. "Fuck me. You can't do stuff like that. If I had known…"

She shuts me up by kissing me. Lazy, slow. Tantalizingly sweet—so fitting for her. Her hands run down my chest before they land on my belt. Her hoarse voice whispers in my ear, my spine tingling at her boldness. "We don't need this right now."

Our heavy breathing echoes off the walls, mixed with my groan as the belt's metal buckle hits the floor. Maya undoes my zipper slowly. My cock stands to attention with precum seeping from the tip. She pulls my dick out of my pants, her thumb brushing against the pearly drop.

I groan. "Shit."

"*Shh*. You're too loud," she says before stepping away and pulling a condom from her purse.

Her preparedness makes me smile. "Thought you'd get lucky tonight?"

"I expected it." Her eyes gleam at me.

"Always dreamed of fucking the sass out of you." I push her up against the wall, done with talking.

My lips find hers while my hands stroke her core, pulling a gasp from her. It doesn't take much work with her, and I love it. Love the way she pushes me for more. To feel, to live, to breathe her in and never let her go. To keep Maya all to myself because fuck the world, they don't deserve her. *Shit. I don't either.* But I can't help my selfishness, the possessiveness I feel around her. A desire to mark her up and leave a trail of bruises from my lips. To bring her over the edge before pulling her back up, shattering around my dick the same way she smashes into my walls.

She puts the condom on me, rolling it along my shaft, making the simplest things look erotic.

I lift her up, and her legs wrap around my waist. Maya's thighs clench around me, squeezing me the same way invisible hands grip my heart. But I don't want her to let go. She can take over my whole life with a smile on her face and I'd thank her for it. Her back hits the wall as my lips find hers, smashing, nipping, and tugging at the soft flesh.

I slide into her slowly, wanting to enjoy the sensation of the first thrust. My eyes close when my dick is fully sheathed inside her. Her breathy sigh pushes me to move after what feels like a full minute of me regulating my breathing.

I pull out to the tip before sliding back in with an unhurried pace.

"Oh God. Noah." Her hands claw at the back of my tux.

My lips move to her neck, finding the spot that drives her crazy. I suck and mark her because I want every fucker to know she drives me wild.

"You're soaked for me. Does it turn you on knowing anyone could walk in on us right now? Find me fucking you against a wall. They might want to watch. Shit, I would."

I squeeze her ass when she tries to lift herself up.

"No," I growl. "I'm in charge."

Thank fuck I work out every damn day and she doesn't weigh much because I don't want to break our connection by moving us to a table. At least not before her first orgasm. Turns out I tend to be selfish everywhere but in the bedroom.

"It's too much." Her strained voice makes my dick pulse inside her. I get what she means. Our relationship is more than a physical attraction, not limited to a lust-induced fuckathon. I don't fear the emotional tie linking us, instead choosing to embrace it because I'm the only one who fucks her and loves her like this.

Love. One word I didn't understand until Maya.

We intensely gaze into each other's eyes as I slide in and out of her, pulling a few moans from her while she tugs on my hair. Sex has never felt this close for me. Like Maya chips away at my exterior, leaving a piece of herself behind forever.

My lazy tempo continues. I want to brand her, make her mine, drive her as crazy as she makes me. She comes the first time when I brush against her G-spot. I hold her while her body shakes, gripping her ass and not letting go.

I live for hearing her yell out my name and bringing her pleasure. Obviously, I'm an egotistical bastard, but she likes me anyway, so be it.

I eventually increase my pumping, hitting her in all the right places while I struggle to keep my own orgasm back. She needs to come again because I crave it more than my own. Like chasing a high.

"Yes. Just like that. Fuck, Noah." Her hands run through my hair and tug at the roots. I love how she tells me what she enjoys, encouraging me and feeding my self-esteem all at once.

"You're stunning when you come. I don't know if I've seen anything as perfect." I leave a searing kiss on her plump lips.

I carry her to an empty table nearby that looks sturdy enough, needing to adjust my angle. One of my hands finds her clit while the other palms the material over her breasts.

"Do. Not. Stop," she says between my thrusts.

I groan at her request, my dick throbbing inside her at the desperation in her voice. My pace becomes quicker and messier. A mix of her pants with my deep inhales rings in my ears. Her eyes meet mine, half-open and hazy, a masterpiece of lust and love.

And with a few sweet words of encouragement, she explodes around my dick again, milking me. Her nails scratch at the material of my tux. Fuck if that's not sexy.

My dick slides easily in and out of her, her arousal coating me. I increase the pressure and pace. Hurried thrusts match my limited sense of control, becoming more rushed with each push. My heart beats rapidly in my chest. I detonate inside her with a roar of pleasure, my spine tingling at my release. Lazy pumps until I have nothing left to give.

My body relaxes, and I lie on top of her, both of us catching our breath.

"I think you shave off a year of my life every single week," her voice croaks.

"What a year well spent."

Her chest shakes under me, and I smile into her neck.

We both take care of each other. I help smooth out her hair while she fixes my bow tie. We're quite the pair, she and I.

"I have one last request." I grab her hand. She glances up at me, her curiosity apparent. "Will you dance with me?"

She nods her head enthusiastically while shooting me a radiant smile.

I pull up the music-streaming app on my phone before placing it on one of the tables. Thomas Rhett's "Die a Happy

Man" croons through the tiny speakers, loud enough for us to hear. My hand grabs hers as I pull her toward an empty area. With one hand on the small of her back and the other wrapped around her hand, I sway us to the music.

This is the best I can get for now since we can't dance together in public yet. The moment feels fitting after the sex we shared, her head lying against my chest as we move around in a small circle. I kiss the top of her head before I spin her around.

She unabashedly throws her head back and lets out a sultry laugh. I make it a goal to make her laugh like that every single day for the rest of my life. She turns me into a sappy motherfucker who can't help it around her, endlessly searching for ways to make her happy and satisfied.

I gather up courage as the song continues because I want to let her know. Because I never want another day to go by without her hearing it.

"I love you." My voice rasps over the music.

Maya always looks beautiful to me. But the moment I admit I love her? She gives me what is hands down the most gorgeous smile I've ever seen, one meant only for me.

I keep saying that. But I'll never forget this one.

"I love you too." Her voice carries over the sweet melody.

I pull her in close after she says the three words I've wanted to hear for weeks, committing the moment to memory.

CHAPTER THIRTY-THREE
Maya

B razil. Home of Noah's beloved Juliana Santos-Carvalho.
I'm joking. No more bitter feelings about that
comment since Tequila Talks was a few weeks ago. I'm
more mature than that. Plus, Noah loves me. Back in the
ballroom, he caught me off guard, looking excited to say those
three words. Now he never goes a day without saying them.

Lying to my brother about my current whereabouts fills me
with dread. I let him know this morning that I was flying to
Brazil earlier than expected with Sophie, telling him we want
to explore Rio de Janeiro together before the next Grand Prix.
My lie isn't too far off from the truth. See, I am in Rio de
Janeiro…but I'm actually here with Noah.

Shocker. I know.

But we have a week off between the last race and the
Brazilian Grand Prix. We came to the country early, enjoying
the trip he planned. He shows me how he cares, doing sweet

things that make me appreciate him even more. Like buying me one of every candy bar when I got my period and sex was off the table. Or how he made sangria when I felt homesick, which led to us getting drunk and playing another round of two truths and a lie.

I carry my camera around while we wander through Rio's streets, filming private moments of us. Nothing like the hustle and bustle of a big city. Noah shows an interest in my camera, asking people to take photos of us, claiming he wants memories of our first trip together. He hates every camera except mine. I can't imagine being famous, not being able to enjoy fundamental privacy.

We both dress up, currently incognito because avoiding fans has become our new day job. I don't want pictures of us out there on the internet. At least not identifiable ones, so I put myself in charge of the outfits.

"Is the fake mustache really necessary? It's kind of itchy." Noah scratches his face for the fourth time today. I hate to say it, but mustaches don't suit him, especially not the handlebar kind.

"Stop your complaining. I'm the one wearing an Albrecht team shirt. They're, like, the worst in the whole F1 circuit, so I got the short end of the stick."

His throaty laugh makes me chuckle along with him.

Noah taps the brim of my hat. "I told you to wear the wig instead. You refused."

"It's hot outside, and wigs get scratchy." I don't even know why I bought that atrocity. It makes me look like a porn star, and not exactly the well-paid kind.

"We'll have to save it for another day."

Noah's heated smile sends a shiver down my spine. He kisses my neck at the bottom of the Christ the Redeemer steps, people pushing past us, grumbling in Portuguese.

"You have lots of kinks. I'm not sure I would've agreed to this relationship if I had known all this beforehand." I step away from him and give him a one-armed shrug. His sexual appetite alone leaves me sore for days because once is never enough with this man.

He smacks my ass while we climb to visit the statue. By the time we reach the top, my lungs ache and my legs wobble.

"You never look this sweaty after sex with me. Am I not working you hard enough?" Noah's smile matches the mischievous shine in his eye.

I shoot him a half-assed glare. "Not all of us like to visit the gym at five in the morning. This is the most I've worked out all year."

He shakes his head at me. "Don't discount all the times I've fucked you. Better than any cardio you'll do at a hotel gym."

"Look at you, solving all my problems." I genuinely smile up at him.

My phone rings, vibrating inside my leggings' pocket. I may not work out, but at least I look the part.

"Let me take this. It's Santi." I walk away before Noah protests. He stays put, checking out the view while I sit on a bench.

"*Hola, hermana*. You forgot to check in earlier." Santi's voice carries through the small speaker.

My hand holding the phone shakes as uneasiness settles

in my stomach. "Sorry about that. We got busy." *Not a lie per se.*

"How's the weather over there? Heard a storm may be coming in before the race."

The sun shines down on me, not a cloud in sight. I hang out in the shadow of one of Christ's open arms, which is ironic since I'm lying to my brother.

"Don't worry about that because it's bright and sunny here. You still have a few days before you need to come over anyway."

"How's little miss Sophie doing?"

"Good." I choke on the word. "Hanging out at the famous statue before visiting Sugarloaf Mountain."

I promise once this season is over, I will tell the truth no matter what. Noah tells me how much he wants to date me after the season ends. Hopefully, my relationship with him is worth the nausea I feel every time I lie to my brother.

"Well, lucky you're having a good time. Noah stood me up at a sponsor event, which meant I had to spend five hours talking to people by myself. I hated every second of it."

My chest tightens. "Oh no." *Wow, Maya. Please act less surprised.*

"Yeah, no shit 'oh no.' He acts tough and entitled, too good to pick up the phone and let me know he wouldn't be saving my ass from dead-end conversations. But whatever. I survived."

The three of us need another tequila bonding session.

"At least you love those types of events. Sucks he didn't show." *Sucks he was in bed with me while you were schmoozing.* I might as well shower in holy water to cleanse myself from my deception.

"Yeah, maybe for the first hour. But I can't even take a piss without someone asking me a question about the season or my teammate."

I laugh at the mental picture Santi paints me. "Well, I better get going."

"Right. Your travel buddy has replaced me."

Santi clenches a fist around my heart without knowing it.

I fight to get the words out. "Never. You're always my number one."

"I better be. Catch you later." He hangs up the phone.

Noah grins at me from across the cobbled platform. I offer a weak smile and a small wave, taking deep breaths to ease the tension building in my head.

I hope all this worry is worth it because unlike Noah, I don't welcome trouble with open arms and a kiss.

"You disappeared three times already tonight. You even abandoned me with Charles Wolfe. Of all people, that's low, Maya." Santi's voice comes out whiny.

I shoot him a sweet smile and shrug my shoulders. He dislikes that sponsor, sharing how the guy gets drunk and has a preference for hugging it out. Brown eyes glare down at me with a hint of amusement.

"I'm sorry. I got distracted." I bring my drink up to my lips because I have to keep my hands busy. If not, my nervousness will give me away.

"You've been more than that lately. I'll have to talk to Sophie because she takes up too much of your time, making me feel needy and jealous."

He fails to notice me choking on my drink.

Way to keep it cool, Maya.

He continues, oblivious to my internal struggle. "It's getting out of hand. Give me my sister back already. We only have two races left, and I barely see you anymore. Not even at the press conferences."

"Well, those get boring. I almost fell asleep at one... standing up, I might add." I don't include how Noah had kept me up for hours the night before.

His cold gaze assesses me while he remains silent.

"I'll spend the rest of the night by your side. I'll even help you avoid Charles; I don't think he likes me very much anyway." I link my arm in his, ignoring how my throat feels like I chugged sand.

"You better. He hugged me twice, his sweaty face rubbing against mine. Feel pity for your older brother." Santi winces.

I rub his arm in assurance. "Aw, poor baby. I'm here now, and I'll keep an eye out for him."

Not soon after, Noah finds me again. But this time, he frowns when his eyes land on Santi next to me. His eyes scream trouble. The delicious kind of trouble, but trouble nonetheless with my brother here. I subtly shake my head from side to side in hopes of discouraging his advances. His lips tip up at the corners.

"Noah, good to see you, man. It feels like you barely hang around these things. You missed Charles today. He hugged me." My brother gives Noah the usual guy hello: hands shaking, backs being clapped.

Guilt eats me alive like a corroded battery in the pit of my stomach. How does Noah keep his face neutral all the time? I need to set up a meeting with Bandini's PR manager because I could use some insider tips.

"Yeah, these events haven't been doing it for me lately. Especially Charles. He's a nice guy but a bit touchy-feely." He smirks at my brother.

We both know what *has* been doing it for him lately.

Spoiler: it isn't Charles or winning races.

Even though Noah wins most of the races anyway. Commentators think Noah may be the best of our generation and F1 history. Fans obsess over him, attending races with huge posters, some including women's numbers. They line up for hours to get him to sign their stuff. Boobs not included.

My brother and Noah chat while I insert random comments that come off half-assed at best. Noah and his nearness distract me. His tux makes me lightheaded, and the look of his roguish smile muddles up my insides. Thankfully Santi doesn't notice anything. I'll tell him soon enough because I can't take the lying anymore.

Soon after, Santi and I call it an early night, wanting to get extra sleep before the qualifiers.

For the first time in a while, I stay with Santi because of his admission about being lonely. He does so much for me, and I lie to him, keeping a secret hidden that he should be aware of.

I don't sleep a wink. Instead, I end up tossing and turning, never finding a comfortable position. Turns out sleep is for the innocent.

"I don't like the way he looks at you," my brother growls before taking another sip of his beer. Noah stares at us across the pit lane, smiling before turning back toward a man he's talking to.

Noah sucks at keeping his cool. He's already talked to us twice at this kid's event, a kart race fundraiser for children with cancer. When Santi and I hopped in two karts, Noah decided to join, claiming he wanted to spend time with his teammate.

Preferably the teammate he spends his nights with.

And damn him for making my heart melt onto the pavement as he played with kids, throwing them in the air and catching them. A total dad move that makes my ovaries happy.

My brother stares at him, dark eyebrows tipped down as his fingers clench around his beer bottle.

He glances over at me. *Crap.* I forgot he said something in the first place.

"He looks at everyone that way. Don't bother getting annoyed." I take a sip of my water, wishing to chug Santi's beer instead.

"No, he doesn't. His eyes stay on you too long. I might talk to him because you're my sister, and he's a man-whore who needs to keep his hands to himself."

My brother is about fifty orgasms too late on his threat.

"You're making excuses because you want to like him, but you both have a dumb rivalry."

Some may call it a stretch, but they bonded over tequila. If that doesn't scream future friends, I don't know what does.

He grumbles under his breath. "Thank God you're not into guys like him."

Should I be afraid of how often my chest constricts around Santi?

"Why?" I whisper.

"Do you really need another reason besides the fact that he fucks everything that walks?"

I fail to hide how my body cringes, but he misses it, too enthralled in glaring at Noah. Santi's words stab at my armor and leave me bleeding.

"Well, people change. I don't want to cast judgments when he's been nice to me this season." I tip my chin up and cross my arms. People can only walk all over your heart if you let them.

Santi lets out a bitter laugh. "This is one of the reasons I love you. You're innocent and trusting of the world and the people in it." His statement makes my heart deflate like a balloon.

"Maybe you need to trust your teammate more instead of looking for everything wrong with him. You can learn something from me." *Whoa.* I have no idea where those words came from.

Santi stares at me, unblinking and unmoving. He changes the subject after chugging the rest of his drink. But the air around us remains heavy, a dark cloud looming over me, guilt hitting me like hail.

CHAPTER THIRTY-FOUR
Noah

It takes everything in me not to explode. I grind my teeth and clench my fists as my feet stomp across the pavement, coming face-to-face with my father.

And look, he brought a film crew.

"Noah, just the man I was looking for. Sports Daily wanted to do a special on me, marking the twentieth anniversary of my last World Championship win." His sinister smile makes a chill run down my spine like my nerves know what a slimy piece of crap he is.

My head nods along like I give a shit. Cameras film me, making it impossible to hide my scowl at the unwanted attention, unlike any type of filming Maya does. My dad surprises me by coming back after I chewed him out during our dinner a month ago. He disregards how I told him to stay the hell away from me because he never does anything I ask. *Lucky me*. Looks like I got my listening skills from my dad.

"Excited to compete in the Brazilian Grand Prix tomorrow?" His bright smile doesn't reach his eyes.

"Sure." My lips remain a tight line, not the least bit interested in this chat.

I manage to walk one step away before he pulls me in, his thick arm wrapping around my shoulders and holding me in place.

"Want to tell the cameras how you've been preparing for your racing lately? Fans wonder what makes you tick, what makes a winner stand out from the rest. Interesting strategy of taking a whole week off before the race." His eyes glint in the sunlight. I hate the look on his face, a smug smile meant to intimidate and control me.

"Just the usual, resting and prepping while keeping to my schedule. Don't want to mess with perfection." A weak smile breaks out across my face as I shrug my dad's arm off me.

"You better be careful. Don't want secrets getting out about how you win races." His sly smile makes my stomach churn.

I step away from the bright lights of the camera, putting distance between my jackass of a father and me. First the issue with Santi's contract, and now he threatens me. A never-ending cycle with us. Me pushing, him punching. A screwed-up relationship that will never be normal, but thank fuck I have new sponsorships and a fresh start.

His game doesn't interest me, and for once, my decisions

can affect someone else. I feel like an idiot for telling him about Maya and me because the way he looks at me tells me this thing with us won't be over until he says it is. The ultimate control freak. And worse, he gets off on it.

Fuck me, I really screwed up this time.

Brazilian
Grand Pix

CHAPTER THIRTY-FIVE
Maya

A rainy race day. The worst kind of news for drivers and fans alike.

The track shines, slick from the downpour, and the crew scrambles about as they swap regular tires for wet ones. Some drivers perform better than others in slick conditions, and my brother isn't one of them. It takes a lot of skill to successfully navigate cars with limited visibility and grip on the track.

The pit crew scurries about with a nervous buzz as they prepare the spare parts needed for the cars. Extra pieces lie outside for any minor crashes, just in case the Bandini boys have a collision.

Santi and Noah discuss game plans with Sophie's dad. I linger, getting in the way of random mechanics who kindly work around me, not asking me to move until I knock over a power drill. They escort me to the computer area where I can wreak less havoc. Sophie sidles up to me.

"My dad bet fifty bucks that Albrecht doesn't make it past thirty laps. Want in?" Her green eyes shine, complementing her tan skin. She rocks French braids, a jean skirt, and another slogan T-shirt.

I chuckle. "Do you ever learn from bets?"

"No. That's why I bet they wouldn't make it past seventy laps." She blows a pink bubble before popping it.

"There are only seventy-one laps."

"Exactly. My dad raised a smart cookie." She taps her temple, sporting a megawatt grin featuring her two dimples.

The drizzling rain lets up, allowing drivers to compete, but not enough for the tracks to completely dry before the start of the race. Sophie's dad announces how the Grand Prix will begin in twenty minutes. Noah and Santi meet with engineers near the entrance of the garage, reviewing driving strategies for these conditions, both men in my life working together. Once the crew gives the all clear, Santi comes to our spot in the computer bay.

"It's going to be fine. You worry too much lately. Just a little sprinkle, like a sun shower." Santi pulls me in for a hug.

Wet pavement mocks me. I give the rain a death stare like I can change Mother Nature's mind.

"I wish they didn't make you race in these conditions. It's kind of dangerous. I think of Albrecht crashing every time."

Santi chuckles. "They wouldn't let us race if the risk was that bad. Nothing more than the usual kind, like crashing into barriers with minimal damage."

"They prep for this. Plus, my dad will chat away with them, giving the best possible advice." Sophie flicks a braid over her shoulder.

I give them a tight smile. "Be safe out there. I'll have headphones to hear everything with the Bandini team." I leave out the part where I'll also tune into Noah's radio.

"Attagirl. We'll see you soon." He taps my hat with his car number.

I wave at Noah over Santi's shoulder, wishing I could hug him before he goes out there. Our secret is wearing on me and messing up my sleep cycles. Two races left until I can tell Santi everything, and I'm praying for the best reaction because he gets rattled easily.

Noah offers me a glorious smile before getting into his car.

"Damn, girl, I don't know how you ended up with that one. Sex on wheels." Sophie winks at me, except it comes off like a twitch.

I let out my first laugh of the day.

Nothing special happens during the beginning of the race. The grid has Liam in P1, with Noah, Jax, and my brother following behind. I don't know how the other teams don't get bored being on the back of the grid. But I guess they live their best lives anyway, happy to compete and do what they love every day. F1 calls them the "best of the rest."

The drivers take off, a few cars skidding and sliding across the wet pavement. Thankfully, both the McCoy and Bandini teams make it out of the grid perfectly intact. Our boys drive down a narrow straight with Liam in the lead. Sophie smiles and claps her hands together when Noah fails to overtake him.

Bad news rings through the radio and television. Santi turns rapidly, and with the slick track, he crashes during a tight turn. His car stalls next to a barrier wall with the left wheel dislodged and rolling away. He retires as a one-lap wonder.

My brother lets out his frustrations on camera. The radio buzzes with chatter as Sophie's dad calms him down, soothing him like a parent would during a child's tantrum. What a sucky job to work with hotheaded drivers.

"My dad deals with anger like a champ. No wonder he handled my teenage rage so well," Sophie mumbles.

"He puts up with these two all season long, so his patience must be endless."

I try to imagine Sophie's teen outbursts, resembling something along the lines of Tinker Bell stomping her foot.

My eyes remain glued on the television. "Santi's going to be pissed for retiring early."

Santi stands next to his car, the camera crew catching him smacking the red metal frame.

The safety car drops my brother off in the garage ten minutes later. I give him a quick hug and some words of encouragement before he heads on up to his suite, claiming he needs a break and meditation. My heart hurts at how defeated he looks, his shoulders hunched over as he disappears.

Sophie nudges me. "That went better than expected. No thrown helmets or dramatic sweeping of tools off a rolling cart."

"Does anyone else comment on your vivid imagination?"

"Duh, Liam—all the time. Says I should write stories and make money off my madness." She nods like she has considered the idea.

Liam and Noah fight for the first-place spot. They each pull off risky moves, trying to get around each other. Anticipation and nerves mix around inside me. A few times, their tires lose traction, but they regain momentum, pulling back onto the track before they stall. Liam's car spins out once as he expertly misses a barrier and gains enough force to keep driving. Another ten laps to go. Noah attempts to overtake Liam at the turn, but the track looks too wet.

My stomach churns at the live coverage, a helpless witness to the noise of crunching metal and squealing tires and the gasps from the pit. Sophie's dad yells into his radio, but his words are hard to make out.

Liam's front wing and tire clip the underside of Noah's car. My blood pumps loudly in my ears, making it impossible to hear shit out of the radio. I'm silently sitting on the edge of my seat as time slows down, frame by frame, and the crash happens.

Noah's car flips on its side and proceeds to barrel roll. Once. Twice. Three fucking times. It bounces again before it drags across the track, slamming into the barrier at an estimated one hundred and seventy miles per hour. *Holy shit.* The complete underside of his car is exposed, tires spinning and liquid leaking down the metal.

Tears flood my eyes at Noah's lack of response to any radio calls. Wetness streams down my face. Sophie's dad speaks into the radio, the only voice in the quiet garage.

Smoke billows from Noah's car despite the drizzling rain. It rises, darkening the air above him. More silence from the radio. Orange flames lick at the red paint of the Bandini car, marring it, making it look all wrong.

Noah speaks into the radio.

"Fuck, there's a fire. I'm upside down. Please get me the fuck out of here! Now!"

My heart sinks at his heavy breathing, his voice betraying his fear.

Flames engulf the cockpit of the car. Bile builds up in the back of my throat, my body fighting with everything to keep it down.

Sophie's dad speaks into his microphone. "They're on their way. Keep calm, Noah! We'll get you out of there. Take a few deep breaths. They're bringing the fire extinguishers now."

"Where the fuck is the safety team? The crane? My suit is on fire! There's a shit ton of smoke coming from the car, making it hard to breathe." His labored breaths garble the radio.

Sophie's dad takes control of the situation and asks if Noah has any injuries. My heart throbs at the panic laced in his voice.

I can't do anything but watch. I am helpless, out of control. The safety team finally shows up with fire extinguishers, white foam pouring over Noah's car, running down the red paint like a cloud. They control the flames in record time, but it still feels like forever. I tune out the commentators on the television. My legs move of their own accord, sitting myself down before my knees buckle.

The crew brings a crane to dislodge Noah's car from the barrier.

I sob at his desperate pleas to be let out, upset about how long it takes. God, it feels like torture. Knowing he feels weak, knowing I can't do anything but sit, watching the safety team do everything. Not being able to help the person I love is ten levels of fucked up.

I take a deep breath when the crane lifts his car. His body crawls out from under the hunk of metal with the help of crew members. An image I'll never get out of my head. He throws his helmet across the grass, the headpiece bouncing around, body shaking as he takes in a lungful of fresh air.

Invisible needles pinch at my heart, watching him get upset on the grass. He lies there vulnerable, no longer his usual tough, competitive, and brave self. Tears run down my face, mimicking the ones on TV. No privacy during a time like this.

My sad tears turn into ones of relief as the safety team checks him out, giving the all clear. It's sheer luck to walk away from a crash like that unharmed.

Sophie hugs me, her arms squeezing me tight, the smell of coconuts and summer wrapping around me. My nose runs and my vision clouds as the safety team drives Noah away from the crash.

"He'll be okay. The cars are built for these types of things, plus there's all the new safety precautions."

I give Sophie another hug, grateful for her friendship in a time like this. My body freezes at Noah's voice. I push Sophie away and hurl myself into Noah's arms.

His body tenses before his arms wrap around mine, not giving a shit who watches. He breathes in the scent of me, tears springing from my eyes again, hitting me with all types of emotions. I cry into his chest as he holds my shaking body close to him.

"I was terrified. I'm glad you're okay," I mumble into his chest.

"I'll always be okay and come back to you. Those cars are built for a bomb. I love you." He squeezes me as he whispers the words in my ear.

I take another deep breath, Noah's terrible smell invading my lungs. Like a mix of burnt rubber, smoke, and sweat. I try not to gag as I hold on to him.

Once I calm down, I pull away from him and assess for any injuries. Besides his flushed cheeks, he appears okay. Thank God. His hazy eyes look down at me, shining under the fluorescent lighting.

I let out a long sigh. My spine straightens at the buzzing of pit equipment. After everything today, I need to talk to Santi. With one race left, he deserves the truth because I care about both of my Bandini boys.

We pull away from each other, and my eyes fall to the floor. *The slate color looks fascinating.*

I toe it with my sneakers while everyone congratulates Noah for making it out safely. His chuckle bounces off the garage walls. Needing a moment to collect myself, I head toward the suites, telling him I need to use the bathroom.

CHAPTER THIRTY-SIX
Noah

Today's crash is single-handedly the worst one of my F1 career. Even nastier than Abu Dhabi two years ago. I hope they don't release the radio tapes for my sake because what an embarrassment.

Maya left ten minutes ago, not returning after saying she needed to go to the bathroom. That should have been the first warning sign that something wasn't right. She would've come back after my shitty crash.

A cold feeling trails up my spine as I head up the stairs toward the private suites.

I walk into the hall, confronted with Maya's tear-stained face, an angry Santiago, and my sneering father. Leave it to my dad to have impeccable timing. Calculated, waiting for the perfect moment for my defenses to be down, and I can't do anything to stop him.

I dread looking at Maya. Her eyes hold mine for a second before they shift, looking back at Santi.

"Noah, just the man I was searching for. You must be busy after that little tumble. But I was catching up with Santiago, giving him a few pointers, ways to do better on rainy days."

My fists clench at the sight of my gloating father. I thought I had already hit rock bottom, but man, was I wrong. The man who disgusts me leers at me.

"I'd like to speak to Santiago and Maya alone if you don't mind." Because I sure as fuck mind my dad standing here, getting off on all the drama.

Tension cloaks the room. Uncomfortable, unwelcomed, and so fucking wrong on a day like today.

"Actually, I thought we could all chat about the final championship, mainly because you're coming out about your relationship. How mature of Santiago to be okay with all this." My dad nods his head at Santiago.

My stomach drops at the surprise etched on Santiago's face. Maya covers her face with her hands, red creeping from her neck to her cheeks.

"Shut up." I glare at the man who is dead to me. *Finished. Done. For-fucking-ever.*

Santiago's head whips from my face to Maya's and back to mine. His fists ball up as he puts the pieces together. He eats up the distance, pushing me against the wall, his fists gripping my race suit. Up close and personal with his flared nostrils and sharp eyes. I don't put up a fight because I deserve this and more. He presses my body into the wall, my arms remaining flat against my sides.

"You *fucked* my sister?" His words pass through gritted teeth.

I hate how pissed he looks, how his lips curl and his cheeks redden. I hate causing him pain even though I love his sister.

"Look at that. Nothing like team bonding." My dad's voice drips with appreciation.

I don't need to look over Santi's shoulder to know how much my dad enjoys this. Why use Viagra when he has a lifetime supply of drama to satisfy his urges?

"How could you? I bring her along, hoping you're nice to her instead of your usual asshole self, and what? You screw around with her like she's nothing and then get her to lie to me. Is that your kink? Fucking up families because you come from a shitty one?"

Maya groans as she tugs on Santi's shoulder. "Stop, Santi. It's not his fault I lied. I didn't want to tell you, not him. *Let go.*"

Santi doesn't budge. He glares at me, his fingers twitching as he grips my suit, itching to hit me. I recognize the look from my father. But I'm a big boy. I can take it.

"Why only beat you on the track when he can get in your head just as much?" My dad lays it on thick, twisting everything special I have with Maya, selling his dirty story to my teammate.

Santi's fists tighten. I wait for him to take a hit, anything to put me out of my misery. I despise how upset Maya is.

Her eyes are red and puffy, her skin a sickly color as she watches us.

"I didn't fuck around with her. I love her. I'll keep loving her through everything, no matter what you or anyone else says or whatever you try to do to break us up. It's insulting for you to even think I'd be with Maya to fuck around with your racing. She's the endgame. I don't hook up with her for a shitty trophy, and sure as fuck not for a championship win. I want everything with her. Everything after *this*."

Maya takes a deep inhale, her eyes wide as she looks at me. I smile at her, even though I have a raging Santi pegging me against a wall, a second away from decking me in the face.

"You're a piece of shit. I trusted you. And *you*—" He looks at Maya for the first time over his shoulder while he holds me. "I'm disappointed in you." Those four words do Maya in, her eyes leaking fresh tears.

"Don't take this out on her. *Please*," my voice croaks, "blame me." I don't mind begging if it saves Maya from her heart smashing all over the Bandini suite floor.

The most honest moment of my life.

"Seriously, all this drama for a stupid cunt?"

Santi's hands drop me. His reflexes startle me, turning in a blur of red. The sound of flesh meeting flesh reverberates off the walls. It all happens in a second. My father clutches his face with a fired-up Santiago standing over him. In all my years, I've never hit him, but for once, someone has.

"You're a piece of shit. No one talks about my sister that

way. *Ever.* I don't care who the fuck you were, but I know the sad excuse of a man you are now, and let me tell you, you don't live up to the hype."

No words come from my mouth while Maya stares at the two of us.

Santi's body shudders, his self-control wavering. "Maya, let's go." He grabs on to her hand like a child.

My heart clenches as fear pumps through my veins, unable to handle her rejection if she finds this relationship not worth the trouble, not worth pissing off her brother, not worth a risk flooded with cons and promises that have yet to be followed through on.

Except her feet remain cemented to the floor.

"No."

A simple word fills me with hope.

CHAPTER THIRTY-SEVEN
Maya

No more lies, no more secrets, and sure as hell no more people telling me what to do or how to live my life.

My brother's eyes flare. His mouth opens, but I hold up a finger, needing to talk before I lose courage.

"Santi, I'm sorry for lying to you and keeping my relationship with Noah a secret. I...I love him. And I don't want to hide it anymore, like something shameful because it's nothing close to that. I need to grow up, and you need to let me. Mistakes included. Not that I think this is one, but no matter what happens, I can't live my life worrying about disappointing you, Mami and Papi, or even myself. I love you, but I need to take a chance on my relationship, and you have to accept it."

Words rush out of my mouth, raw and unfiltered like my feelings for Noah. Santi gazes at me in disbelief.

He shocks me. His arms wrap around my body, pulling me in for a hug as he mumbles into my ear, "I'm so fucking proud of you. But also, I'm pissed as fuck. To find out your secret from this dipshit on the floor, to know my teammate crossed boundaries...definitely not over it. But I want to be happy for you because you deserve everything in the world and more." He lets me go. His eyes shine under the suite lighting. "Don't ever lie to me again. And you—" He points at Noah. "You better do right by my sister. If you make her cry, I swear I'll make you regret ever being born from your crappy dad." He looks down at Nicholas Slade, who has yet to sink back into the pits of hell from whence he came. My brother walks away.

Secrets no longer get in our way, eating me up inside. I let out a shaky breath, my lungs no longer cut off from fresh oxygen.

Noah's dad stands, his usual bravado absent except for malice in his eyes.

Noah takes over, stepping between his dad and me. "You're no longer welcome here with Bandini. If you come around again, I'll have you banned. We're done. Don't call me, don't text me, and for fuck's sake, don't talk to Maya or her family. Go spend your sad existence somewhere else. It's over. *We're over.*" Noah's blank face expresses nothing as he looks into his father's eyes. No anger, no love, no sadness. Nothing but emptiness.

He grabs my hand and pulls me away. With no need to look over my shoulder, I turn my back on lies and Noah's past. I glance up at Noah, and for the first time in hours, I smile.

Despite wanting to spend time with Noah after his crash, I

need to speak to my brother without an audience. My lies hurt Santi more than he lets on because he has the softest heart.

I order us carry-out dinner since the way to his heart is through his stomach. When I arrive at our suite, he grabs the bag from my hands without giving me a backward glance. He sits at the large dining table and pops open my takeout box instead of his. His eyes assess the contents before sliding it to the empty seat across from him.

His eyes remain glued to his food as he shovels fried rice into his mouth. I sit and toy with the plastic-wrapped utensils.

"Santi, I'm truly so sorry for hiding the truth from you. I was going to tell you after the Abu Dhabi Grand Prix because I didn't want to upset you. You and Noah have a rough history. But I hated lying to you, and I never want to do it again."

He blinks at me. More shoveling of food and scraping of plastic cutlery against Styrofoam. I deserve his silence and anger.

"I went to Rio early because Noah planned a trip, not because I was with Sophie. I used her as an alibi multiple times, and I'm sorry." I don't know what else to say.

He takes a few deep breaths. "We always tell everything to each other. I hate how you lied to me...but I get it. I only want you to be happy, and I'm willing to put it past us." He takes a big gulp of water. "I can accept Noah as your boyfriend under one condition."

I hold my breath, waiting to hear what he says. In usual Santi fashion, he makes me sit with my discomfort, taking a few more bites of his dinner before putting his fork down.

"If you two break up, you still have to come to my races.

No bullshit about it being awkward or how Noah broke your heart. You want to act like a big girl, then you need to deal with the consequences if you have a falling-out." He rubs his stubbled chin while he assesses me.

I can agree to those terms. Noah acts confident enough for the two of us about how this relationship will work out.

"Deal."

CHAPTER THIRTY-EIGHT
Noah

The Abu Dhabi gala reeks of extravagance and wealth; crystal chandeliers shine around me as I mingle with sponsors. Everyone wants to talk about the final Grand Prix. About who will come out on top. Whether I will choke or dominate behind the wheel. My head pounds from the barrage of questions, wishing I could escape with Maya because takeout and a movie sound great right now.

Maya busies herself with Sophie, getting drunk on champagne, while I schmooze with minimal booze.

I wrap up chatting with a sponsor, eager to spend time with Maya, when Sophie's dad pulls me aside. He wears a suit with his graying hair slicked back, a grimace marring his face. Not exactly the best hello.

"Noah, follow me. I need to show you something." His eyes tell me not to argue.

My brows furrow at his request. I follow him out of the

ballroom, curiosity piquing my interest as we walk into another empty room. My lips lift at the memory of Maya and I sneaking off to empty rooms. Except once my eyes land on the other Alatorre sibling, my smirk turns into a frown. Santi made sure to avoid me at all costs this past week. Nerves make my hands clench as I tamp down the tendency to run a hand through my thick hair.

"All right, you two. I don't like how tense you both have been. Fans notice, the crew comments on it, and I sure as hell don't want to deal with it. Get everything out now. I won't allow any more drama on my team, especially with the final GP coming up. If I wanted to be waist-deep in shit, I would have worked for McCoy. Santi, I'll allow you one punch. Make it count because everyone knows Noah can be a smug fucker."

My eyes bulge. James is giving Santi an all-access pass to take a shot at me? *What the fuck?*

Santi shares my same surprise, his eyebrows drawn together, making him look like he's thinking too hard. I'd laugh if I didn't want to piss him off more.

"I don't know what to say." His Spanish accent draws out his words.

A tic in his jaw says differently. I should pass Santi my therapist's number, give him some help in the emotional expression department.

"Oh, cut the crap. He slept with your sister behind your back. Now he dates her, even *loves* her—all while competing against you. Of course you have shit to say. Get it out or hit him. But fix this crap." James taps his shoe against the floor.

Sophie's dad stands tall, not backing down from this

challenge, commanding respect from us as our team principal. *Cue the feels.*

"Okay, fine. Noah, it pisses me off how you disrespected me and went behind my back. You have a terrible track record with women, and I don't want my sister to become another number in your long list. Someone to pass the time with until you get bored. Not to mention the fact that she's my *sister*." Santi crosses his arms, his fears and distaste for my past hanging around us like a third teammate.

"I'm sorry for hiding it, but I'm not sorry for doing it in the first place. Don't expect Maya to be either. I want to put it past us, because I love her, and I want to be with her. *Forever*. I can't help my crappy past and decisions, but I can control my future. And she's it."

My confession hangs in the air, willing to admit everything if it stops his moping.

He walks up to me, his clenched fists a warning. *Shit.* His eyes glare at me. I stand there, ready to take a punch, anything for this to be done with.

"I don't need to hit you to feel better. I love my sister too much to mess up your pretty face." He shoves his hand out in front of him, and I take it. His fingers grip mine tightly. I let him pull his man card, not interested in another pissing contest with him. I'll save that for the track.

"I'm proud of you both, settling this like real men. Now get out of my sight. I don't want to hear about any more drama from either of you, so help me God, because I didn't ask for two sons. I deal with my daughter enough." James's voice has a hint of pride in it. We look over at him, catching his grin.

Santi and I walk out together, the tension following us from Brazil no longer a problem.

Santi claps me on the shoulder. "Let's grab a shot? Cheers to the end of the season and to new beginnings?"

"Best idea you've had all year."

CHAPTER THIRTY-NINE
Maya

"Just so you know, I think I threw up twice in my mouth looking at you two," my brother says. He barreled over after his practice round. The pit crew went on their lunch break, meaning we have a silent garage to ourselves, perfect timing for my filming.

I smile. "Aw, feel free to use the nearest trash can when you need it."

"Quit harassing my girlfriend, Santiago." Noah trails into our conversation. He makes his smug presence known, his palm tapping my ass before sliding into the back pocket of my jeans. Can't say I hate it, now that I reap the benefits of his wicked smiles and dirty words.

My brother groans. "You're the one who just smacked her ass right in front of me. Do you have a death wish?"

Noah grins while my cheeks heat. He lives to get under my brother's skin, despite the number of times I tell him to stop teasing Santi. But at least they both laugh.

"I can't help our burning love for each other," Noah purrs with a dramatic clutching of his heart. *Beautiful asshole*.

Santiago gags. "Did you lose your balls between Brazil and here? Because if so, my chances of winning the championship just got a whole lot better."

Noah drops his head back and laughs. "I think Maya found my—"

I rush to cover his mouth, standing on the tips of my toes to reach him. "Nope. Absolutely not. Dirty jokes are off the table forever and ever."

Noah licks my hand and winks at me. I pull away, not trusting myself around him because he has a way with words and his tongue.

"Seriously, can't you both make out somewhere in private? Preferably far away from the pit garage where I don't have to see you pushing my sister up against stacks of tires."

Santi scared the shit out of us yesterday. The piles of tires fell like dominos, drawing everyone's attention toward the three of us. My cheeks remained red the whole day after that display.

"We learned our lesson with that one." Noah shakes his head, fighting a grin.

Unlike him, I let out a laugh, unable to rid myself of the mental image of a fuming Santi pummeled by massive tires.

"I'm sorry. We'll be better. That means no more funny business." I give Noah a pointed look.

"Things we do are anything but funny." Noah waggles his brows.

My brother runs an agitated palm down his face. "I hate to

say it, but I may prefer broody Noah versus lovey-dovey Noah. That guy kept to himself during race weekends rather than shoving his tongue down my sister's throat at every possible opportunity."

We all know he likes Noah. These two have never been friendlier, with us all eating dinner together each night this week. They even hung out on their own when I went to interview Liam. I came back to the suite to find the two of them playing video games, duking it out with an F1 simulation. I sat between them and spent the night watching TV with the biggest smile on my face.

I situate the two men of my life in chairs facing back-to-back.

"Okay. Moving along." I click the Record button on my camera. "Hi, everyone. Welcome to my last vlog of this F1 season. We're in Abu Dhabi, where Santi and Noah just completed their practice round. With only two days left before the final Grand Prix, I wanted to take advantage of Bandini's off time. Today, we are playing the Newlywed Game with our two favorite Bandini boys. The game goes as follows: Noah and Santiago each have two cards. A blue card means Noah, and red means Santi. Every time they both agree on an answer, the team gets a point. After ten months together, let's see how well these two know each other. The goal is to win as a team, so think of your answers carefully. Three strikes and you're both done, proving to the world Jax and Liam are the best teammates." Those two scored thirty points together, surpassing my expectations. I doubt Santi and Noah will make it past ten.

I take up a seat next to the camera, choosing to stay out of the frame.

"Okay, first one. Who has had the least number of speeding tickets?"

Two red cards go up. Noah and Santiago turn around and smile at getting the answer right.

"American cops pull you over for everything." Noah rolls his eyes.

My brother faces the camera. "Because only an amateur gets caught."

I continue or else we will never finish at this rate. "Who has the bigger butt?"

My brother holds up a red card while Noah lifts up a blue card.

"Oh, you disagreed. One X." I cross out the question.

Noah sighs. "Come on, Santiago. Your ass could never fill out my jeans."

My brother stands up and shows his butt off to the camera. I laugh to myself while Noah gets up to compare, the two of them not coming to a conclusion. Clearly their bonding has reached new levels when they ask my opinion, but I shrug my head. Not touching that debate.

"Who holds their liquor better?"

Two red cards wave in the air.

"Stick to beer. No one wants to see you taking up shop at the nearest pit trash can again."

The three of us laugh. Noah's poor decisions don't hang around us, not after he admitted the truth about his dad to my brother two days ago. My boyfriend, the same man who acted like the whole world could go fuck itself, gave my brother a hug and told him thank you for punching his dad. A freaking thank you. If I didn't already love him, I would have offered my heart at that moment.

"Who is the biggest baby when sick?"

Two red cards go up. Glad my brother sees his man-child ways because the stomach flu I got the last time taking care of him was nothing short of terrible.

"Who is more stubborn?"

Two opposite colored cards hang in the air.

"Another strike and a prime example of how stubborn you both are."

"You do know it took you, like, eight months to figure out you liked my sister, right?" My brother flicks his blue card for emphasis.

Noah smirks at the camera. "Not as bad as you taking ten months to realize you wanted me as a friend rather than an enemy."

Oh shit.

"I didn't need a referee for Liam and Jax's game. Which, by the way, you are going to lose because you can't agree on anything."

"Well, at least we can agree on how we both love you," my brother says with a telling smile.

My chest tightens at the two of them looking at me. I never in a million years would have imagined them getting along like this, willing to put aside their differences to make me happy.

The two of them lose the game after a total of nine points. Unfortunately, they couldn't decide who cares more about me. *No, I'm just joking.* They couldn't agree on who deserves a World Championship more, with Noah raising a red card while my brother raised a blue one.

Yup, that happened. Jax and Liam may have won the game, but these two won each other over, a seemingly impossible task. And if that doesn't deserve a trophy for the Constructors' Championship, I don't know what does.

CHAPTER FORTY
Noah

My phone rings on the nightstand. And thank God Maya left the suite ten minutes ago because the curse words flying out of my mouth are nothing short of abhorrent.

I don't know what pushes me to answer the phone. Whether because of brewing emotions inside me or because I have a kink for masochistic tendencies. My finger slides across the glass, my head pounding to the beat of my heart.

"Mother. What can I do for you?"

Why hit her with pleasantries when she has the emotional intelligence of floral wallpaper? If you're trying to make the connection, don't.

"My son."

A classic. Nothing like reminding me of who signed my birth certificate to manipulate me.

"I'm busy and about to leave for my qualifier. What do you need?"

"You can work on your delivery a bit, Noah." Her voice carries like a melody through the phone. A siren who calls to men with wallets and trust funds, luring them in before ripping their hearts out.

I grunt, unable to produce words.

"Well, I'm spending time with Clarissa and Jennifer in Dubai, and we thought about visiting for the race. What do you think about getting us some tickets? Preferably in the VIP section I like that is far away from the loud stands."

Because God forbid, she actually has a view of the finish line.

Every time my mom asks for tickets, I get them. In the whole scheme of things, I never thought to say no because it was easy to do. Easy to give in to my toxic parents. Simple to not put up a fight, not wanting to make waves like my dad despite how sick it made me feel to be used over and over again.

But like I did with my dad, I want to give her one last chance. Being around Maya has made me a forgiving person.

"I can message my assistant. How are you doing?" I hold the phone to my ear, having no interest in asking about any tickets.

She scoffs. "Is it that man who prattles on the phone forever?"

If she means Steven, who likes to ask her about her day, then yes.

"Yup, the same one I've had since I started with Bandini. Can you believe it's been seven years since I began racing with the team?" *Bet you a weekend on my yacht she doesn't catch my mistake.*

"Nope. But the end of the season means your birthday is coming up. How are you celebrating your twenty-ninth this year?"

I'd say she blacked out for her entire pregnancy, except she couldn't drink. Surprisingly she remembers the month I was born, most likely because my father drops a large sum of money in her bank account as a "thank you for birthing my spawn" gift.

"Actually, I'm turning thirty-one. But numbers blur after so many years." *Insert obligatory eye roll here.*

"Exactly. My mistake." Her laugh sounds similar to nails scratching a chalkboard.

I hate every second of this call, of the battle waging inside me to not hang up the phone. But I want to show myself why I need to let go. Why I can't fall back into a damaging relationship with my parents because their love is conditional. And if I learned one thing in therapy, besides the fact that crying makes my face puffy as fuck, is how love doesn't come with conditions. No ifs, ands, or buts. It should make you a better person—not because you have to be but because you want to be. I want to be the fucking best for Maya and myself. Need to love myself and all that jazz.

"Yeah, your mistake. Did you know I met someone while competing this year?"

"That's sweet." She distracts herself with talking to someone else in the background.

That's sweet. Although an upgrade from my father's comments about Maya, she can't say much more than that?

"Clarissa is asking if you could also access some VIP

passes for the after-party? We personally like the one with the champagne company, but we aren't against others."

Looks like she can procure more than three words at a time. But like a gumball machine, she only works when you put money in her.

"You know, I don't think this is going to work."

Time to rip off the Band-Aid. Because why the fuck not, with everything else in the Slade family going to shit.

She sighs. "What do you mean?"

"You, me, your ex-lover Nicholas. The whole thing. I can't do this to myself anymore, trying to be a son I thought both of you wanted. Instead, you only contact me when convenient. And shockingly, you withheld your one-stop user card for the whole year until now. But in case you didn't know, I got into the worst crash of my career two weeks ago. And how many times did you call on me to check? None. Hell, how many times have you called me this whole season? Besides the one misdial?"

Her silence does nothing but encourage me.

"I appreciate you for giving birth to me, for being whatever you tried to be. But it's over. You should have protected me from *him*. The first time he hit me, you walked away because you didn't want to threaten your allowance. Time and time again, you let me down. So by all means, let it be my turn. I can't get you tickets. Not now. Not next year. Not ever again. If you have an interest in calling me to get to know me as a person, let me know. If not, have a good life."

I wait, holding the phone to my ear, willing her to say anything. Closure is a funny concept. Everyone talks about how cathartic it feels, but no one describes the pain you experience before. The courage needed to push through tough situations. How much it rips a person up to know they need to let go, not because they want to but because they have to.

My whole life, I lived chasing an unattainable prize of my parents' love. I sped down racetracks and life, willing it to go faster, but now I want to slow down. Enjoy the moments with people who matter, who want to remember my birthday, or who know five facts about me that can't be googled.

The dial tone greets me.

I clutch my phone, my lungs taking in the fresh air. For once, I have no ill will toward her, only wishing her the best. Everything falls into place. My therapist said I needed to face my past to embrace my future. Looks like I went to hell and back, scoring an angel along the way.

CHAPTER FORTY-ONE
Maya

Let me get this straight. You invited my parents to the final Grand Prix two days ago? And they said yes?" I struggle to get the words out.

Noah dropped this bomb on me while we watched a movie on our hotel couch. He casually mentioned how my parents boarded a flight last night to come visit us, like we all planned it.

"Yes. Can you believe it? They want to see their two kids after months of being away." His eyes sparkle.

"But why would you do that?"

"Why not?" His lips tip at the corners.

I tilt my head at him. "Don't answer a question with a question."

"Can I answer with a kiss instead?"

Noah pulls me onto his lap, the couch dipping under our combined weight. His lips press against mine, a tingle spreading to my spine as our tongues caress, teasing each other. The charged energy between us never wavers. A constant current, all at the touch of our hands or the press of his lips.

I break the kiss. "Under all that attitude, you sure have the biggest heart."

"*Shh*. Don't let anyone in on our secret."

Noah kisses me stupid, my mind blanking as he shows me how he feels. I love everything about this man. He continues to throw me for a loop and surprises me whenever he can.

His lips move from my lips to my neck before trailing down the V of my polo.

"As much as I want to continue, we have dinner plans with your whole family tonight."

"They are here?" I rush to stand, leaving a lusty Noah behind.

"Better get a move on. Dinner's at seven." His dazzling smile reaches his eyes, lines showing at the corners.

I squeal and hug him before hurrying to get ready. Noah keeps to his side of the bathroom, thankfully, because he tends to distract me.

"I still can't believe you flew them out here. Santi thought about it, but my parents said no when he asked. How did you convince them?"

"Are you keen on learning my tactics?" His eyes dance from the bright lights.

I wave a hand in the air. "I became a victim of your skills a long time ago. Why hold back on me now?"

He crosses his arms and leans against the vanity. "I asked them to do it for me."

My face must show the confusion that runs through me.

Noah sighs. "I told them my parents aren't coming, and it would mean a lot to me to have my girlfriend's family here, no matter who wins. Because I would like to get to know them before I whisk you off on a two-week vacation. But most of all, it will make you happy, which in turn makes me happy."

Oh wow. Okay, I didn't expect that.

I stride toward him and wrap my arms around his neck. Looks like I get to be the distractor today because Noah's sincerity and kindness deserve all the rewards.

We made it to dinner only ten minutes late. I count our delay as a success because if someone had seen my hair after our bathroom romp, they would have called me a lost cause.

Santi scoffs at the role of a fifth wheel, choosing to become the life of the conversation instead of sitting back.

"You know when I gave Maya some rules about our trip, I didn't anticipate Noah being an issue." My brother flips through his menu.

"Isn't the first rule to never underestimate your enemy?" Noah holds back a smile.

"You got me there. I thought you were too much of a jackass for Maya. She tends to go for the nerdier guys."

"That's so not true. Name a nerd I've dated." I cross my arms. Seeing as Noah has slept with enough women to populate a small island, he can sit and handle this conversation. Mainly because I don't believe my brother's words.

"Xavier, for one."

"How was he a nerd?"

"Well, he did like to remodel those computers," my dad chimes in.

Great. Did everyone think Xavier was geeky?

"He also loved watching *The Twilight Zone* with Mami. Talked about how he posted on Reddit boards about it and stuff." Santi hits Noah with a smirk.

I see what he does here.

My mom smiles at the memory. "Such a sweet boy, offering to read the Bible with me."

My brother shoots me a look. *All right, the Bible study group was a bit weird.*

My dad joins in on the fun because why the hell not. "Don't forget about Felipe."

"What was wrong with him? Do you all have *chisme* sessions without me?"

"To be fair, he was gay." My brother hits me with a family secret I had no clue of.

Noah chokes on his wine. "You dated someone without knowing they were gay?"

My eyes narrow at him. "Seeing as this is all news to me, clearly not."

"Sorry. We have to air all two pieces of Maya's dirty laundry in case Noah wants to run in the other direction," Santi says before sipping his wine.

My mom butts in, ending Santi's game. "Noah won't run. He's liked her since Barcelona."

Noah and I look at my mom with wide eyes.

"Oh, don't look at me like that. The way you looked at my

daughter is one I recognize in my own husband. You two were just too stubborn to admit it."

My dad grumbles under his breath.

"What's that, *mi amor*?" She smiles at him.

He looks Noah in the eyes. "If he breaks her heart, I'll run him over with the car he loves more than anything."

"*Loved* more than anything." Noah sends me a wide smile that I save for my memories.

CHAPTER FORTY-TWO
Maya

Noah preps for the final Grand Prix race despite the crash two weeks ago, all smiles and jokes as the crew works in the garage. Such a badass. He landed the third position on the grid after a decent qualifying round.

Pit mechanics and engineers act as the backbone of a team, fixing any damage from Noah's previous crash; the car looks brand new with not a dent in sight. Noah thanks the crew as his fingers graze the red hood.

Worst-case scenarios flash through my mind as I hang out with Santi for his last race. I clasp my fingers in front of me, my sneakers rocking back and forth against the concrete floor. Abu Dhabi. The final Grand Prix and home of the infamous crash between Noah and my brother. With a close Constructors' Championship standing between Bandini and McCoy, it all comes down to this race.

Noah runs an unsteady hand through his hair while he talks

to the engineers. Despite me asking him about his nervousness, he feigns indifference. He gives me a quick peck on the lips before he takes off with crew members toward the track.

My brother tugs me in for a good luck hug.

"Try not to crash into my boyfriend this time," I mumble into his chest.

"I was planning on knocking Liam out. Seemed like a safer bet because that guy can't hold a grudge to save his life."

Our bodies shake from laughing. We break apart, and Santi hops into his car, waving at me as the crew pulls him away.

I hang out in pit row, preferring to be close instead of lost somewhere in the crowd. Earlier, Noah reserved grandstand VIP tickets for my parents before Santi even had the chance. My heart swelled at the look of appreciation my parents offered him, both of them unaware of how much it means to Noah to have someone rooting for his team. Noah, a man denied love and affection, craves my family's acceptance more than anything.

Race cars zipping down the track do little to calm me. Noah's car speeds by, a red blur with an engine reverberating off the walls. McCoy cars follow behind, creating a vortex of sound and dirty air.

Noah deserves the World Championship, and honestly, I want him to win, hoping it can help us overcome these worries.

Sorry, Santi. I'm loyal to my boyfriend too.

A few cars crash throughout the laps. One of the drivers from Albrecht can't catch a break this season, leaving behind a crumpled mess of a car after turn three.

Cars lap around the track. Sports announcers talk about

Noah's swift recovery after his tragic loss in Brazil, his racing a testament to his will to win. My heart taps against my chest, unrelenting during the first few laps. No hiccups yet. I take my first steady breaths once Noah makes it through his first ten laps with no issues.

Round and round cars go, careening through the track. Drivers complete laps in less than two minutes. The race rankings are close, with Bandini seconds away from McCoy, Santi trailing behind Noah with Liam in the lead. Noah's engine roars as he pulls in for a pit stop to get new tires. His last one for this season. He takes off again, spitting himself back out onto the track, eating up any time lost.

Noah completes his forty-fourth lap, only fourteen circuits left between him and the winter break. His car hangs behind Liam, putting him in second place. He can't win the World Championship if he keeps the runner-up position.

His car jerks, the movement unfamiliar. Like he hesitates. Noah's reputation for overtaking cars is missing, his usual swagger on the racetrack not coming out.

"Maya, I need you to get over here." Sophie's dad waves me over.

I don't hide my surprise when he hands me the headset that communicates with Noah. He presses the mute button, taking a deep inhale while rubbing his temple. His intense green eyes bore into mine.

"Noah wants to talk to you."

"Is that even allowed?"

He shoots me a look. "This is worth the possible race fine. Trust me."

Despite his approval, I don't reach for the mic.

James sighs. "The nerves got to him, and he thinks you can calm him down. Forget about the fine and help him out. His place in the championship rests on you working with him. If he doesn't get over this, he may never come back to race because fears like this can ruin a career."

Okay, no pressure. Understatement of the year. But I don't have a second to linger on it. I grab the headphones, situate the microphone, and unmute myself.

"Hi, this is Maya. Do you copy?" I try to imitate team radio videos that Noah and I have watched online.

Noah's chuckle sounds through the headphones. "Hi, this is Noah. I copy."

"Well, I'm going to be shit at this job. But hold on. There's a red car behind you moving pretty fast. There's one car in front of you also going exceptionally fast. About three clicks away."

"You're nailing it. Keep it up. Not sure what three clicks means but…"

I laugh into the mic. Can't wait for sports announcers to listen in and comment on our conversation.

Wanting privacy from the crew, I walk up to the railing that overlooks pit row. A television hanging above offers an overhead view of the track. Cars squeal in the distance. Useless lights blink all over the computer screen, offering me nothing but confusion.

"Hmm, there's an amazing driver with the number twenty-eight on his car. But he won't overtake the driver in front of him. What's going on?"

Noah makes it past another lap. He holds back, not acting aggressive enough to win the whole thing.

"Tell me more about this great driver. I don't know if I see him out here." His voice strains.

My heart dips at the thought of him panicking in the middle of a race. "They say Noah Slade's basically the best. Likes to break records, on the racetrack and in the bedroom. You gotta be careful with him."

He lets out a hoarse laugh.

"This is going to be a terrible team radio video. I'll end up being talked about online for sure. *Perdóname* Mami *y* Papi. Ignore this."

Noah speeds up after turning. *Good.*

"So anyway, please stop distracting me. And quit the seductive laughs too. Did you know this guy agreed to help the girl grow her vlog? He may be part of the reason she has over a million subscribers now. But I don't think the guy knows he's stuck with her. Stage-five clinger. She's already signed a contract with the team to come to the races next year, since they want her to film more behind the scenes action to promote the brand. A whole ordeal."

His voice expresses his surprise. "You didn't tell me. Congrats, Maya. I'm so proud of you. I knew you could do it. Bandini is lucky to have you working on social media."

"*Shh.* This story isn't about me." I laugh at his slipup before continuing. "Pretty crazy. Imagine the girl's surprise that number twenty-eight doesn't want to drive faster. Take more risks. He took a chance on their relationship, and it all panned out. I wonder if he could do the same thing today?" I imagine fans commenting about how cliché I am on our video. *Oh well, I won't be crying myself to sleep. At least not in that way.*

Noah's deep breathing and gear changes ring through the radio. The roar of the engine excites me. His car accelerates, pushing closer to Liam's, closing the gap between McCoy and Bandini.

"Pretty sure the girl told the guy that she doesn't date losers. But I can't be too sure about that one because I haven't asked her. But you can never put it past these racing fans, all fun and games until the guy doesn't end up on the podium. I think girls have a thing for trophies and race suits—a combo deal."

Noah chuckles into the mic. With only a few laps left to overtake Liam, the championship is starting to slip from Noah's fingers.

"But that's a lie. Because this girl loves the guy. Like the 'forever and always' type of love. The 'kids playing around outside while the parents have a quickie upstairs' kind of love. Have you heard of that type?"

He stays silent. His rhythmic breathing and the hum of the engine encourage me to continue.

"It's pretty insane. Can you imagine that kind of love? I can because I experience it. The story doesn't end with a happily-ever-after because it starts with it. Because they have the rest of their lives to finish their story. Crazy, huh?"

Noah speeds up at a turn, pushing his car to the limit, sparks flying from his rear wing. He overtakes Liam in one of the last corners.

"Great job, babe! That was an amazing one. I knew you could do it."

"Maya?" his voice rasps.

"Yup?"

"Keep talking. I love hearing your voice."

Happy to oblige.

CHAPTER FORTY-THREE
Noah

lift the American flag in the air. *World. Fucking. Champion.*

I can't thank Maya enough for helping me at the end there. Almost lost my shit behind the wheel, poorly controlled tremors running through my body until she came on the radio. But her voice and words pushed me to the limit and gave me courage.

The crowd wildly jumps around with energy and excitement. I call Maya over from the roped-off VIP section. Security guards let her through, grinning and shaking their heads as she runs up the steps of the stage and launches herself into my arms. The best hello sealed with a kiss. I twirl her around as she giggles, her arms wrapping around my neck while her addicting floral scent invades my nose. Someone passes me the trophy, and I hold it and her in my arms. One of the happiest days of my life.

Our friends shower us with champagne. Maya screams as

the cold liquid splashes against us and runs down our bodies. I drop my head back in laughter, guzzling champagne that miraculously makes it into my mouth. Fans scream as I give Maya a mind-numbing kiss that tastes like champagne and happiness.

Amazing how quickly life changes.

I thought winning the World Championship was the best thing, the only goal I had for a long time. Shit, was I wrong. I realize today that the best thing includes winning with your loved ones.

Not my shitty father. But with Maya, my team, and my friends. This is the best feeling ever.

Well, the best for now.

CHAPTER FORTY-FOUR
Maya

I f someone had told me a year ago I'd be standing on the F1 stage, hugging Noah Slade and my brother with each arm, I would have laughed until I cried. My brother stands next to me with the biggest grin on his face after placing third in the entire World Championship. He and Noah shower each other with champagne after winning the Constructors' Championship together. Old rivals hugging like friends.

Funny how life has a way of working itself out. I joined the F1 schedule because I had nothing going for me, a postgraduate with a trail of failed attempts at jobs, stuck living in my brother's shadow whether I wanted to be or not.

I can't help looking over at the man who called dibs on me, the one with wavy dark hair and blue eyes that hypnotize me. A World Champion with a heart of platinum to match the trophy he carries above his head. The same man who says "I love you" instead of "good morning" every day. A self-proclaimed "sappy motherfucker" who begged me to wear his race car number today because he needs to mark me in every single way. A human wrecking ball who came into my life unannounced and smashed through all my expectations, leaving behind rubble, dust, and a fresh start.

But most importantly, Noah Slade, the love of my life.

Abu Dhabi
Grand Grix

EPILOGUE
Maya

ONE YEAR LATER

Noah and I relax on his balcony, staring out at the Amalfi Coast, blue waters glistening under the morning sun. He messes around on his computer while I appreciate the view. I welcome the melodic sound of water splashing against the rugged coast. We hang out in our pajamas, enjoying our coffee—our morning ritual while on break.

A year has passed since Noah won his fourth World Championship. Our team radio from the Abu Dhabi Grand Prix became a viral video on YouTube, fans supporting our relationship immediately. My parents welcomed Noah into our family, taking him in, no longer allowing him to spend time meant for families alone—holidays, birthdays, the works.

F1 still plays a huge part in our lives. I travel around the world with Noah, joining him at every race. My vlog remains popular among fans. The Formula Corporation asked me to work with the other phases like F2 and F3, but Noah claims he can't win without his good-luck charm, threatening to hold me hostage if I skip out on his races.

Salty air hits me in the face, rustling my dark waves.

Did I say how much I love Noah's house in Italy? Something straight out of a movie.

I scroll through my phone to check morning updates when I get a strange notification. *Weird.*

I look up into Noah's blue eyes. "Did you click the wrong date for me to upload my next video? I got a notification that it just went live."

"I don't think so. That's strange." He shrugs.

My point exactly. He grabs his laptop and places it on the table. A black screen with an odd title plays in front of us, nothing like the uploaded video I had scheduled.

"That's not it because I picked a different thumbnail. Do you think someone hacked into my account? And what does *More to Come* even mean? I like to be punny. I'd never come up with something like that."

He chuckles. "I'm well aware. Before we report it, let's watch it."

Noah, always a thinker. Exactly why Bandini pays him the big bucks.

The video starts up with a short clip of me at Santi's first Bandini race in Australia. Someone took a video of me giving Noah a death stare. How embarrassing, but appropriate for how I felt about him at the time.

"Oh my God. Who would even upload this? Look at how

I'm staring at you. And why were you laughing behind my back?" How interesting, Noah checking me out on day one. *What a player.*

The scene changes before Noah gives me an answer. This time, a shot of us at a press conference plays. Noah grins at me while I bob my head, making fun of one of the reporters. He barks out a laugh when I roll my eyes. Liam and Santiago glance at him while reporters look around, wondering what made Noah react the way he did.

How cute of him to look at me like that. I had no idea he checked me out that much, hanging on to whatever dumb thing I'd do next. It makes me feel all warm and fuzzy.

Next scene plays, a clip from the vlog I did with Noah and his car. He sits near the cockpit while I ask him a bunch of questions. My heart warms at the clip, enjoying how he glances at me with an enamored look on his face. *Either that or he wants to take my clothes off. A true toss-up.* I never looked at the video this closely, not checking for signs of Noah liking me. Noah gives me a beaming smile when I laugh and talk into the camera. He barely pays attention, his eyes remaining on me.

My stomach flutters at the clip. I feel off-balance, being hit with many emotions at once—happiness and nostalgia mixed together.

I have an idea of who created this *More to Come* video. The big guy next to me remains suspiciously quiet, not one peep coming from his seductive lips. But I don't pause the video because questions would ruin the moment.

Another video starts, this time of the podium when Santiago won the Grand Prix in Spain. Noah ignores everything happening on the stage. He gazes off to the side, the camera panning off to find what he smiles at, catching me with my back turned, hugging my parents. The Spanish flag is draped over me as I jump up and down.

My heart beats rapidly, my throat closing up, unable to get any words out. Suppressed happy tears cloud my vision. Noah was always into me, even when I thought he was only interested in hooking up, but his eyes betray the way he's thinking about me. It's a sucker punch right in the feels.

Various video clips play, including one of me whistling at Noah as he walks down the runway in Monaco. I embarrassingly yell how I'd like to take his tux off. He winks at me, but I miss it because Sophie distracts me by covering my mouth with her hands. I'd die of embarrassment if Noah didn't squeeze my hand in a silent way of telling me he still finds me cute. Not sure how this video saw the light of day or how Noah got it in the first place. Sneaky man.

Another plays of me dancing up on the podium after the kart race Noah planned. My scream shakes the computer's speakers as Noah sprays me with champagne like a real F1 driver, even making me chug straight from the bottle. Peer pressure is a thing. I dance around on the small step, my arms thrown up in the air. Noah laughs along with me before he winks to the camera. *Ovaries, meet your master.*

His thoughtfulness makes me want to cuddle up to him and never let go. Put a "do not disturb" sign on our front door, sealing us off from the public for an unforeseeable lifetime.

The camera catches him smiling wide as he carries me over his shoulder to the car. Claps for the cameraman because he conducts a perfectly executed zoom of Noah smacking my ass. *A+ filmography.*

Damn Noah and all his cuteness. My throat feels like I swallowed a rock, unable to say much as I watch all our memories. *Why does he have to be such a sappy yet seductive man?*

Tears escape my eyes. Noah occasionally rubs them away with his thumb, my skin heating up at his touch.

He stays silent. The whole thing almost feels like too much. *Almost* being the keyword, since I need to lap up this romantic display and enjoy every second. *Duh.* I'll replay this video a hundred times—to my children, my grandchildren, my next-door neighbor. Everyone in walking distance.

A clip plays of me screaming for dear life while he drives the atrocious green Bandini car. He stares at me and laughs while one hand turns the steering wheel, our car drifting as I grip on to him like a lifeline. *Must have blacked out because I don't remember that.*

A short scene of my Tequila Talks episode plays. Noah answers the question I ask about his dream girl, but he intensely gazes at me while he responds. I stare straight at the tequila bottle and pick at the label instead of meeting his eyes.

I swear my heart has never beat this fast, questioning another cardiac arrest. A swirl of emotions churns inside me: happiness, excitement, thankfulness. A whole freaking spectrum.

The screen shows a film from a Brazilian fan based on the terrible quality and backdrop. I crack up while walking up the stairs to the Christ statue. Noah trails behind me, alternating between checking out my ass and looking up at the sky like it can answer his prayers. No such luck though because he's stuck with me.

Sappiness leaks out of me along with my tears. "Die a Happy Man" plays low in the background over the part where Noah twirls me around in the air after winning the World Championship. Our smiles mimic each other. A beautiful mess surrounds us, with champagne splashing everywhere and confetti launchers exploding on the stage.

I love this cocky, self-assured, yet equally selfless and loving man. No other can ever replace him. I never thought it was possible to love someone like this. Unyielding passion and endless appreciation. Like he hangs the moon before dancing with me under it. Noah never lets a day go by where he doesn't tell or show me how he loves me. A broken masterpiece no longer defined by his past.

Music cuts out to a black screen. I wipe the tears from my face and look over at Noah.

Except he isn't in his chair anymore.

He looks up at me with the smirk I love while he's down on one knee, holding a ring box.

THE END

EXTENDED EPILOGUE
Noah

I never imagined getting engaged.

Fuck. Really, I never imagined having a girlfriend, let alone having someone I wanted to spend the rest of my life with. But here I am, about to get married to my rival's sister. I've become domesticated as fuck with weekly family dinners and yacht trips with my future in-laws.

Okay, maybe my version of domesticated is a bit different than others. I never had genuine people to share my wealth with, and now that I've had the chance, I can't go back.

I want to share everything with Maya. Fuck prenups and shit emphasizing the potential for a relationship to fail. If my marriage ends in a divorce, Maya might as well walk away with half my shit anyway. Why the fuck not, seeing as my heart is the most valuable thing she'd take.

Sappy as shit, yet true.

I knock my knuckles against the door of our bedroom.

Our bedroom. The very one we custom made like the rest of our house. The same house we plan on raising our kids in, hopefully with Liam and Sophie living next door. Maya having her best friend a house away would make her happy, which in turn makes me happy.

Sophie opens the door an inch, not giving me much space to see inside. She eyes me skeptically from head to toe. "You're not supposed to be here."

"Why the fuck not?"

"You know the tradition." She moves to close the door, but I'm quicker, obstructing the doorway with my loafer. The same loafer that is about to walk down the aisle.

Did I mention I'm getting married today?

I scoff. "I don't believe in bad luck."

"Oh really? Too bad, so sad because your future wife does." She kicks my shiny loafer with her glittery sneaker. My foot fails to move, making her growl in frustration.

I smirk. "I thought religious people don't believe in luck."

Sophie lets out the biggest sigh of her life. "Noah, go away."

"But I want to be the first to see her."

"You missed your chance since I've seen her first. Now, shoo."

I let out an irritated breath. "Okay, I want to see her before anyone else, minus you. I'll allow the maid of honor exclusive rights to what's mine. Sharing is caring, after all."

Sophie stares me down for a solid thirty seconds. "Fine. Let me ask her. Do *not* come in here without permission."

I shoot her a wide grin. "Perfect." I remove my shoe so she can close the door.

"Stupid, pushy, entitled men." She frowns at me as she closes the door.

I tap my shoe to the beat of my heart as I wait for Sophie to speak to Maya. Fuck traditions. Everything about my relationship with Maya has been anything but traditional.

I was being honest with Sophie, wanting to see Maya first. It's not due to possessiveness. More so because I have this innate need inside of me to value every moment with her. To see her in private before any fucker gets to watch her walk down the aisle. It's no secret I'm a selfish fuck, but Maya accepts me for all my flaws, so be it.

The door to our bedroom opens. My head shoots up, catching Sophie discreetly stepping out before shutting the door again.

She shakes her head at me. "I don't know what magic voodoo your dick has, but Maya agreed to see you. Don't mess up her hair. Don't mess up her makeup. And for the love of God, don't have sex before your vows. I'll be back up in twenty minutes to take you back where you belong. You know, outside with everyone else." Sophie shakes her finger at me before walking away, the sound of her sneakers echoing down the hall.

I grip the handle with a shaky hand. The idea of a future with Maya makes me edgy with anticipation. The good kind. The best kind. The kind of high I want to chase for the rest of my life with her.

I want to be everything she needs in a partner. I've grown up with terrible examples, and I never want my family to feel the same kind of disappointment I did. To feel unloved and used because of a title and a talent.

I've gone above and beyond with everything in my life, so it's no secret I aspire to be the best husband and father one day. To be the person Maya and my future kids can count on to fight their battles and protect them. To love them unconditionally because I want to, not because I have to.

I take a deep breath and open the door. Maya looks out the window of our new backyard, giving me the chance to stare at her. And fuck do I stare. I stare so damn hard that I'm afraid I'll need glasses by the time I'm done.

The lace material of her white dress clings to her body, emphasizing the curves I love. I'm tempted to tug on her dark, wavy hair falling against her back. She turns, hitting me with what I swear is hands down the most beautiful look she has ever given me. Even better than when she told me she loved me for the first time.

Because this look? It's a silent promise that she'll love me forever.

My eyes roam over her, cataloging every last detail. A sense of happiness I've never felt before hits me, with my eyes clouding and my fingers shaking.

Me. The biggest asshole on this side of Europe, tearing up over my fiancée. I run a hand through my hair. "You look so fucking beautiful."

She drops her head back and laughs, the sound a sweet melody to my ears. I walk up to her, grabbing onto her left hand. I fidget with her engagement ring in a calming gesture to remind myself she is all mine.

For better, for worse.

For richer, for poorer.

In sickness and in health.

With orgasms forever and always.

Okay, the last part is part of our private vows. Santiago would probably pop a vein in his face if I mentioned anything related to his sister and our bedroom. Religious people—all shy and shit.

"You don't look too bad yourself, Mr. Slade." She smiles up at me. Her unoccupied hand goes to fix my bowtie before lingering on my chest. "You couldn't even follow this basic tradition, huh? Why am I not surprised?"

I lift her hand up to my lips and kiss her ring. "I plan on starting new traditions with you."

"Like what?"

"Like this one." I tug her into me, wrapping one hand behind the back of her head as I pull her lips to mine.

I kiss her with every ounce of love I feel toward her. It's an unspoken promise to love her every damn day of the rest of our lives. To be the person she can rely on most in the world, no matter how hard life may get. To offer her endless years of happiness.

The kiss is invigorating, knowing Maya's the only woman I want. Today. Tomorrow. Forever.

I pull away too soon, not wanting to ruin her makeup.

"I like your kind of traditions." Her smile hits me with a warm sensation in my heart.

"Well, I have one more."

She tilts her head at me, her curious eyes making me laugh.

"I have a little gift for the future Mrs. Slade."

Maya's eyebrow raises. "I don't think I'll ever get used to that name."

"You have decades to try." I smile as I grab onto her hand and lead her toward the bed.

"No funny business before the wedding!" She stops.

"You don't want to see my surprise?"

"I've seen everything there is to see of you already. I can promise you that."

I shake my head at her as I tug her toward the bed again. "Close your eyes."

Maya's eyes close on command. I grab onto her waist and hoist her onto the bed, letting her get in a comfortable sitting position.

She attempts to open her eyes.

"Keep them closed or you don't get your surprise."

She lets out a resigned sigh. I kneel on the floor and tug my gift out of my pocket. I lift the hem of her dress up, causing goosebumps across her skin.

I grab her left leg and slide up the custom-made garter I had created for her. Ever since I turned into a sentimental motherfucker, I really go all out. I'm a glutton for punishment, leaving a path of light kisses down her thigh until I reach the garter. She lets out a light sigh as I pull away and stand.

"Okay, all done."

She bends over and checks out her new gift. "Whoa. Explain."

I trace the garter belt. "This is made from the fabric of the Barcelona Grand Prix's checkered flag. That was the moment

I was truly screwed with you because I gave up a win to make you smile."

Maya's smile expands. "I knew it!"

"If you tell Santi, I'll deny it. I didn't know it at the time, but I was already a goner for you."

A single tear runs down her cheek as she assesses her gift.

"Shit, you're not supposed to cry." I wipe it away, hoping I didn't mess up her makeup.

"I can't help it. I love you so damn much it hurts." She looks at me with a wobbly smile.

"The good kind of hurt?" I step in between her legs, grasping her chin in my hand.

"The best kind." She runs her hands down the lapels of my tux.

I place a soft kiss on her lips. "I love you so fucking much. Enjoy your last thirty minutes as Maya Alatorre because after that, you're all mine."

She rolls her eyes. "It's only a last name."

I smirk. "No. It's only the beginning of forever."

Also By Lauren Asher

DIRTY AIR SERIES

A series of interconnected standalones

Collided

Wrecked

Redeemed

DREAMLAND BILLIONAIRES SERIES

A series of interconnected standalones

The Fine Print

Terms and Conditions

Final Offer

LAKEFRONT BILLIONAIRES SERIES

A series of interconnected standalones

Love Redesigned

Scan the code to read the books

Acknowledgments

From 2019 Lauren: Thank you to everyone who read my debut novel. I am grateful for the bloggers and readers who gave my work a chance. You deserve your own champagne shower.

From 2023 Lauren: To all those who believed me and showered my debut series with love and excitement, thank you from the bottom of my heart. This series—along with the Dreamland Billionaires—changed the course of my life, and I have you to thank for making that possible.

Mr. Smith – I am appreciative of your endless support, including the times you forced me out of my house to eat and socialize. Your patience, help, and positive words pushed me to believe in myself and pursue this dream.

Julie – You welcomed me into the book world with warmth and kindness, and I can't express my gratitude enough. You're a fantastic individual who has been an integral part of this process. Thank you!

To my beta readers – Thanks for giving my F1 world a chance. With your feedback and comments, *Throttled* became everything it is today. I am forever grateful!

Erica – If you hadn't beta read this book in 2019 and helped me build the confidence to pursue publishing, I'm not sure Throttled would be a book available around the world right now. Your everlasting impact on my life will never be forgotten.

Mary – It is crazy to think this book began it all for us. Thank you for making the most beautiful covers—and amazing memories to accompany them.

Jos – Thank you for taking a chance on my book even though it wasn't in Kindle Unlimited at the time. Incredible to think how a one-click decision created such an amazing bond between us!

Jess – Thank you for helping double check my Formula 1 facts. Your eye for details truly blows my mind, and I appreciate you!

To Christa, Dom, and everyone at Bloom Books – I appreciate you giving me the ability to share my stories with readers everywhere. It is still hard to believe an opportunity like this happened.

To everyone else who helped me during this process – Thank you from the bottom of my heart! Without you, none of this would be possible.

About the Author

Self-diagnosed with an overactive imagination, Lauren spends her free time reading and writing. Her dream is to travel to all the places she writes about. She enjoys writing about flawed yet relatable characters you can't help loving. She likes sharing fast-paced stories with angst, steam, and the emotional spectrum.

Her extracurricular activities include watching YouTube, bingeing old episodes of *Parks and Recreation*, and searching Yelp for new restaurants before choosing her trusted favorite. She works best after her morning coffee and will never deny a nap.

PRAISE

"Eloquent, insightful, and intensely engaging.
The Zipper Club is both scary and inspiring,
offering valuable perspective for all of us who have
hidden our shame and fought to appear normal. I
held my breath from the first page to the last."
ANNITA SAWYER, AUTHOR OF
SMOKING CIGARETTES, EATING GLASS

"In the way a good memoirist can, going inward
(deep into his own defective heart) in order to go
outward, Mannella reveals we're all of us members of
The Zipper Club."
BOB COWSER, JR., AUTHOR OF *GREEN FIELDS*

"Like a pitcher's muscles charged by the kinetic
chain that leads to a perfect fastball, Mannella's *The
Zipper Club* rushes the reader along his—and his
heart's—frantic journey through pride, craving, and
destructiveness, to the pivotal moment we feared
would come. A rawly honest, extraordinarily
detailed, and astonishingly beautiful account of one
hard-beating, passionate young life."
JANE ALISON, AUTHOR OF *THE SISTERS ANTIPODES*

ABOUT THE AUTHOR

Thomas Mannella was born and raised in Naples, New York, where he currently lives with his wife and sons. *The Zipper Club: A Memoir* is his first book. For more information, please visit *thomasmannella.com*.

The Zipper Club
Copyright © 2016 Thomas Mannella
All rights reserved.

Print Edition
ISBN: 978-1-925417-12-8

Published by Vine Leaves Press 2016
Melbourne, Victoria, Australia

Cover photography © abhijith3747, determined
Cover design by Jessica Bell
Zipper graphic designed by Freepik
Interior design by Amie McCracken

National Library of Australia Cataloguing-in-Publication entry (pbk)
Author: Mannella, Thomas, author
Title: The Zipper Club / Thomas Mannella
ISBN: 978-1-925417-12-8 (paperback)
Subjects: Heart--Diseases--Patients--Biography.
Heart valves--Diseases--Patients--Biography.
Dewey Number: 362.196120092

THE ZIPPER CLUB

THOMAS MANNELLA

Vine Leaves Press
Melbourne, Vic, Australia

TABLE OF CONTENTS

For Maddox and Nico, and for Missy.

"Literature is a form of fondness-for-life.
It is love for life taking verbal form."
George Saunders, *The New Yorker*

AUTHOR'S NOTE

This narrative is based on my experiences. Some names have been changed, characters combined, and events compressed. Certain episodes are imaginative re-creation, and those episodes are not intended to portray actual events.

Q. Mr. Faulkner, you seem to say that a writer should write out of the heart …

A. It's the heart that has the desire to be better than man is. It's the heart that makes you want to be better than you are. It's the heart that makes you want to be brave when you are afraid that you might be a coward, that wants you to be generous, or wants you to be compassionate when you think that maybe you won't.

From *Faulkner in the University*

THOMAS MANNELLA

PROLOGUE

Watch me drop my T-shirt on the sand. Sunglasses on, I turn and walk and after a moment I pause, staring at the water. I am twenty-eight and used to have solid abs, but now that part of me is softened, slender but with less definition.

A finger-wide scar runs from beneath my left pectoral, parallel to my ribs, wrapping around my left side and turning upward, following the edge of my shoulder blade all the way to my spine. This scar is two feet long and twenty-two years old. A twelve-inch scar runs from the top of the breastbone to four inches below the terminus of my sternum. A scar on top of a scar. Twins. Stacked, wide as a crayon line. The original, sliced through and replaced with new tissue, is twelve years old. The other is six. See how it has been stretched and is slightly wider at the top, and also flatter there from the stretching?

Look closer.

See how it is wrinkled at the bottom from the month I could not get the wound to close and heal? The month I smelled like infection. A month both years ago and always yesterday. Run your eyes along this strip of skin, the rough trench in the bone below the surface. Notice the four one-inch perpendicular scars scattered below.

For years I observed the expressions of people who believed me when I told them the scars were from an alley knifing, which is not true. What actually happened set a fire under my skin, buried me alive under hot sand, shredded my insides with a rusty serrated knife. I preferred eluding explanation so I didn't have to own up to my insecurities, atavism, fate.

I didn't own the marks; the marks owned me.

Now when somebody asks, I tell them the truth—most of the time. I share what I am able to remember. That takes longer to do because I am a little braver than I was before, and can say more.

My son, Maddox, scampers to the shoreline, his one-year-old-fingers wrapped tight around the handle of a red bucket, and, as always, my titanium heart valve clocks my time. It is a sound I used to be ashamed of and would try to hide. A sound that I have come to know and for which I am deeply thankful. The sound of my life.

Tick.

Tick.

Tick.

I watch the water.

A little voice calls to me and I turn to find it.

PART 1

THE ZIPPER CLUB

1

The first nosebleed I remember was massive and required emergency room treatment. I was five. My legs dangled over the gurney, a plastic bag of ice on my neck and a metallic slickness on my tongue. The towel against my nose sopped with blood, but more than blood gushed out of me. Like floodwater after a storm, the torrential flow rushed away the feeling that bad things could never happen to me, as well as my parents' perceptions of healthy, safe children. Over the coming years it would carry off pieces of my innocence like debris up the funnel of a cyclone. The hot blood flowed into the towel and I got older quickly. I got scared.

This moment is a vestigial memory preceding my first hospital stay in May of 1988. I attempt to grasp it now, like wind rushing through my fingers.

"A portion of his aorta is constricted," the doctor had told my parents. This narrowing increased the blood pressure in my upper body, and so, while eating a Happy Meal, blood had poured out of my nose and onto my tray, mixing with the ketchup in which I dipped my French Fries, and, with shocking speed, drowned Ronald MacDonald on the paper placemat.

I needed surgery to remove the coarctation.

At my pre-operation appointment, a plump nurse held my tiny forearm against her skin and stabbed it with needles. My parents signed paperwork, some of which acknowledged that the surgery could be fatal.

"Highly unlikely, of course," the doctor said. He used blue and red ink to draw a tornado of arrows on diagrams of the heart. He charted normal and abnormal blood flow

through the chambers, before-and-after pictures, me now and me later. The narrow piece of my aorta would be removed and the two ends of the tube spliced together.

"Will the scar eventually go away?" Dad asked. I slouched in his lap, my head on his chest, and felt his deep voice resonate like a protective lullaby only his touch could deliver. "Will it fade?"

"The scar will be there forever," the doctor said.

I spent the night prior to surgery in the hospital and received the first of many toys to assist my recovery. A plastic walking eyeball accommodated my need for the gruesome and shocking: its guts hung out of its chest and green warts cauliflowered its lips. I cuddled this action figure, making space for its head on my pillow.

I was no longer inviolable so Mom, who allowed me to experience measures of independence whenever possible, slept on a cot in my room. I saw her squinting through the dark to where I hugged my new mutant. Surely my parents had explained to me the reason for my visit, but how could I comprehend the severity of the situation? I rolled away from her. The stiff hospital linens tugged at my Teenage Mutant Ninja Turtle pyjamas, my brown hair. Beyond the privacy curtain the nurses' station glowed. I spun the plastic wristband to read my name and then reached out to part the drapes. A lone custodian swabbed the floors with antiseptic water, and dipped his mop into a yellow wheeled bucket again and again until he rolled out of sight. I let go of the curtain and waited as long as I could, and then rolled back toward Mom. My eyes adjusted to the darkness and found hers, still staring at me.

The next morning Dad helped me slip my arms into a papery hospital gown and Mom cinched the cloth strings in a bow at my back. Most of all, I wanted to go home to Naples, New York, the small Finger Lakes town in-between

the hills where I grew up. I wished I was instead playing with my little brother, Nicky, in our backyard, picking blackberries from the tangle of thorny bushes behind the garage, killing the yew along the porch with our Kool-Aid piss, or chucking black walnuts into the sky and fleeing before they returned to Earth. Dad paced between the window and the door to my room, and Mom combed her blonde hair. The minutes burned fast, like fire eating straw. I wanted another cartoon. Another night to sleep. Another hug.

Then, I was wheeling through bright hallways, my parents walking alongside my gurney. A lumpy heat burned the back of my throat. If I moved under the blanket I might cry. I took a deep breath to push away my tears. No matter how easily Dad smiled his squinty-eyed smile or Mom ran her hand against my cheek, I was aware of the forthcoming separation. I didn't know the word at the time to define this aching presence, but travelling to the operating room felt like an abduction. Mom was an arm's length away but she might as well have been on the moon.

The OR was behind schedule. All of the proper waiting rooms were occupied so the bed-driver ushered us into a supply closet. This raised my hopes that the whole deal was off and I could go home to show Nicky my new toy—check out the cracked yellow toenails, I'd say!

Like a sudden clap of thunder a nurse knocked on the door.

"Time to go."

We said goodbye, and then I was on the move, alone.

In the OR I didn't have time to cry. "We don't want you to be the *only* one who doesn't look silly in there," a nurse said, adjusting a hairnet on my head.

The transportation team parked my bed against the operating table and lowered the side rails. I closed my eyes.

Machines hummed. Water spattered in a sink. Laughter cut through the beeps of various volumes and frequencies. *The hairnet*, I thought.

"You just hold still, honey," another attendee said in a voice muffled by a paper mask. She rolled me on my side, scooted me to the edge of the bed, and then settled me on my back again, this time on the operating table. I was stiff and cold. Nylon straps crossed my legs and waist and two buckles clicked. *Abduction*. A blanket settled over me. I shivered. With a large Q-tip, the nurse painted the left half of my chest the colour of water poured from a rusty can.

"Hello, there." A wide mask, neck, and chest appeared overhead. "I'm going to help you take a nap. What flavour you want: grape bubblegum, cherry, or cotton candy?"

This nurse's question paralyzed me. I said nothing.

"Bubblegum's what most people choose."

"Okay."

"All you have to do is breathe." He fitted a plastic mask over my mouth and nose. The soporific did taste like grape bubblegum and before I could wonder how long it would take to work, darkness fell over me.

2

My family later told me that the nurses updated them in the waiting room. Then the surgeon himself appeared. Before he spoke a word my parents began sobbing. They assumed I was dead. He hastily explained that the smoothness of the procedure allowed him to visit.

The operation took all day and when the bubblegum spigot dried up, familiar voices wobbled through my mind. Each waking glimpse revealed flashes of brightness as my bed clipped along under the corridor lights, my world framed by talking heads and IV bags on poles. Someone joked that, after I was discharged, the wires connecting me to the machines would stretch from the hospital all the way home. I might have chuckled were I not so desperately parched. Finding my lips and tongue, I murmured, "Thirsty."

"We'll get you some ice chips in a short while," a nurse said, apparently oblivious to my dehydration. Her cheerfulness conveyed understanding, though I doubt she understood. I was so thirsty that I would have given her my mutant eyeball *and* my brother for the opportunity to lick condensation off a toilet tank.

In a swirl I arrived in the ICU. Sun flooded through a window and this light greased my dreams of the neighbourhood fun I was missing. I chewed ice chips served in plastic cups, which did little to slake my thirst or hunger, and wondered if my brother and friends were building forts and battling our imaginary enemies while waiting for my return.

After a few days I transferred to the paediatric cardiology ward. In this strange place, I was scared into politeness by

the unfamiliarity of my surroundings, the intermittent presence of my family, and the uncertainty of the duration of my stay. My manners earned me extra attention and sympathy; a night nurse even made me a puppet out of a latex glove that looked like a ghost rooster.

In her bid to document my childhood, Mom became a devoted photographer and heart surgery was a prime subject. Whenever I groaned about her camera, she responded, "They're for the museum—you know, after you become President. Now put your arm around your brother."

Among the photos from this time is a shot of Dad in bed with me. His hair is black, his polo shirt pink, his body muscularly slender. His feet overreach the end of the bed and his presence all but swallows me. I was responsible for the large splotches of perspiration under his arms. That morning, the bandages covering the continuous locking stitch of my incision were removed.

"This might be a little painful," the cheerful nurse said, "so if you need to rest, just say, 'rest.'"

If by "say" she meant "scream with the ferocity of someone being lowered into a vat of boiling oil, bringing the suffering party to the brink of unconsciousness without causing death," then I followed her instructions perfectly.

"Rest!" I howled, again and again.

The nurse spoke softly.

"You're doing great."

"Rest!"

"I know it hurts."

"Rest!"

"I'm so, *so* sorry."

"REST! REST! REEEEEST!"

My mind and skin were on fire. Dad was melting. He paced back and forth, rubbing his face in his hands, because sometimes only words are available and they are an insuf-

ficient medicine.

I screamed louder before the nurse even grasped the edge of the bandage. Its adhesive qualities acted like trillions of microscopic sutures bonding bandage to skin. One might have picked up an airplane with a small square of the tape that encased my left side.

I remember the moment the nurse finished. She snipped the knot at the end of the thread that stitched me together and, from nipple to spine, the line slipped through my skin in a fluid tickle.

"You're a member of the zipper club now," she said.

 THOMAS MANNELLA

From my elementary school, where Mom also taught second grade, I received garbage bags full of gifts: nuggets of pyrite and a turkey feather; the Ghostbusters' vehicle, Slimer, and a bucket of slime; a cassette tape titled "The Witch of Naples"; flowers and chocolate chip cookies; and balloons and cards enough to paper the walls. The girls in my kindergarten class drew us holding hands under the sun and rainbows; the boys drew us shooting each other with machine guns, blood gushing from the holes. The bandage fiasco faded with each pile of loot delivered to the hospital.

I walked around the nurses' station for exercise. To soften the violence of coughing or laughing or sneezing, which strained the incision, I held a bundled towel to my side. There was also a breathing device to expand my lungs—a plastic cylinder with a ball inside attached to a tube that I sucked on, trying to lift the ball as high and for as long as I could. I walked a strip of medical tape on the wall with the fingers of my left hand, stretching the tightness from my side, reaching higher and higher to my family's praise. They marked each new apex with a black pen. This progress was observable from my bed, like the interlocking teeth of a zipper. I counted the lines and began to understand that I was healing.

One day Nicky visited with important news.

"You missed it," he said.

I knew this would happen.

"What?"

"Hail."

I didn't know what he referred to, but was crushed.

"Don't worry, I saved you some in the freezer," Mom said. "The biggest anybody had ever seen." I couldn't wait to touch my piece of the sky. Mom reached for her camera and nodded toward Nicky saying, "Put your arm around your brother and smile like you love each other."

When it was time for everyone to leave I leaned over the bedrail, kissed Nicky, and jealously watched his cow-licked head bob out the door. Without Dad beside me I felt small in the bed. Mom tucked the blankets under my legs tightly, so that my heels touched together. Even though I knew I would be discharged the next morning, lonesomeness rolled in like a thundercloud. I wanted to go with Mom to Naples. To sit beside Papa in his rocking chair, holding half a book with my left hand, the other half in his right. To hear Grandma say, "You have a face only a mother could love." To dig networks of matchbox car tunnels in the dirt and bury my feet under the sand at the lake. To walk by Sutton's Spoons on Main Street, where fishing tackle and Woolrich vests were displayed in the powdery window-panes, and the green and white striped awning sagged after storms, its hem filled with old rainwater warmed by the sun, waiting for me to swat and douse Nicky.

Mom kissed my forehead and each of my eyes, and then was gone.

I had never felt so alone.

Closing my eyes, I held tightly to my coughing pillow and waited for the dreaming sleep that would carry me like paper in the wind to tomorrow and all that I loved.

On the one-year anniversary of my surgery, Dad took me to my first baseball game, the Rochester Red Wings vs. the Columbus Clippers at Silver Stadium. Our seats were behind home plate and we spent much of the game talking to a scout with a radar gun who sat in front of us clocking pitches. I ate cotton candy and the peanut shells piled up at Dad's feet. By the time the stadium lights blinked on we were walking across the gravel lot to the car.

"So, how was that?" Dad asked.

"Maybe we can bring Nicky next time."

Driving home, the summer sky faded from blue to a deep black sliding off the car windows. The dashboard glowed. Even though Mom had told him not to, Dad cracked the sun roof and lit a cigar. I settled in, enjoying the sweet burn of the cigar and the leather seats and the cool June air, the wind ripping overhead, and the stars in the sky. Sleepy and comfortable, I almost nodded off, but a star came loose and fell across the opened roof.

"Dad, did you see that?"

His cigar was a small nub now, pinched between his teeth. He blew smoke out of the corner of his mouth and stared at the road ahead. Everything was quiet except for the wind and the world above.

I knew that, having seen the star fall, I was allowed to make a wish. My thoughts turned to my friends and school. In the year since my surgery, my neighbourhood play had resumed its uninterrupted vigour. Balls to throw. Sticks to transform to sorcerers' staffs with magic words. Cat crap to excavate from the sandbox, and pinecones to

collect and stockpile in our forts on the margins of the neighbourhood. I was oblivious of my own history, lost in the enduring present of our collective imaginations.

At recess I sweated enough for Mom to pack me an extra T-shirt to change into. My classmates and I were allowed only seconds at the water fountain, which was never long enough for me because I wanted to delay changing in front of anyone. Self-conscious about my incision, I didn't want anyone to tease me or think of me as different. Weird. Ugly. Although I couldn't have put it into words, I had hoped to prevent everyone from discovering a secret defect about me. So I lingered at my desk or near the window until my friends finished drinking and sat on the carpet to listen to my teacher read a story. Then I wandered to the boys' closet. I opened the cubby door so slowly and quietly I could feel my heart beat. I held my breath and reached into the dark for my backpack on its hook. I unzipped it and felt inside for the fresh T-shirt, careful as a member of a bomb squad. I wanted nothing to blow up. Now came the hard part. I looked to the reading corner to make sure nobody watched me. Then I turned away and shut myself in the closet as much as I could without actually getting inside. I *would* have gotten inside if I weren't so tall. Concealing my scar behind the door, I wrestled out of the sweaty T-shirt, careful not to bump the door open with my elbow, and quickly pushed my head and arms into the new one.

One day I realized I had been unsuccessful in concealing my scar.

My best friend, Dave Irwin, and I sat on either side of Missy at lunch. Compared to us, she was tiny, blonde-haired and blue-eyed. She was beautiful and we had fallen in love with her on the first day of first grade. Since there were two of us and only one of her, the only logical thing was to make her choose.

"What you have to do," I said to her, "is pick one of us to be your boyfriend." We had decided this over the weekend while playing *Super Mario Bros.* on Nintendo at his seventh birthday party.

I had done all I could to win Missy's love. In class I sat the same way she did with one arm on my desk holding my pencil, the other in my lap. When she dangled her legs under the chair, I tried to do the same, and even though mine were too long I held my knees in the air, and did my best to swing-away. I prayed she noticed my devotion. I rushed to stand by her in line for art, music, lunch, the bathroom, the library, the drinking fountain, tried to sit next to her on the carpet during story time, our knobby knees almost touching. I answered our teacher's questions and looked at Missy to make sure she noticed. I exhausted myself scoring runs in recess kickball. I stared at the ribbon tied in her hair and waited for her to speak to me.

In bed at night I imagined she lay beside me and, consumed in waking dreams, I bubbled with smiles and warmth, the blankets becoming soft grass and my ceiling the stars and the moon. In my dreams our hands clasped. We did not speak or even look at each other because that was unnecessary; our love, I imagined, was incommunicable.

"I pick Dave," she said.

I knew why immediately: she had seen me changing my T-shirt. It never occurred to me that maybe she thought Dave was cute, funny, or strong, kicking his soccer ball farther than everyone else on Field Day. He carried Missy's lunch tray to the dishwashing window and together they chose a new table where they could sit across from each other for the rest of their lives.

So, riding home from the baseball game with Dad that night, I wished I had never had a scar.

5

Papa built a wood-panelled bar in his study. The back bar walls were mirrored, German steins and sword swizzle sticks lined the shelves, and martini glasses dangled from the ceiling. Sometimes I tested my luck with the nickel slot machine on the bar top, pulling the lever for all hearts. *Ding. Ding. Ding.* Two Mexican pistols hung on the opposite wall above a sabre disguised as a glittering gold cane. There was a large TV, surround sound speakers, and the rocking chair where I learned to read. The Rec Room. Here, surrounded by his records and remotes, books and booze, Papa was most comfortable. A classical music aficionado. War veteran. Scholar.

Macho.

I raced my Matchbox car around the corner of the bar and a black handle on the bottom shelf caught my eye. Tucked behind a carton of copper BBs was a shining handgun and it looked exactly like the one the A-Team's Hannibal used to shoot bad guys on TV. I could tell it was heavy without picking it up. I reached for it. Tested my grip on the handle. Fingered the trigger. Papa turned down the TV volume and stood. I clumsily stowed the gun. I had admired the antique rifles hanging on the basement wall. I coveted the Swiss Army Knife dangling from a hook in the kitchen. I knew Papa had served in Europe in World War II and, impressed by his arsenal, I couldn't contain my excitement.

"Papa," I said, "What's this gun for?" I imagined him sniping villains on rooftops, parachuting into battle while discharging round after round into enemy lines, defending

pretty girls like Missy. Heroic stuff.

"This gun?" Papa said, retrieving the weapon. "I use it to shoot cats." He placed it high on a shelf beside the steins and swizzle sticks. I imagined Nicky's cat, Cello, caught in the crosshairs.

"Cats?"

"Yes," he said, "stray cats that crap in my yard." He shaped his fingers into a gun and aimed it at a cat eating Friskies in a TV commercial. "Bang," he said.

I was horrified. He holstered his finger gun, leaving me to follow his gimpy swagger into the kitchen for lunch.

Maybe I wanted Papa to be a war hero so badly because that is what *I* wanted to be, to earn Missy's love, to not be scarred, defective—to be brave. In our boyhood quest to be tough, *to be men*, Nicky and I made a survival kit, a duffel bag stuffed with supplies that could sustain us in the wilds surrounding our home. We had no guns. Instead we provisioned bandaids and black electrician's tape for treating flesh wounds; lengths of twine from our neighbour's horse barn for detaining enemies; matches from a tin canister in Mom's pantry for fires; dog biscuits from Irwin, for sustenance (because we were roughing it); pencil-drawn maps that marked the summit of East Hill, the creek, the cemetery, our house. The prized possession of the kit was Papa's multi-tool pocketknife.

"Be careful," Grandma had said when she handed it over. She probably hoped the knife would keep us out of her kitchen. When Papa saw us sharpening the tip of our hunting spear with it, he said, "I'll have to show you *my* knife." Of course, it was *our* knife now and we performed many emergency surgeries in the woods with it. Amputations. Appendectomies. Lobotomies. Tracheotomies. Transplants. Nicky and I were prepared for anything. The knife was vital, isolated as we were within our imaginations

and dependent upon our wits for survival.

Possessing a scar that wrapped around my side from sternum to spine, I was the patient. I removed my shirt and revealed the gummy white line from my heart surgery. In the forest with Nicky, I felt more comfortable about my scar than anywhere else. There were no secrets between us. So I laid on a mattress of leaves, the roots of a maple tree my pillow, the terraced hillside of an abandoned vineyard a reclining hospital bed. Nicky pressed the cold steel of the dull blade to my skin and opened me up, re-enacting my aortic coarctation operation or whatever procedure was necessary that day.

I always survived.

6

Pete Linton rigged a ladder to ease our approach over the chain link fence to the high school athletic fields, specifically the cinderblock wall of the swimming pool, on which the outline of a soccer goal was painted. Irwin, Pete, Nicky, and me, kicking the ball against the wall for hours after school. One of us occasionally booted the ball onto the second story roof. Although an impressive display of power for a fifth-grader, this achievement ended the game until a school custodian could retrieve it. The idea of getting the ball ourselves didn't occur to us—at least not right away.

One Saturday we awakened at the rising of the sun, filled our bellies with Cheerios and toast, Fruit Roll Ups and Little Debbie Cakes—whatever was closer and most easily swallowed—and exploded out our doors, shoelaces dangling, or hopping one-footed as we pulled and stomped on permanently tied sneakers, racing down our driveways, bits of early light touching our cheeks, the crumblings of sleep stuck in the corners of our eyes, bed-head feathers waving in the breeze, the anticipation of hours of wall ball so glorious that we sprinted through our neighbourhood screaming at the top of our lungs at 7:00 a.m.

A few minutes after arriving at the wall, I blasted the ball onto the roof.

"Dang it!" Pete said.

He placed his hands on his hips and walked to the wall. A drainage pipe ran from roof to ground. Pete grasped it and tugged. It appeared secure. He gripped the pipe, knuckles scraping against the sandpapery blocks, and shimmied his way twenty feet to the top. In a fluid motion he reached for

the gutter, pulled himself onto the roof and disappeared. Moments later he smiled down on us, bright eyes and white teeth. A sunny glow spread behind him. I squinted. He disappeared and then, miraculously, the soccer ball sailed down to us.

A few nights later, at Little League, we experienced another phenomenon.

Pete's dad, Mr. Linton, coached our team. He wore the same cap that we all did, the same blue T-shirt that was our uniform. His jeans had holes in the knees with strings of dangling denim. His white sneakers were grass-stained at the toes from mowing the ball fields. He directed us from the first base coaching box.

"Play's to first!" he shouted, cupping his large hands around his mouth. When we overthrew the extended mitt and the ball skidded into the weeds, he tucked his scorebook under his arm and clapped his hands. "We'll get it next time." He was six and a half feet tall. When he spoke to us, he took a knee and looked us in the eyes.

"Time!" he called, and gathered us at the mound after we squandered our lead and walked the bases loaded with one out. Wayne Pirmann, our pitcher, pounded the ball into his glove. I removed my catcher's mask. Bubblegum snapped and the team fidgeted.

"I need you all to listen," Mr. Linton began. "This is important. Two old men had been best friends for years, and they both live to their early 90's, when one of them suddenly falls deathly ill. His friend comes to visit him on his deathbed, and they're reminiscing about their long friendship, when the dying man's friend asks, 'Listen, when you die, do me a favour. I want to know if there's baseball in heaven.'"

Mr. Linton knelt beside Pete and draped his arm around his son's shoulders. "The dying man said, 'We've been

friends for years, this I'll do for you.' And then he dies. A couple days later, his surviving friend is sleeping when he hears his friend's voice. The voice says, 'I've got some good news and some bad news. The good news is that there's baseball in heaven.'"

Mr. Linton paused, glanced around.

"'What's the bad news?' the surviving friend asks."

"'You're pitching on Wednesday.'"

We busted up.

"Don't worry—we've got the last at bat," he said, ending our powwow. "Throw home first."

"Play ball!" the ump shouted.

The next pitch passed me. I found the ball in a cloud of dirt and threw to Wayne, who covered home. He tagged out the runner trying to steal. Two outs. And, as was customary in our league, there was confusion on the base paths. Pete screamed for the ball and when he received it, dashed toward a bewildered runner between second and third and planted the tag. We cheered wildly, amazing ourselves with our swift-thinking, our mighty arms, and our destined victory.

Joyful chaos erupted from the dugout. We turned our caps inside-out for the rally, freshened our bubblegum, jumped, screamed, pounded the cinderblock walls, and nearly blew the roof off the joint. We tried our best to rip the protective chain link fence off the front of the dugout. Was somebody video-taping this for the news? Were major league scouts in the bleachers, anticipating greatness? Did they have their radar guns ready to clock the incredible speeds of the pitches we were about to crush over the fence, one after another after another without mercy?

Our first batter swung at the first pitch, nudging a sleepy fly ball to the shortstop. Out number one. On the bench we focused on the yelling and cheering and protective-

chain-link-fence-demolishing, on the parades and confetti that would soon be ours.

In an 0-2 hole, our second batter flailed at what should have been ball one. Two outs. Our cheering edged toward pleading but there was still one more chance and with that shred of hope we attached baseballs to the upturned bills of our inside-out hats with wads of Bazooka Joe and sustained the rally one more time.

Pete stepped into the batter's box. The chalk lines were erased and, even though his feet were already buried in the ruts, he scraped his cleats back and forth, digging in. The other team disbanded from a meeting on the mound. There was a lull in our noise-making and through the cinderblock walls, crickets chirped, keeping time among the clover and dandelions in the fading evening light.

We were not prepared for the coming events.

Their pitcher was rattled and after working the count to three balls and no strikes, we were back to shrieking, assuming that Pete would take the next pitch and then walk to first base as the potential winning run.

"A walk's as good as a hit," Mr. Linton said, clapping.

But Pete swung at a low pitch and lined a shot into right field. He was off. We screamed our vocal chords raw as he approached first base with no sign of slowing down. The right-fielder scooped the ball, fumbled it, scooped it again and threw to second. Pete was only halfway there when the ball hopped off the dirt toward the infielder's mitt. Our words exploded from the dugout in multi-coloured capital-ized jagged dialogue bubbles, like in the original Batman and Robin television show: *SLIDE! POW! GO BACK TO FIRST! CRACK! GO GO GO!* We were electric and Pete was, too. Sparks flew off the fence and arched from the clouds in the sky to the backstop to the soles of his shoes. He was a flash of lightning, a boom of thunder, as he

gained speed around second base. The infielder swiped at the air around our hero's white-hot ankles, setting his glove on fire, melting his hand, and the searing light burned us blind like a spotlight of blazing mercury. Halfway home, with no regard for the whereabouts of the baseball whatsoever, Pete continued to outrun the final out. His determination washed over us like a Gatorade shower. The infielder overthrew the third baseman and it was really happening—Pete was in fact rounding third base, stomping home plate, continuing to run without slowing down until we were all together in a squirming pile on the dirt where the dugout used to be before it disintegrated under the pressure of our decibels.

The following week, I clung to this moment, turning the vitality of it over and over in my mind as evidence that Pete was still alive. But, no matter how forcefully each of his heroic footsteps beat the base paths in my memory, his death was the inevitable coda that cut me each time. I didn't know where to put that feeling, how to patch it up or hide it away. I could not fix it with Papa's knife. It could not be controlled, only endured—another scar.

7

It was the sort of accident everyone should have seen coming, knowing the audaciousness that filled Pete's veins. The idea was to play the game to take our minds off of everything. We were only ten, maybe eleven years old. We did not speak while warming up. Under the low gray clouds of a sticky June evening, some of us hid our faces in our mitts. We chewed the leather strings to mush. Mosquitoes hummed near our ears and bit our necks, our scrawny biceps, the soft bare flesh behind our knees. We didn't care. I hoped it would pour so we could quit and go home. It didn't. I pulled the brim of my cap low over my red eyes.

Who knew the score? Were we losing by ten runs? Twenty? Wasn't there a mercy rule? Pete was scheduled to pitch. Thick smoke from the concession stand grill pushed down on me where I crouched behind the plate. I caught ball four again, and another run was forced home.

"Time," Mr. Linton said and we ambled out to the mound. Wayne's face was streaked with tears. Mr. Linton towered above us and through glistening eyes searched the diamonds, the surrounding hills, the warm breezes passing through the branches of the maple trees beyond the splintering outfield fences. The breath of the wind was a magic we felt but could not understand. It was the calming gentleness of untainted boyhood. Then it was gone.

Standing on the pitcher's mound, I thought about a photograph on our refrigerator. Pete, Irwin, Nicky, and me, posed atop a pile of snow taller than a school bus. Snow-panted and scarfed to our eyeballs, that day we had

made the most of it, wrestling each other off the top and launching snowballs at passersby.

"Hey!" I remembered Irwin whispering, his cheeks burning red. "Get ready!"

Miranda, the most beautiful girl we had ever seen, was walking by. Pete told us how he had kissed her, which we knew was true because he was bold in a way that none of the rest of us could ever be.

"FIRE!" Irwin commanded, a moat of snot running over his upper lip and into his mouth. Snowballs disintegrated in midair from the force of the explosions, raining shrapnel on our unsuspecting target, and others burst at her feet. Miranda stopped walking and turned to face us, smiling and waving a cotton-candy-coloured mitten, her shiny black hair spilling from under her knit hat, like delicious strands of liquorice. We threw wildly, off our heels, two-handed, without even looking, but our supply depleted rapidly. Pete rose and spread his feet for balance, clutching the ice ball we'd been spitting on all morning to make solid.

"Hi guys," Miranda said sweetly. "What are you doing up there?"

She was pure evil.

The snowy street flared in the sunlight and time warped into slow motion. All sounds were silenced. In one magnificent motion, because he loved us more than he loved Miranda—first kisses be damned—the ice ball rocketed from Pete's hand and, as if we were underwater, made contact without a sound. Nobody cheered. Miranda crumpled to the ground like a sheet settling onto a mattress. She lay on the sidewalk and stiffened. I imagined the ice packing into the shape of her ear. I imagined broken bones. Blood. Death. Miranda's mouth was open and she was crying without making a sound as we cowards escaped into the network of tunnels we had burrowed into the snow-

drifts, crawling all the way back to Pete's fort where we waited for our mothers to find us.

Standing on the pitcher's mound, I wanted to return to that snowy day. I wanted to hide under the snow with Pete and Irwin and Nicky while all the trouble blew by. I wanted to be together. Or, if not that day, then another winter day at the fort, when Pete stood outside the railing, one foot on the deck, the other on the roof of his neighbour's garage, smiling at us, his hands in his snow pants pockets, saying, "Check this out." He worked his way around the outside of the railing to the soccer field side of the fort, facing us, and shimmied backward so that he only touched the deck boards with the toes of his boots. He crouched and leapt backward, throwing himself into the sky. With an airy, reckless beauty, he seemed to ride an invisible current, an unseen stream of energy to which he gracefully submitted his body, arching away from us and floating like a cloud in the air above the distant high school bell tower before falling, falling, falling, and the puff of his body popping a drift. He waved his arms and legs to make a snow angel, wings growing at his sides.

Standing on the mound, I was angry at Pete because he died. This feeling slashed at my heart. Then I was angry at myself for being angry at him because I loved him so much. But there was nothing on which to focus my anger and confusion. There was only a moment a few evenings ago when phones rang at all our homes at supper time. *There's been an accident at school.* Soccer ball. *The roof over the pool.* Soccer ball. *I'm so sorry to tell you.* For some time after, we were terrified whenever the phone rang.

Walking to school the morning after Pete died, we had passed his house, and instead of picking him up, we looked through his backyard, at the fort, through the chain link fence and over the soccer fields to the cinderblock pool

wall, the outline of the goal, the pipe that ran up from the ground to the edge of the roof, to the top of the world and beyond, like a branch reaching for the light. Small towns compress landmarks into single visions. We started walking again and turned away from school, toward a nearby maple Pete liked to climb. I still do not know whose idea it was, putting Papa's knife to tree bark, this small act of remembrance. Three boys and four initials. Puffy letters like clouds in the sky.

Standing on the mound, I had these thoughts, and those of Pete running home.

8

One afternoon during the following autumn I left school in the fading light, walking past the soccer fields and the village road that lead to our childhood homes, toward Pete's maple. My sneakers scuffed the sidewalk and, in the distance, somebody kicked a ball off the wall. In some outlying place the smoke of the coming season plumed from a brush pile in the tangy vineyard air. Finally, at the melding tree, I drew my hand across the bark that scabbed over our initials. I grabbed a hold of a branch, nobody to give me a boost, and pulled myself off the ground, grabbed another, then climbed higher and higher through the branches that reached out from the trunk like the veins and arteries of a circulatory system, reaching upward in the syrupy amber light until I could climb no higher. I settled into a crook in the limbs. I watched the sun dip behind the hills, thankful for the gentle breeze passing through the tree, through me, and all I wanted was to listen to the echo of that ball in the coming darkness, forever.

I was eleven years old.

Pete would never be older than eleven.

I missed him.

Irwin, Nicky and I talked about Pete whenever we were together. We sometimes packed lunches in our survival kits and hiked up to the cemetery to be near him. On the hill, I was unnerved by the immensity of the sky. I feared floating away into the vast spaces above, disappearing into the atmosphere forever, yet I spent many afternoons on my back searching the wispy language of the clouds.

Every night Mom prayed for us to be healthy and safe,

but I was troubled to think that Pete's parents had done the same for him, too. I also knew that I would soon reach an age—twelve—that I would not have reached without heart surgery in kindergarten. Because of this, Pete's death pushed me beyond missing him and feeling sad. Now I wondered about my own death. Twelve seemed like a limit that I was about to pass and I needed to know everything would be okay on the other side.

Beyond the slope of the cemetery hill, the fields and vine-yards patched the valley floor like the fabric of a monk's stole. To the north, clouds spilled out of the space above the lake. On one occasion, our sky searching was affirmed when thick rays of light escaped a bright seam in the clouds, beaming down and tracing the earth with an illuminating finger. The rays paused on us. Flushed with warmth and light, we squinted.

Nicky and I called these Jesus Rays. Riding to church in the Chevy wagon with Mom one morning, we noticed them striking the hills. Giggling, Nicky turned to face me in the back seat, holding his hands above his head, palms open toward the light. He raised his brows, rolled his eyes backward in their sockets, and released holy arpeggios.

"Ahhhahhhahhhahhhahhhahhhmeeeeeeeeeen," he sang in a minor key.

I laughed.

"Nicholas Mannella!"

"What, Mom? I'm praying." He pointed. "See, Jesus Rays."

"That is *not* praying."

The architect of St. Januarius Church designed a grape leaf-shaped roof. From the ridge, the shingles sloped downward like leaf blades, and the pews inside were acutely angled toward the altar like veins. The thick concrete walls were speckled from floor to ceiling with a

thousand multi-coloured, paten-sized glass panes representing the variety of grapes grown in our valley. But, to Nicky and me, this was The Jellybean Church.

I sat in the hard wooden pews each week and observed the elderly parishioners: saggy-skinned Judge Cribb, drooling in the front pew; Gladys Jones with her walker and hissing oxygen tank; a guy with bib overalls whose pacemaker ticked during homilies; Ralph Parker, whose drunk grandson levelled the mailboxes on both sides of our street last year with his granddad's Cadillac; a short Honduran lady to whom I was never introduced, but who always smiled at me like a close relative; Guy, the owner of the hardware store, whose three-legged dog hobbled the streets of town as if looking for the missing limb; and the intimidating Ethel Gottschalk.

She waited in the back, often flashing me a dentured smile, which I reluctantly returned in exchange for a doughnut and hot chocolate before Sunday school after Mass. The establishment of the slightest greeting was a tremendous risk. Avoiding eye contact with her until after the host and wine were carried up the aisle for the priest to bless was critical; to do so before communion meant flirting with captivity. Sometimes she greeted me at the door and asked if I would bring the gifts to the altar.

"I've two seats saved for us." She stared into my eyes with a face as pitted as the church's concrete walls. Ethel smelled like cigarettes and liked to hug. She was buxom, too, making the smothering especially unpleasant. I couldn't say no to Ethel. I feared suffocation almost as much as disapproval. Everyone in the pews sought an eternity in Heaven, and I wanted to make a positive impression, especially on people like Ethel, who had a better chance of reaching St. Peter first and could put in a good word for me. I also recognized the possibility that God loved me and cared

about me and had fixed my heart. If so, I owed him big-time for helping the doctor find the problem and for my aorta being successfully repaired. In Sunday school, we had learned that the blood of St. Januarius-Gennaro, patron saint of Naples, Italy, had been gathered as a relic after his martyrdom. In an event known as The Blood Miracle, this sample liquefies annually, defying what is scientifically known about blood: soon after it is removed from the body it coagulates and spoils. Of all the saints, perhaps Januarius was who I needed to protect me, he of holy blood and powers greater than science.

The readings, gospels, and homilies bored me. The music was pleasing at times, but usually droning. I was too ignorant to understand what such a religion could do for me—a channel to access myself and accept my own flaws and the flaws of others—and that limited my motivation to try to understand it. I was only eleven. As far as I knew, God was the best shot I had at communicating again with Pete, as well as a safeguard against future heart problems. I felt I *must* pray to get what I wanted: to demonstrate appreciation for my life, to be healthy, to make up for being damaged, to keep people from thinking of me as different.

Delivering the gifts did have two advantages. For one, Ethel and I sat in padded folding chairs, not pews, and sit is all we did. The other parishioners shifted their weight, kneeling and standing, for what seemed an eternity.

Secondly, in the padded seats I could observe the entire swath of jellybeans. This was no reward at five o'clock Mass on Saturdays in December or the holy days on which it rained or snowed. It never took a lot of light to make the beans glow, but when the sun rose over the valley hills on springtime Sundays, I knew why the architect had chosen spots for so many. The sun pressed light through the coloured glass; and above the altar, the kaleidoscope burst

into a warm rainbow of Jesus Rays. My eyes shut and I slumped in my chair. Then, squinting at the congregation, I noticed Nicky had done the same.

At the cemetery, the clouds smothered the Jesus Rays. A breeze embraced my body with the warm dampness of grass and tilled earth. I thought about Pete running home last year, stomping the plate. In remembering him, I sensed that the pain of loss is not something that can be given away. Loss is something that owns tiny pieces of you until you figure out a way to own all of it yourself.

Standing in the water, the waves breaking against my legs in a steady pulse, I noticed the others pointing at acrobatic seagulls scavenging our refuse. The birds darted and dipped to snatch lunch scraps from the sand.

Wayne gripped a rock.

We cheered the first attempt.

He cocked his arm and let it fly.

Contact.

The seagull squawked, dropping the apple, its wing bent brokenly, and began its spiral into the frothy waves below, landing softly, noiselessly.

Wayne began to cry, and his tears became thoughts.

The bird never knew what was coming and neither did we. What seemed an impossible game now filled me with regret. Before killing the bird I thought we knew who we were: the U-12 Finger Lakes Travel soccer team, the best young players from the area, for which our parents shelled out money for uniforms, coaching and tournament fees, halftime snacks, and gasoline to travel the region to compete against other upstarts. Between tournament games we ruled the beach, running full tilt into the water, clamouring over spits of rock along the lakeshore, kicking soccer balls, throwing Frisbees, and burying each other in the sand. Our energy was limitless. I thought we were strong, gentle, kind. But I had just caught a glimpse of a previously unrecognized ugliness, and this realization wiped away my perceptions of us as innocent boys. Each wave that broke against the beach carried the seagull closer to shore, closer to us, until its broken body came to rest on

the wet sand, the wind touching its feathers, then touching our hair as we turned our backs and tried to leave it behind.

At soccer tournaments, I played game after game after game. The first whistle in the morning woke us like an alarm clock and the dewy grass soaked our cleats. My ears filled with our voices, calling for the ball and yelling encouragement, and our parents' voices, cheering us on and berating the officials, whistles chirping across the surrounding fields. Our shadows shrank to dots at noon, and then slowly stretched to duel with the blades of grass, the white painted sidelines, one another. We darted around, swooping toward the goal on corner kicks, and flocking to the ball in our defensive third to protect our lead. A centre back, I cleared the ball off the goal line, chased strikers around the eighteen, and found my teammates on free kicks. I was depended upon to think clearly, to be physical without being reckless, and to be fast and strong. I was the last player back and I loved this pressure to prove my reliability.

My forearms and the back of my neck tanned in the intense summer sun, and my knees took on a deep brown between the hem of my shorts and the top of my socks so that afterwards, I watched the pieces of grass float between my feet and down the shower drain, looking at my striped skin with wonder. I was perpetually moving, laughing, playing, hungry, happy. Only in retrospection do I notice the light fading, the quieter air of a July dusk near the lake settling upon us as we removed our cleats and shin guards on the sideline, our feet glowing white and wrinkled. My teammates spilled Gatorade down their throats and pulled their jerseys over their heads, stuffed them into bags for not washing, or tossed them to their mothers. But not me. I remained uniformed until I reached our car, threw my bag in the trunk, and concealed myself behind an open door, or

in the back seat, quickly wriggling out of my Finger Lakes threads and into a dry T-shirt before anyone could see my naked chest.

Riding home, I was blissfully exhausted. Along the winding roads, Mom at the wheel, the wind ripped through the opened windows, tearing at my shirt like a flag in a hurricane. I observed the things we passed: crumbling barns on fading farms, the music of cicadas, cold air pouring down the lakeside gullies and spilling across the road, through our windows, our hair, our lungs. In the visor mirror, Nicky asleep on the back seat. Mom navigating our way home.

Me wondering if anybody saw.

10

For my twelfth birthday my parents gave me a new stereo. A slick JVC CD changer with multiple trays, dual cassette decks for dubbing, and a digital menu panel with lights in a rainbow of colours. It was beautiful. The speakers were allegedly powerful, too. The only downside came when I looked briefly into my crystal ball and saw that in two years, on his own twelfth birthday, Nicky would receive a stereo that was vastly superior due to inevitable advances in audio technology.

In my bedroom, Dad removed the sound system from its large box, recklessly snapping the Styrofoam packaging. White kernels littered the carpet and clung statically to his sweatshirt. In one swoop he had my dresser angled away from the wall to plug in the stereo.

"Nice," he said. The panel glowed invitingly and he stepped back to admire it.

For me, the anticipation of this moment had accumulated like a ball of snow rolling downhill all winter. The waiting, the desire, the glory of solitude in my sanctuary with Pearl Jam, Nirvana, and Soundgarden.

Dad had other ideas. Hunched beside the stereo he chose a CD he had brought to christen the music machine. When I saw what he was doing, I was flabbergasted and assumed it was a Genesis album—this was the group we listened to on the rides from Naples to Rochester and back again during weekends with Dad. We cruised the city streets in the black Acura Legend, to Dick's Sporting Goods for sneakers and baseball mitts, Blockbuster Video for *Dumb and Dumber* and *Ace Ventura: Pet Detective*, Rocky's for

meatballs and red sauce, and to Redwings games, where I dreamed of catching foul balls and someday grinding my own cleats into the dirt behind home plate. Often, we three bachelors ate Pizza Hut for dinner and then again for breakfast, sprawled on the couch at Dad's apartment, watching SportsCenter repeatedly, simply enjoying one another's presence.

My parents had divorced soon after my heart surgery and when they told Nicky and me, I had no idea it was coming. They never fought in front of us, either while they were married or after they separated, and never spoke negatively of one another in our presence. As parents, they were a united pair, and have remained so. Perhaps this is what shocked me most about their split.

I had immediately thought of the only other kid in my class whose parents were divorced. Gary Gaspar was, to the best of my recollection, a cliché of poverty and neglect. His shirts were too baggy, his pants too short. Either he didn't know how to tie his shoes or he didn't care if they dangled onto the bathroom floor. After school he walked to the bowling alley where, he bragged, he consumed unlimited pizza and Coke—his teeth were spotted with black rot— and played video games while he waited for his mom to finish her shift at the shoe rental counter. He sat beside me in school and smelled like cigarettes and unwashed bed sheets. His skin was sallow. He left class for remedial help in math and reading. He couldn't throw a ball well. He didn't smile much. As immature as my judgments about Gary were, he was not somebody I aspired to be like. Yet, sharing the commonality of divorced parents, I felt more like Gary than I ever imagined I could, and less like my friends than I ever wanted to. Another scar to hide.

Thinking about my parents splitting up was like punching a bruise. I didn't want anyone to tease me or think of me as

different. Stupid. Sick. Neglected. Like my zipper, I didn't want anyone to discover my new defect. I knew that in this way, Nicky and I were different from all of our friends, so to keep the divorce a secret I chose to ignore it. I simply never acknowledged that Dad lived in another town. That I only stayed at his place a few times a year. That I was ten before I knew that he made amazing omelettes. That he had girlfriends. I even ignored the fact that my attempts to keep the divorce a secret never fooled any of my friends.

Once, after Dad brought Nicky and me back to Naples on a Sunday evening, the Acura broke down. He left it at the bottom of our street and walked back up the hill to the house. It was too late to call a tow truck so he spent the night on the living room couch. The next day I came home from school and there he was watching TV, still waiting for the tow truck, the only times in my life I would see him like this just after school.

"Hi, champ," he said when I walked in the room, "how was school today?" I loved him speaking those words from that couch.

Unlike when we spoke on the phone during the week and ended our conversations by saying, "I miss you and I love you," on those car rides back to Naples we just watched the road and trees scroll by and listened to Phil Collins until it was time to hug goodbye and then say only, "I love you, too." Sometimes in the car Dad sang in a rangy voice. It was more imitation than authentic. I slumped in my seat because even when you're young you know whether or not your parents are rock stars. At the time I didn't realize he might have been messing with me, not even when he dropped us off at home and told Mom about his performance on the ride, apparently proud of his clever histrionics.

"Your father used to be in a band," Mom told me after he

left. "*Fortune Tellers* they were called." That impressed me a little and I tried to imagine him onstage.

"What instrument did he play?" I asked.

"None. He was the singer," she said with a rueful laugh. "They were pretty awful."

The CD tray slid open and into the new stereo Dad placed the first album, a ceremony I planned to orchestrate myself, but he caught my eye with a teenage twinkle in his own. I kept quiet. A bluesy guitar lick jumped at us. Then, drum kicks and the bass line. Dad twisted the volume knob to the max and howled. I couldn't distinguish his voice from the stereo voice. The lead guitar bit again, the rhythm section filled, and Dad was leaning back on one leg, the other bent at the knee in the air and with his giant hands he picked out the notes of a vigorous air guitar solo. Then he turned the volume down.

"Nice," he said again, but I didn't know what to say, could never have predicted that routine. "After classes finished on Friday afternoons," he continued, "I used to put my speakers in my dorm window and play that record as loudly as I could." In the most beautifully clichéd way, he appeared younger at that moment.

The stereo sat atop my dresser, the top drawer of which contained a wrinkled photograph of Dad holding me afloat in the high school swimming pool. I was four years old at the time. The picture, my go-to charm when I needed to see him at bedtime, was one of the only concessions I allowed myself regarding an acknowledgement of the end of my parents' marriage. In that photo, in his arms, I had felt so secure. Looking at it each night confirmed reality, because looking at it meant he was not downstairs. Only alone in my bedroom did I feel less different, stupid, sick, neglected, less like Gary. After each glimpse, I buried the photo under my T-shirts at the back of the drawer. On the

other side of my bedroom wall I imagined Nicky, with his own picture, did the same. We never talked about it.

Suspended in the water, suspended in time: in that picture everything was okay. I could almost smell the chlorine, hear the lifeguard's whistle skip across the water and echo off the walls, feel Dad hold me tightly with one hand around my waist while reaching under water to snatch Nicky off the bottom and hand him back to Mom on the deck. I remember how, after that lesson, I chased Dad. The sun stretched over the crackling summer grass and wind whipped my damp hair and I almost had him. Dad zigged one way and then another and I kept after his knees. The plastic bag holding our wet towels and trunks twisted and crinkled in his hand. I was chasing the sound and the chlorine smell that covered us and I was chasing him. From the school pool, up the hill, across the soccer field. Dad looked back at me, just out of my reach and I giggled and pumped my legs. My whole world was that sprint. A gust of wind pushed against me and I charged forward, reaching with my hands, but Dad was pulling away, a blur of denim I watched explode to the far side of the field. I stopped running and waited for him to come back to me.

"Who was that?" I finally asked when the music stopped.

"Led Zeppelin," Dad said, drumming his fingers on the doorframe. With that, he snapped his gum like a snare shot, left the CD in the stereo, and walked out the door, whether to the past or the future I could not tell.

Soon after I realized I didn't need to hold the picture of Dad and me in the pool anymore to see it, I began to grasp for other images of him from my childhood, but there was not as much as I'd hoped for. To aid my memories and to make myself indestructible I scavenged his free weights from the basement floor. They were covered in foundation dust and cat piss but I didn't care because they seemed to

have been waiting for me to find them. The bars were only a little rusty, the plastic weights filled full with sand. I curled to Led Zeppelin in front of a mirror and watched the blood fill my biceps. Lifting the same weight, I'd hoped, would create a conduit between us.

11

Eating breakfast, I was absorbed in SportsCenter, watching the highlights of Pete Sampras's 1995 Australian Open Quarter Final match against Jim Courier. After losing the first two sets, Sampras won the next two. In the fifth set he did something I had never seen a grown man do: he wept. Notorious for his composure and lack of emotional displays, Sampras wiped his eyes. He bounced the tennis ball again and again before his service toss and wandered at the baseline between points, taking towels from ball boys but looking for something else. During a changeover Sampras buried his face in a towel and sobbed.

"Pete, you all right?" Courier called across the net at one point. "We can do this tomorrow if you want."

Sampras shook his head "no" and tossed the ball and crushed another unreturnable serve. The SportsCenter anchor explained that Sampras's friend and coach, Tim Gullikson, collapsed at the tournament and had returned to the United States. Within the year he would die of brain cancer.

Sampras won the match and my devoted admiration. It was the gutsiest performance I had ever seen. Sampras had an enormous heart. Without being able to articulate it at the time, I sensed that the emotional scar of losing his coach did not own him, and I began a quest to associate myself with his courage in as many ways as possible.

To appropriate the soul and strength of Sampras, I clipped articles and pictures about him from newspapers and magazines and plastered them across my bedroom walls, and tacked posters onto my ceiling when there was

no wall space left. I watched all his matches, waiting for him to make his move in the final set: a service break of his opponent at four-all, then four bombs to close out the match on his serve. He rarely lost and I loved that, too.

So much of Sampras's success derived from his fitness and uncommon flexibility. I was rigid with tight hamstrings and spent hours stretching with one leg against the door frame. I ran through the neighbourhood in all weather to improve my stamina because tennis was something I wanted to be known for. I, too, wanted to persevere in the face of adversity. I wanted to obliterate weakness and insecurity with athletic prowess and emotional courage.

Although enrolled in junior high school and too old to participate in the local youth tennis program, I hung around the courts during the summer to rally with Brian, the instructor. Brian had a wicked Western forehand and when I hit with him I felt rich. I didn't know he'd had abdominal surgery until lifted his T-shirt to reveal the scar across his stomach. In the very act of showing it to a court rat like me, he seemed to accept his scar and everything that came with it. Seeing it—and seeing him whip ground strokes—transferred a new power to me. I felt less scarred. I even showed him mine.

I asked Mom to build a tennis court in our back yard, which happened to be exactly the size of one. I knew because I'd measured. I wasn't hearing voices, but was as determined as Ray Kinsella in *Field of Dreams*. If I built it, maybe he'd come.

"Just one," I said.

"You can play around the corner," Mom replied.

So I brought three tennis balls to the school courts, hit three serves, walked to the other side to retrieve them, and hit three back, over and over and over again. I practised picking up a tennis ball with the outside of my sneaker and

the tip of my racquet head. Sometimes I hit tennis balls off the school wall next to Pete Linton's pipe, waiting for the day when I would not be ambushed by the feeling of missing him.

"What about your brother?" Mom said, and Nicky started coming to the courts with me. Soon we could keep the ball moving and tennis really felt like tennis. We recognized the subtle body language we each used to call shots and serves in or out and played entire sets without speaking more than a few words. Our communication had never been clearer. Nicky took his shirt off on the hottest days like the men on the nearby courts, his chest hairless and smooth. Unless we were alone, I left my shirt on, my acceptance of my scars still as elusive as returning a serve off of Sampras's own racquet. I couldn't have put it into words at the time, but I wanted to be able to show everyone my scar like Brian had showed me his, without it defining him, his scar instead being *a part of* who he was.

That summer Mom, Nicky, and I drove to Chicago just to visit Nike Town, where there were shrines to Sampras and loads of his gear. Posing for a photo next to a life-sized shot of my idol, wearing my Nike tennis shorts and holding a plastic Nike shopping bag containing a Pete Sampras Nike shirt, I didn't even smile, because this was real. At Nike Town I might have been closer to him than ever before, which was exactly what I needed. In our family, the name "Pete" referred to one person and was spoken with the same tone we might use when referring to somebody who would be welcomed to join us for a meal anytime.

I used my index finger like a windshield wiper to flick away the sweat from my forehead just as Sampras did before serving. I mimicked the rhythmic way he bounced the ball before each serve. I dangled and spun my racquet just as he did awaiting the return. When the high school tennis

coach invited me to practise with the team even though I was too young, I broke up with baseball forever.

During tennis practices I tried running leaps at the service line to swat overheads out of the air, just like Sampras on Centre Court at Wimbledon. Even though they didn't feel right against my palm, I wrapped the handles of my racquets in the purple-blue Tourna Grips that Sampras endorsed. I played with his racquet model, a Wilson ProStaff Original 6.0, even though the head was only 85 square inches and far too small and unforgiving for an amateur like me. And far too heavy. I placed lead tape inside the frame at three and nine o-clock to weight my equipment just like Sampras. I got unyielding looks when I asked a sporting goods store employee to string my racquet far above the recommended 55-65 lb. tension, just like Sampras. I thought I wanted to be like Sampras, but what I really wanted was for him to want to be around me because *I* had a strength that was unique and admirable. And if not Pete, then someone like him who would call me up and ask me to hit, or talk, or just be together. I wanted to be so strong that I didn't need a lower tension to generate more power, but instead needed a higher tension to harness it. I wanted to be so strong that I could cry in front of millions of people at the thought of losing someone or something I cared deeply about.

12

Adolescence sometimes felt like arriving at a party naked when everyone else was clothed. In these moments I was transparent—with even my most guarded thoughts visible. Alternatively, adolescence sometimes felt like arriving at a party clothed when everyone else was naked. Then I was on the distant periphery, miles away from the thing that everyone else knew, the thing that would have included me in the moment. Worse was to feel both ways simultaneously, when my hormonal gumbo was too hot to handle. It could not be controlled and I could only wait for the emotions to run their course.

When, soon after entering high school, I suspected that a few of the guys had gotten laid, a dark self-consciousness and sense of failure settled inside my chest. Even though I, of course, would want my friends to know I was getting with a girl, it was an unspoken policy that we would not kiss and tell. When campfire conversations turned to girls, and my friends verbalized assumptions about my accomplishments, I remained tight-lipped and let them assume I was *the man*. I knew the truth. My Led Zeppelin weight-lifting program had garnered no sex. Neither had my pursuit of Sampras's chi. We all were doing whatever preening we could to score the hottest girl possible and if anyone actually did, the pressure on the rest of us multiplied. Yes, some of us wanted to love girls and to have them love us back, but more than that, there was a yearning to discard our inexperience, again and again. Perhaps only subconsciously, I sensed this urgency because I needed to prove, at least to myself, I wasn't damaged goods. That my desires were real and normal, and

I was capable of delivering. But, because of my fornicating friends, I believed I would never go to another party where I wasn't wearing clothes in a roomful of naked people. My subconscious echoed: *You loser.* Like sex was some problem I needed to deal with alone, yet it required a girl. I was a failure and I questioned myself as such.

My suspicion of their virgout talents did not erase my angst and life continued as before. At my annual cardiologist appointment to monitor the coarctation repair, I weighed in and was thrilled to see that the weightlifting had added a few pounds. Yet, in the examination room with cartoon animals painted on the ceiling tiles, the characters mocked me and my lack of mature experience: *you are still a virgin child and will be treated as such.*

I was wired to the EKG machine and the electronic box scribbled red lines on a roll of graph paper. The nurse tore my reading free and tucked it in a folder thick with paperwork dating back to my kindergarten surgery. When she finished I quickly put my shirt back on. In a second examination room I disrobed again and a technician spread warm goo across my naked chest for the echocardiogram. Under the dim lights, I listened to my heart *woosh woosh woosh*, like small, fast waves beating a lakeshore. In a third examination room I waited while the cardiologist reviewed the data, comparing the new red line and *woosh woosh wooshing* to the old. I waited for him to return, to say, "Looks good—you want to schedule next year's appointment today or have us call you in six months?"

But that isn't what happened.

The cardiologist opened the folder thick with my paper work and spread several documents across the table. He wore a stern expression. He asked the nurse to grab Mom and Nicky. He made small talk—"How is school?" "Do you like your classes?" "What do you plan to do this

summer?"—and when Mom and Nicky arrived he stopped questioning me and began explaining that it was only a matter of time.

Both the EKG and echocardiogram indicated the aorta was fine, but there was another problem, one that was in fact common among people with aortic coarctations, and more significant. The aortic valve in my heart had morphed from its natural tricuspid design into a bicuspid sieve. Instead of the normal three leaflets, I had two, and two don't close tightly. Two leak.

I stared at the gray linoleum tiles between my sneakers while the doctor continued.

If I stopped lifting weights, if I stopped putting undue stress on my heart, if I experimented with medicine to lower my blood pressure, perhaps my heart could function more normally, instead of ballooning.

"But that's like building a dam out of paper towel rolls," he said.

"Life-threatening."

"You will need surgery," he said. Cutting me open and replacing the valve.

It didn't matter that I felt fine, that I had no physical symptoms. Shock thrummed at a high intensity. The wall clock hands swept away the minutes. I was angry and less brave than I wanted to be. I was profoundly damaged. And confused. I was in prime physical condition and could only wonder, *How can I be in a life-threatening situation?*

In my mind, there were many facts refuting the diagnosis. I could run all day, logging heaving minutes in all sporting contests. I had six-pack abs. I believed my endurance was unmatched, so much so that, like many of my teammates, I sought additional challenges. Instead of relaxing the day before the first basketball practice of the season, I ran laps around town. Instead of fifty crunches after running UCLA

line drills in practice, I did one hundred. How many extra leaps had I taken in-between wind sprints and pyramid runs trying to dunk a basketball? How many times had I waded through thigh-deep snow on the Finger Lakes Trail, climbing the switchbacks with a load of gear on my back to spend the night in the woods with the guys? How could I need such a surgery? I had worked so hard to make myself indestructible, lifting weights to Led Zeppelin in my room—but I had failed.

Physically, I felt invincible, but the trajectory of my athletic career, indeed the arc of my life, was instantly disrupted. Possibly derailed. I had assumed I was done with all of this heart-problem-bullshit and that I would play a sport in college and, if I worked hard enough, beyond. Realistic or not, *this was my goal.* I was fifteen. My eyes traced the paths of my shoelaces as they wove through the holes of my indoor soccer sneakers. The cartoon animals danced above.

I could not accept surgery as the greatest of additional challenges or a gift cure; I only understood it as an inconceivable inconvenience and at worst, the end of my life.

The doctor continued, describing surgical options, his terms shifting from *if* to *when* the operation would occur. That seemed the only question that remained. I listened to what I did not want to hear.

"In all likelihood," he repeated, "it's only a matter of time before the valve must be replaced and the most successful surgeries of this kind occur when the patient is healthiest, before the heart has enlarged so much that it cannot return to a regular size."

Suddenly, we had planned to replace the valve in a year, in-between basketball and tennis seasons. This was as hollow-feeling a choice as any; action to continue my life seemed like a defeat.

Riding home along the lake, the wind whipped the

water into whitecaps as turbulent as my thoughts. Surgery would be a tremendous kick in the nuts, especially now, absorbed as I was in the social vacuum of high school. It was also a direct alarm to my vulnerability. Anxieties from the previous heart surgery surfaced again. My body was making decisions for me. I was not in control.

But the fear … .

Would I show it or hide it?

I decided to keep my problem a secret from everyone. I locked the news inside, the ways I felt damaged and without any means of validating my worth as a friend, a brother, a son. *The things that had given me so much of my identity were about to be taken away*, I thought. In the days that followed, I tried to convince myself that the news was good—this was a treatable circumstance; I didn't have terminal cancer, for instance—but I was inconsolable.

I deconstructed the weightlifting equipment and threw each piece to the bottom of the basement steps where they thudded in the dirt. Time fell away. The surgery date approached. At last, I had no choice but to disclose to everyone my forthcoming absence from school, from sports, from life. *The things that had given me so much of my identity were about to be taken away.*

And maybe what happened next happened because I never wanted to be owned by another scar, because fate tampered with my innocence and prodded me, demanding, *So what are you going to do about that?*

PART 2

A MATTER OF TIME

13

An abandoned horse barn on the hill behind Wayne's house was our best prospect for privacy. Devoid of all life forms, save for some hardy mice, and with a view of the surrounding vineyards, distant lake and hills, we elected to renovate this structure during the winter of our sophomore year of high school. Despite lacking electricity and plumbing, it seemed as good a place as any to party on the weekends.

Our contracting skills were shabby at best. Alden Burnham rigged a climbing harness to a nearby tree and we hoisted him to the snowy barn roof to cover gaps with tarpaper he found in his basement. We scavenged plywood sheets and 2x4s to patch the walls and the holey upstairs floor, and Billy Tanis mooched some cash from his mother for nails. We furnished The Barn with folding chairs, a yellow velvet flea market couch, a three-legged table, Army surplus blankets, spray paint, and black light posters even though we didn't have any black lights. Eventually, we ran an extension cord from Wayne's house across a field and up the ladder to power lights or a stereo, depending on our needs at the time: light for descending the ladder or The Grateful Dead for partying in the dark. As far as forts go, it was haggard, but it was ours.

We inhabited The Barn on weekends, drinking whatever we could scrounge: dented cans of Labatt Blue from unplugged basement fridges; milk jugs of Genesee Cream Ale pulled from a reliable kegerator; blends of bourbon stolen a centimetre at a time from bottles in our parents' liquor cabinets and stashed in shampoo bottles.

Some nights we lay on a mattress in the back of Irwin's pickup truck and watched the stars stream by for hours, the wind ripping at our hair and clothes as we travelled the lake roads. We sledded the local ski resort during the witching hour. We indiscriminately fired paintball guns out of the truck windows like a band of vigilantes. We appropriated signage and danced in our underwear in the field, the bonfire gritting and hissing in the wind. We suffocated with laughter.

The most exciting nights came in March, when the snow melted and the daylight spilled later into evening, when we invited girls to The Barn. Girls curious about what we had created and what we did there, girls we were attracted to and who were attracted to us. In the mornings afterward, everyone followed the extension cord to the house to cook bacon and eggs and wait for our parents to pick us up and take us home to finally get some sleep, or to the Y for another round of hoops. Every weekend at The Barn we revelled in the freedom.

Then, at the peak of such fabulous fun, it was April, and I would have surgery to replace my deformed heart valve. Like a prisoner, I would say goodbye to my friends and family, enter a strange institution for a time, confront my demons head-on, and hope for a healthier life upon release.

I was also petrified to tell anybody about my condition out of embarrassment and an awkwardness around their sympathy. I could not accept concern from others because that would confirm I was damaged and weak. At the Jellybean Church, when the priest asked the congregation to pray for me, I nearly melted in the heat of unwanted attention. It was like being spotlighted by a Jesus Ray: *See, everyone? This is the boy with a damaged heart.*

On several occasions I donated my own blood at the hospital for transfusions in the operating room. I discussed

the procedure with my surgeon and the potential consequences with my cardiologist. I thought about the bone saw biting my sternum and tried to imagine the pain. Of course, there was a chance I could die; simply mentioning death outside of these appointments seemed like a self-fulfilling prophecy despite the relatively low odds. Most distressing was the forthcoming exile from what I knew to be my life, an existence that revolved around my friends. I worried they would forget me. The trespassing and vandalizing, the partying: I knew all of it placed undue stress on my leaking valve, but I participated anyway because I felt a pulsing need to be included and thus remembered. What leaked through my heart valve was not just blood, but conflict itself.

After the final blood draw, I hiked the barn hill with Wayne and Burnham. We pushed our way through thickets of blackberry brush, cockleburs and bentgrass, over shale and snowmelt toward a small clearing above the village. The sun burned through thin clouds as we rambled along and smelled the mud and tasted the last of the icy shadow snow. If ever there was an opportunity to acknowledge my feelings to my best friends this was it. I wish my fifteen-year-old self had the confidence and the language to tell them I was frightened, and to lean on them, but I didn't say a word.

"My, oh, my, what a view," Wayne said upon reaching the clearing. The lake. The hills. The budding trees. He reached out and squeezed my shoulder. I held my distant gaze. He squeezed harder, and then harder, until I turned to him and smiled. A moment later we trooped downhill.

Back in Wayne's kitchen we feasted on peanut butter and grape jelly on toast. He sifted through his father's vinyl collection, spinning Pink Floyd's "Fearless" over and over again, the hardcore Liverpool F.C. fans singing "You'll Never Walk Alone" in unison from the terraces of Anfield. The chanting was a message I wouldn't understand for years.

The night before the surgery, Nicky and I turned on the tennis court lights for a night-time session. It was early spring, cold. The muddy hill beside the courts smelled somewhere between oozing and frozen. We wore wool hats, flannel button downs, and shorts, and if we were worried about breaking our strings in the cold because we both hit ground strokes with so much topspin, neither of us mentioned it. We opened two new cans of tennis balls instead of one and took turns inhaling fumes straight from the can, our pre-match ritual.

Each shot kept time. Strings, the hard courts, the net tape, the fence. Little clouds trailed each of us. We danced between the lines, chasing drop shots, slicing backhands at the net, and whipping beautiful crosscourt winners into the dark corners of the court. Aside from the occasional, "Nice shot," or soft curses rebuking ourselves for mistakes, we spoke little to one another. Nicky blew snot rockets through the chain link fence. I straightened my strings like Pete Sampras would.

I won the match, as the older brother should, and approached the net after the final point. Arriving at the net first, I watched Nicky remove his hat, cowlicks reaching for the sky. He walked to me with his head down. I should have reached out and wrapped my arms around him and hugged him tight to my chest. I tried speaking out loud, but I couldn't. I smacked his outstretched hand and tossed him a sad smirk.

"Next time," he said with a smirk of his own, as if there was ever a doubt we would play again.

We turned our backs to walk home and the lights snapped off behind us and glowed blue in the darkness. The sky glittered with stars.

"Next time," he repeated. "Next time I'll beat your ass."

15

The hospital linoleum glared and the gown I wore felt soft with use. In an empty white room, on a gurney, I hugged and kissed Mom and Dad. Then they disappeared. I sensed they kept a secret from me, for me. Nicky was at school. Had our positions been reversed, I could have gone to school only if I was convinced the surgery would be a sure success.

What might it feel like to die? Would looking into the blinding lights above the operating room table be the final conscious moment of my life? Then nothing? Gone. What would death look like inside of me? Blood where there should be no blood? No breathing when I should take a breath?

What would it feel like to live?

The aloneness gripped me. The part of me that was five-years old inundated my psyche. I was afraid. Maybe my heart had let me down. Or maybe I had let my heart down.

A nurse placed a plastic mask over my face.

I didn't know to look at the smooth surface of my sternum one final time.

I heard a voice. Sensed commotion, bright lights, but I could not open my eyes, or if I did, I could not see.

In a picture Mom took of me in ICU, tubes extend from all parts of my body: my neck, my throat, my ribs, the backs of my hands, my abdomen. My face was the colour of water in a metal pail. My chest was punctuated with brush-strokes of iodine, and my braces glinted coldly in my mouth, cracked lips parted with a plastic breathing tube. I appeared dead. It is easy to imagine the

pillows of a casket surrounding my body after the under-taker has pulled the tubes out of my veins and peeled the tape off my skin. In the photo, my body rests at the same height as a body might during a wake.

I heard a voice again. It was Nicky. "I love you, man," he said and leaned forward to plant a kiss on my forehead. "See you tomorrow."

In ICU I remained sedated for two days, a bovine valve opening and closing in my heart. No more leaks. Maybe because my grandmother was a dentist, my family took turns brushing my teeth even though I received all nourishment through an IV. They cradled my jaw in their palms and scrubbed while I slumped in a chair. The surgeon visited, placed a meaty hand on my leg, and asked me how I felt.

Terrible, I wanted to say, but hadn't the energy or the temerity to mention the pain. Besides, he stepped in where my heart failed and defied the course of natural selection to give me new life. I *owed* him mine.

I weaned off the heaviest doses of morphine and each pulse of blood increased the pain, an exhausting, throbbing hurt in my chest. ICU nurses swaddled me in blankets like a newborn, but the pain wove in and out of the morphine haze, a fuzzy yellow light that became the air and the fabric of the blankets themselves, as if somebody dyed my blood yellow and it seeped into the lenses of my eyeballs through veins in my eyes. I couldn't blink or think it away or ingest a pill to shrink it. Any movement delivered pain that closed my eyes. So did not moving. An IV needle in a vein on the back of my hand caught up in the yellowness of the blankets and was nearly torn free. I felt the needle move inside me. I didn't mind because for several seconds I did not notice the fire in my chest. I slammed the morphine button, amplifying the gauzy glow.

A few days into recovery, the doctors removed the cath-

eter, which felt like taking the thickest, hottest piss of my life. I then transferred to a regular ward. Upon arrival I felt cold, then colder. I shivered. Outside the sun fell away and the window blackened. I had trouble speaking, my lips and tongue frozen. A nurse hung a bag of my own blood on the IV stand and began to fill me up. Then a bag of plasma. I warmed, felt the gnawing at my sternum again. I closed my eyes.

I hadn't the strength to displace the elephant sitting on my ribs, the shards of glass impaled deep within. I attacked the morphine button relentlessly. Like a junkie, I lived for the next quarter hour, when my desperate thumb-jamming on the plastic knob would deliver another dose. I preferred the outlines of things to be blurred.

The next morning Nicky told me Papa struck a tree backing out of our driveway and shattered his taillight; I learned not to laugh because the physical hurt was so profound. Friends huddled around my bed, brought red wool socks and The Doors' *L.A. Woman*, updated me on progress at The Barn. I could not explain how I felt beyond saying, "It hurts" or "I think I'm feeling better." I let them fill the silence. Told them I'd see them soon and waited for another night in which the nurses responded slothfully to the call bell, my requests for water, Sprite, ice chips, morphine, help sitting up and adjusting my pillows and bedding, the piss jug, to unstick the stuck TV remote, and various other interruptions of my semi-rest to check my vitals. My greatest ambition was to wait for the pain to subside.

In my wildest delusions, I could not have predicted that in just a few weeks I would be gasping for air, climbing the stairs to my second floor classes at the high school, where I sat in a Codeine haze, my friends nudging me back to the present during biology. And in six weeks playing a Sectional

tennis match, working the tightness from my chest with each serve, resuming on-court Sampras mannerisms and displaying a toughness I thought he would admire. That I would reach the point where my biggest concern was taking a shower unassisted or walking to the end of the street without holding a pillow to my chest to cushion the rattles of a cough. Before all of that, those long hospital hours crawling toward sunrise delivered intense pain.

I was discharged on the afternoon of the sixth day.

At home again, I popped Codeine pills and sank into the couch to watch Sampras play an uncommon Davis Cup doubles match. Waiting for the meds to kick in, I moved gingerly, but in the miraculous way of all healing I realized that the pain in my chest had dissolved a noticeable amount. It had reduced from pain to discomfort. I was baffled. The change was psychologically invigorating and I wanted to test it, to push myself, to find the limit of this good feeling. I could sit on the couch without cringing, but what else could I do? Swing a tennis racquet? Have a good laugh? I walked to the bathroom and closed the door. I took off my shirt, contorting slowly so as not to strain my ribs, and stood in front of the mirror. I looked at the crusty red line tracing downward from my throat to my belly button. The two black-blooded drainage tube slits just below. *They sliced you open and reconfigured your insides,* I thought, amazed. Where was the change? What molecules had made friends inside the bones and nerves and tissues of my body? It was like turning a ship—difficult and slow—but I was healing.

Two weeks after surgery I looked across the backyard. Mom gardened and an April breeze wrapped my depleted, hunched frame. I had shed twenty pounds, most of it muscle. The past few afternoons I had sat behind the garage with Tim O'Brien's *The Things They Carried.* In my hands the book was warm and heavy from the sun, and in my heart, I felt that O'Brien had written it for me. In "Speaking of Courage" I *was* Norman Bowker, home from battle and unable to talk to anybody about my expe-

rience of surviving because nobody could understand. I was isolated from friends, family, and the town in which I grew up that now seemed changed and changing, leaving me behind. Two weeks in isolation seemed like two years. I was comforted to know others had been alienated, too, but it also broke my heart with self-pity. I loved and hated feeling this way. I needed to acknowledge this separation and depression because they were real emotions. I shivered while I read and hoped the sun would make me look less feeble, and give me strength.

I finally said to Mom, "Burnham called. People are hanging out tonight at The Barn." I wanted to be with my friends more than anything in the world.

She footed the spade into the dirt and turned to me. "Absolutely not. You've only been home a week."

What she didn't know, and what I didn't know how to explain, was that while surgery had saved my life, the separation from my friends was killing me.

I told Nicky he couldn't go to the party, for which he has yet to thank me. There was torrential rain and a washed-out road through a tunnel of trees. Burnham, Wayne, and I rattled along, following a string of taillights. Boys and girls swarmed the property, darting between the stream of cars and the rain, red Solo cups in hand, sloshing, stumbling, the anticipation bubbling. Valley View Farm was a game preserve, hundreds of acres of wilderness for hunting and shooting sporting clays, but not tonight. Tonight—the Fourth of July—was going to be the biggest party of the year. Independence Day. I felt as good as I had felt in months and was ready to celebrate my freedom.

The kegs sat on a covered porch of the main lodge, and we filled our cups to spilling all night long. A guy with a beard collected money and pumped the tap. Because the rain pounded the metal roof and the stereo blasted Pearl Jam and everyone was drunk, we shouted our conversations. Maybe we weren't even conversing, just yelling. I recognized a few kids from a rival soccer team and watched them suck clouds of smoke out of a bong the size of a fire hydrant. Before long every girl looked twice as beautiful as she had in school a month before.

Although it wasn't my first time drinking, inexperience mixed with ambition, and I didn't wait for the first few cupfuls to settle into my bloodstream. I drank quickly, as if the kegs would empty before I received my portion. I felt it was my right to make up for lost time, to drink and drink and drink, so I chugged crisp, icy beer until my brain froze, the cold receding and surging with each round, freezing

again and again until it froze for good, totally numb, and I stumbled to the car. My universe spun. I finally made it, and coated the upholstery with puke.

I recall a voice. Tumbling out of the car and into a mud puddle, the voice again, laughing, and the voice leaving before I could ask for help because I had lost the ability to speak.

I came to hours later, sprawled on a brown and orange crocheted couch inside a wood-panelled lodge in the middle of nowhere, wearing my own vomit. I can still see the pale blue sky of early sunrise through the mud and bug-spattered lodge window. The police were everywhere.

"They were about to call an ambulance for you," Wayne said. I was not only dangerously drunk, but heart surgery was only a few months in my past, to which he had alerted the authorities. I staggered to my feet and outside.

Apparently, the cops had been on the property for hours. When they ran out of handcuffs they detained the rest of us with zip-ties. They set up a finger-printing station on our beer pong table to officially book us, and they hunted in the woods for revellers capable of running and hiding. Some kids crouched behind the chimney, trying to disappear on the roof, and when the tow trucks dragged away cars, others tumbled out of their parents' minivans.

Cuffed to Burnham, we all were marched through a wet field at sunrise and stuffed in the paddy wagons. I was far from sober despite profuse intestinal heaving. On the way to jail everyone sang a boisterous rendition of "99 Bottles of Beer on the Wall." I used my remaining strength not to finish puking. It was an Olympic display of willpower, especially considering the sour stench of my T-shirt. It could have stood on its own.

At the station, we packed into a yellow cinderblock hallway because there were too many of us to fit in a cell. We

sat on the grimy linoleum with our backs to the wall. The bravado of the paddy wagon singers had transformed into a silent, hung over reality, the uncertainty of our circumstances settling in. The cops, in an adjacent room sorting things out, let us wallow in our misery, and summoned us one by one to be photographed.

"They're calling our parents," Burnham declared.

Doom overwhelmed me. I couldn't piece the night together. I thought it was the drinking—the blatant disregard for my own health after I had already endured surgery to improve it—that would devastate my parents more than even attending the party, so I decided to cover it up. In the bathroom I scrubbed the ink from my fingertips, washed my face with dispenser hand soap, and swished some around in my mouth. I avoided looking in the mirror. The only clear thought I had was that Mom and Dad were going to pick me up and then kill me.

Eventually the large, gray metal doors opened and there they stood—my parents seemed to have aged years. I looked at the ground and stumbled forward, my shirt reeking.

"You told your Mom you were staying at Burnham's," Dad said. I squirmed.

"I—."

"Don't. I spoke to the police," Mom said. "They nearly requested an ambulance for you. You could have died last night."

The jig was up.

18

Summer passed and I sought redemption. To compensate for the damage to the property during the party, I operated the spring-loaded flywheel device that launched clay pigeons for the patrons of Valley View. And I did whatever I was asked to do at home. I begged for labour in hopes of being absolved.

At court I pled guilty to trespassing under the agreement that my records would be sealed. I also received fifty hours of community service.

With a garden hose coiled around my shoulder, I peddled to the elementary school to meet Burnham for our first community service session. He screwed one end to the spout and I dragged the other to Pete's memorial tree while the cicadas hummed. Unlike the tree we had carved our initials into years before, this one was young, a sugar maple, not yet ready for us to climb. A painted wooden plaque with Pete's name and the dates of his life was planted in the ring of mulch. The paint had already started to fade. Burnham turned the spigot a hair, and I leaned against the slender trunk in the shade, waiting for the water to dribble out.

"Is it drowned yet?" Burnham asked after a while. He reclined in the shade of the elementary school wall, a guitar screaming through the headphones hugging his neck.

I nudged the crispy grass with my sneaker. "Still thirsty."

"Excellent," he said. Then, "I've commandeered beverages for The Barn."

"Perfect," I said, without hesitation, surprising myself. I needed to show everyone that I deserved their approval and

care, their love, but it was as if my mind was an Etch-a-sketch, my memories of Valley View simply erased with a shake. All I cared about was being with my friends, whatever the cost.

He grinned like the Cheshire Cat and stared upward at the clouds drifting by.

"About forty-nine more hours to go," he said.

A few weeks later, on the day we completed the last tree watering, my mug shot arrived in the mail with my sealed criminal record. I studied the photo and could smell the puke, could see it splattered across the neck of my T-shirt. My face was ashen. My lips puffed over my braces. There were dark circles under my eyes. Based on those details, I tried to imagine what I looked like in a semi-conscious state on the hunting lodge couch. Probably no different, I realized, than I did in the picture Mom took of me after heart surgery in ICU. On Independence Day, I looked dead, too.

In the adolescent years that followed, in the name of exhilaration and escape and friendship, the partying would continue, a mounting strain on my heart. Sometimes it felt like pissing into the wind. Sometimes like hugging a person I loved. It was an irresistible mix. I wondered about the payoff, the magic that seemed to fill the gaps in my common sense, the ways I tried to take control. The accidents of adolescence were in my past—and also in my future.

19

Rebuilding my stamina after heart surgery was more difficult than I anticipated. During my first summer soccer game, my lungs felt the size of grapes, my windpipe as thin as their stems, and I ran around sporadically, gasping for air. I didn't know what it meant to have been placed on cardiopulmonary bypass during surgery. The chambers of my heart had been connected to a pump, commonly known as the heart-lung machine. A dose of blood-thinner was administered to keep my blood from clotting inside the machine, where it was oxygenated and cooled to 82 degrees Fahrenheit to induce total body hypothermia. Cardioplegia was chemically induced with a potassium solution, stopping my heart. In this way, my blood cells were able to continue cellular respiration and my heart was stilled so the surgeons could replace my leaking valve. Then my chest was stapled together and sewn closed.

I played centre midfield on the soccer team during my junior year, an aerobically challenging position, and by September, five months after surgery, I expected to be at full strength. I still struggled. For air. For endurance. For confidence. As with every season under Coach, our expectations were high—we had won the Section V Championship the previous year with an underdog squad in thrilling fashion, a golden goal in overtime—but maybe I was an entitled player on an entitled team.

Coach subbed for me and pulled me aside during a night game.

"Are you okay?" he asked.

I felt the squirt of adrenaline. I knew he was concerned

and I did not want to disappoint him again: after Valley View, I had disclosed my culpability at his kitchen table.

He tried to look inside me.

"I'm fine," I lied, staring across the wet grass, the shining ball skidding under the lights. I was scared to have my effort questioned, to appear lazy or uncaring, to not have his trust. And then, because of these uncertainties, I thought, *Maybe something is still wrong with my heart.*

Whenever we could, Nicky, Irwin, Billy, and I trudged into the woods. We explored the twisting veins of the Finger Lakes Trail system without maps. We built stone benches in the clearing beside the water tower on West Hill and cocktails of our own ingenuity, watching the sun sink, the light fade, the stars blink on. We discovered disc golf and charted courses through the trees, skinny dipped in murky ponds, and tested our balance on crumbling, forgotten stone walls. Thunder and lightning and drenching rains chased us out of the woods from time to time. We hiked over West Hill with a tent and sleeping bags. We got lost. We found our way. We rarely saw anyone else. These hills, it seemed, were ours. We kindled campfires with old homework assignments and by the light of the flames we strummed guitars and blew harmonicas, sang about life gone wrong in New Orleans, and laughed. When coyotes howled we answered them. When their screams drew nearer we shut the hell up and listened carefully, mouths opened, eyes as wide as rabbits'. We watched satellites trace the sky, lying on our backs in the tall grass, studying space for UFOs and shooting stars, the wood smoke dancing sweetly in the wind.

Autumn nights in Western New York are spectacularly crisp, and one night I drifted away from everyone, wallowing a bed in the heather and field grass to look at the stars. Alone, I tried to figure out how I felt. Free and alive? Brave or cowardly? Self-destructive? Imbecilic? Normal?

"Tommy Boy!" Irwin called from afar. I remained silent

in my wallow long after he stopped calling, my free hand resting on my chest, and the pine smoke weaving through the reedy grass. I studied the stars. I found no answers.

Time and again, my conscience settled on my new valve, the Fourth of July, and our campfire monkeyshines, and the guilt I felt filled the spaces between. I knew unhealthy choices made recovering from surgery and reaching my potential on the field more difficult. And I knew I would be suspended or kicked off a team if I was to break training rules, break trust, and be caught. I loved sports, and needed them to prove I was strong, but I believed in the magic of all moments with my friends to carry me beyond my defects. Those experimental happenings consistently relit the wick of adolescent gunpowder that detonated in the sky like so many beautiful explosions, so many signals that guided our way. I was sixteen—I would not be denied.

So in practices I tried to compensate. I ran harder and longer, in every drill, every scrimmage, my atonement a physical penance, pursuing every 50-50 ball, every header, never backing down, through a soccer season that ended without any team trophies and an early exit from the Section V Tournament. We felt the emptiness of defeat settle in our guts to simmer for a year until the chance came for redemption. A heaviness gripped my chest.

I found old photographs of Mom and Dad in a desk drawer. Mom's hair was long and straight and blond, and Dad's mop covered his ears. In one shot they appeared oblivious to the camera, each biting into a powdered donut, the sugar dusting Dad's moustache, and even though he was wearing a leather jacket I noticed how much bigger he was than me. Even though he was older than I was, I felt inadequate. In another picture he cut to the basket and I saw the cords of muscle in his legs and his arms, his wild hair. With my new heart valve, the doctors had given me the green light to lift weights again, so I ratcheted-up the reps for basketball season.

Chuck Norris and Christie Brinkley were all over television promoting Total Gym fitness, but I couldn't afford the programs or the equipment. Some of my friends cut firewood. Others stacked bales of hay. One was naturally muscular, the youngest in a family of many brothers, and to be avoided during impromptu wrestling sessions in the P.E. swimming unit unless you could hold your breath for minutes at a time. I knew nothing technical about weightlifting, but I knew I needed to get stronger. In Dad's old basement workshop I found a rusty pair of pliers and a flathead screwdriver to loosen the iron clamps on the ends of his dumbbells. I secured disks to the bars and began regularly waving them around in my bedroom, *Led Zeppelin IV* blasting from my speakers. I gripped the weights tightly in each hand and tested the hinge of my elbow, the endurance of my biceps and triceps, extending my arms for arbitrary numbers of reps until I felt satisfied with my effort.

With a metabolism as high as mine, and as active as I was,

and as amateurish as was my bodybuilding scheme, it was impossible to tell if I gained any muscle or strength. Not one person told me I looked like I had been going to the gym, because I hadn't. If anything, I had spent many afternoons listening to classic rock in my bedroom, ruining my jump shot with ignorant attempts to increase arm strength and muscle mass.

On the whole, our team was small and scrawny, a bunch of soccer players balling for the winter, so we ran a fast break offence. We spent far too much time composing warm-up tapes, but we were a smart team, a quick team, scrappy and willing to play defence. On Friday nights on our home floor, basketball was beautiful, applause bouncing around the gymnasium, the opposing coach calling timeouts to regroup as we high-fived our way to the bench. We slugged cups of water, towelled our faces, wiped the dust off our sneaker soles. The horn sounded. Cheerleaders dashed across the gym, pompoms, hands and skirts fluttering in the air. The ref blew his whistle and we returned to the court to run some more.

College coaches showed interest in me and although they weren't Division I, being recruited was exactly what I'd dreamed about. They mailed me program information, invited me to their practices and games. A few came to watch me play. I shook their hands. Sent them game tape. Dreamed about playing college ball.

I was, in fact, growing bigger and stronger, and believed I could compete at a higher level. More importantly, I wanted people to forget I ever had open heart surgery, to delete that defect from my resume.

Girls from other schools—I was thrilled to learn—knew who I was. They cheered my name, pumping me up like a steroid. I once walked into the guest locker room at a rival school and, written in soap across the mirrors and walls,

were messages of love, phone numbers, and the words, "We're **EASY** …to reach." Reading this, I felt strong and my confidence soared.

But at my next cardiologist appointment Dr. Tarchini expressed concern. In the echocardiogram room, a transducer—a microphone-like wand—slid smoothly through gel and over my bare skin, directing ultrasound waves into my chest, my tissues and blood, reflecting these transmissions in different ways to create images and sounds on a computer monitor. The sonographer recorded many pictures. Based on the results and what he heard using a stethoscope, Dr. Tarchini determined that the bovine valve was already leaking. The valve that was supposed to last several years *at least,* but now the backflow was enlarging my heart after just eight months.

"This typically does not happen so soon after surgery," he said gently, cautiously. I said nothing. Ejection fraction, he said. Diastolic function, he said. He described treatments. I would take a beta blocker, atenolol, again. I would stop lifting weights. I would have a stress test, for which I would run on a treadmill to determine the effect of the atenolol on my blood pressure and whether I should continue playing sports.

"Have you experienced any chest pain, heart palpitations, or light-headedness?" he asked.

In a heartbeat, I decided that if I ever replied *yes*, whether it was true or not, then I would be prevented from playing sports.

"No."

A month later, testing showed that the atenolol reduced my blood pressure when resting, but aggressive physical activity still caused my heart rate and blood pressure to jump to concerning levels. My solution was to go to appointments as infrequently as possible, because every

time I was examined I hoped not for a discovery to help me lead a healthier life, but feared a diagnosis that would restrict me from being a boy who loved sports and romping around in the woods with his friends.

I kept this information to myself and pretended I was as normal as my friends. This way, it seemed easier to be the person I aspired to be: not weak, but strong; not erratic, but dependable. I wanted no sympathy. I knew all too well who Hank Gathers was. The 6'7" Loyola Marymount transfer had been one of the only Division I basketball players in history to lead the nation in scoring and rebounding in the same season. Gathers was a physical specimen with exercise-induced ventricular tachycardia, for which he was prescribed a beta blocker, like me. Gathers skipped cardiologist appointments. Gathers didn't take his medicine, especially on game days. Gathers dropped dead on the court amidst another dominating performance, moments after a rim-rattling dunk. Whenever ESPN ran stories about athletes at all levels of competition succumbing to sudden cardiac arrest, I felt anxious because I knew I would not stop playing. In my subconscious, my ability to justify my actions approached omnificence.

Over the phone, or in letters embossed with collegiate crests and mascots and Latin mottos, DIII basketball recruiters described how I would fit in their programs. They proposed dietary plans and training programs and, because they felt less real to me than my friends, I told them the truth: I could not lift weights. The silence that spread between us thickened, clotted, swelled, and made it simple for me to read their minds. Instantly, I ceased to be worth their time. The rejection I felt cannot be overstated. My identity was falling apart.

"Oh, no kidding," they said.

"Yea."

"I'm sorry to hear that," they said.
"Take care of yourself," they said.
"Let's be in touch," they said.
I never heard from them again.

21

One Friday night we attended a Rusted Root concert at a local college. On the way, Burnham told us about hoisting a girl up to his bedroom window with his climbing harness and rope in the middle of the night.

"Made quite the pulley system with the leg of my bed frame," he said. "I reeled her right in." I pictured his red face as he tugged on the rope, his heart pounding, one hundred and ten pounds of girl dangling above the ground and scuffing footprints on the house siding. "At the end of the night I hardly had the strength to lower her back down."

Since surgery, each moment I spent with my friends was a degree of repatriation. I brimmed with anticipation: for the music, the girls that would certainly be there, and the booze that Billy had filched from his parents' cupboard. Donning jeans with colourful patches, band T-shirts, and hemp necklaces worn smooth by the oils of our neck skin, we buzzed along the road.

Outside the car windows I first noticed the basketball arena where I had sat behind the team bench last month as a guest of the coach and a hopeful recruit, then rows of dorms and soccer fields. A moment later we parked beside Jim Neville's truck.

"Let's see what you got!" he said as we huddled around the tailgate. Billy furtively distributed paper cups and my eyes darted around for security officers—not one to be seen, although they could have been hiding anywhere. Adrenaline leaked inside me. It pulsed outwardly from my chest and, in cahoots with the guys, I relished the excited, nervous burn. Billy uncorked the bottle and poured the

first round, but something was wrong.

"What is *this*?" Irwin asked, taking another sip.

"I didn't even look," Billy said, "I was in such a hurry to snatch it before we left – my dad came home earlier than I'd planned." Holding the bottle under the yellow parking lamp we read the label: Arbor Hill Sparkling Raspberry Grape Juice. Our hearts broke.

"Juice?" Irwin said.

"Shit," Billy said amidst a chorus of groans. I heard boozy yells and watched masses of college revellers stumble up the concrete steps to the venue and felt like the biggest rube of them all. These kids, I assumed, had fake IDs or reliable connections or were actually of legal drinking age, with stashes of beer and booze and drugs I had never even thought to try. These kids were ready to rage. They partied in their own cars, their own dorm rooms, and their own houses. For us, this was an opportunity to *be* those kids, to connect and have a great time and a story to tell to our friends who couldn't come to the show, about the night we threw down with the college crew during the '99 Rusted Root winter tour. But we failed to seize the moment. Amateurs. Never had I felt *so* sixteen.

"So this is kind of like the time you sold me that bag of oregano," Irwin said.

"Shit," Billy said again, because there was nothing else to say.

At the door, security patted us down and pushed us along, past a boy holding a girl's hair and rubbing her back as she vomited into a hedgerow. Blue trash bins filled with bottles and cans, and several tall, brawny men wearing tight black T-shirts and walkie-talkies scrutinized the procession with iron faces, and searched purses and pockets. With ticket stubs in our hands, we entered the field house. People swarmed the stage front and the taping section, cramming

against the temporary tube-metal barriers that enclosed the mixing boards to erect their own condenser microphones and battery-powered preamplifiers to personally record the show. This, we knew, was where we'd find the best sound, and so we wove through the crowd to the front of the barriers, dancing over power cables duct-taped to the floor and past hippie chicks wearing batiked skirts and corduroy purses, nose rings and henna tattoos. Slowly the air filled with fog from the dry ice machines, incense and smoke from the revellers, and the conversations of a thousand fans.

"Grape juice," Irwin said, stuffing his ticket stub into his wallet and shaking his head.

"Grape juice!" we shouted.

"Shore could use a barrel of that there sparklin' bubbly!" he said.

The room suddenly went dark and Rusted Root strolled barefoot onto the stage. The lead singer pressed his palms together in front of his chest and bowed several times. The crowd roared, and before he slung his guitar strap over his shoulder the drumming and dancing had started, resonating within me, my heartbeat matching the tribal pulse. The music percussed the intercostal spaces of my chest, and during deep respiration I felt the lower limits of resonance in my ribs. I raised my hand to my sternum and from my wrist tapped my fingers in time with the drums and the bass, and then used the flat of my hand, drumming my chest from top to bottom, and side to side, percussing my chest all around and in synch with the polyrhythm that carried us along. This dancing drenched us in sweat. Submitting to the music, surrounded by my friends, I felt my heart beat in time with more of its kind than I ever could have counted, steadier than it ever had before.

Across fields, over crumbling fieldstone fences and rambling wire, we trudged toward the cabin, our refuge of choice that cold winter night. Billy and his pup, Deeohgee, Irwin, Nicky, and me.

The snowfall was tremendous that day, the sky through the trees a hard winter blue. The drifts were captivatingly deep and we broke trail as the sun plunged into the horizon. Guitars and pillows hoisted above our heads, we danced the dance of river waders crossing to shore. Darkness filled the sky as afternoon took its curtain call and the first stars blinked to light.

The world was still.

Inside, we twisted newspaper into kindling, struck a match, and in no time were spoiled by a luxurious wood-stove glowing at the seams. Our coats and mittens, knit hats and scarves, were strewn about, and the snowmelt from our boots evaporated quickly, leaving sooty rings on the floor.

We melted candles and sculpted the wax into goblets and goblins. We imitated the Cowardly Lion from the *Wizard of Oz* and quoted Garth from *Wayne's World*. We made plans to live at the cabin over the summer, year round, plans to drive to Ithaca, to California, to fly to Germany, to play soccer, to longboard down Main Street at midnight, to eat bagels and Rockcastles at the Grainery, to see Rusted Root, Phish, David Grisman, Smokin' Joe Bonamassa, The Allman Brothers Band, plans to climb Adirondack mountains and to kiss girls. We patterned the foggy windows with fingertip pictures, condensation masterpieces on

black canvas that was a winter night. We tuned our guitars and sang. "Angel from Montgomery." "Melissa." "Mustang Sally." "Running on Faith." "Gimme That Ol' Time Religion." "Simple Twist of Fate." "Wish You Were Here." Working through our repertoire, the temperature climbed. We drummed with newfound vigour, clapping and clubbing the table with sticks and with spoons, sock-stomping around the room in an improvised dance. The indoor/outdoor thermometer read eighty and twenty. We stoked the fire anyway and tingled with warmth.

Then, without hesitation, we got naked, raced outside and dove into the snow.

We howled. We backstroked nowhere. We reached toward the sky to unscrew the stars and retrieve the unknown. We never wondered, *What good is it to swim naked in the snow?* because we just knew it was. Kicking the powder, we raced into the cabin, breathless and scratched red-raw from our dip in the tree trunk shadow-streaked snow.

In the months to come, the weather warmed and girls visited the cabin. We told them about moments like these while the wine sank in the bottle and the fire nestled into embers. We all slept in a pile on the floor in a nest of blankets and sleeping bags and sweaters, and in the dark my hand found its way, after so many years, to Missy's delicate hand.

THOMAS MANNELLA

I asked Missy to Prom. Billy took Kayla. We were not dating them, but they were our dates. They were the girls that other girls probably hated because they could hang with the boys. Girls who were flirty without being slutty. The ratio was almost always two girls to many more boys. They were friends. They partied with us at The Barn and crammed into cars for late night trips to the north end of the lake for billiards or diner food or a movie, loops around the city pier and long wanderings around the grocery store picking donuts out of the pastry cases. They let us drive their parents' new cars and, when we jokingly jerked the wheel back and forth, spinning on dark and snowy roads, and the car ploughed into a fencepost, denting the door, these were the girls who collaborated on a reasonable story and stuck to it. They played Knock-Out in the gym after school, winning their share of rounds, and they filled the mandatory "two girls on a team" rule for coed volleyball tournaments, becoming skilful setters to our spikes. We peppered these girls with bits of paper in class to make them think about us instead of physics or calculus or *The Canterbury Tales*. Missy and Kayla were the girls we spied on and ambushed, hurling snowballs at their house windows from dark spaces, trying to make them scream. The girls who peeled our oranges at lunch and let us take care of them when they drank too much at a party. The girls who let us sit in their living rooms and at their kitchen tables to blather our nonsense for hours and hours as we tried to impress them. As we started to *like them* like them. With us these girls walked the aisles at the House of Guitars,

not knowing much about guitars themselves, but just to be along for the ride, to see what we were up to because they didn't have any other girlfriends, and because maybe they were starting to *like us* like us, too. They were the girls who got us to watch *When Harry Met Sally* and who jumped concert gates to the front rows with us and challenged us to admit we liked *this* girl or *that* girl, and that we kissed *her* or *her*. Girls whose hands we eventually held in cabins in the woods or in dark movie theatres or longboarding down the middle of main street at night, whose hands held ours, secretly and then openly, now and many years from now. Girls we were friends with first. Girls we delicately competed for. Girls a few of us would someday want to marry.

But this was just the four of us on Prom night, wearing gowns and tuxedos in an upscale restaurant where we'd never eat again. The girls were indecisive with the menu. The friendly banter between us evaporated. We drank the ice water quickly and waited for refills.

Billy ordered honey-glazed tiger shrimp. The sauce was equally sticky and slippery, and the knife and fork were like chopsticks between his fingers. He poked and sawed. He slathered his lips and cheeks, but he did not quit and soon we were laughing. Missy removed the corsage I gave her and set it on the table and, while Kayla helped Billy plan the next shrimp dissection, I mustered up all the bravado I had to tell Missy that she looked great—and she did in her black dress, her eyes blue and pleasantly slitted. Her presence heightened my own senses, my consciousness of our surroundings. But I was afraid these were things boyfriends, not good friends, said, and the moment slipped by.

"I swear I'm not stalking you," Missy finally said, "but I think we have the same doctor."

"Really?"

"Dr. Tarchini." She named my cardiologist—our cardiologist, apparently. I had become accustomed to ignoring the existence of my cardiologist; if somebody else mentioned surgery or the heart or the word *cardiologist*, then I would reflexively lock down, deftly changing the subject. But Missy said his name and I did not short circuit or hide.

"I have an arrhythmia," she continued, "and knew you had surgery and figured your doctor was a great one because you seem to be doing so well."

"I had no idea," I said, as much about her condition as her perception and consideration of my health. Who was this girl, self-accepting in ways I had never been, willing to disclose her weakness to me here and now? "How did you get his name?"

"I asked your mom."

"You talk to my mom?"

"Sometimes."

"Are you sure you're not stalking me?"

Missy laughed.

"Maybe a little," she said, churning her spoon in her ice water, our link strengthening a beat more. The waiter began setting plates of food in front of us, but my mind had already drifted far away from the fancy table. I imagined Missy sitting in the same exam room at the same hospital as I had, Dr. Tarchini speaking to her in his calm, confident voice, the cartoon animals dancing across the ceiling tiles.

The way she reached out to me felt safe. In doing so I felt a little less alone.

And if I could have chosen somebody with whom I would like to feel a little less alone, for the first time I knew it could be her.

24

"Any big parties planned for this year?" Mom asked as we neared Independence Day and the anniversary of my Valley View arrest.

"Of course not," I lied.

By mid-July the heat settled in and we caravanned two hours down the New York State Thruway to our first Phish festival at the County Airport in Volney, NY: Camp Oswego. The traffic near the venue pumped intermittently like blood in a narrow artery. At the festival gates, a hippie passed our procession and held in plain sight a tuberous cola bud the size of his forearm. It wasn't the size of the specimen that astonished us, but rather that one could so casually sell drugs apparently undaunted by the prospect of getting in trouble. Perhaps we were about to taste lawless utopia.

Unfortunately, the security guards made off with more than a few cases of our beer. While the rest of us established camp, Irwin and Neville walked several miles to retrieve the confiscated supplies. Upon their return, Irwin dropped the empty cooler, took a seat on it and lit a fresh Camel. He examined our digs with a wry grin.

"Bastards," Neville said.

Fortunately, we had packed plenty more beer and with no adults around to wag their fingers, we focused on indulgence. It was impossible to know how to pace ourselves under such conditions. Vast swaths of excitement stretched into the weekend, so we just went for it because this festival seemed an impossible thing to do: marking our calendars and saving money and getting permission from our parents

to procure tickets. Finally, the day had arrived. We plunged into the scene.

It was not possible to wake early on the first morning and resume the merrymaking because we never actually slept. The drum circles in the car yard lasted until dawn and at sunrise we toasted cheese sandwiches outside our tents, washed them down with a formidable amount of beer, stood for an hour in an ice line, and sought refuge inside a mist tent, like lizards in a desert oasis. From time to time we refilled the water bottles and scouted for girls and listened to bands performing on the side stages. Or we strolled the avenues of a bustling, unauthorized, and haphazard marketplace, rehashing the night while the sun burned off the residual weariness until the main event: Phish in the afternoon.

Our enthusiasms included drinking beer, which we did without interruption. Despite the chaos, I remembered to take my atenolol each day and hoped doing so would offset anything else I mixed into my bloodstream. In the time-honoured tradition of male adolescents attempting to gross-out their counterparts, we crassly shared with each other the particulars of our latest bowel movements. We were all deranged. Maybe it was the element of survival and the absurdity of a situation so far removed from our normal lives that made our descriptions hysterical. Maybe we were just drunk. It was blissful, this autonomy.

Pungent clouds of smoke—tobacco, clove, marijuana, campfire, cook stove, and meat grease—domed the base. The dirt blackened our toes. The air smelled like summer-time and music. We were in high school, so it of course smelled like freedom.

Our wandering led us to an airfield of crackling grass where marshmallows the size of beer kegs were impaled upon twenty foot chopsticks, stuck in the heat. Underneath

a cluster of marshmallow trees a pair of girls appeared like a mirage. Four smooth legs folded on the ground among dozens of empty balloons.

"Nitrous," Burnham said.

The girls stared into the cotton sky and like a flock of vultures we made a gliding approach. Before any introductions were made, one girl slumped to the ground, her eyes rolled back into her head, and she convulsed rhythmically. Colour emptied from her face. A half-deflated balloon was pinched between her fingers. I was stunned. She wore a skirt and exposed the naked space between her legs. Her friend watched with a wooden face. Just before we ran for help, she stopped twitching and regained her composure, sat upright again, bits of broken grass and dirt Velcroed to her hair, and looked at me in an implacable way that suggested I was to blame. I backed away. Billy offered his water to her, but she waved him off and inhaled the rest of the balloon.

We remained quiet for a long stretch of airbase runway, plodding along in the brutal heat. Often, when behaving recklessly, I calibrated my choices against those of others. I felt I could handle anything my brother and my friends could; who else would I have measured myself against? But seeing the nitrous balloon girl lose consciousness, seize, and struggle to regain manual dexterity after coming to, I believed we were different than her, safer, more responsible because we were just slamming beers and wandering around; we were mainly there for the music. *That girl could have died!* I thought, but in the true spirit of adolescent self-reflection, I never applied the same logic to myself, to my heart. Maybe I would have benefitted from a video of myself at Valley View, staggering, falling, splayed in mud and puke. Or a video from the operating room, my chest opened wide. Instead, sweating along the runway, I recalled

the photograph of me after heart surgery and my Valley View mug shot and Pete laid low in the funeral home, and now the girl in the field with the balloon, the paleness in our drained cheeks. We all shared the same ephemeral existence.

To escape the sun we entered a small house and stumbled into the angles of its whimsical construction. Screwed onto the walls were children's toys—dial phones, bells, jack-in-the-box clowns—and we played in the shade. A poem was painted on the ceiling in vermiculate turns of colour:

There was a crooked man and he walked a crooked mile,
He found a crooked sixpence upon a crooked stile.
He bought a crooked cat, which caught a crooked mouse.
And they all lived together in a little crooked house.

Indeed. Between the heat and sleep deprivation and partying we were as crooked as a barrel of fish hooks. We exited along with a tumble of children's playtime bubbles and returned to Shakedown Street, where there was enough hemp for sale to lasso the stars. A topless woman with nipples dangling like shoestrings and the hairiest armpits I had ever seen sold sunglasses and canned beer. Shirtless djembe players wandered about looking for a jam amid the deeply tanned hula-hoopers and ball and stick jugglers, hacky sackers and hand baggers and stilt-walkers glittering in wacky sequined suits. All of it resembled a vivid carnival scene out of Dr. Seuss. The circus was in town and many of these peripatetic folk were on tour themselves. Music poured from every nook. Happiness and pleasure saturated the air. On the corner a dreadlocked man sipped a joint and held a foofy little dog and a cardboard sign that read, "Friend for Life: 25 Cents." Billy, the most parsimonious among us, hugged him, paid his quarter, and smiled contagiously.

Back at camp we washed spaghetti noodles down with

warm beer. Strewn about the grounds were empty bottles and cans, Frisbees and hacky sacks, a trampled rain fly, several pairs of Birkenstocks, and a scummy pan lid that buzzed on the ground with each boom from our neighbours' rave speakers. A preppy kid wearing a pink-collared shirt stumbled into our lair, bug-eyed and mumbling.

"Have you seen my friend, Molly?" he asked, "Molly? Molly? Molly?" and was on his way before anyone could reply.

Then it was time. We filled the Nalgenes and loaded our backpacks. I took stock of our crew. A Backwoods cigar smouldered in the tuning pegs of Neville's guitar while he improvised a Son Seals song with a beer bottle slide. Billy bounced with excitement, as sure of this as anything he had ever done, and Nicky nodded along with the music that played inside his head. In the spirit of survival, Irwin and I donned skirts made of patchwork silk and only after a final toast were we ready to go. A ragged troupe we were, but eager to claim our piece of the scene. The last time we saw Wayne and Burnham they were napping under the tarp, two heads, one pillow, but now they too were gone. We assumed we'd find them before we left. And as for the others, well, I hoped they were comfortable in this sweltering heat, among this staggering crowd. Chance was the only way to communicate with these stray friends, so to the venue we went and settled in at the gates.

In the middle of acres of blacktop under the sun, it was as hot and damp as the inside of a possum's mouth. The runway pinched to a point on the horizon, its terminus obscured by the shimmering heat. We sat back-to-back and passed the water in the woolly air. My last electric-yellow piss had occurred ages ago.

"It's in the triple digits, easy," Irwin said.

Nicky's dehydrated expression confirmed what did

not need further confirmation: our asses were literally burning. Water was scarce but I couldn't fault Billy for pouring a puddle to sit in. If there was a freezer, then I would've stepped right into it. We could've fried an egg between our feet, but supplies were rationed a mile away at our shantytown camp—tarps tied together with bungee cords and a few collapsing tents within a ring of our parked cars. There was little to say so we sipped warm beers while our skin cooked, tracing the hazy arc of the sun with our eyes. A bearded and robed wayfarer wove through the crowd distributing papers. One fluttered to my lap.

7 - 16 - 99

Holmdel, NJ

<u>Set I</u>

Sample in a Jar, Beauty of My Dreams, Dogs Stole Things, Limb By Limb, Billy Breathes, Vultures, Back on the Train, Maze, Cavern

<u>Set II</u>

Also Sprach Zarathustra > Mike's Song > I Am Hydrogen > Weekapaug Groove > Simple > Guyute, Loving Cup > Golgi Apparatus

<u>Encore</u>

Born to Run

We huddled together, read the names, and because Phish's song bag was so immense and unpredictable and could probably fill an entire tour without repeating a tune, we wondered what they might play that day. I cracked another tepid beer. So much of Phish was a mystery that I wanted to uncover. Radio didn't play Phish, yet they sold out festivals like this, and each bootleg concert tape was filled with songs they only performed live.

Suddenly, the crowd cheered in anticipation, a swelling rush of joy.

"The music hasn't even started yet!" Billy shouted, slapping my shoulder. The crowd pulsed and buzzed and the sun skidded behind the distant horizon. Wayne slithered through the crowd with Burnham. They carried water and our spirits soared. Then the crowd crushed forward and we were on the move, shoulder to shoulder, pouring through the gates and toward the stage, thousands and thousands of us dashing down the runway, taking off. We ran like antelopes until there was nowhere else to run, twenty yards from centre stage. Around us, blankets patched everyone together, lighters chirped like crickets, and clouds formed above the airfield.

Beside us a man searched the sky.

"Pods," he repeated. "Giant seeds, right there."

Nobody listened and he didn't seem to care. He shook his head slowly, amazed.

"Water, inside," the stranger said, "but to retrieve it …" His words fell away, perspiration catching in his bird's nest beard. He reached upward prayerfully toward clouds and atmosphere that were but a shade apart, a shipwrecked sailor contemplating coconuts in a tree. The racks of stage lights were pod-like, indeed. *This is the highest person I have ever seen,* I thought. On his T-shirt was printed an image of a concert audience, which to my eyes was like looking through a window in his chest at the actual crowd. A caption below it read, "More Friends Than Jesus," but with *Friends* spelled *Phriends* in honour of the band. In this devout congregation, that was exactly how I felt. This was what I had been terrified to miss the summer before, on the mend from surgery and out of the loop. On the outside of an inside joke. It felt damned good to be a part of the crowd.

"Want some?" I offered Pod Man my water. He met my gaze and licked his lips.

"Oh, boy, oh man, my god." He sighed with relief. "Shit

….." He guzzled rapaciously, as if for the first time. " …this was way easier than, you know …," he said and pointed feebly at the pod lights. "I *never* could have done it alone. Thank you." And that said it all.

A large beach ball smashed Pod Man in the face, instigating a noiseless laughter that crumpled him to the ground. There he slept on a blanket and sucked his thumb. Perhaps that's what we were all chasing, I thought: rapture, those means and moments that allow us to experience something more beautiful and pleasurable than anything we could imagine. But maybe he was just tripping balls.

Similar objects appeared above the assemblage: Scooby Doo, a killer whale, a cactus, a lizard, a hot dog, and colourful beach balls of all sizes. Some were scribbled with songs requests. The sky divided into swaths of pink and purple. A distant scream initiated thousands of replies, rolling in like surf before splitting open and melting into the evening air. Fog machines on stage. Blue house lights. Another cheer, cresting and breaking. Tangled in anticipation, we waited for the lowest trough in the wave to start our own, to connect to thousands of people who responded to our roars. We smiled. Phish took the stage. I stripped off my T-shirt and dropped it to the ground.

I'd been told that you couldn't truly experience Phish unless you attended a show. It was true. Guitarist Trey Anastasio and bassist Mike Gordon synchronically bounced on trampolines while playing and burst encroaching balloons with the tuning pegs of their guitars. Jon Fishman was a donut-patterned-dress-wearing wizard on the drums and Page McConnell, ear to the ivory, locked into the grooves. This—the music, the energy it produced—was why people followed Phish around the country. It was why they mattered. I listened to them listening to each other. I danced miles. They channelled our energy, thousands of us,

into sound. At night, glow sticks rained from the sky, some exploding, speckling me in phosphorescence. I smeared red lines down my chest like some kind of warrior.

Between sets we sat on the trampled field grass under a smoky and murmuring sky. Everything about Oswego felt sacred. In the presence of these musicians and this crowd I belonged to unified and unique group. If I had been excluded from this festival, the part of me that desired to be with my brother and the boys I considered brothers would have died a little more. To what lengths, then, might I go to compensate?

The next day Phish jammed on. A permanent cloud of smoke hung over the airbase. Pipes and joints, pills and balloons, circulated through the crowd, and strangers became instant friends in this sharing. Nitrous balloon girl lingered on the periphery of my consciousness. Did she experience a gauziness similar to the morphine and Codeine highs of heart surgery and recovery? A funky, roaring jam was a strange place to be thinking about such a vividly painful moment of my past, yet I felt so, so good to juxtapose my past with the present: live Phish. My chest was sawed open? No biggie. There was a chance I could have died? Whatever.

I felt perfect.

Connected to the band like a screwdriver bridging battery terminals, the music leapt to the crowd and we became one surging circuit. My senses blurred: I heard the liturgical stage lights and saw the music, the synaesthesia beautiful and pure. Bright sound exploded with the sizzling intensity of each jam, or washed us in cool blue beams. At various moments the airbase became a sunny Sunday in the Jelly-bean church, covering me in Jesus Rays. At the apogee, the fireworks unzipped the night air, ropes and knots of colour, electric pinwheels spinning in the dark. The final chord rang

out and was swallowed by applause. My synapses burned.

Retreating to camp, with his arm around Billy's shoulder, and in his finest drunken voice, Irwin said, "I could really use a beer."

"Heads-up," someone called. Irwin lifted his eyes in time to see a can flying at him. He reached out and caught it against all odds.

Eventually, we shuttled through a labyrinth of campsites and port-a-johns at sunrise, bleary-eyed and home-bound. Cavalcading more than an hour west on the Thruway was impossible, despite the lure of our beds only a second hour away, so we caught a few winks at a rest stop before crawling to Naples. For the next twenty-four hours we slept, waking for meals and to watch news reports of the riots and rapes, the violence and fires that marred the weekend's other outdoor music festival, the thirtieth anniversary of Woodstock, fifty miles east of Oswego, satisfied that we instead had chosen the peace, the love, and the music.

25

We were the Big Green Machine, the only school whose mascot was a dude with a Mohawk who drove an armoured tank with fearsome tread, a giant hammer, and metal pincers. This soccer season would be my last in Naples and my expectations were lofty, as were those of my teammates. Coach felt the same, and on the first day of practice set a hypodermic needle on a table in front of us.

"This," he said, pointing at the syringe, "is the only thing between you guys and a state title." Clearly, he knew more than we thought he did. Then he turned and walked away, leaving us something to prove. The choice was ours to make.

The boldness of his proclamation cannot be understated: only four teams in the State of New York would win their final game of the season, one for each classification of school size. But he knew what it took to be one of those four teams, having won a state crown ten years before, and taking another team to the state semi-finals since. He knew our potential as soccer players, and had been grooming us since elementary school, covering tournament fees, and the cost of uniforms and soccer balls out of his own coaching salary, his desire deep, his belief in ours shaken.

I obstinately ignored my leaking two-years-young bovine valve; maybe I should not have played. Aware of my athletic ambitions, Dr. Tarchini administered another stress test. He connected my chest to wires and recorded my heart rate and blood pressure while I ran on a treadmill, the speed and incline of the machine steadily increasing. Afterwards, he doubled my atenolol dose to ease the labours of my

pumping heart. This, we hoped, would slow the deterioration of the valve.

"Pills are the least invasive treatment," he said again, doing his best to care for me, but there was some shit I knew I was never going to get a second crack at; I wasn't going to lose soccer. So I avoided contact with his office the rest of the season, cancelling appointments, stalling. I disregarded the inevitable. My heart ballooned with each beat, each relaxation of my left ventricle allowing blood to flow in two directions through the regurgitant aortic valve. The persistent regurgitation caused the ventricle to pump harder and harder to compensate for the leak, its walls thickening and losing elasticity. The increased pressure from the increased work load could cause my previously repaired aorta to bulge, an aneurism to form and rupture, another blood-filled balloon set to burst.

The paresthesia in my chest came and went. I had frequent palpitations doing homework, of all things. Once, a bolt of pain divided my chest, demarcating a stark line between feelings of danger and normal non-feeling feeling. *It's scar tissue and cartilage moving around*, I told myself and it might have been, so I ignored it. The potential for tragedy was hidden and high, the surge that could make me the next sad story on the news entirely real.

That autumn we won all of our Finger Lakes West games except two and, unremarkably, finished in second place in our league. But perhaps losing focus and failing in this way allowed us to relive the disappointing loss at the end of the previous season, and to regain our poise in time for the single elimination postseason tournament. Across New York State, winter sports seasons began: basketball, swimming, volleyball, skiing, ice hockey, wrestling. We defined a new goal—survive and advance—and continued playing soccer.

The days passed, the snow fell, and the superstitions piled up. Throughout the postseason we ate our game-day breakfast at the Redwood Diner, and August was the last time several of us had washed our jerseys. Burnham's uniform was especially rank. We massaged our cleats with mink oil. We stopped shaving; some of our faces were fuzzy and others were unchanged. Dressing for games became ritualistic: left shin guard, left sock, left cleat, right shin guard, right sock, right cleat. Tape. We also used the tape to bind the speakers of our D-battery-powered stereo together, blasting ZZ Top's "Got Me Under Pressure" and Smash Mouth's "Padrino" as our bus rolled along the valley roads. Regardless of the temperature, we opened the windows hoping to smell skunks. Why was this lucky? Because we deemed it so. Our focus was such that every moment, every sensory detail associated with soccer and the team, took on significance, and we had the responsibility of bestowing these experiences with positive value that helped us win. We were in control. So we ran through the same series of passes and stretches with the same people in the same spots on the field each game. We cleared the goal posts and danced with the corner flags. In synchronization, we clapped twice as each opponent was introduced over the PA. At halftime we ate apples. And after the final seconds ticked off the game clock, we collected our shin guard tape into a growing globe, a talisman with its own seat on the bench. The same sort of hospital tape that held IVs in my arms and legs, tubes in my side, stomach, and neck. My heart did not register in my conscious thought during a single moment of a single game. Soccer was tremendously fun, and I just played.

During practice the soccer balls deflated in the cold, the panels slick and stiff. Our keeper dove across the goal, landing on frozen footprints, and then jumping to his feet

to hurl the ball away, grinning and daring us for more.

The team warm-up gear was inadequate so we wore long underwear and wool hats, knit mittens and puffy coats. We scuffed our spikes in the frosty grass, blew snot rockets everywhere, and rubbed away the ice that stitched our eyelashes together. The jug water was a cold burn going down. Below the practice field, steam beckoned from the gymnasium chimney, yet we were thankful to be outside. Coach defied the weather in tight green polyester shorts and a green trucker hat, and his assistants wore insulated Carhartt bibs, hunting socks, and real beards. We were at ease on rock and snow and spoke our own language:

"Cookie jar!"

"Goose egg!"

"Away! Away! Away!"

I would not be denied these teammates, this time, for any reason. I would not be owned by my leaky valve, would not quit because playing was dangerous. My heart belonged to my friends.

A shootout following a drawn score after regulation and overtime gave me greater apprehension.

So on the sunny afternoon before our first playoff game, I punted my ball over the Linton's fence, pulled Pete's ladder from beneath fallen leaves, rusted and tangled in Goldenrod, and climbed over. Alone on the rocky field I drilled PKs until I was satisfied. I sat on the eighteen, where, as sweeper, I began each game, and smelled the sugary grass, the valley walls dropping the last of their leaves. A bleacher-like hill surrounded the field and after practice each day we sprinted up this hill to condition our bodies to the limits of their power. We personified clichés: grit, hustle, heart. That devotion, I hoped, made my choice of a tissue valve worthwhile instead of the biggest mistake of my life.

1999 Section V Class C Boys Soccer Tournament

Quarterfinals: Wayne drove the first goal to the back of the net with his head and I was breathless from celebrating and relief. We quickly scored twice more and drowned Kendall in our adrenaline.

Semi-finals: Windswept the lighted field with the season's first snow and our bus rolled to a stop. Maybe due to the wintry weather or the magnitude of the game the team was unusually quiet. If we lost the season would be finished. We lacked our usual energy. Following Coach, we stood to exit the bus, but he stopped on the bottom step. He turned, climbed back inside, and addressed the team with his powerful voice.

"Gentlemen," he said, "one more thing: practice tomorrow at 3:30!"

We exploded.

The air screamed off Lake Ontario, ripping the words from Coach's mouth and scattering them about: *Hang. Tough. Mannella.* After a scoreless regulation, Burnham single-footedly ran the ball across the Red Creek goal line in overtime, initiating a big green pile that swallowed him before he could get out of the eighteen.

Finals: Wayne buried Geneseo with a first-half blast and we hoisted the Section V trophy amid a percussive booming from our fans: cowbell, trash can, chain link fence.

We had advanced to the state tournament, and so reporters came to the practice field and asked us to put the magic of our enduring season into words. To explain that we had been together, on this field and with this ball, since we were little boys. That we played for each other.

When it was my turn to speak, there was no way to explain my appreciation for this team, or to explain how my risky behaviour was filling me with life. To lose would

be crushing, but not playing would be far worse. I would rather drop dead on the field than be kept off it. And as long as I kept the palpitations and chest pains a secret, I believed they would cease to exist.

1999 New York State Public High School Athletic Association (NYSPHSAA) Class C Boys Championship Tournament

Section V Qualifier: Despite temperatures in the twenties, an attendance record was set under starry skies. Wayne struck first on a direct kick, later kneed one into our own net off of a Mynderse throw-in to tie, and then completed the weird hat trick with a miracle upper-90 rocket in quadruple overtime, minutes before an imminent shootout. Another one bit the dust.

Regional Qualifier: The Big Green 1, Lake Chautauqua 0. Wayne was a machine, a cold-blooded assassin from the penalty stripe. We rode on, this time to Poughkeepsie, NY, for the semi-finals.

At a pep rally the morning of our departure the community celebrated us, overwhelmingly so. Years later, watching grainy video of this event, we all appear outwardly humble, heads sheepishly tilted to the floor under waves of applause as we gather around the tape ball in the middle of the gymnasium floor. Throughout footage of the pep rally and the games we played, it was also clear that we couldn't keep our hands to ourselves. Without exception, we draped our arms around each other's shoulders when walking onto or off of the field, to or from the bus, bear-hugging after heady plays and blunders alike, after goals and games when we were mobbed by fans. Communication was necessarily physical. The video footage shows that we were unable to walk past one another without high-fiving or fist-bumping or back-slapping. It shows me kissing Wayne on top of the head after his quadruple overtime game-winner against Mynderse, Coach speechless and laughing with disbelief, and our crew dancing with the enthusiasm of newlyweds,

as if we had not just played the longest game of our lives.

After the pep rally, we passed through the elementary school bus loop to read the signs the younger kids made, to hear their excited, high-pitched screams, and to remember what it was like to be in their shoes a decade ago when the first Big Green state champions left for the finals in the autumn of 1989.

Our five-hour bus ride to Poughkeepsie made a lot of time for thinking. For eating pans of brownies and grape pies. For festooning the aisles with snacking debris. For vomiting in the tiny bus bathroom. For cards and music and flatulence. But mostly for gazing out of the window, lost in thought.

Like ancestral ghosts the 1989 Naples Big Green New York State Champions lingered in my consciousness, cloaking us in an electric and vaporous sanctity. At over-night birthday parties in elementary school, we had studied their yearbook pictures. We dreamed of victory. We carried their names with us like destiny in a jar. Ten years after, I felt we were in the right place at the right time, born into this moment. Time to unscrew the lid.

Semi-final: As trains rumbled along the Hudson, we secured a 2-0 win over Seton Catholic at Marist College courtesy of Irwin's 40-yard first half bomb and later a magical cross that Nicky placed on Burnham's noggin. Afterwards, leaving the field with the guys, I turned to Wayne.

"After tomorrow's final, we'll have played in every game possible this season."

He smiled his widest smile.

Final: In stark contrast to Mattituck—our professionally-organized, undefeated opponents with pre-game cones and pinnies for three-v-one—we were a collage of unmatching gear and random juggling and passing configurations, a

cob job tinkered to near perfection. The Big Green had not played in front of a crowd as large or on turf as beautiful as the Vassar College pitch. The tape ball emitted the positive juju from the bench, a bundle of home field dirt and the sweat of our accomplishments thus far. The Tuckers, all gelled hair and shining boots, looked groomed for a night in Manhattan; the Big Green, semi-bearded and scruffy, looked like we had walked out of the woods and all the way to the game.

For a long while both teams darted around the field in flourishes of chaotic energy and neither side capitalized on scoring opportunities. Minutes before halftime, Burnham was dumped in the Mattituck box and earned us a penalty kick.

I recall an absence of sound. Wayne placed the ball on the hash and paced his strides, and stopped and turned, and lowered his head. I crouched at midfield many yards directly behind the ball. Ever since we were five and six and seven years old, red-faced under a summer sun and wearing green t-shirts as uniforms that celebrated the '89 team, we had been traveling through time and had finally arrived at our destination.

Beginning that summer after my first heart surgery, our energy had gathered like an unstoppable engine hurtling us through the stars and accumulating into a moment that was dense and forceful, carried by a town and a team. This moment was greater than any individual adversities, any surgeries in my past or in my future, because it was about all of us, it was about Naples, and while the blood slammed through the bovine valve and thudded deep inside my ears I felt nothing malignant. I simply concentrated on the idea of the ball crossing the goal line.

It seemed to require no conscious effort on his part, this PK weighted with extraordinary pressure, the fibers of

his muscles and his mind balanced, fluid, and sturdy, the evolution of his ability now fluently and instinctively beautiful. The whistle blew. He ran forward. Planted his left foot and struck with his right. The ball rippled the net like a stone in water.

The crowd exploded. I could not hear myself whooping and hollering, and I knew I hadn't felt this good since we were boys and Pete had outrun the final out and scored the winning run. I was but a small part of this cacophony, a vessel in this delirious system. I decided that nothing had ever felt so good—this moment was worth hundreds of open heart surgeries—but after an eternal defensive effort extending throughout the second half, we slid a shot into the Mattituck goal with seconds remaining and I realized we couldn't lose.

On the ride home, Wayne said, "They're going to have a parade for us, man."

After dark we pulled into the boat launch lot at the south end of Canandaigua Lake. The night air burst with the blaring of every emergency rescue machine in our town and those of our closest neighbours. Our legs cramped badly and stiffened, so we carried one another to the party, letting loose with brio what was left of our ragged voices. At the centre of this dissonant merriment was a wooden trailer hitched to a tractor to drive us the final miles into Naples.

In the village we paraded down Main Street past the people of our town: folks who volunteered for us, paid for us, lobbied and cheered and cooked for us, held and taught us, birthed us or claimed us as their own and cared for us whether they were related to us or not, people who were patient with us and forgave us and loved us because we were Naples, which was awash in pulsing red light and rhythmic chanting and cheering and singing, a place at the

heart of the Big Green Machine. Choosing the bovine valve was a gamble that I knew had paid off. It wasn't even about winning games. During heart surgeries and arrests, foolishness and ill-fate, I accepted the town's support. I owed Naples something, and I hoped that the solidarity of this celebration might be part of that.

Riding the wagon, seventeen years old, I could never have stared a decade down the road and confronted the circularity of life. That one day I would coach my coaches' kids and teach them in the classroom at my alma mater. That I would speak about moments like these at Coach's funeral. That because of those words, the tape ball would become a curiosity for a new generation, drawing them into my classroom, wanting to see it and touch it. And before I'd realize what was happening, I'd be answering their questions and telling stories and it was 1999, my body quivering with adrenaline and ready to run. I'd try again to decide what it all meant, why I could not look at pictures and videos and a mouldy bundle of tape and dream about our adolescent soccer selves, why I could not even recall those interminable moments in writing without choking up, alone in front of the computer screen on November nights. I would wonder if I was living vividly and foolishly in the past. But there is no ignoring what remains. I do not feel regret or sadness or a longing for what was. Instead, I feel an overwhelming sense of belonging. I love those people and that time and that is a magic that will never pass me by.

26

Marcy is the tallest mountain in New York State at 5,343 feet and is a 15-mile round-trip from the car lot on the Van Hoevenberg Trail. Climbing it requires a good deal of gear-schlepping. Before the trip, Mom stood beside me while I placed my backpack on her scale to make sure I would not carry more than 50 lbs. of stuff. Doctor's orders.

"Give the tent to Nicky," she had said when the scale topped out at fifty.

I knew it was important not to worry Mom, which was why I did not tell her about the pains that shot through the left side of my chest on last year's trip to climb The Great Range. Knowing that cardiac muscle is without feeling, I again chalked the pain up to scar tissue and cartilage moving in my ribs, doing my best to ignore the discomfort whenever it did occur, and hide any trace of concern. The pain certainly wasn't debilitating, but it preyed on my psyche. Even though it rained on The Great Range trip and we got lost and hiked an extra half dozen miles and only summitted three peaks and drank mud before we decided to bail, I enjoyed the challenge immensely and was happier still to have avoided tragedy, and to do it again. After that trip, when Dr. Tarchini asked if I experienced any chest pains or palpitations, I said, "No."

This year, fancying ourselves fit enough from soccer and youth, we found the acclivitous trail to the top of Mt. Marcy as advertised: forested and smelling of sap and black mud. Rocky outcrops, lichens, and alpine shrubs dominated the peak. By Indian Falls we scrapped our plan to explore Lake Tear of the Clouds—the highest lake in the

state and the source of the Hudson River—on the south slope, feeling knackered. It began to rain the misty rain of the region, adding to our discomfort.

Mountain runoff purified with iodine tablets and handfuls of trail mix could only carry us so far. Sooner or later a hot meal was essential. With this in mind, we proceeded skyward, scrambling to the summit in a wind strong enough to lean into without falling over. Irwin and I, food partners on this leg of the trip, huddled behind a boulder above tree line to fiddle with our cook stove. Ramen Noodles were on the menu, so we set the stove to boil after much fine-tuning of the wind screen, positioning our bodies and backpacks around it to shelter the flame from sudden gales. Somewhere behind the adjacent rocky outcrops the others presumably did the same. The iodine tablets we used to kill bacteria and giardia in our drinking water turned our bottles yellowish-brown and made the water taste shitty. Only when dehydrated did I drink the treated water without plugging my nose, which was the case at lunch. There is a neutralizer tablet that allegedly conceals the metallic bitterness, but we were too cheap to buy those, too, so until the noodles boiled, we replenished fluids with iodine water.

In my impatience and under Irwin's drooling stare, I finished the cooking on the harder side of al dente, but *to hell with it*, I thought, emptying the powder packet of salty goodness into the steaming pot, my wrinkled fingers trembling. A mountaintop was no place to be picky about noodle firmness.

In addition to whatever foodstuffs our band of woods-boys had dined on last night at base camp, Irwin ate more, walking the two miles back to his truck and commuting to the nearest McDonald's for a Supersized version of Extra Value Meal #1. Billy kept him company, riding shotgun

and on the hunt for girls. But from our position in the clouds, Irwin's eyes emitted what can only be described as desperation, ravaged as he was from the climb. The chicken-y vapours bubbling from the broth danced in the air between us.

"It's ready," I said, giving our lunch a final stir and closing the fuel valve.

Irwin rose and presented his soup bowl with his chubby fingers. He hadn't even the energy to smile as I ladled fifty cents worth of deliciousness—exactly half—into his vessel before depositing the remaining portion in my own. What happened next horrifies me to this day.

As I buried my face in the savoury steam and made love to my lunch, I peered in the direction of my ursine friend. Inconceivably, Irwin balanced his bowl on his knee while he rummaged through his gear. Perhaps it was the physical rigour that had sapped his mental strength, too. Sadly for us both, the bowl teetered and then lost its battle with gravity, descending in slow motion to the great stone table on which we sat, splashing everywhere at once, including the crotch of his pants. Irwin said nothing and let the wind lash his face.

It seemed entirely unreasonable to pretend I hadn't noticed; we were alone and no more than a tent's width apart in the dim noon light, so I could not polish my meal off in a flourish as I wanted to. I remained silent.

"FUCK!" Irwin screamed into the gloom.

I waited. Nobody rushed round the corner of the boulder to answer his cry.

I had not experienced a single chest pain on this trip, but I knew that if something tragic happened, Irwin would be the first to sling me over his back and carry me to base camp, lunch or no lunch. He picked individual noodles off the summit, dangling them worm-like in front of his lips, and blew pieces of dirt away.

"Hey, man," I said, just as he sucked the first dirty noodle from the tines of his hand. I reached for his bowl and spilled half of my lunch into it. "Got your spoon?" I asked before handing it back.

"I think I left it at camp," he said, reaching for his bowl, "but I don't need it." In one head tip, he emptied lunch into his gullet before leaning back against the boulder, closing his eyes, and dreaming of all the meals that awaited him.

On the shore of Marcy Dam Pond the next morning, we stood with the water and the reflections of Adirondack trees at our backs. It was cold, even for dawn, and we were eager for breakfast at a diner in Lake Placid: coffee and bacon, fried potatoes, eggs, and Woodstead Hot Anything & Everything Sauce smuggled along from Naples. A hiker not of our group offered to photograph us, so we gathered shoulder to shoulder on the pebbled shore—Nicky, Billy, Irwin, Neville, Wayne, Burnham and me. Then we hiked out, enamelled cups clinking all the way.

27

We spent much of that winter outside. Late nights of candle light and guitar picking at the cabin. Campfires in the snow. Radiohead's *OK Computer* sifting through the moonlit trees. Night-time hikes along the hillsides with Nalgenes of Wild Turkey, or thermoses of black coffee, or crooked Backwoods Cigars, and a few dogs breaking trail. We pelted tree trunks with snowballs to mark our route when we weren't pelting one another. Walking through the woods, we plotted our lives: the colleges we would attend, the places we would travel, the sort of girls we would marry.

In April, Missy and Kayla joined our backpacking crew on another Adirondack adventure, this time to climb Algonquin Peak. We had planned the trip all winter, from the cost of gasoline to the gear we would take to where we would eat in Lake Placid to celebrate our achievement: summiting a 5,115-foot mountain and sleeping a few nights in the fog and wet snow of early spring. Missy rode shotgun in my car, counting change for Thruway tolls, and handling the map and the music. More than once my single-sided Allman Brothers tape ended and the silence extended for long, comfortable stretches. I watched her watch the landscape roll by.

We were lucky to score a forgotten lean-to, hidden far from the trails surrounding Marcy Dam, so far in fact that we decided not to walk all the way back to the falls at the dam to rig a line on which to hang our food above the water.

"Why would we hang our food?" Missy asked.

"Bears," I said. I pawed through my pack and kept my eyes down.

"Bears?"

"And wolves, and coyotes, and maybe mice."

"You'd better keep me safe tonight," she said, settling her sleeping bag beside mine, zipper to zipper.

Ascending Algonquin proved slippery, the snow both slushy and icy, the trail a bobsled luge in places above tree line, but at the top we toasted ourselves with Nalgenes of gritty snowmelt brewed with Iodine tablets, and watched the clouds scarf the distant mountaintops. Any concern I might have had for myself, for my heart and the remoteness of my location should I suffer any sort of cardiac accident, was entirely replaced by concern for Missy: Was she comfortable? Was she having fun? Would she want to do this again, with me?

The descent took hours and darkness settled on us. To dry off and warm up back at the lean-to, we built an illegal fire, ignited a fleet of MSR Whisperlite Stoves, and feasted on our remaining noodles and peanut butter.

In the morning, the coals lay dead under a blanket of sticky spring snow. Motivated by breakfast fare in town, we packed our gear hastily and prepared to depart. As I surveyed our environs for any forgotten items, I noticed several prints in the mud and snow close behind the cabin. I crouched to examine them. An expert I was not, but to my eye these tracks looked fresh. And large.

"What are you looking at?" Missy asked, suddenly standing behind me.

"I don't know," I said. Five toe pads, claw imprints, a large circular depression.

"Tommy. Seriously? Tell me those aren't—"

"Let's go," I said, taking her hand and leading us down the trail for what I hoped would not be the last time.

For a stretch, the muddy path unfurled between the pines like an aisle through the nave of a great church. As we

walked, our strides became languid. I don't know if it was because of the rhythm of our footsteps, or Duane Allman's "Little Martha" that—after hearing it several times on the long drive to the mountains—now played like a recessional in my head, or the way the wind bent the trees like a waving crowd congratulating us and wishing us well, but as we passed through the woods, I interpreted it all as a positive omen. And so we proceeded to the car, to Naples and beyond, side-by-side, and hand-in-hand.

THOMAS MANNELLA

In May, Billy and I reached the final match of the individual Section V doubles tournament, only to find Nicky and his doubles partner across the net. Naples versus Naples. Brother versus brother. Billy and I won the first set and then choked, dropping the final two sets and the championship, the bragging rights, and our pride—to the underclassmen. I could not comprehend what had happened. A senior, I'd blown my last opportunity at the title. We shook their hands and congratulated them and walked off the court.

Having ridden to the match together, Nicky and I also rode home together. I thought about the wooden Chris Everett raquets our aunt had sawed the handles off of when we were young boys, the electrical tape Papa wrapped around the raquet necks to secure the leather grips, the homerun derbies we held when the courts were full on summer evenings, crushing tennis balls onto the high school roof. The ride home was much longer than the hour of time it took us to return to Naples. When the Phish bootleg ended I didn't flip the tape, and we cruised in silence.

If I was older and more mature I might have congratulated him then, discussed the match, and been happy for him, but the stakes—the emphasis athletic success acquired in my quest to prove that my heart did not make me defective—were too high. I didn't know what to say and, apparently, neither did he. My swagger, the thing that made it possible to skip cardiologist appointments and play soccer, the thing that justified partying in the woods with my friends despite my condition, faded a little right then.

Maybe some of it transferred, though, bleeding into my brother.

Days later, I walked into Nicky's bedroom to borrow his headphones. He was sprawled on his bed, looking at the wall. I looked at the wall, too: hanging above the light switch was a large poster board on which was printed the entire Section V Tournament bracket, the capitalized last names of all the doubles teams in red text. With a blood red Sharpie, Nicky had written his name in the "CHAMPIONS" box.

"You *fucker*," I said, but I couldn't say it without laughing. At Nicky's pomposity, his confidence, his ability to break the tension between us by slapping me in the face with such audacious abasement.

"I told you that night," he said, "'Next time I'll beat your ass.' Except this match *counted.*"

That night, I thought. Our match before my surgery a few years ago. Inhaling the fumes from brand new cans of tennis balls. The cold April air and our billowing breath. The stars above on the walk home.

"Come here," I said.

"Why?"

"Just stand up and come here."

He rose from the bed uncertainly. His cowlick waved in the air. He was nearly as tall as me.

"Come here," I said one more time and, with no net between us, I stepped forward and wrapped my arms around him. "*That match* counted, too."

We left Naples on a chartered bus for our senior class trip in Virginia Beach and twelve hours later were sprawled on lounge chairs, killing time by the pool. Even in the presence of people I had known my entire life, I kept my T-shirt on to conceal my incision, a flash of self-consciousness after all those years. A few guys, a few girls partied on the balcony above. College kids, maybe, older than us. They held plastic cups and looked beached: salty and scruffy and tanned.

Pool water sloshed onto the cement deck and Wayne's board shorts clung to his thighs. A guy with mirrored sunglasses and windy hair invited him up. Irwin followed.

A moment later they smiled down. Then Wayne stood on the railing, curling his toes over the edge. He held onto the ceiling with both hands. He crouched. He jumped into silence and landed in the water with a terrific splash, clearing the edge of the pool deck by a few feet.

Wayne absorbed the applause as he climbed the ladder and wiped wet rags of blond hair away from his forehead with his hands. Unlike Wayne, who was lithe and bouncy in his step, Irwin's vertical leap was unimpressive and he weighed substantially more.

"Make sure you jump out," Wayne instructed from below, "and tuck your legs—the water is shallow."

Irwin footed the railing, crouched and shoved off. He fell like a stone and crashed into the water with only a sliver of daylight to spare, missing the wall by inches. He surfaced, giggling. The balcony crew cheered and laughed in disbelief.

The boys prepared to jump again, but a security officer appeared on the deck.

"Excuse me," the officer said. "You wouldn't know anything about people jumping into the pool from a second story balcony, would you?"

"No, sir," the jumpers said.

"Are you sure about that?"

"Yes, sir."

"Let's check the security tape together, just to be sure," the officer said, beckoning them to follow. At the amusement park the next day we photographed the boys locked in replica pillory stocks.

On the last night of the trip we took a dinner cruise. Several other schools were aboard, along with a DJ and a dance floor. It was June and the light hung around in the far-reaching way of beachside postcards, casting long shadows across Chesapeake Bay. On the roof deck the soles of my shoes absorbed the bass pumping below. The ocean wind tossed my necktie over my shoulder and the ship cut a path through the glittering water.

"Hey," Missy said, pulling me from this reverie. Her small hand rested on my back and, still leaning over the railing, I turned to meet her blue eyes. Wispy blonde hair, a short, tight black dress, a thick scar across her knee from the injury that had ended her senior soccer season before it even began.

"So, did you make up your mind?" I asked, tapping the back of my hand against her scar.

"I can't even feel that," she said.

"I know," I said. "I can't feel mine either."

We had decided not to date one another. We believed the geographic distance between the colleges we would attend in the fall was an expanse too great for a boyfriend and girlfriend. We would each jump into college alone.

"The coach still wants me to come to preseason in August, so we'll see how my knee handles three-a-days."

"You're lucky," I replied, referring to the physical I could not pass because of my bovine valve, the practices, games, and career I would not have as a member of the St. Lawrence University men's soccer team, the reigning DIII National Champion. A part of me wished I'd never been recruited.

"I am," she said, smirking and checking me with her hip. "What kind of a mascot is a Saint, anyway?"

"About as intimidating as a Cardinal."

"I guess not everyone can be a Big Green Machine."

"*A part of* the machine."

"Then that makes us both lucky."

"It does," I said, and wrapped my arm around her shoulder.

"It does," she said, resting her cheek on my chest.

I kissed the top of her head, and together we watched the sunset ships pass by.

PART 3

OPENING UP

30

Newly graduated, I now needed cash for college, so the day after commencement I began employment in a box factory. Unfortunately, this job entailed monotonous eye-stabbing boredom. After filing the necessary paperwork, I was hired and given a tour of the campus: a parking lot filled with late model American sedans, the stink of synthetic adhesives, and weeds flaming up through the blacktop. Inside, rows of belt-fed machines conveyed stacks of thin cardboard through a series of folding and gluing apparatuses that produced envelopes for photographs, compact discs, and other items of similar shape and size. I exchanged my youthful summer hours and the opportunity for creative thought and meaningful interactions for a paycheck and a bunch of wretched experiences that just might nudge me toward the Dean's list so I'd never find myself working in a place like that again.

Each work day was the same. I savoured every second of the morning commute, the sun, the air, the softness of the driver's seat. Captive as I felt inside the factory, I envied Nicky's job as a golf course bag boy, Brother Wease and his radio show crew laughing, even the DOT workers alongside the expressway shovelling road kill into the bed of a pickup. At the factory I punched my time card at the door and for the next three hours performed a task called "breaking out": after the pre-envelop sheets were printed and cut and stacked on pallets three feet high, the templates needed to be separated from the excess material at the perforated seams and restacked on an adjacent pallet. The paper was so sharp that I never felt the first razor edges

slide across my hands, but when I sweated the sting became distracting. I tried not to smear the templates with blood. I wondered: was this why I endured open heart surgery? To work day shifts in a factory, paper-cutting my hands to ribbons?

More unsettling was the attention paid to me by two co-workers.

Wally was a lanky, white-haired fellow of about sixty with twisted yellow teeth similar to the popular dentures displayed in stores selling zombie costumes for Halloween. His magnified eyeballs floated behind thick lenses in a way that suggested an altogether unique atmosphere inside his head. I presumed his gaze friendly, with the exception of the crinkled upper lip that was more sneer than smile, and I left the staring up to him. My concentration was devoted to Aretha and preventing her from brushing her body against my legs or my arms or my ass. Like a black Mama Cass with maroon hair extensions, Aretha was a lot of woman. And she did *not* ride the bus all the way to the factory to ruin her bedazzled finger nails. She waddled about and blabbed all sorts of gibberish, her hoop earrings knocking against her chin and her massive breasts against each other, her fatty parts poking out here and there and, unfortunately, making frequent contact with me. The first time or two I thought nothing of it. By the end of the morning I choreographed my paper cut party so that the pallet remained between us, and managed to stay a comfortable distance from Wally's warbling eyes. Our foreman later explained that the factory worked in partnership with an organization that offered vocational services to individuals with disabilities. Even Wally and Aretha knew to wear gloves during break-out.

I preferred to wait as long as possible to take my morning break because that decreased the working time until lunch.

At quarter after ten, I spent my fifteen minutes in the shimmering parking lot with Greg Church. He smoked unfiltered Camels and promoted Scientology. A sociology major at the University of Minnesota, Greg had enviable stubble, distant eyes, and hair inspired by Charles Schultz's Peppermint Patty. I sought his company, hoping to strike a workplace friendship through our common age and academic ambitions, but that never panned out.

"I'm seeking my Dianetic engram," Greg said.

I fanned cigarette smoke away from my face. "Your what?"

"Stimulation of the protoplasm of my tissues that can be traced to a reactive injury," he said, and pulled a messy pile of crinkled papers from the back seat of his minivan. He pointed to a passage by Scientology founder Ron L. Hubbard: "Hubbard redefined this concept as being 'a mental image picture of a moment of pain and unconsciousness' that when stimulated increases power." I returned the paper to Greg and stepped backwards. "This job," he said, thumbing toward the building, "will pay for my professional hypnosis sessions."

From then on I spent break in the car, waving hello to Greg in his van, where he studied a religion created by a mid-century science fiction writer.

Free hypnosis was available daily when we took our places on the assembly line. For entire afternoons I placed unfolded templates onto the conveyors every twenty seconds, fighting the urge to stare at the clock, wondering about college, or replaying entire athletic seasons in my mind. I often thought about Missy, who was completing summer course work nearby, and the next time I could see her. Sometimes I considered my future. I wasn't developmentally disabled like Wally and Aretha. I wasn't brainwashed like Greg. I would leave the factory at the end of the summer and never come

back. My life, my heart valve, didn't seem like a raw deal at all.

On other days I stood at the opposite end of the conveyors and pulled the folded products off the line, daydreaming about similar things. Either way, the rote nature of the physical and mental activities numbed me and I relished machine jams when paper stuck to a belt or a wheel, then crumpled and caused a massive accident, the others smashing up behind the first like cholesterol in an artery. Before the screeching belts snapped or the friction between rubber and paper ignited the envelopes, somebody pressed the red emergency stop button and we worked to pull the ruined bits free. Operating the loading end of the line I sometimes nudged a stack of templates one way or the other, hoping for mechanical calamities. I pushed my luck one afternoon, initiating three jams in an hour, and Joe shut down my line.

"Grab a putty knife from the back room," he said. With delight I skipped to the tool closet. Joe removed the main belt and for the rest of the day I scraped glue from every roller on the machine. I rubbed the wheels with alcohol until they sparkled. The pleasure I took in this was perverse, and I hoped to do it again.

As much as I couldn't wait to sit in my air conditioned car for thirty minutes at lunch or punch out at the end of the day, I knew I would never feel the relief of leaving a dreaded thing behind until I exited the parking lot for the final time at the end of August.

That summer I lived in Rochester with Dad to reduce the commute to the factory. Our work schedules were such that our paths rarely crossed. In fact, for two months I had little interaction with anyone I knew. Sometimes after my shift I walked to an elementary school near his apartment and sat against the goal post of the soccer field watching the pink

bellies of the clouds pass by. There in the grass I invited nostalgia to make me dizzy, to keep me company, reliving our sporting glories and those I would not get to pursue in college because my heart made me a liability. Other times, alone and bored, I browsed book stores, studying Adirondack trail maps and creating routes to hike in the fall. I composed wandering emails to my future room-mate. I reunited with the boys I played travel soccer with when I was twelve for one last hoorah, but the games were sporadic. I counted the days until I would arrive at St. Lawrence University with money to blow, far away from the factory and Wally, Aretha, and Joe.

Alone one midsummer night, I sorted through a box of photographs my family had given me after graduation, searching for a few to bring along to college. Choosing images felt like taking a test without any correct answers. Each photograph I held captured a fragment of my past and the act of looking increased my awareness of what I had already left behind by moving to Rochester to work. Standing atop a snow fort with Pete. The tape ball. Hiking to the summit of Algonquin. I could have sorted through these photographs any time, but I had chosen this isolation to do it, and looking at picture after picture, I practically dared myself to keep it together. Finally, when the sun set and the apartment had grown so dark I could hardly see the photographs, I stopped sorting and sat listening to cars drive by the open window. A moment later I lost it. I couldn't ignore the separation from all the people I had known since my life began, from the town where I had grown up. The people and the places that had given me so much of my identity seemed so far away, and this remoteness was too heavy to carry. Finally, I let something go. It felt good to cry. I wished I had acknowledged these feelings sooner, but something inside clamped down on my emotions. Since I

was in kindergarten, I needed to be stronger in my heart than anyone I would ever know. Maybe this was part of the adventure of leaving: dwelling on memories, being thankful for people and places, confirming my past before changing directions. I wiped my face on my T-shirt sleeve, berated myself with a few names, and opened my laptop to email my future roommate about bringing a couch to college.

31

Charlie Silcox was a cross-country runner from Vermont. Despite our communication we ended up with two mini-refrigerators and no couch, so for the first semester we often sat on the floor. This circumstance put our eyes at level with the window sills, where we gazed down on the main entryway of our residence hall. Before long we were dumping buckets of water onto people we'd just met. So amused were we with dousing the other residents that we soon began attacking unsuspecting Laurentians in the shower. The bathrooms were coed and it was often impossible to differentiate the male and female screams of our victims. We even ambushed each other.

I didn't know what to do about showering, because of the zippers on my chest. I had just been introduced to the SLU Class of 2004 and didn't want to be recognized for the most insecure aspect of my identity. The possibility that nobody cared whether or not I was scarred never occurred to me, but even if it had it would not have been an idea I could have embraced with conviction.

Among the females in the vicinity of our room I found several beautiful. I hoped to impress them with my kindness, my humour, perhaps even my past athletic prowess. To that end, I also hoped to keep them in the dark about my ugly scars, but how? I couldn't sport my towel like a girl, wrapped up to my arm pits. Wearing a T-shirt to the showers might suggest I was hiding something, which of course I would have been. The other guys walked around shirtless, sometimes even when they weren't showering. They tossed a lacrosse ball on the lawn in front of our

building, the sun gleaming on their smooth chests, muscles toned and tanned, just waiting for girls to pounce. In the hallways they stopped to have conversations, wrapped only in a towel from the waist down, flirting with this girl, making dinner and bar plans with that girl. I could never do that.

One afternoon there was a knock at my door. I looked through the peephole at Randy Quayle. His back was to me and his hair draped his shoulders like Jesus's. He wore only jeans and Birkenstocks, no shirt, his skin perfect and clean. I hesitated. Rumours circulated about his sexual eagerness, his collections of sex toys and porn. Earlier, he had invited me to join a massage club he'd started.

"I have some young ladies coming over tonight and I'd like you to join us." Skeevy was the first word that came to mind. Also, predatory. Randy swung his torso forward, bending at the waist, and gathered his hair into a rubber band as it dangled to the floor. His massage club was not how I wanted to meet girls. I told him I'd pass.

"Would you go on a beer run for me?" I'd said.

"You bet," he'd said, and slapped my ass.

Standing with my eye to the peephole now, I heard Randy singing outside my door—James Brown's "Sex Machine," from the sounds of it—and, remembering my request for beer, I opened it.

Randy turned around.

"Hey, buddy!" he shouted, and leaned forward with arms spread to wrap me in a bear hug. Just before our embrace I looked down. Where I should have seen the zippered fly of his jeans I saw instead a wad of skin. I leapt back.

"Dude?" I asked, pointing at his crotch. Randy erupted in laughter, clapping his hands together while his ponytail flailed about.

"You've never seen a Texas Belt Buckle before?" he asked.

"No!"

"Neither had Marcy's mom!"

He explained how he had thought he was pranking our dorm mate when she knocked on his door, but in fact it was Mrs. McAliley, lost and looking for her daughter.

"I had to come tell you," Randy said.

I gestured toward his crotch: "You mean you walked here like that?"

"Yeah. I'll have your order after dinner."

He walked away without zipping his fly closed.

I was amazed at how comfortable Randy was with his body. Nudity could be a joke. Massage parties, a joy. He seemed to devote his life to these pleasures and, to a sufficient degree, he indirectly allowed me to accept a naked-chested walk to the showers as less of a big deal. *It's not like I'm exposing my junk*, I thought. So, walking to the shower that night, I did not strut or dally, nor did I rush to conceal. But I walked at a moderate pace, my arms at my sides, my chest available for anyone to see.

Later, I approached Randy's door.

"It's unlocked," he called from within.

Atop a nest of pillows and blankets, Randy sat in the middle of his harem, holding a tray of oils in glass bottles with cork stoppers. A harp-and-wind-chime number played on the stereo and incense burned sweetly.

"Everything's in the fridge, buddy," he said, and gave another giggle, wiggling his eyebrows like Groucho Marx at the girls surrounding him. "You sure you can't stay?"

"Maybe next time," I said. I hefted the cases of canned swill before walking deftly back to the confines of my room to fill our mini-fridges. I paused for a moment in the doorway to scout for the RA or campus security and before stepping out, I looked back at Randy.

"Thanks," I said. And then I said it again.

The dorm windows were tall and wide, brightening our domain, so Charlie assembled his two-person tent in the middle of our room to nap in darkness during the day. He had already constructed a suit out of tinfoil for a sorority mixer, so the tent didn't surprise me. It was not dismantled until final exam week, when procrastination came to a head and Charlie needed the square-footage to shoot his final project for film class: a Claymation scene based on Bob Ross's show *The Joy of Painting*. Perhaps he would not have required midday naps if it weren't for our nightly pillow talk.

Pillow talk may seem like an activity reserved for middle school girls at slumber parties, but as eighteen-year-old guys we participated, too. Our lofted beds were positioned against opposite walls, the mattresses three feet from the ceiling with the desks underneath. The first session began early in the semester after Charlie smashed his head on the concrete ceiling while sitting up, and it went something like this:

"Shit!"

"Are you okay?"

"Yeah—Anna's wicked cute, huh?"

Anna was the first recipient of a cold water attack and as a result seemed to have an unlikely crush on Charlie.

"We could have used that tent a few weeks ago," I said, referencing one of our first nights as roommates. After bouncing from room party to room party and drinking much of the beer Randy had bought us, we had found ourselves at our desk chairs under our lofted bed mattresses,

a beautiful girl on each of our laps. I recall all of us trying to dance to Jeff Beck. One of us spilled a full can across the floor. When the girls stumbled to the bathroom together, Charlie and I tried to hash out a plan. Neither of us, we decided, should have to leave. Additionally, in our uncoordinated stupor, any intimate attempts in our lofted beds would be dangerous. Our solution involved the desk chairs and blankets as a barrier down the middle of the room with our mattresses on either side. It was better than nothing.

"The tent would've helped," Charlie agreed.

Over the weeks, pillow talk drifted from girls to roommate courtesies. I'm a non-confrontational person, but one night I worked up the courage to mention the funky smell of Charlie's bath towel, which had yet to be laundered.

"Your towel reeks," I said. "How can you even dry off with that thing?"

In the darkness I watched Charlie tumble down from bed and remove the specimen from a hook on the back of the door.

"Check it out," he said, placing the foul cloth on the floor where it stood as stiffly as the tent. The next night, with the help of a few PBRs and Sergi's deep-fried pizza rolls—AKA Fat Bags—we ceremoniously burned the towel near the fourteenth green of the college golf course under the moonshine.

Occasionally we discussed academics. I decided on English Writing as a major and had the unfortunate luck to be enrolled in Professor Stelios's American Literature class. Stelios was a man who proudly proclaimed to have given a lecture to an empty room; that his students had left campus early for holiday break deterred him not. Worst of all, he tortured us with lectures on the various printings of Fitzgerald's *This Side of Paradise*, a subject on which he was regarded as an expert. It was a brutal

class. In my mind Stelios completely resembled a pelican in silhouette—a throat full of seawater that was tough to swallow.

I was the only freshman in his section of juniors and seniors. Perhaps this is why, when I was called upon to stand in front of our group and present a biographical analysis of James Fennimore Cooper, I was insanely nervous. To begin with, I dreaded public speaking. I chose seats in the backs of classrooms. Also, our class met late in the afternoon on the third floor of Richardson Hall, a one-hundred-and-fifty-year-old un-air-conditioned brick edifice. The room was an oven.

Stelios took a seat among the rest of the class and even before I approached the podium I was sweating. I read from a scripted report, wiping the perspiration from my temples, my cheekbones, my forehead, my upper lip. My voice echoed in my ears. Suddenly there was an explosive mumbling from the group. Everyone turned and looked at Stelios, who exaggeratedly mumbled gibberish into his hands and pretended to mop his brow. I attempted to continue my presentation while he mocked me with predatory persistence, again and again unleashing his disturbance. Finally, I stopped speaking amid the abuse.

"Mr. Mannella," he blurted through his hands, "I cannot understand your mumbling."

My classmates snickered.

"Please," he continued, "refrain from covering your mouth with your hands and teach us *something*."

During pillow talk I confided in Charlie my humiliation. Where was John Keating, the inspiring teacher played by Robin Williams in *Dead Poets Society*? I could not even recall how I finished the presentation after Stelios crushed my confidence.

Looking back, that was the greatest adversity I faced during freshman year.

Knowing the heart-related challenges that I would face in my remaining years of college, freshman year seems like a carefree blessing. A gift, and Stelios a problem for someone without problems. Recalling it as such, I am compelled to submit additional proof. In September, I caught Phish with Missy and the Naples crew; I cheered Nicky and The Big Green Machine as they captured another Section V soccer title; I entertained my hometown friends at St. Lawrence; I met wonderful people at college. It was a lovely fall.

I did work the night shift at the box factory between semesters despite swearing never to return, but I needed the money and, this time, I knew what the money would buy me at SLU—admission to Greek parties, Fat Bags, backpacking trips to Lake Placid, concert tickets, a new ID, and nights with meat and potatoes, axes, and a keg at a cabin in the middle of the woods alongside a frozen river with my new friends. My college life was glorious. When my bank account ran low in April, I rushed fraternities for the free food and drink. During Spring Party Weekend in May, while the Beta guys rode a beer-soaked Slip 'N Slide through their house and across their yard, a girl slid into my arms with a look that said, *I need you to take care of me*, and I was right there to oblige.

A gift, indeed.

But these untroubled times were making me a fool again.

On a whim, Charlie and I pooled our remaining cash to fill my gas tank and drive to Mt. Azure for one last hike of the spring semester. The late-afternoon light sharpened above the mountains and the seasonal road rattled our teeth. We forgot flashlights for the descent, but there was no place we'd rather be. A muddy trail. Patches of crusty snow in the darkest shadows of the forest. The smell of the earth.

At the trailhead we found a pile of rocks and a note

tacked to a tree asking hikers to lug stones to the top to be used to curtail erosion at the summit. This we did, and as we walked we rehashed the semester.

"Fuck couches."

"Two fridges are better than one."

On the peak we added our rocks to the pile at the base of the fire lookout tower and climbed the ladder-less structure to the top. The rickety platform swayed in the breeze. The sun sank into the horizon. The sky flared orange. This North Country sky I had become so comfortable under: I could all but hear the train whistle the many miles away on campus, as if I were gazing through our tall dorm windows with all of the time in the world to look and to listen. The minutes ticked past and the brightness bled from the sky, draining from orange to a depthless purple, the light dying quickly until it was time to move on.

This year without worry I could not recognize at the time, our jaunt on Mt. Azure nothing more than a beautiful hike with my friend. Fresh air in my lungs, sweat across my back. I felt terrific physically and ignored thoughts that related any carousing to the destruction of my health. Freshman year, my third year of living with a bovine valve, the year smack in the middle of the range of years the doctors had told me such a valve tissue might last *at a minimum*, was about to conclude.

I believed there could be nothing but more of the same to come.

Climbing down the tower, I marked my descent by noticing the pile of rocks growing larger and larger until I was upon it. This mineral accumulation meant absolutely nothing at the time, but now carries symbolic weight: increasingly I would carry the accumulating burden of a calcifying heart valve, a slow gathering of debris without the power to reverse course. Thinking I had arrived at the

summit of only one mountain, I in fact had arrived at the summit of two. I simultaneously descended to the trailhead of Mt. Azure—and to the limits of good health—in darkness.

Landscaping with a legit outfit kept me in Naples during summertime, close to friends and physically fit. Busting each other's chops was a big part of spending sixty hours every week with the same guys; therefore, we called the portable toilet at the shop "Billy's Toilet" even though he hadn't worked there for a while. In fact, he'd been fired soon after I arrived, which made me feel a little guilty. I suppose we'd found the best way to honour a person who was so desperate to not shit their pants that he'd knocked on the mansion door of our most lucrative lakeside account to ask the owner to use their commode. It was easy to imagine the confusion and subsequent repugnant expression on the homeowner's face upon seeing his fuzzy, green legs, and his sweat-soaked shirt, and hearing his request:

"Excuse me, Mrs. Winthrop, I'm quite sorry to disturb your cocktail hour on this lovely summer morning, but I'm afraid if I don't immediately have a place to grow a tail, then there will be a tragic depositing all over your lawn."

She sets her sweating glass of Riesling on the hallway table and folds her arms across her chest. "Pardon?"

I wasn't around when this happened, but that was the story the guys told. They had the whole spring to spice up the dialogue each day at lunch. It probably wouldn't have been such a big deal for Billy had he not already let himself into a few other homes to do the same thing—nearly everyone in Naples knew each other, so on those other occasions he probably felt as comfortable tracking mud and leaves down the hallways of other accounts as he would in his uncle's house.

My first day replacing Billy on the line trimmer was treacherous. I zipped along the boulders at the lakeshore in the wavy heat and at the end of the day my hands buzzed. The pins and needles did not subside by late evening, so I started to worry. I asked myself the question that always came first: *could it be my heart?* I was sensitive to subtle changes in my physical state ever since the valve replacement surgery, and this fuzzy numbing freaked me out. Maybe it had to do with poor circulation or maybe it was a side effect of the intense heat. I tried to recall which arm went numb before a heart attack. I wanted to identify any damage to the bovine valve now and proactively deal with the consequences so that I would not be blindsided like I was in high school. But would I be assertive enough to speak up if I needed help, or would I stubbornly wait for the problem to pass because I was afraid of seeming vulnerable and out of control?

"Cramming three pounds of shit into a two pound bag, Tommy Boy," Staudt, the foreman, said the next morning. The pins and needles had indeed subsided by then, but as I loaded the truck with pitchforks and wheelbarrows for a day of mulching, my left index finger went numb. I began to sweat. I shook my hand. I clapped it against my hipbone and breathed slowly and deeply. I talked myself into a trance, focusing on what I'd read online about the symptoms of carpal tunnel. And cardiac arrest.

I tried not to panic, but thought about all the heavy things I had lifted throughout the summer that I was not supposed to lift at all. Concrete pavers and landscaping boulders for retaining walls. Trees and shrubs for planting. Lawnmowers into our trucks. Root balls from diseased plantings and chunks of sod and barrels of organic debris and load after load after load of mulch. I imagined a tear in the tissue of the bovine valve at the seam where it was

THOMAS MANNELLA

attached to my cardiac muscle, gradually separating and disrupting the function of my heart. A levee about to burst. I thought about all of the parties at college and the stress I placed on my heart and how it all sped up the clock on a ticking time bomb.

Bovine valves could last up to twenty years without deteriorating, but now a third finger went numb. If not a tear, I thought, then calcification of the valve, as the doctor had cautioned, in which case the whole bloody replacement would need replacement. My heart skipped a beat and another. The palpitations became regular and I tried not to freak out. Even though it seemed a useless game, like trying to stare a hole through the sun, I couldn't help but think of all the things I did not do to preserve this valve. The guilt was tremendous.

All of this I kept to myself. I tried to defeat these problems with defiance and denial. Instead of slowing down, I worked my ass off. *Screw it,* I thought. I lifted and pushed and forked hundreds of pounds of mulch and equipment, up hills and over walls and into trucks for the rest of the summer so that when I left for St. Lawrence everyone knew me as the hardest worker on the crew and not some soft-palmed college pansy. Mulching a property became a contest, Staudt and I attempting to lap one another as we made trips between flower beds and truck beds for loads of mulch to dump. I ignored tingling hands because moments of inclusion made me feel alive and worthy. I was one of the guys. And I wouldn't be if I was snivelling and weak.

I didn't have a crystal ball or magic cards, no way to make time stand still, and no way to chase it down to glimpse the future, so I also learned to laugh like nothing was wrong at all.

34

Mondays were cemetery days. Throughout the valley the crumbling headstones sank into the ground and we were in charge of keeping them grass-free and visible.

At the truck, I lamented the missing guard on my Husqvarna line trimmer's motor: I had just married the sizzling metal to the underside of my forearm and melted a circle of skin into my elbow. Sweat trickled into the boiled flesh wound. I searched the glove box for a Band-Aid without success. In the distance the mowers spun through the acres. Roger, my co-line-trimmer, was scalping the hell out of the ground, missing tufts at every plot, not giving a shit, so I cleaned my sunglasses on my T-shirt, twisted up my earplugs, and headed back out.

Soon I paused to watch the sun rise. It climbed over the hills and beamed through the green maple leaves, warming the headstones. A moment passed. I bit a callus off my palm and spit it sideways. Staudt made a bee-line toward me on his Zero-turn mower, his man boobs jiggling all the way.

"Tom-ass," he said, killing the engine. I turned to explain the burn on my arm, the callus, or some other reason I was not working at the moment, but he surprised me with a compliment. "Great job out there, way better than that ass-wipe Billy Tanis." He spun around and I mumbled a thank you to his backside.

Everyone running line trimmers was careful out of respect for their own legs. Time made the headstones flaky and frail, and trimmer line nibbled pieces away that bit into our bare skin. Sometimes it was hard to tell if the stinging was stone or a bee. Grass shrapnel covered our sunglasses,

our legs fuzzy green. My thoughts were vapid whenever line-trimming, except here at the cemetery. Up and down the rows I read the names on the stones. There was one I sought in particular.

Irwin, I knew, had placed his New York State Champion soccer medal on Pete's headstone, where the metal rusted in the rain and the ribbon faded in the sun. I took a long look at it and the school and valley walls beyond, the grassy space atop the cemetery hill where the Jesus Rays had beamed down on me. My heart beat against my earplugs. The line trimmer sputtered and stopped. I removed the earplugs and tried to stop thinking about Pete, to just enjoy the morning sun, but I couldn't. I jump-started the trimmer and continued, listening to the liquid slamming of my heart, sweating and trimming for hours, draining consecutive tanks of 2cycle, absorbed by the past and he who was no longer around. I decided by the time we loaded the trucks for the next cemetery that burying was not for me, and thought of the places I'd like my ashes spread when the blood stopped flowing.

35

"Did your mommy buy you a new box of crayons for SLU?" Staudt asked on my last day of work.

"I'm a sophomore, so I got coloured pencils this year," I said.

My bank account replenished, I packed my car and drove to college, expectations blowing through the roof.

An upperclassman now, I participated in an unsanctioned pre-semester welcoming ritual. Freshman orientation customarily culminated in a candlelight ceremony on The Quad. A single candle was lit and the flame spread between the few hundred newbies circled in the grass and holding candles. To enliven the hokeyness of this symbolic ceremony, I joined dozens of Larrys in hiding at the outskirts of The Quad in a garden behind the chapel. There we prepared for ambush. We drank beer for courage and watched the candle-lighting begin, our cue to disrobe in the dusky light. Males and females alike, we stood together wearing only running sneakers, backpacks, and sunglasses. We whispered and waited for the moment of attack. Cans in hand, the guys stood together and planned our routes through the freshmen while some of the girls tied bandanas around their faces. Amazingly, despite being naked, I was more concerned with somebody noticing the scar on my chest than anything else.

And then somebody did:

"Whoa, what happened to you?" someone asked, pointing at the centre of my chest.

"Knife fight in Mexico," I replied, my voice slippery drunk. I took a long swig to avoid saying more, gave a smile, and threw the empty can at their face. Everyone laughed.

"Now! Now! Now!" someone shouted and we were off, burping and tearing out of the garden shadows and onto The Quad in a wild, adrenaline-fuelled sprint toward the University Centre on the other side. We revelled in the first year girls' screams, laughing hysterically as we ran by, or boldly hugged and danced beside them for a moment, or stole their hats, performed cartwheels and barrel rolls and leaps in the most twisted display of parkour these initiates had ever seen. A second group of streakers burst from a dormitory stairwell opposite the garden and flashed past my group in a rush of skin. I saw Randy trip and splay across the lawn and a moment later Charlie caught his toe drunkenly on the curb. He dove forward like Pete Rose sliding into home plate, shredding himself on the blacktop.

I was the first across and I was alone. Campus security pursued a nude peloton on a golf cart with roof-mounted spotlights; the bastards were ready for us. I dashed in the opposite direction, plunging into the shadows of an ever-green, breathless, and reflexively put on my T-shirt first, a little boy changing in his classroom coat closet.

Looking back, this event seems auspicious, a mark of qualitative growth from self-consciousness freshman to experienced sophomore, from nervous-to-be-seen shirtless to streaker. Maybe it was the liquid courage. Maybe it was the North Country air. Maybe it was the passage of time, the way fears that once were new become old and begin to fade.

Over the summer there had been less to distract me from the changes I perceived in my heart; at St. Lawrence, I disregarded the way I felt while working for Lawn Doctors. Naples drifted from my consciousness and so did my heart. This was easy to do attending a school where all the students looked like nothing bad had ever happened to them.

Maybe I looked that way, too, or so I hoped.

Many of them drove expensive cars, wore expensive clothes, their parents' credit cards and vacation homes at their disposal. There was also the self-confidence of so many of the students, their possession of greatest excess. They were never rattled, always certain that the future held their best days, their greatest accomplishments. Their money was a shield, an invincibility that forced me to set aside my defective valve so I wouldn't be passed by. But in a blink it was springtime and, not even halfway through college, I was back in the hospital.

36

In hindsight, without membership to a team and the consistent physical challenges of athletic practices and contests I had relied upon for so many years to prove my strength, my toughness, my ability to succeed, I allowed sports to be replaced with reckless and unhealthy attempts to establish the same characteristics. However, I could not articulate this idea to Irwin, Billy, Wayne, and Burnham, who sat in chairs around my bed at Strong Memorial Hospital, listening to me recount the circumstances that had laid me low. I could present the facts, but not the insight.

Throughout sophomore year, I filled the windowsill in my Scholar's Floor dorm room—Dean's list students only—with bottle caps. On Tuesdays there were dollar beers at the Hoot Owl. On Wednesdays at the Glass Onion I flipped quarters to win drinks. Thursdays and Fridays I attended themed parties hosted by sororities at the Tick Tock: Halloween parties, 80s parties, duct tape clothes parties. In the wee hours, after the bartenders signalled last call and our fraternity friends barred us from deep frying chicken tenders in their kitchens, we roamed the town in search of after parties. I cranked out Power Hours and played epic beer pong tournaments at Greek mixers and basement raves, and basically carried on like everyone else I knew in Larryland. In October, I made my first weekend trip to Buffalo with my SLU friends for what became an annual bender. On Saturday there was Anchor Bar and the Wellington Pub, Checkers and Chippewa Street until last call at 4:00 A.M.; on Sunday, there was the parking lot at La Galleria to tailgate, and draught after draught to hoist

with the rabid Bills fans inside Ralph Wilson Stadium in the All-America City.

My grades remained excellent and I was on track to graduate *magna cum laude*, so I used my academic success to prove to myself that my behaviours were not a problem. But what was typical collegiate experimentation and bonding with the guys did not weigh typically on my health. I pushed closer and closer to the edge of risk: a heart valve that no longer functioned and overburdened cardiac muscle that grew too thick and tough to efficiently pump.

There were pick-up hoops, during which I capably matched up against players from the SLU team who were honing their skills during their offseason. Adirondack hikes and broom ball tournaments added to the tomfoolery of so many college nights, but none of it provided the outlet I subconsciously craved to compensate. And by the end of January, something wasn't right. It wasn't the dried-out and fuzzy-headed punishment of over-indulgence that gripped me. Instead, my throat was perpetually sore. My head ached and I had fevers I couldn't shake. I went to the student health centre. I followed their instructions and alternated doses of amoxicillin and ibuprofen, 600 mg of each, for the headaches and the fevers. I was optimistic. I was encouraged not to party on the meds. I kept partying. The headaches became severe and the fevers intense enough to soak my bed sheets at night or my shirt during class in a matter of minutes. I wore hoodies to disguise the sweat soaking my T-shirts, the damp V reaching down my back. I returned to the health centre and tested negative for mononucleosis and strep.

"It feels like I'm swallowing glue and nails," I said.

"Gargle warm saltwater," the nurse said, and as rudimentary as it seemed, I stole a shaker and plastic cup from the dining hall and did so enthusiastically, but to no avail. At

Rite Aid, I bought over-the-counter cold and flu medicines, trying most without relief, wasting my money. I made a third trip to the health centre at the end of February and was prescribed a stronger antibiotic. *Finally*, I thought, *this will cure me.* The headaches made academic concentration extremely challenging. The fevers were frequent and my throat was raw and bumpy, my mouth tacky with salt.

"Do not consume alcohol while taking this antibiotic," the nurse warned, but alcohol was my greatest source of relief. With my meal card I purchased plastic bottles of orange juice from the campus snack shack and from the liquor store plastic handles of Mohawk vodka. I drank one quarter of the orange juice and then refilled that amount with the vodka for a stiff Screwdriver. Several of those and I was primed for a night of Long Island Ice Teas at the Tick Tock and cans of Natty Ice at after parties in dilapidated houses in dark parts of town. For the stretches when alcohol whittled away my symptoms, I felt a notch below good.

Mornings after nights like these were rough. At brunch I rehashed the night's events with my friends: who hooked up with who in the lounge; who evaded the police in a footrace down the railroad tracks; who was blacklisted from the bar for vomiting in the fireplace. Laughing along, I'd try to swallow a piece of breakfast, but the rawness of my throat would take over and I couldn't force down the food. I'd jokingly chime in the conversation as the latest fever barrelled over me like a runaway keg. Whatever was happening, I was not in control. I couldn't shake it and I wanted to scream. I was frustrated. Sometimes, when I was alone, I wanted to cry.

Nicky and Missy visited me for the biggest party of the year: Snow Bowl. The Outing Club sold promotional T-shirts—"Come pack the bowl with the OC!"—and on

the sunniest of winter days, they bussed everyone to a retired ski hill near campus for a good old North Country Bacchanalia. The Greeks raced homemade toboggans down extremely steep hills at extremely unsafe speeds: couches on skis, pirate ships the size of ambulances, bikini-wearing snow bunnies atop keg-pontoon sleds. Everyone crashed into the forest at the bottom. Larrys launched themselves into the sky off giant kickers, their snowboards and tele-marks glinting in the sunlight, and dropped a hundred feet to the base of the hill. Smooth landings and bone-breaking crashes were applauded with equal enthusiasm. With the exception of the on-call EMTs, it was challenging to iden-tify a sober participant. Snow Bowl weekend was also an informal recruiting trip for Nicky. I hoped he would join me at SLU the next year, so I mentioned nothing of my illness and used all of my energy to show my guests a good time.

Despite feeling awful, I drove to Myrtle Beach with my friends for Spring Break. On a gambling boat, I drank Bloody Marys until I went blind. At the beach the next day I drank beer after beer and at night mixed the stron-gest punch palatable—several handles of cheap vodka, fruit punch, and chunks of pineapple, orange, and water-melon stirred up in plastic garbage pail. After the trip, I was happy to have a few days in Naples before the end of break. Each swallow felt like a rough-grit sandpaper block being dragged down my throat, and as the semester went on, I actually allowed myself to mildly complain to my friends from time to time. But they did not know how serious my situation was because I didn't tell them.

Because I didn't even know myself.

In March, I placed a final call to the health centre before a weekly independent study meeting with three upper-classmen and a professor. I was honoured to be part of

the group and as we discussed revisions to our report on sustainable campus energy practices, the Environmental Studies Department secretary came into our office.

"I have a message for Tom," she said. "It's from the Health Centre. Dr. Rosario called and said you need to go to the hospital immediately."

The group looked at my clammy, pale, unshaven face. Embarrassment rushed through me. I felt exposed.

She handed me a slip of paper. "He suggested you go back to your dorm room and call this number."

"I believe you have bacterial endocarditis," Dr. Rosario said over the phone. He explained that such an infection can begin as a form of strep and likely entered my bloodstream through a cut in the mouth, or by passing directly through the heart itself. The infection had likely settled on the bovine valve, rendering it ineffective or causing it to calcify dramatically and leak.

I packed for home.

Driving past the dilapidated farms and through the rusting towns of St. Lawrence County, I inventoried the facts. I was nineteen years old. A good student, formerly brimming with vitality. One who now partied aggressively and often, although no more than my friends. I now had reason to believe that I had felt ill for a long, long time because something was wrong with my heart valve. Would I need to have another surgery? I had no regrets about choosing the tissue valve in high school so I could play contact sports. If a mechanical valve had been used I would have needed to take Coumadin—rat poison—to thin my blood to prevent clots from forming on the valve, which would have increased the risk of internal bleeding and bruising had I been injured playing a sport. No regrets at all, but I sure wanted the bovine valve to last longer. In the rear-view mirror I caught a glimpse of my gray, sweaty skin. My self-consciousness and self-loathing jumped at the

sight. Four hours later, I met my family at Strong Memorial Hospital.

The admitting nurse was beautiful and not much older than me. Her brown hair shined and her olive skin glowed, and when she spoke I believed she cared about me. I forgot some of the worries I stewed over driving home, like my friends and professors having no idea why I left, and answered her questions.

"Describe a typical weekend this semester," she asked.

I elaborated on my recent hiking and hooping, but left out most of the rest.

I knew that this nurse was collecting information to diagnose my condition, but I could not answer her honestly with my parents sitting there. In fact, I didn't want to answer honestly in front of myself: to do so would be to admit that my partying might be a cause for my illness. I wanted to get better, but couldn't tell the truth.

My blood was tested for mono and strep again, but also cat scratch fever and other rare diseases like polycythemia vera. Dr. Tarchini was puzzled, but confident he would identify the problem. In excellent physical condition from high school athletics and genetic inheritance, I had lived with strep-like symptoms for months. The final diagnosis was indeed bacterial endocarditis, which I was told can kill a person within hours.

Ultimately, I was attached to a pic line that fed antibiotics through a vein inside my left bicep directly to my heart. The process of inserting the line into my body was painful, like stabbing the inside of your upper arm with a pen cap. The lidocaine did little to deflect the pain and so I felt a lot of pressure. It was not easy to be still enough to keep the needle from tearing my vein. The access point was sealed under a clear plastic patch and the nurse demonstrated how to wrap my arm in plastic bags to protect the entry point during showers, change the dressing on the pic line, and contact a visiting nurse for assistance. Then, with my new device, I went home.

Medicines showered the valve until July. I replaced cartridges of antibiotics in a pumping machine the size of a hardcover book, and three times a day I detached myself from the machine, hung a drip bag, attached the bag to the tube that disappeared into my arm, and fed a different antibiotic into my bloodstream. I nearly embolized myself each time. Sterilizing the apparatus and keeping the line free of air bubbles was stressful.

The strep symptoms alleviated and I returned to SLU for finals while continuing my treatment. The pumping machine ticked and revved during my exams and I did my best to ignore the noise and the students who stared at me when they heard it. In the evenings, because almost everyone had left campus for the summer, I sat alone in my empty dorm room with a fresh bag hanging from the IV pole, waiting for another dose to pass through me so I could study and rest.

At these times I tried not to become discouraged, but that was difficult. A tube passed through my shoulder and down to my heart. What would the pic line feel like slipping through my body when it was removed? I wondered how I was going to pack up my stuff for home with the device attached to my arm. I wondered what caused the infection: a cut in my mouth, or the filthiness of my dorm, or the time I dropped my Atenolol on the bathroom floor and dusted it off and ingested it anyway, or the dirty ball we played beer pong with in the basement of the fraternity? Could I have prevented this problem? Who knew?

I would not be able to resume landscaping until July, which would reduce my college fund for next year. Missy and I had planned to drive to Montana that summer, too, to climb mountains and hug trees, but that seemed unlikely. I had missed Spring Party Weekend and the celebrations that accompanied the conclusion of academic obligations and the coming of summer. I never reminisced about the past semester at SLU with my friends before parting ways, and I wondered what bonding I was not part of, as well as the unwanted pity I might have been given. The bag dripped. I felt depressed. On the final day of finals week, I completed my last exam and left for home.

Back in Naples, I watched Nicky win Sectional tennis matches and fill his name in the tournament bracket champions' box again. I hiked with Irwin and Billy, breathing in the clean air of spring, millions of crickets popping off the forest floor as we traversed the switchbacks of the Finger Lakes Trail. Never too old to build a fort, we made plans to repair Lucky's Lean-to, a high school project built of sticks tethered with twine. There were fallen trees to buck-up and firewood to split, stone benches to mend, maybe even a garden to plant, and starry nights ready for gazers like us. The anticipation of these plans filled me with strength.

It was the planning—the process of thinking about and organizing activities to achieve a desired goal—that turned me on. And that the plans were made with my friends. My future filled me with excitement. Near the west end of Academy Street, Pete's maple looked so healthy, so alive with soft green leaves. The edges of our initials carved long ago in the bark sweated sap. Whenever I walked past it, I patted the trunk for luck.

The soreness in my throat slowly melted away and time passed in a pile of discarded antibiotic cartridges that the home nurse collected in a red biohazard bin at the end of each week. Yet unable to work, I took long, aimless drives with Missy along the creek road, the lake roads and back roads, rambling on about Montana: how long it would take us to drive there, how dry it would be and how hot, how deep the snowpack might measure on the glaciers in August, how the buffalos I had read about cleaned themselves with dirt, and how together we'd experience it all. The only thing I didn't know was how we would pay for it.

When she wasn't chauffeuring us through the valley, Missy worked as a hostess at a lakeside restaurant. One June evening she called, insisting I stop by.

"I know your birthday isn't for a few more days," she said, taking my hand and leading me to the docks, "but I got you something." The light drained from the sky, the hill across the lake mirrored in perfect blackness, reaching toward us across the water. She handed me a small cardboard box.

"What's this?" I asked, removing a bell on a Velcro strap.

"That's for Montana. So we don't surprise any bears that could eat us."

I smiled. "Thank you."

"This is the loudest one you can buy," she said.

I gave it a shake.

"I can't wait."

I had made the Dean's List, but at the appointment to remove the pic line, the doctors confirmed that the damage was done—the endocarditis had changed the valve. It needed to be replaced sooner rather than later, and although I had a little time, it was difficult to know how much.

My family spotted me the money I had not time to earn, and in August Missy and I headed west. I think of our trip as the final step in our progression from friends to a boy and girl in love with one another, long-distance relationship quandaries be damned. I am disquieted to think that the endocarditis almost prevented me from spending so much time with her. My defective heart almost deprived us the opportunity to finish falling in love.

Missy handled the map and music and I took the wheel. In the deserts of the high plains we opened the windows despite the heat and held a straight line toward an unreachable horizon, tractor trailers and Harleys blowing past us at 85 m.p.h. Wisps of hair danced around her blue eyes, her delicate face, as she looked out the window. I watched her. In Montana, we walked between mountains and through meadows, our bells ringing over stone and snow. We saw no bears, but many yellow and pink monkey flowers, glacier lilies, fireweed, pristine red cedar and hemlock. There were eighty degree days and thirty degree nights. We ate buffalo burgers in roadside diners and Ramen noodles beside my tiny cook stove in the dark woods. Of all that we saw, I remember the white bear grass most clearly, growing abundantly across the Continental Divide, and one of the most important components of western ecology because its rhizomes survive wildfires: it thrives in periodic burns.

In October, I came home for a weekend to catch up with Billy for the first time in months, to loosen our jaws with liquid truth in the ambrosial valley. I saved my deepest breaths for the stretch along the winery road, that sweet-smelling space.

Before arriving at Billy's house I passed Pete's tree to touch the scarred bark. I sensed a vast chill in the swath of air above the nearby vineyards. My visit was unannounced but would not be a surprise.

Billy sat on his porch in a chair he had salvaged from The Barn. So often, this was where he took to intoxicated slumber, as satisfied as a hummingbird after a sugar-pool bath. He sought immediate rewards at the expense of those that were large and delayed, and that, I thought, was why he had so recently been in jail.

Deeohgee, Billy's chocolate lab, barked.

"Howdy, pardner," Billy said, smoke spurting from his mouth with each syllable.

He set a bottle at his feet and we greeted each other with a brotherly hug.

That evening we ascended West Hill to the headquarters of our cherished post: Lucky's Lean-to. Light touched our faces through the treetops. We had done this since we were young boys and tonight we were prepared to sleep outdoors. I looked through the trees toward a scene I'd scrutinized throughout my life, rows of vineyards striping the valley floor like rumpled corduroy.

We built a fire. In the coming dark, the wood smoke dissolved among the branches. We talked about the land on

which we trespassed. We toasted bread and melted cheese and roasted a purple onion on the flames. We washed our food down with local vintages and I took the opportunity to remind him of the time in high school he brought grape juice to the Rusted Root concert.

"Well, shit," he said.

West Hill had been terraced long ago for vineyard cultivation. As we ambled along a ridge we found our boots tangled in sprawling vines or rusted wire. Widmer's Winery had abandoned the steep slopes where we slept—the same terraced hillsides where Nicky and I once performed heroic surgeries with Papa's knife—and about that we were ambivalent; less grape growing, but more space to wander. The duties of adopted ownership honoured us.

Billy tossed pieces of bread to Deeohgee and poked at the fire.

We drank more wine.

"Thanks for visiting me in the hospital this spring," I said.

"Anytime, brother. Thanks for replying to my letter."

It was the first I had ever written to somebody in jail.

We stared into the fire.

Then Billy opened up and described his demise.

The details of his arrest remained mysterious and he said he replayed them in his mind many times. That summer, a few nights after he was fired from Lawn Doctors, he drank several bottles of wine. In the middle of the night he found himself stepping over the sill of Mrs. Carpenter's porch window and slipping between lace curtains one leg at a time, into the darkness. In her kitchen he finished off another bottle of Meritage and rummaged through the old woman's cabinets for alcohol. He then came upon a stairway. He didn't remember climbing the steps so much as floating up to the foot of her bed. Moonlight dusted her shrouded body in pulsing phosphorescence and cast barred

shadows from her headboard onto the wall. He drifted through the room in a semiconscious state collecting items to redeem at a pawnshop out of town. A bronze incense tray decorated with robed men, a jewelled rosary, and an antique painting of "The Last Supper" framed in gold that he lifted off a nail. Booze money. Drug money. Food money. Rent.

The residential street was dark and silent until he misjudged the distance between his car and the Volvo parked behind it, reversing into its headlight with a crack and triggering an anti-theft alarm. The neighbours roused to investigate. He sped away. At the village limits a deer materialized in the road, hypnotized by his headlights. Spooked, he jerked the steering wheel and rolled his car, skidding into a guardrail at the top of a gully. Mrs. Carpenter's belongings scattered across the pavement and glimmered in the high beams of the responding police cars.

"Trespassing, theft, DWI," Billy said. "There was so much poised against me."

"I felt the same way in the hospital," I said.

In jail, he thought often about the company of friends and what they shared, the company of fools and what could be learned. He wondered if any of us would visit him or send him letters or remember him in conversations. Regret flooded his thoughts. Jealousy soaked his core like wine into a cork.

"Wondering what you all were doing outside the walls consumed me," he said. Billy tossed a few sticks on the fire and rummaged through his backpack.

He held a Tawny Port up to the firelight.

"Bottled at the bottom of this hill," he said, handing it to me.

"The good stuff, for special occasions only." I pulled the cork, drank, and passed the bottle back.

"We only get one sip of that divine nectar," he said,

taking his drink.

"Can't ask for seconds at the altar."

We looked at one another in the eye for a moment. A breeze pushed the surrounding trees back and forth, their silhouettes waving at the sky. Branches snared starlight and pulled gleaming rivers of cosmic glow together. We remained silent, absorbed in the flames licking the cold air and the confessions and celebrations, communions and blessings of our time together. To complete the ritual, we passed the bottle once more and searched for escape in the elusive sky. Accomplices. We each had a lot to leave behind.

Around midnight, with the moon above us, I reclined on a bed of leaves, swaddled in my sleeping bag. I listened. The snap of the fire. The slosh of Billy draining his drink. The scratch of a lighter and the push of air bending the treetops.

Billy began a monologue about the land, continually returning to its pre-human form despite our interference.

"We can't control it," he said, "which is control in itself." Vegetation sprouted randomly in this earth. Erosion and maple trees rounded the stepped corners, roots gnawing and pinching away like a fist closing in the mud.

I told Billy goodnight and cozied up to the fire.

"In a month," he slurred, "many of these trees will be bare, their naked branches reaching out to the sun during the day and stars at night, waiting for the quiet of the snows."

Suddenly he vomited into the fire, a purple jet of puke.

Deeohgee barked.

This was routine.

I laughed with a grimace.

"Shit, man," he said, "Goddamn!" He wiped his lips and chin with his sleeve.

In the morning we woke to fingers of light poking

through the forest.

"What do you say we go to the bagel shop for breakfast," Billy said.

"Nah."

He stretched his arms and scratched the unruly nest of black curls atop his head. He eyed the chunky splattering of food and wines near his pillow.

"How come you never want to go to breakfast with me?"

"I guess I'm not hungry," I said, petting Deeohgee with one hand and separating the coals in the fire with a stick. "I digested my dinner."

Billy mumbled something I didn't understand and we packed up and walked home in silence. He seemed simultaneously offended and apologetic.

"Hike tonight?" he asked as we parted ways.

"Sure."

That evening, I ascended his porch steps again, hoping the dust had settled.

"I see you're feeling fine," I said.

"Glad we could do this again." He handed me a folded page from his journal:

And when I die
Don't bury me at all.
Just pickle my bones
In alcohol.
Put a bottle of wine
At my feet and my head
And if I don't rise
You'll know I'm dead.

I refolded the paper and slid it into Billy's shirt pocket. I clapped my hand on his shoulder, unsure what to say.

Soon we rambled up the terraced hill again through the black night. Without flashlights our pupils adjusted perfectly.

We followed our feet, the stony trail to the water tower

mapped across our minds. I looked downhill through the woods, smooth maple trunks playing peek-a-boo with the village lights, the night air tangy and wet in the almost-winter woods.

At the water tower we sat on a rock bench and gazed at the village below, passing a jug of good ole Naples hooch between us. Tractor-trailers passed through town silently, floating light-bulb rectangles like display cases about to illuminate the unknown.

"Yessir."

"Mmm, hmm."

The truck shifted gears, leaving town, and disappeared between hills.

It got late but going to bed meant saying goodbye, so we wandered back into the woods, taking the long way home. We trickled downhill like rainwater, paused in the middle of the vineyard, and craned our necks upward for shooting stars and the constellations that told us that this was home.

The alarm clock screeched like a smoke detector and I wanted to know where I was. It was almost noon and last night my hazing culminated in a wild party—I officially became a social bro at KDS. I was in a sorority.

I lifted my heavy head off the pillow. Scattered across the floor, my personal effects formed a maze of sorts. Wallet. Pants, one leg inside-out. A toppled desk chair. I still wore my button down, half-buttoned. Severe pain shot through my left hand. The back of it bulged significantly, like half an orange slipped under the skin. I was horrified. I sat up and felt more pain in my hip. Baffled, I looked to the floor for answers. There were none.

I tried to piece the night together, but couldn't remember much beyond the KDS sisters duct taping two 40s to my hands until I finished them, the girls screaming and dancing all around the new crop of social bros in our undershorts. My hand felt broken, for sure, but how did I break it? I decided to meet the guys at Meadows Diner even though they always ran out of bacon. Maybe they had some answers.

On the pedal to the diner, I thought and thought until I discovered the missing pieces of the puzzle—the pain in my hip and the toppled desk chair. Getting into bed each night, I climbed my chair to my desktop, then to my lofted bed, and last night I must have lost my balance and fallen, breaking my hand. I was relieved I didn't catch a piece of the desk with my face on the way down. Another problem emerged. I needed an X-Ray and a cast and to get treatment I needed insurance information from Mom. How

would I explain any of this to her? That her son, the one who had left school to be treated for endocarditis last year, behaved so carelessly, as if the infection in his heart had never happened?

Years had passed since the first valve replacement surgery, and with the physical changes to my heart came continuously evolving mechanisms for coping with what I perceived as self-weakening. As a young boy, I tried to be brave, but that need for courage transformed into a combination of concealment and compensation in high school. Now, a new phase of defiance solidified in my core. The more scarred I felt, the greater my denial. I detached myself from the endocarditis and the slowly deteriorating bovine valve in my heart by partying at SLU as college folk do. This made me feel—and, I hoped, appear—to others as if I were normal. Unfortunately, my behaviours had the effect of accelerating time.

Soon, I would run out.

Through separate programs at our respective colleges, Missy and I studied in London the following semester and explored Europe. In Dublin we tasted Guinness from the source. In Spain, there were beaches and bullfights. From Venice to Rome I searched for my namesake, and came face-to-face with Van Gogh in the Netherlands, his *Self-Portrait as a Painter* the last piece he produced in Paris. There, we found ourselves bombing down the streets in an open-door police van just before sunrise.

That night, we had eaten with friends at a fondue joint that served wine in baby bottles, and then strolled along the Seine. The air held the fragrance of the thousands of spring flowers and leafing trees of April, the gentle ebb of the river water below, our voices. In the field between the Eiffel Tower and the Institut des Hautes Etudes de Défense Nationale, we tossed a Frisbee in the dark until our shoulders ached. Finally, on the cusp of morning light, we walked to our hotel.

I pushed the door buzzer and the proprietor responded in French over the intercom.

"Room 24," I said in English.

"Sors d'ici," he snapped. Missy and I exchanged looks of confusion.

"We're in room 24," I tried again.

"Je vais appelar la police!" he shouted, his final communication.

"I think he plans to call the police," Missy said. Her French was rusty and mine nonexistent. *But why would he call the police?*

Exhausted, angry, and locked out, we decided to find the cops ourselves.

Without any trouble, we slipped into the stereotype we had hoped to avoid: incompetent American tourists searching for someone who spoke English. With the exception of bums passed out in storefront foyers, fingers of urine trickling down the sidewalk from their cardboard mattresses, the streets were empty. I began considering a plan that involved us sleeping in a park until morning when Missy noticed a man approaching us from the shadows of a nearby apartment block.

"Look," she said, "he's drinking a Fanta."

Indeed, he carried a can of the fizzy orange refreshment. At that point, nothing could have provided greater proof of his reliability, sobriety, and heroics, so we approached him. It was unclear whether or not he understood the explanation of our predicament. Fanta in hand, he gestured for us to follow him. We proceeded, a few steps behind, block after block, believing he would help us. Eventually, he stopped to use a payphone. Awash in a pool of yellow streetlight, he conversed briefly with someone, and then cradled the receiver.

"Police," he said, pointing to the ground on which we stood. A moment later I heard sirens in the distance. They quickly grew louder. Suddenly, as if in an action movie, a SWAT team van whipped around the corner, lights flashing, and screeched to a stop in front of us. Guns drawn, police officers in black riot gear jumped out, some speaking into shoulder-mounted walkie-talkies, others to our guide as he sipped his soda.

"Montez! Viens avec nous!" one of them finally said to us. We stood still. "Come!" he said, motioning to the van. We jumped in. There was no time to close doors or secure seatbelts. We accelerated down the street, the wind tearing

at our clothes, our hair, Paris a blur beneath the running boards. We must have given the address to the hotel, because in moments the squad leader rang the buzzer, shouting into the intercom, hammering the door with the butt of his weapon. The door unlocked and, to our relief, we entered. Then both the proprietor and the police began screaming at us.

"Americans! Eh!" the officers shouted, disgusted with us and our communication. Apparently, the police thought we had been mugged and robbed by the proprietor. We didn't care what they thought, completing the stereotype, and slept soundly that night, safely reunited with our passports and backpacks in the city of love.

If we had simply walked to our hotel after a beautiful evening and been buzzed inside together without issue, then I doubt I would remember this night so clearly. The food and the wine, the river walk, the Frisbee and the lights and the springtime air, the trust Missy and I placed in a strange man drinking Fanta, and in each other: all of it composed another moment binding us together. The small adversity that we faced became the common language of shared experience. A memory doesn't become a memory if you don't talk about it, and so whenever we recalled our night in Paris thereafter, we didn't need to speak French to share this story, or even an audience.

In fact, most often the only thing we needed was each other.

41

What of this next story have my friends heard? Nothing. Not on a hike or at a bar, on a boat or by a fire. Not a word.

My calcifying bovine valve lasted until graduation from St. Lawrence, but by then I was in bad shape. Over the year leading up to commencement I did my heart few favours. As usual, I acted as if everything was fine, that I had no reason to hold back. My grades remained excellent and I worked for Lawn Doctors over the summer to whip my ass into shape, but my collegiate lifestyle and weakening heart were catching up to me. It felt like slowly being horse-collared from behind. By Christmas of my senior year my energy had dissolved. I continued the charade of a happy twenty-year-old: Tommy College would not cry mercy. Then, at a cardiologist appointment in January, Dr. Tarchini said what I had been waiting for years for him to say.

"After you graduate in May, the valve must be replaced."

He had warned me that choosing a tissue valve was risky because it could harden and cease to perform. When I was fifteen, five or six years seemed a lifetime away, and in some respects it was. I repeated to myself that this second valve replacement surgery was real. No pretending I was okay anymore. Unlike the first valve replacement, this procedure was not preventative. The fibrillations occurred frequently; leaking backflow at the valve was extreme; my heart had swollen to a dangerous size. My demise had transpired gradually and, because of my denial, I was relatively unaware of how dire my condition was until Dr. Tarchini confronted me. For months I laboured on the basketball court or mountainside, baffled by my lack of wind. I was so

breathless after so little exertion, but any associations to my leaky bicuspid valve and my ballooning heart eluded me. I couldn't acknowledge my fate lest it become real.

A writing major, during my final semester I turned down an invitation to publicly read my work because I was ashamed at how I could not stop myself from sweating. My heart worked overtime, pumping harder and harder to compensate for the blood that sloshed back through the leaking valve, the walls of the chambers growing thicker and thicker. I found it all but impossible to remain composed in confined spaces while carrying on academic conversations with people I respected and admired, because in these moments I perpetually wiped perspiration off my temples, from under my eyes, and off my forehead. This profuse sweating matted my hair and soaked my clothes every day for a year, until it became as normal as breathing except that I pleaded for it to end. I'd excuse myself to the lavatory during every class, meals at the dining hall, at the pub with my professors, and during meetings with my advisor, to walk around in the North Country winter air, mopping my forehead with paper towels and imploding with frustration, considering the next excuse to escape to my townhouse where there were clean, dry clothes.

In March, I drove to Key West with the guys for Spring Break. One of the side effects of my fat heart, I realized on that trip, was vertigo. At the wheel on the New Jersey Turnpike, my vision blurred for a long moment. I endured the whirling dizziness and hoped I wouldn't pass out in the rush hour traffic, injuring or killing my friends, other travellers, myself. I shook my head, squeezed my eyes shut, and then stretched them open several times, even slapped my own face, and after a few moments the dizziness subsided. I was a selfish fool who was too proud to admit a weakness and relinquish control.

Thirty hours later we made it to Key West. It was party time. Day after day we drank Red Stripe on the beach, threw a Frisbee, floated in the ocean, and napped in the sun. On Duval Street it was Happy Hour every hour. We ate raw oysters on weathered porches and our tabletops grew empty bottles like glass leaves on mangrove trees, our heads as heavy as sand-filled balloons. There was no end in sight: I bounced from bars to clubs to rooftop lounges, double-fisting vodka tonics and Dark 'N' Stormys, scarfing street meat after last call and clambering back to our crib with booze and mustard on my shirt, and sand in my pockets. Every day I was the last person standing. I thought I had something to prove. Sunrises were my specialty, a drink in hand at the edge of the mangroves, the docks, the Southernmost Point in the United States, before crashing on the windswept, sun-soaked peninsula jutting into the water, milky blue with salt.

Finally, on a bare-chested walk on the beach it just came out: "What's up with the scar," Charlie asked. Four years. He had not asked me in all the time I had known him. Unlike when I had been similarly questioned before streaking through The Quad during freshman orientation at SLU, I told him the truth, and that I'd have another surgery the first week of June.

"The new valve will probably be mechanical," I added. I remained amazed that after four years together one of my best friends hadn't mentioned the zipper on my chest. Was my scar like somebody's dead father that nobody ever talked about? How strongly did I emit a *Don't ask* vibe? I didn't want to ruin our pleasant jaunt in the sun or stifle the energy that buoyed our trip. I didn't want pity, either. Instead, I was relieved to tell the truth, to acknowledge my scar, and grateful to hear how much my friend cared.

But, in what was perhaps my final collegiate hurrah, I

endured a final bender during senior week, still acting as if I wanted every person in the goddamn world to know I was normal. I was not normal. I was sick. It is entirely accurate to state that I was close to dying. The balloon could have popped. I had not applied to graduate schools and instead of being thankful for the opportunity to replace the valve, my post-graduate prospects depressed me. Epically hungover and exhausted, I crossed the graduation stage on a sunny May afternoon, snapped some photos with my family and friends, packed my belongings into my car, and left my home-away-from-home.

A few days later, alone at the computer on the night before surgery, I tried to scare myself into being brave. My fingers tapped keys, and my attention was aroused by a video of an aortic valve replacement. Squeamishly, I paused and replayed it, again and again, eight hours paired down to as many minutes.

Of course there was a lot of blood. The camera was mounted above the table and focused on the patient's chest, oriented vertically on the screen and bathed in iodine-tinged light. The ribs were draped with linens except for the skin encasing the sternum. Twenty seconds, in a latex-gloved hand skated a blade across this smooth surface. I watched the weight of the body on either side of the slice separate this supple membrane and like a paper cut, the blood was a moment before arriving. With rough precision the surgeon passed a spinning blade over cartilage and bone, sawing the sternum in half. I imagined bits of body spraying under the saw guard. The video cut to the next scene—the double-walled sac protecting the heart, the pericardium, was scalpeled. Two clamping instruments pulled apart the sides as the blade progressed, revealing the beating heart. I was immediately struck by the sharpness of

these tools and their proximity to tissues wet and tender, vital and thin. And the simplicity. It looked like an X-Acto knife with which I once cut up a frog in biology class.

Inside the myocardial chamber, the aorta was cannulated—its fluid was drawn off with a tube—and the blood came, pulsing out of the artery and filling the pericardium. The blood spattered the latex hands until the tube was secured in the hole to divert the flow. Like fitting a casing on a sausage press nozzle, the aorta was stuffed with the cannula and sutured to it. Soon the insentient patient was surviving on the extracorporeal cardiopulmonary bypass, an apparatus that circulated blood and oxygen throughout the body, bypassing the heart. The beating heart was a spirited and dynamic organ. The steadiest of hands could not manipulate a scalpel, needle, and surgical thread without shredding it to ribbons or perforating its jumping walls, thus the importance of the heart-lung machine.

Bloodways were vented and clamped. Tiny guy-wires appeared to steady the chamber tissues in the video frame like ropes tied to a hot air balloon. The wires were there to deliver electrical impulses to stimulate the heart if necessary after the void was closed. The blade carved back and forth under the gentlest of pressures and the surgeon excised the valve, leaving as much cardiac muscle as possible to anchor the new tap. The defective valve was white and lifeless, and as rubbery as boiled calamari. Two pairs of latex hands held metal sticks and wires steady and another inserted replacement valves of various sizes, testing for fit. This was not a gentle process. Once chosen, the new bovine valve was attached to the end of a probe and crammed into the hole.

I looked away, tempted to stop the video. There was no sound, no verbal direction from the surgeons, or clinking instruments, or humming and beeping machines. No banter of last night's dinner, next week's fishing trip, the

THOMAS MANNELLA

sexy new intern. I could only hear my computer breathe and feel the laboured *dub-dub, dub-dub, dub-dub* inside me.

Tweezers poked and looped and pulled the thread to sew the valve anchor into the heart walls, tugging it tight. The camera window pulled back to reveal the steel clamps that maintained the thoracic cavity's yawn at a width of two fists. The cow tissue took a last dip in the sterilizers before the sutures were placed in the valve sewing ring. All of this I could see, but what about smells emanating from the body? The exposed slabs of pectoral muscle? The veins of fat cushioning the inner chest? The blood burning at points of cauterization?

If you have ever looked through your closed eyelids at the sun, then you know the colour of the blood-soaked linens, the way the bright light played on the redness through a videographer's lens. The knots were tied and pressed firmly with a finger and I could all but feel the prodding from within. This recognition pinched my breath, as finite and sudden as bursting a perfect bloody bubble.

In its stillness, the heart looked less alive than the latex hands, a similar shade of disposability and engineering. The aorta halves were piped together and rhythm returned. The heart resumed its dance. The surgeons wiped the cruor off of their fingers into their workspace. The pinkish halves of chest muscle were inspected for adverse bleeding and cauterized before the hole was shut and stapled at the bone and sewed at the skin. Each tug of the thread raised the flesh until the twenty-inch incision was zipped closed.

So, I thought, *me. Tomorrow.*

In that instant I separated from the illusion that my life was perfect.

I smashed into the truth.

It had taken so, so long.

Outside the window bright stars held steady in the sky.

I wondered: *How did one organize an open heart surgery and all the tangential protocols and possibilities? How was a surgical team assembled? What if the surgeon passed out? Did surgeons take breaks? How many bags of blood were available? What happened when a patient couldn't be taken off the heart-lung machine? How did surgeons prepare to stand for hours at the OR table? How could they sleep the night before surgery knowing the next day they were the life support? If I could pick my surgeon—if I could pick somebody to save my life—who* should *I choose?*

In the pre-op room, he slid the curtain aside and stepped forward. He smiled at me. Instead of shaking my hand, he grabbed my ankle and patted my foot. He registered the tension in my throat from holding everything in and the ways in which I could never be as brave as I wanted. He leaned his strong body over me and when he secured my hand in his and held my shoulder with the other and spoke to me the words I needed to hear, I understood his power.

"I am very, *very* good at what I do," Dr. D'Allesandro said. My chin dropped to let air in. I didn't want to cry, and I wanted to believe he would be brave for me. To my parents he said, "I will care for your son as if he were my own." I believed him. He wiped tears off my face and stood again to leave, and with my sleeve I wiped away the rest so I could look at my Mom and Dad, Nicky and Missy. The time to live or die had come.

I was wheeled to a prep space. I put on a gown and felt self-conscious about what it covered and what it didn't. I clung to the sheet and followed a resident nurse's instructions. I sat up in bed and slouched out of the gown. Another resident with an electric razor sheared the hair from my chest, exposing the scar that already existed. Iodine was slathered on my sternum in a cold wet tickle. A third resident dabbed numbing cream on my wrist and explained what it was. I wished to swallow gallons of the stuff.

I was a body on a board. It was time for the arterial IV but my wrist was not numb. The resident opened a package of blue arm-length plastic tubing as skinny as guitar string.

I stiffened. With a cone-shaped device like a pen cap he punctured the skin on my wrist below the stump of my thumb and taped this portal to my arm. He pushed the tubing into my arm through the portal. Blood ran down my arm and onto the sheets. The room was very cold. I sweated profusely. Nobody wiped away the blood. I was rigid from head to toe and my arm flashed with electricity and fire. I wanted to scream at this sadist. My breathing was shallow and I looked from the blood to my toes and back again. For a moment I was distracted by a nurse wrapping an ID tag around my wrist and another nurse swaddling my thigh with a blood pressure cuff. Nobody talked to me. I was paralyzed by flashes of electric prickings at my elbow.

The tubing felt like it poked through the artery and was stabbing raw nerves, but I couldn't move. The IV nurse muttered an apology and removed the tubing. It was coated with blood. This nurse got a fresh piece of tubing. He inserted it into the portal and I felt swelling pressure along my arm as if the tubing plunged all the blood in the artery back up into my arm, resisting compression like a hydraulic press, blood leaking out of the plastic portal, a metal file grating raw nerves or a hammer tenderizing the bundle of fibres in my elbow or both. There was not a trace of numbness. There was seasick pain.

In his most cheerful voice I heard the nurse ask me how the numbing cream was working—did it do the trick? He must have known the answer because he perspired along his receding hairline, his zitty chin and greasy nose. I sweated more. I shook my head no. Not working. He pulled out the second tube and examined it. Blood dribbled down my arm. I couldn't look away. My respiration was ragged. Then he tried to insert the IV a third time. I hated this nurse very much. But I was defeated. He said he might have to work an IV into the other arm. I could not possibly hate him

more but then he said, "I'll insert the IV once you're under anaesthesia."

I wanted to scream. *I'm not your practice cadaver.* I detested him even though he was part of a team of people trying to fix me.

Moments later I was wheeled away and surprised not to be anaesthetized before being placed on the operating table, because six years ago I was knocked out in advance and spared the OR scene. Now I was a twenty-two-year-old paediatric cardiology patient about to be operated on by somebody who normally repaired the flawed hearts of infants.

In the operating room there was only me supine on a table. Nobody talked to me. Nobody asked how I felt. Everyone prepared, like roadies before a concert, sliding cabinets here, opening and closing drawers there, testing electronics and counting supplies, tuning instruments and flowing in chaotic choreography throughout the room before the main act arrived, the man with the steady hands about to take centre stage. There was no pillow under my head and I was cold from sweating so much. Above me hung racks of austere lights. Somebody mentioned the gas, told me there was oxygen in the mask to help me breathe and remain calm, but I knew better. A nurse fitted the two prongs of the oxygen hose into my nostrils and tucked the tubing behind my ears like headphone cords. Before mumbling a reply, the sky darkened as if millions of winged creatures had passed in front of the sun.

43

It has been said that open heart surgery feels like somebody with the best of intentions has shot you in the chest. This is accurate, but instead of an exit wound I felt the radial distribution of shrapnel inside of me. What was worse was that I knew exactly what was coming.

In ICU, life sped up and slowed down because of the drugs and the waiting. The universe folded inside out. I had been sawed open and was conscious of little else except my inability to prevent the pain.

Sitting up was climbing Mt. Everest. Breathing expanded my thorax and felt like swallowing shards of glass. I needed to breathe to live, therefore I needed to hurt. I burrowed inside fractions of seconds of distraction: the perception there was a heater in my mattress, the crinkle of a magazine page, a nurse knocking at the door, the jostle of an IV stand as a drip bag was replaced, the sensation my lips were cracking, my mouth was dry, and something was crammed down my throat. I floated in a cloud of hurt. To have had a valve replaced before did not help. I would not recover as quickly as before because of the pre-existing scar tissue, the areas of trauma traumatized a second time.

Time warped on and I became sensitive to my whereabouts in the semiconscious moments between doses of sedatives. Morphine slithered through my veins but it did not assuage my discomfort. The valve became me and I became the valve.

I never promised to attend any churches or believe in any gods. I cared a lot about living and I wanted to live normally, productively, actively, but that seemed a distant dream. My

subconscious was the only mental engine connecting me to pre-surgery thought, so I tried to speak, to ask if the surgeons did the Ross procedure – replacing the diseased aortic valve with the pulmonary valve and then replacing that with a cadaver valve, an advantageous procedure putting my own tissue in the more critical position. No, my family said, the match between the valves was poor. The new valve was mechanical. I muttered awkwardly because among my newly acquired accoutrements was a polyvinyl chloride tracheal tube several millimeters thick that was in my throat. There was also a catheter tube, IVs in my arms, an electronic clamp on my finger registering vitals, blood pressure cuffs on my limbs, and drainage tubes sutured into my stomach and neck.

The next day a nurse shoved pills up my ass and washed me with sponges. Rolling onto my side to accept the suppositories was a monumental effort requiring me to constrict chest muscles that gripped my sternum, pulling at my bones. In agony I held my breath but that maintained the tension, so I exhaled, which also hurt. There was no escape. Shove as many pills up my ass as you like—just lift the house off of my chest and throw a bucket of water on the fire inside.

I took amnesiac medicines so I wouldn't remember most of the torment, but chemistry only covered so much. The drugs could not clot a conversation between my surgeon and another doctor, their words floating through the doorway past beeping machines and blinking lights to the bones of my inner ear: *ten hours …internal bleeding … twenty-five percent …BP …significant …ET …going back in … IloveyouIloveyouIloveyou.*

The surgeons realized the door to my room was opened. They closed it.

My memories expanded with the days. Blood drained through two tubes inserted below my ribcage and accumu-

lated in a calibrated plastic box. As my intravenous pain-killing regimen was reduced I became wary of the box's contents. I marked the passage of time with each fluid check and over the days it changed from red to pink to yellow-clear.

An oxygen mask replaced the breathing tube. Unfortunately, the large volume of oxygen overwhelmed the delicate membranes in my nostrils, triggering a torrent of blood from each. I was back at the beginning, a worried, helpless five-year-old with a gusher. The nurses pressed a hamper's worth of towels to my nose for hours. Missy assisted the ICU crew. I tilted my head backwards and several finger-sized clots slipped past my nasopharynx and into my throat. I choked violently. The dynamic tremors pried my stapled sternum. I was fearful of reopening myself. I received an injection of platelets and bundles of gauze were packed up each nostril. The bleeding finally stopped. I shook and shuddered uncontrollably and the thin hospital blankets did not warm me so Missy lay on top of me to hug the coldness away. The next morning I was too weak and sore to hock a loogie, so we all took turns suctioning the phlegm and blood clots out of my throat with a large plastic eyedropper.

On day four I moved to the paediatric ward. The walls displayed cartoon fish and my toes touched the footboard. I transitioned from urinary catheter to piss jug to lugging my drainage box to the bathroom. The nose plugs made eating difficult; chewing and swallowing completely closed my airways. At night, I slurped paltry amounts of green Jell-O and drifted off into hallucinations, night skies dripping onto a green city, black rain, shifting shapes, tarry figures that pulsed under the stars. These chartreuse dreams were strange and beautiful. Missy slept in a chair beside my bed. The next morning my nose plugs were removed

and I was overpowered by an unclean odour that defied the imagination: the oily stench emanating from my body.

One evening a voluble volunteer visited me to play board games. In my reticence, I parried his attempts to strike a conversation and he left with the boxes under his arms. I felt relieved because to befriend him would mean that I wanted company, that I was lonely and homesick. The Lakers and Pistons played in the NBA Finals but the game was just noise on TV for all I cared. A few days ago I could not have imagined standing, but even my progress couldn't placate a crankiness that was replacing the politeness I employed in ICU when the only thing I could control were my manners. I also could not get used to the clicking and thudding of the new valve.

A nurse encouraged me to move about so I shuffled to the window. A rainstorm had passed through the city and I stared at the dark clouds drifting away. Then, the faintest of rainbows arched across evening like a gateway to the vast spaces of the world to which I suddenly longed to return.

And that was all it took. A fucking rainbow. A small glimpse of the vitality that awaited me.

Watching the rainbow, I anticipated leaving the hospital with eagerness. Maybe something so simple, so fleeting, made me feel more alive because death had seemed so possible. Most of the gratitude I felt for my life came from my memories of friends and family: hiking a muddy trail with the guys; riding with Mom to soccer tournaments or cruising nowhere with Dad in his car; the sound of a train rolling past campus at dusk while I walked to the library; crowd noise swelling to welcome Phish to the stage; a soccer ball rolling through the grass; the crackle of a fire and the sway of bear grass; exploring Paris with Missy; night-time tennis with Nicky; a handful of forks and a grape pie; the grip of cold lake water. These memories made me feel I

had had the experiences of somebody twice my age. I felt thankful. I felt loved.

A fucking rainbow. That's all.

Five days after surgery the doctors were satisfied with the clarity of the fluid draining into the box and decided to remove the tubes. A nurse peeled away the rusty bandages from the two entry points. With shining scissors, he snipped the sutures anchoring the plastic hoses to my belly. Firmly gripping one tube, he pressed his other hand just above the one-inch slit and, in an aggressive and unannounced motion, yanked the bloody thing out. A thick burn crept into my flesh.

"The second tends to be more difficult than the first," he said. A black clot oozed from the slit. I focused my consciousness on a bundle of red balloons in the corner of my room and braced myself as he clutched the other tube.

Without the tubes I was wheeled to the electrocardiogram room to check the new flow. I was nervous because this test was administered on the same machine and in the same room in which my demise was monitored over the years. The technician smeared warm gel on my tender chest. She gently slid the wand from place to place and took pictures.

"This is where the traditional shape of a heart as we know it comes from." She pointed to the screen. I saw the two halves. She printed the image and tucked it under my arm, saying, "Beautiful, I think." This was the loveliest valentine I had ever received.

I gained strength and discarded tubing and wires and angst, keen to go home. Dr. D'Allesandro shook my hand on the morning I was discharged, my sixth day in the hospital. What do you say to the people who have saved your life? Might telling everyone I can that the men and women comprising the Paediatric Cardiology Unit

at Strong Memorial Hospital are the most extraordinary people in the world, to me, to my family, suffice? Even if my insurance paid the hospital hundreds of thousands of dollars, receiving the opportunity to live a healthy, meaningful life is priceless. There is nothing that can be said or done to equal the magnitude of that act. I thanked Dr. D'Allesandro anyway, but he got the last word, thanking me, and drifting quietly down the hallway.

Missy loaded me into her car and drove us to Naples. Over the following days, simple movements like getting into or out of bed were excruciatingly difficult and painful. Laughing stretched my chest; as before, it hurt so much I cried. In the hospital I had received a tutorial in the ways Coumadin, the blood-thinner I would take as long as I had a mechanical valve, would change my life. I would bruise easily, and therefore was not allowed to play contact sports, ride motorcycles, climb trees, or drink alcohol in excess. The titanium valve would not ossify, but I needed to listen to its click because changes could alert me to clots settling on the valve or tissues growing into it. I was my own greatest safety net.

I lived in pyjamas and wore profound bed-head for weeks. My shoulders were hunched, my chest pulled together at the incision, which was a wound that would not heal. The twisting, folding, and stretching of my abdomen kept several inches of the trench open and the matter inside it turned yellow and gray, and reeked of infection. At my one-week check-up, a nurse scraped the gunk out with a gauzy cloth and then scraped it again. The blood seeped and trickled.

"Bleeding will clean the wound and allow it to scab and heal," she said.

Afterwards, Missy and I walked the roof deck of the parking garage where the wind was warm, and the traffic

murmured below. Beyond the horizon of hospital buildings I observed the flowering greenery atop Cobb's Hill Park and Washington Grove, lilacs and leaves surrounding the reservoir. These were some of the get-well bouquets that mattered most to me. As with the rainstorm and the rainbow, noticing them infused me with optimism. I pushed against the taut skin, muscle, and bone of my chest to stand taller than I had in days, in months, really. A ballsy mood I did not expect to feel emerged, too—something I forgot I *could* feel because of the months of self-conscious sweating, dizzy spells, evaporated physical prowess, and lack of control. This confidence had been there all along, just waiting for me to open up.

THOMAS MANNELLA

Surviving surgery was a strange fantasy, because the consternation that lurked in my subconscious and caused me to ignore the debilitating nature of my leaky valve also blinded me to the beneficial results of a valve replacement surgery. I did not know how good I could feel.

My heart returned to a normal size and the work required of it had been greatly reduced compared to the pre-surgery overdrive that overheated my system; continuous sweating became a thing of the past. I felt calmer. Normal. Before surgery, I required ten hours of sleep a night after even indolent days. Now I couldn't sit still. I slept less each night and filled my life with relentless activity: hiking, biking, reading, writing, friends, travelling, concerts, and work. Normal heart function felt like taking steroids.

It took months to become accustomed to the clicking in my chest. When I held a book, each beat made the pages tremble, but this concession was worth every molecule of life pumping through my body. I no longer pretended to be normal because I knew, and embraced, what was my new normal. Feeling so good after feeling so bad was a dream I had dared not dream before the surgery.

Each month my blood was drawn to check my Coumadin level with a PT-INR test. PT, or prothrombin time, is the measure of how quickly blood clots, and INR stands for International Normalized Ratio, which is the standard unit used to report the results of a PT test. The higher the INR reading, the longer it took for the blood to clot. The target number for my Coumadin therapy was between 2.0 and 3.0, and I typically fell in this range.

I had a standing order at the hospital. The secretary pulled my paperwork and I read the *New Yorker* or scrolled through my phone until my name was called, and a nurse directed me to a cushy chair between curtain walls.

"Full name?" she asked, looking at my paperwork.

"Thomas Nicodemus Mannella, III."

"Date of birth?"

"June 20th, 1982."

"Which arm do you prefer?"

"Doesn't matter," I said.

She looked at both my arms.

"You have wonderful veins," she said. I looked, too. I did have kickass veins.

She put on rubber gloves, wrapped the rubber strip around my left bicep, and tightened it.

"Relax your arm for me."

I did and she pushed down on the bigger veins to make them stand up. She chose one, tore open and removed an alcohol swab from a small packet, and sterilized the skin over the vein. She paused a moment to let the disinfectant dry. Then she rested her hand against my forearm and pointed the needle tip at the vein.

"Small pinch," she said, the needle stinging like a bee.

A whiter piece of skin stretched over top of the needle that was inside me. The nurse attached the plastic tube to the other end of the needle portal, filled the chamber with blood, and removed the needle.

"You want me to hold it on there?" I asked as she pressed the gauze onto the bloody puncture. Once, the blood didn't flow, and the nurse slid the needle back and forth, in and out, tilting it up and down, searching for the middle of the vein. She was probably training, and so there was a lot of hunting for the sweet spot. I braced myself. Two unsuccessful jabs and another phlebotomist took over. The

best phlebotomist I ever had was an enormous dude, black skin and a shaved head, a former military officer. Drawing blood in a small air-conditioned hospital was easier than doing it in a Middle Eastern desert wasteland, he had said, with explosions, or the constant threat of explosions, all around, in his case sometimes so close he felt the sand and grit land on his sweating arms.

"Freaky shit, man, freaky shit," he had said. I hadn't felt his needle go in. "Someday, when the veins in your arms break down, they'll draw from your leg." I wanted him to draw my blood every time.

If the INR results were undesirable, then my diet was usually to blame. Vitamin K is required for blood coagulation and is highly concentrated in leafy green vegetables, including asparagus, broccoli, Brussels sprouts, cabbage, chickpeas, collards, endive, green tea, kale, lettuce, mustard and turnip greens, parsley, soybeans, and spinach; and fruits, such as avocado, kiwifruit, and grapes. Without vitamin K, uncontrolled bleeding can occur, especially for people ingesting Coumadin daily, like me. Because low levels of vitamin K also weaken bones and promote calcification of arteries and other soft tissues, I needed to eat it to stay healthy, and so I also needed to take a high dose of Coumadin to balance the coagulative properties of vitamin K and inhibit the formation of blood clots on my mechanical valve.

Thinned blood is not normal, after all, so there have been minor complications. Over the years I have banged my legs on coffee tables, night stands, car doors, open dishwasher doors, trailer hitches, fallen trees, scaffolding, and chairs, and they bruise terrifically every time. I bruised my kidney on a water slide and pissed blood for a week. I began playing soccer again because my energy overflowed and not using it seemed a tremendous waste, but when an oppo-

nent kicked my ankle, I developed a large hematoma that remained swollen and painful for weeks. When I had my wisdom teeth removed, I withheld several doses of Coumadin to control the bleeding. The oral surgeon nicked the roof of my mouth and, after I resumed taking my blood-thinner, that tiny cut bled into my throat for days until he patched it with special dental tape. During the mountain biking leg of an adventure race, mud sucked into the chain and gears of my bike, locking the wheels and pitching me over the handle bars. Upon my return to Earth, the rear sprocket teeth deeply gouged my shin. There was a lot of blood, but eventually it clotted. A potato chip slicing the roof of my mouth even sent me to the ER. I was irritated at the inconvenience, but this reaction meant I had grown distant from consciously feeling thankful for my new life, the new valve, new energy, and opportunities. The expectations I had for my own life had transformed. I no longer pretended, but *expected* to feel healthy and strong.

I was so overwhelmed before surgery that I thought little of life after it. I knew my B.A. in English would not deliver the financial bonanza I fooled myself into thinking it might when I chose to major in creative writing. The first sign of post-graduate reality had come one drizzly spring afternoon as I walked across campus. This warning began with a droning buzz that got louder and louder until a long-tenured English professor appeared, creeping uphill in his dingy Volvo. I noticed how the abused suspension caused the vehicle to sag like a loaf of soggy bread. Exhaust billowed behind the jalopy. This professor was widely published and highly respected in academia, whereas my amateur work appeared only in a few journals of little note. As the emissions dispersed, I contemplated life without a muffler.

Two months after surgery, I took a retail job folding clothes and running the cash register at an outlet store. I earned an extra dollar an hour because I had a four-year degree. My new valve gave me abundant energy, but I could not find suitable employment to use it. An alleged perk of the job was a discount on merchandise, but each shift I felt like I was shopping for a shirt and necktie I didn't need for the career I would never have.

One day at lunch with my co-workers, I realized my valve's clicking was not synchronized with the muscle thumping in my chest. I believed I was about to have a heart attack, that a clot had formed on the valve and the consequent arrhythmia was about to end my life in front of my new friends. One colleague noticed my deep concen-

tration as I listened. He gestured toward our boss, who was responsible for the syncopating metronome. I listened to this concert until I separated our clocks. Then, I turned to him and quietly asked, "Do you happen to have a …?" and was awash in the comfort of shared experience.

Back at the clothing store, I walked to the fitting area to pick pins out of the carpet until the end of my shift. In a changing stall, I observed myself in the mirror. My valve clicked away, approaching the three-month marker. Dr. Tarchini had told my family that I might be on the couch until Christmas, but standing there in front of the mirror I felt better than I had in a long, long time. I was almost waiting for this goodness to wear off. In fact, I was a bit worried it might, and then a new feeling startled me: I was wasting it. This job was a reprise of the box factory. *Anything* was better than slowly dying from a leaky valve but that didn't mean I should do just *anything*. I looked at myself in the mirror to make sure I was still there. The valve ticked like a stopwatch. I didn't want *anything*. I wanted *something* and I would not wait around hoping something would find me.

I opened the door and walked toward the registers. Chloe, the manager, stood with a black tote slung over her shoulder. The bag appeared natural on her. I was horrified when she handed one to me.

"All you have to do is carry it like this," she said, pivoting sideways like a runway model. "And whenever you see a customer, offer it to them to hold their merchandise."

"No problem," I said.

You've got *to be kidding me,* I thought.

I held my ground behind the display of crewneck sweaters for the rest of the day, a position from which I could watch the front door so that if anybody I knew entered I could ditch the tote. In hiding, I tried to plan my future. All the

questions I hadn't asked myself during my senior year of college rushed into my mind. *What did I want to do with my life? What would I have fun doing? What career would pay the bills?* I discretely wadded T-shirts I didn't want to fold underneath a display of corduroy pants embroidered with pheasants, and then retreated to the stock room to think. I was frustrated and pissed off to be working at this store, making no use of my degree, having no fun, earning little money. I decided these were as good of reasons to leave as any.

I walked back onto the floor and told Chloe I quit.

"If you leave in the middle of a shift I will write you up for abandonment, which would be a black mark on your record," she said.

What record, I wondered, *my record of shitty corporate employment?*

I had overlooked an excuse, never having quit a job this way before, but my expensive college tuition paid off.

"I was offered a position writing for the *Democrat and Chronicle* and they need me to start immediately," I lied. "It's in my field, so, you know," I said, handing her the tote and striding out the door.

A week later, Papa called.

"I could use a little help around the house," he said.

So, that autumn I moved the radio around his property, listening to "Car Talk" and The World Café on NPR as I painted, weeded, sawed, nailed, and patched.

"This isn't General Motors," Papa liked to say, "so come in the house whenever you want for a root beer." We'd sit at the kitchen table, the old wall clock ticking, and cross items off his list. I was grateful for this working arrangement, but needed something more substantial, something long term and fulfilling, something with a healthcare plan. At lunch a few days later, he slid a cheque across the table.

On the memo line he had written, "tuition." He'd read my mind.

"I'll pay you back of course," I said.

"Keep writing," he said.

I felt relieved and energized—I had a plan.

Talking in the dark with Missy, I recalled a passage I had read about the tradition of wearing a wedding ring on the third finger of the left hand.

"It began with the early Romans," I said, "who discovered that a single nerve led from that finger up the arm to the shoulder, and then straight to the heart."

"That's beautiful," she said.

I had enrolled in graduate school down the road from our apartment and, because Missy was in the middle of a psychology grad program herself, money was tight. Papa had moved into assisted living, and so I found employment at a childcare centre, chasing toddlers and mopping floors after lunchtime. We siphoned Missy's financial aid package to buy groceries, brake pads for our cars, and, impulsively and probably irresponsibly, plane tickets to visit Nicky while he studied abroad in Europe. On Fridays, we hit a local pub during happy hour, not for the drink specials, but because they laid down a spread of free pizza and wings. The socioeconomic safety net of our families lingered in our subconscious, but to actually tap into that resource, to ask for help, felt like a cop-out, inauthentic and immature. We were young and healthy and this rite of passage was just that—a passing moment in our lives. The Roman wedding ring tale was as close as we would get to official engagement stones and precious metals at the time.

Night had long since settled over the city, the expressway humming outside the opened window. Katydids and crickets sang in the dark. My head touched the pillow, and I was nearly asleep when a voice pulled me back.

"What?" I answered. The wind nudged the blinds, a dull light backfilling their fluttering shadows on the far wall.

"I can hear your valve," Missy said.

"Loud?" I asked. I rolled closer to drape my arm over her.

"Yes," she said. "I love it."

47

Within months after each finishing grad school, Missy and I began careers, got married, and bought a house. Unpacking, I found a box holding the contents of my adolescent desk drawer. Guitar strings and a patch cord bound with a Velcro watchband; Papa's knife; a photo of Dad holding me afloat in the pool; and a white business envelope, my signature in red Sharpie overlapping the seams of the seal. I had forgotten all about it.

Between graduation from St. Lawrence and my heart valve surgery, Missy and I had walked around town, through the vineyards, along the creek, to the bagel shop, and the melding tree, but there was a loud silence in our ears. I wanted a will of some kind, legally-binding or not, and so I sat at my childhood desk to write one. I described my idea of a great day: hiking, friends, grape pie, family, jam band, skinny-dipping, stars. I detailed my distaste for wakes, funerals and churches. Cremate me, I wrote, and sprinkle me in the lake and the woods. And I told my friends and family that I loved them. Into an envelope I stuffed the letter, licked it shut, and signed my name across the back. If a youthful death were to deprive me of so many experiences, then I would at least attempt to control these events.

Alone in the attic of our new house, I felt cold and dark with the letter in my hands. My life was so comfortable now, my future full of opportunity and time, yet holding the letter made it disturbingly easy to slide backward through the years and feel the weight of surgery looming, despite having already survived it. I thought to open the

letter and read it again, but instead set it back in the box because I was overwhelmed by the idea that opening it was suicide. The letter was meant to be opened when I died—*if* I died—and since I was alive and healthy, opening it now would tempt fate. Simply touching it stirred in me a sense of fear that I might invoke danger from the slippery universe.

I decided to get rid of it.

I pedalled to a trailhead at the edge of town and stashed my bike in the woods. I hiked West Hill, over-stepping vineyard terraces and rotting posts. I paused at the water tower, the painted grapes fading on the metal, the village view gradually disappearing beyond the hillside growth, and continued my ascent along an old winery road, rutted and trickling water in two tracks. Brown bottles and faded beer cans shot full of holes faded in the mud below empty tree stands. Brown oak leaves carpeted the land, thick and crackling underfoot. A retired van-sized wine barrel I had once climbed in with the guys rested on its side along the trail, partly buried in the ground, its uncapped mouth hidden only by dead grass and the skeletons of Queen Anne's Lace. At last I found what I was looking for—the abandoned earthen winery culvert at the bottom of a knoll, its edges green with moss.

I walked this line without a sound and in moments arrived at Lucky's Lean-to. Hatchet marks scarred a few of the surrounding trees and the bark scabbed over our careless ways. I kicked the leaves out of the stone ring, peeled a section of old vine bark I found nearby, and built a teepee of sticks. The curls of dry grapevine trunk burned instantly. Stabilized on my favourite piece of shale wedged in the crook of an ash, I reclined and watched the flames dance, the smoke twist and turn. This was meant to be a one-beer-fire, but I kept feeding it more sticks and pieces of vine, helping it grow, then die, then bringing it back to life again. Eventu-

ally, I tossed my envelope on top. I closed my eyes before it burned open.

A few months later, I found myself in the cardiologist's office again. I studied the echocardiogram screen and watched rainbows squirt out of the blackness. The technician adjusted the wand in the goo on Missy's belly and keyed the machine to save an image. Then the rainbows resumed bleeding onto the screen. The examination room lights were dim, the cartoon butterflies and elephants in their places on the ceiling tiles, and the mattress, I knew, was heated. Being in the room made me tense, but not for my own sake. This was a fetal echocardiogram.

"Let me show you something," Dr. Tarchini said as he sat down to manipulate the wand. I felt the pressure of memory on my own throat, searching for the angle behind my ribs to take pictures of the valve. Time clicked by.

"There," Dr. Tarchini said, "that is where velocity and direction align." He turned a knob and we heard the baby's heartbeat thumping rapidly. He smiled. We listened. "Everything looks normal," he said, and a higher degree of calmness swept through me. "The baby's heart is functioning perfectly." Our son would be born free from congenital heart defects.

I realized that I felt like I did when I was eleven years old, when I had reached a limit set by the forces of nature, and lived past that limit because my aorta had been repaired. Watching the pulsing fetal echo screen, I felt I had passed another limit by living beyond college and another surgery. I had entered adulthood, a time I couldn't imagine a few years ago because I was too sick and confused and focused on the defective valve to plan a future. Yet here I was. I was married and had a job, owned a house, and was about to become a father. The things I had wanted to happen to me—the things that I could never have put into words—

had actually happened: I had a future and it was wiggling on the screen in front of me. For the first time ever, in that examination room I felt excited, eager and confident. I knew this for sure without having to think about it at all.

I called my brother to tell him the good news.

"How's little Nicky?" he asked.

"We haven't chosen a name yet."

"It doesn't have to be 'Nicholas'."

"It won't be."

"Nixon."

"No."

"Nicodemus."

"No."

"Just Nik, without a c."

"Maybe it'll actually be a girl," I said.

"Nicole. Nickname Nicki with an 'i.'"

"Maybe you should have your own child."

"I don't think so."

"Maybe you already do."

"Let's not go there," he said. "I'm going to babysit the hell out of that kid."

EPILOGUE

On the beach at the north end of Canandaigua Lake, I crouch with Maddox at the water's edge where things come together, but also separate.

He is curious but cautious, a few months past one, dancing in the wet sand and water. He dips his red bucket into the lake and empties the water on our feet. We reach for tiny shells and ribbons of seaweed. His body is smeared with sunscreen. He grasps for bits of plastic that passed through the slots in the lifeguards' rakes. Maddox is about to plunge into the water, but I reflexively catch his tiny chest in my hand. His skin is perfectly smooth. I hold him, longer than I need to. For a moment I feel his beating heart overlay mine and then speed ahead.

I let go and he pads to Missy, who sits on a blanket in the grass, and for a long moment I stand. The past licks at the edges of memory, advancing and receding like a tide. The water washes back and forth across my feet in a steady rhythm, and I am powerless to prevent myself from wading into my past. The more I ignore it the more I feel further away from myself, as if I have stumbled into somebody else's life or floated away. So instead I embrace it. I own the marks.

The lake curves into the distance, to Naples hidden beyond the bend. In my mind I travel south, my memories as fluid as water, past the vineyards and past The Barn, between the hills and to the village, the houses, fields, and wooded spaces of my youth. Faulty valves and insecurities aside, I find myself wondering how to replicate it all for Maddox as a way of ensuring that the vandals of innocence

build him up as they have me, rather than tear him apart. The idea is lovingly simple yet impossible. I know that this endowment is impractical, and that Maddox's adventure will be his own.

I drop my T-shirt to the sand.

Tick.

Tick.

Tick.

It was only a matter of time.

I watch the water.

Try to see around the bend.

A little voice calls to me, louder than before, and I turn to find it.

ACKNOWLEDGEMENTS

It has been said that many hands tap the writer's keyboard. Infinite thanks to my workshop group at Bread Loaf, who made the generous gift of their time, reading sections of this book and improving it through their critique and encouragement: Ruth Berger, Amedeo D'Adamo, Jacqueline Doyle, Catherine Guthrie, Leah Levine, Nick Robinson, Rebecca Sacks, Annita Sawyer, Elisha Wagman, and Peter Marber. Thank you to workshop fellow, Margaret Lazarus Dean, and workshop leader, Jane Alison: I am deeply grateful to each of you for your help. Thank you to my publisher, Jessica Bell, and editor, Dawn Ius, at Vine Leaves Press, for your steadfast support and patient attention—thank you in particular for being so invested.

To all of the nurses, doctors, and surgeons at the Paediatric Cardiology Unit at Strong Memorial Hospital in Rochester, NY: I thank you for your care, for my life. I am a fortunate man.

Thanks to my outstanding teachers and professors from Naples High School and St. Lawrence University. If you ever wonder whether teachers make a difference, please know that you did for me. Thank you especially to Paul Graham, who worked with me for years to smooth this rough-hewn thing into something more than I ever thought it could be.

In the end, nobody deserves more thanks than my family. To all the Edgertons, Harwoods, Mannellas, and Whites, thank you for sharing your enthusiasm and encouragement along the way. To Eric Doctuer, for tucking the earliest

pages of this book in a folder labelled "Important Stuff." To my dad and stepmom, for believing in me. To my mom, who holds the weight of her family's well-being on her shoulders. To my friends, to my brother, Nicky, to the town of Naples, NY, and in particular the hills that surround it: I love you so much. But most importantly, to Missy. And to Maddox and Nico, forever.

VINE LEAVES PRESS

Enjoyed this book?
Go to *vineleavespress.com* to find more.

CPSIA information can be obtained at www.ICGtesting.com
Printed in the USA
BVOW08s1257070916

461047BV00011B/6/P